UNTIL DEATH DO US PART

BEAUTY IN LIES BOOK FOUR

ADELAIDE FORREST

D1738336

ABOUT THE AUTHOR

Adelaide lives in her tiny house with her husband and two rambunctious kids. When she's not chasing all three of them and her dog around the house, she spends all her free time writing and adding to the hoard of plots stored on her bookshelf and hard-drive.

She always wanted to write, and did from the time she was ten and wrote her first full-length fantasy novel. The subject matter has changed over the years, but that passion for writing never went away.

She has a background in Psychology and working with horses, but Adelaide began her publishing journey in February 2020 and never looked back.

For more information, please visit Adelaide's website or subscribe to her newsletter.

ABOUT UNTIL DEATH DO US PART

In secrets we trust. In promises we doubt.

Our love is built on secrets.

From the moment Rafael approached me, I knew he would destroy me in the end. He built our love on secrets and lies, on manipulation that tears us apart.

I have to trust him to shield me from the flames.

My grief is all-consuming, tearing me apart from the depths of my soul. He's a steady strength at my spine, supporting me through the blackest moment of my life.

Our sins are linked in ways I never expected.

But our enemies are closing in and demanding payment for the blood we've spilled. They want to make us suffer for our crimes, but it isn't Rafael's life at stake.

It's mine.

CONTENT & TRIGGER WARNINGS

Beauty in Lies is a DARK mafia romance series dealing with topics that some readers may find offensive or triggering. Readers of Adelaide Forrest's Bellandi Crime Syndicate series should note that this series is much darker.

Please keep in mind the following list WILL contain specifics about the ENTIRE series and may spoil certain plot elements. Please avoid the next page if you don't wish to know specifics.

The following scenarios are all present in the Beauty in Lies series. This list may be added to over time.

• Situations involving dubious, questionable, or nonconsent
   • 13 Year Age gap, with both characters being of legal age at the time a physical relationship forms.
    • Forced Pregnancy
    • Branding
    • Forced Marriage under threat of death & violence
    • VERY graphic violence, torture, and murder
    • Drug use, attempted date rape, and dubious situations while under the influence
    • Kidnapping/Captive Scenarios
    • Knife Play/Violence
    • Somnophilia

1

*C*onsciousness came slowly, nudging at the back of my awareness as my lashes fluttered against my cheeks lightly. Waking from the deepest well of sleep, the kind of sleep that came without dreams and where nothing existed but the void of everything that consumed my waking thoughts, didn't come easy.

Like swimming for a surface I could never seem to reach, my fingertips always lingered inches away from breaking through and feeling the rush of air in my lungs.

"She's waking up," a familiar voice said, tugging at the haze surrounding me. It filtered through the fog and reached into the waters, grasping those fingers so close to freedom and pulling me out with a sudden heave.

I gasped, sucking air into my lungs as my chest heaved with the force of it. Hugo's hand touched the top of mine where my fingers clutched the arm of my seat, his face reassuring as he filled my vision. With him leaning into my space, I met his deep chocolate gaze until I found a way to breathe through the panic in my chest.

When those breaths calmed, I looked around me and wondered where Rafe could be. My mind raced to consider all the possibilities of what had happened and what would occupy him so thoroughly that he wouldn't be the one to tend to me when I woke up from what they'd done.

The thought had initially been a vague reaction—a phantom of the betrayal I should have felt—as if the muscles of my mind remembered exactly what had transpired before the memory could click into place. I narrowed my glare onto Hugo as the reality of his crime against me came rushing back in an overwhelming flood.

The pained sympathy in Rafe's face as he watched Hugo do something they'd clearly discussed ahead of time gave me the slightest indication that he felt perhaps a modicum of guilt for drugging me yet again. "I did what I had to do to keep you from doing something stupid," Hugo murmured, sitting back in his seat. The white seat that surrounded him was so bright next to the shock of his wrinkled black shirt and weathered olive skin. He looked as though he hadn't slept for three days.

"How long have I been out?" I asked, staring around Rafe's plane. They'd somehow had enough time and the ability to get me out of the bunker and to the airstrip without disturbing me.

"About six hours," Hugo answered. "We thought it was best to let you sleep through as much as possible."

"Where's Rafe?" I asked, gathering the energy to raise my hand to brush a piece of hair away from my face. It didn't lift, refusing to leave the arm of the seat. Glancing down in shock, I glared at the bright white straps crossing over my arms and pulled tight. Jerking against the tight hold, I turned a shocked glare to Hugo. "What the fuck?"

"Just relax, Isa," Gabriel said, stepping out of the front cabin and making his way toward us. He took a seat across the aisle, leaning back comfortably and crossing his ankles smoothly. "We'll be on our way in just a bit."

"Why am I tied down?" I asked through gritted teeth.

"For your own protection. We can't have you running off to do something foolish this close to escaping unnoticed," he said, steepling his hands over his stomach.

"I'm going to ask you one more time, where the fuck is my husband?" I demanded, my voice dropping to a low grate as I glared at him. There was something ominous in his feigned casualness, a lie in the behavior. Of all the brothers, Gabriel was the one I'd thought I could trust to give it to me straight.

I didn't want to think about what must have happened for him to try to deceive me into thinking everything was fine and dandy.

"He'll be here soon," Hugo said, reassuring me and drawing my attention away from his brother. "He and Joaquin are wrapping up some last details and then we'll be on our way."

"But they're both alive?" I asked, hating the weak tremor to my voice. All my bravado faded away in the face of the confirmation that my husband was still alive. That he and Joaquin hadn't died after leaving me in the bunker with Hugo.

"As if Rafael would have allowed anyone but him to carry you out of that bunker," Hugo scoffed. "If there hadn't been more pressing matters, he would've loaded you onto the plane, too."

"What pressing matters?" I asked, casting a glance out the window. Men paced up and down the airstrip next to the plane, but none of them were familiar. They had a wider variety of complexions and skin colors, with all manner of hair color to top it off, in a way that Rafael's very Spanish men didn't have much of.

"Bellandi men," Gabriel said, seeming to echo my thoughts. "They came just in time for the end of the party, so Rafael sent them with us while he wrapped up at the house."

Assault rifles were clutched tightly in the Bellandi men's grip, their eyes alert while they scanned the trees to either side of the landing strip as if they were waiting for an attack at any moment.

From the sheer number of men, it didn't seem likely that Rafe and his men had been successful in killing every last one of the people who'd attacked us, or maybe it was just a matter of being cautious.

They'd certainly given us good reason to be.

"Untie me," I pleaded, turning back to Hugo. I cleared my throat, hoping to loosen the tightness I felt there. The unknown of what might have happened to all the men I'd grown to know even vaguely felt like a crushing pressure on my chest. "What happened to Odina?" I asked, remembering her in a sudden realization that made guilt squeeze my heart. She hadn't been the first thought, or the second, or even the third.

My own flesh and blood had been at that house when all hell broke loose, and I couldn't even be bothered to remember. Even the bond of blood could only go so far, and Rafe's men and the brothers had proven themselves to be far more loyal to me and my well-being than Odina ever had.

Silence rang through the plane as Hugo refused to answer, glancing at his brother out of the side of his eye.

"I didn't bother to ask," Gabriel said finally, raising a brow at Hugo in warning. "I didn't particularly care what happened to that *pendeja*."

I could see it being true, given Gabriel's intense hatred for Odina. He wouldn't bother wasting a second of his day with her, but the lurking sympathy in Hugo's eyes as he studied me set me on edge, making me grit my teeth and clutch the arm of the seat to hold back the surge of emotion.

Would I be able to live with myself if something happened to her? Knowing that for once she had nothing to do with the fight that had come our way, the answer wasn't as clear as I would have liked. I wasn't sure how much more my conscience could tolerate before my humanity would be a thing of the past.

Tires screeched outside suddenly, the sound tearing through the silent, early morning. The sun had only just begun to rise over the horizon beyond the trees, confirming Hugo's words that I'd been out for several hours. I'd lost the entire night to sleep while people battled for their lives.

Hugo and Gabriel both jumped to their feet, moving toward the windows and peering out. "Stay here," Gabriel ordered, making his way toward the exit at the front of the plane.

"I don't have much choice, do I, asshole?" I called, turning my head as much as I could in the seat. He didn't bother to reply, tuned into the seriousness of what he perceived as a potential threat.

Hugo and I watched out the windows as a van pulled to a halt next to the plane. Gabriel descended the steps outside quickly, his posture relaxing at whoever he saw within it. But I knew well enough to know it wasn't one of Rafe's vehicles.

I watched with dread as Matteo Bellandi stepped out of the passenger side, buttoning his suit jacket as he stood in a smooth unfolding of limbs. It seemed impossible that a man could be so composed, given the shitshow that must have happened overnight, but somehow I knew Rafe would be the same. Likely the only thing that could cause Matteo to lose his cool would be a threat to Ivory or the kids.

Gabriel and Matteo spoke briefly, then Gabe nodded and allowed Matteo to make his way toward the plane. "Better you than me," Hugo said, grinning down at me as I grimaced. I fought the binds that kept me restrained. Thinking of being seen that way was humiliating, even under the best circumstances.

What the better circumstances for being tied to a chair would be, I didn't know exactly, but I knew it could have been worse.

Hugo vacated the seat like the traitor he was as soon as Matteo came into view, letting the crime boss take the seat across from me. "Rafael will be here soon," he said, unbuttoning that suit jacket and lowering himself into the seat. He seemed unperturbed that I was tied to mine. He leaned forward, resting his elbows on his knees and studying me too closely. "How are you feeling?"

I raised a brow, scoffing and shaking my head in disbelief. "Like I'd feel much better *not* tied to my seat."

He chuckled, his gaze narrowing on Rafe's name carved into the valley between my shoulder and neck. He didn't say a word about it, only letting out a disappointed grunt.

"Was anyone hurt?" I asked.

He twisted his mouth, nodding his head slightly. "Several people. There were casualties," he admitted. "Your husband had to deal with the immediate fallout. I'll handle the rest once you're safely out of Chicago."

"Your city isn't exactly safe. Shouldn't you be concerned about that?"

"I cannot remember the last time my city was well and truly safe. That's what we're working to achieve; unfortunately, safety doesn't happen overnight or without bloodshed. Pavel will not be the last to challenge our new plans," he answered.

I hadn't known for certain if Pavel had been the cause of the attack, but it seemed like the obvious choice. The confirmation did nothing to calm my frayed nerves. "That doesn't bother you? The fact that people will die because of a choice you made?" I asked, and he sighed as if he understood that my question was only partially for him.

"You and I are not the same. You can stab rapists through the heart all you want. You can seek vengeance for the people who have wronged you and your family, but at the end of the day you're a good person who has done bad things, Isa," he said as he stood. His hand touched my shoulder briefly, a reassuring pressure as he stepped around my seat and made for the exit.

"So if you're not a good person, what exactly *are* you?" I asked, even though I could hardly see him when I craned my neck.

He paused, turning his head to glance down at me and meet my stare with his shock of blue eyes. "The same as your husband. A bad man who is willing to do terrible things and never bat an eye, but who has good intentions."

"What good intentions can you possibly have selling drugs? Guns? Women?" I asked.

"If I didn't do it, someone worse would. With me in charge, I have a chance of giving my children a real future that won't be determined by men like Rafael and me," he said, disappearing from view.

After a few minutes passed, he stood next to Gabriel on the tarmac, watching and waiting. For the car I knew had to come any minute.

For the husband who owed me some fucking answers and to get me out of this prison of a chair.

2

RAFAEL

*J*oaquin drove the armored car along the back roads, making his way toward the airstrip as fast as he dared. Tucked far enough away from the city center, the private airport was off the beaten path enough to be inconvenient in an emergency, but no one could deny how handy it was for making deliveries of weapons or drugs.

Blood and ash covered my suit, drenching the fabric in a way that might have made a lesser man feel queasy. If it had only been the blood of my enemies, I might have reveled in the feel of it against my skin and the knowledge that I'd put an end to the torment of their existence.

Instead, all I felt was dread for Isa and what was yet to come. She still didn't know the truth of all that I'd done and of all that she'd lost in the span of an hour.

The plane came into view the moment Joaquin guided the car around the corner, barreling through the open gates and speeding toward where Ryker's van waited next to my plane. Matteo and Gabriel stood beside it, watching us approach, not flinching when Joaquin hit the brakes closer to them than most men would be comfortable.

He was out the driver's side door as quickly as I was, going for his brother and shoving him backward with a hand on each shoulder. "What the fuck were you thinking?" he growled.

"It was a solid plan," Gabriel defended, raising his hands. "It worked, didn't it?"

"And what if they'd aimed for my head?" Joaquin asked, crossing his arms over his chest. "The vest wouldn't have done much good."

"It was a risk." Gabriel shrugged. "It was supposed to be me, but you insisted—"

"Because I am Isa's personal guard. Don't you think they might find it odd if I'm not by her side in an emergency?" Joaquin shook his head, shoving his younger brother toward the plane entrance. "Get the fuck inside."

Gabriel stood his ground, refusing to allow the brother who'd raised him continue telling him what to do, as Ryker lowered himself out of the driver's seat of his van. He chuckled looking between the two. "Kind of makes me glad I killed my brother," he muttered, turning an amused grin my way.

I didn't return it, focusing my attention on the back doors of the van. Ryker took the hint that I didn't have time for games, grabbing his keys from his pocket and moving for the lock without another word.

As soon as he hauled the doors open, he hopped into the back of the van with agility that should have been impossible considering his muscle mass. Timofey grunted in pain as Ryker grabbed him by the scruff, tossing him forward until the man fell to the ground at my feet.

Tilting my head to the side and staring down at him, I

took pleasure in the fact that his body was so broken, so much thinner than it had been when he'd tried to kill my wife. His face contorted as he rose up the best he could, glaring at me as I pulled the pistol from the back of my pants. "Your brother was looking for you."

He huffed a bitter laugh. "Because that's what real family does. I wouldn't expect you to understand."

"I understand just fine. You're the one who has the misconception that I was ever my father's son," I said, tilting my head to the other side. "Dima would kill you in a heart-beat if he thought it bettered his position with your father. Not that it matters anymore."

"What piece will you send back to my father to prove you've killed me? Will it be my head? My tattoo?" he asked, and only the slight quiver in his voice betrayed the fear he felt knowing the devil had finally come to take him to Hell.

"I haven't decided yet. Any requests?" I asked, earning a chuckle from Ryker as he sat on the bumper.

"Go fuck yourself," Timofey spat, twisting his lips into a grimace.

Apparently giving your victim the choice of which part of his body was sawed off went too far. I shrugged, pressing the barrel of the gun against his forehead and pulling the trigger. Blood splattered the ground behind him as it went through, his eyes going void immediately. The last thing the little bastard saw was my face, and that fact brought me some satisfaction.

That satisfaction wouldn't shift to content until the moment when Pavel and all his sons were wiped from existence.

"Put him on ice. I'll call you once Pavel realizes he got the wrong twin. Then you can pick a body part to send him and burn the rest," I ordered Ryker. He hauled the corpse back into his van, tossing him in with a firm shove and relocking the back doors.

"I'm so fucking tired of looking at his face, I just might peel it off and send that," he grunted, the sound trailing into a laugh when I shrugged. Only Ryker had the patience to peel off a man's skin and keep an entire face intact. I had to admire his craftsmanship.

"Has anyone ever told you that you're a little fucked up?" I asked, turning and making my way to the plane when Ryker's face split into a satisfied grin at what he considered a compliment. Matteo nodded as I passed, our brief tiff over the way I'd treated Isa seemingly forgotten.

"Keep her safe," he said as I made my way up the steps.

As if I needed the goddamn reminder.

*R*afael disappeared from my view as he approached the plane, leaving Matteo and the other man, who'd come to collect Timofey after the first car bomb, behind him. His face lacked the fury I'd expected to see given that one of his homes had been attacked—invaded really—but his steps as he walked over the black top had been calm and measured.

Perfectly timed, the no-fuss swag that I'd come to love during our time in Ibiza showed in his gait. Even though I couldn't see him, I imagined the slow and sensual way he would climb up the steps.

I was certain most people were quick to fear the version of Rafael that came when he sank into the place where he wanted blood. Where he accepted the violence that coursed through his veins as an intricate part of him, constant and demanding, and took pleasure in the destruction.

The few of us who knew him understood that the true version of Rafael to fear came in those moments where he went still. Where his face was calm and collected, cold and unyielding.

Unfeeling.

The devil didn't slake his thirst for blood when he reached the deepest well of his anger, only seeking his vengeance with the kind of detachment that lacked all traces of humanity. *That* was the man who ruled Ibiza with an iron fist and struck fear into the hearts of his enemies.

That was the man who didn't play with his toys before wiping them from the face of the earth without a second thought; the nightmare who didn't care who he hurt on his way to claim *everything.* He wouldn't take time to appreciate the beauty in bloodletting, but would end his enemies with a single bullet to the head and forget they existed before the corpse hit the ground.

I felt the moment he entered the back cabin, the shift in the air immediate and palpable. Even with my back turned to him, I knew each and every one of his silent steps brought him closer. Hugo only confirmed that fact when he didn't touch me before he made his way toward the front of the plane.

Quiet whispers came in the space behind me as they discussed something I wouldn't be privy to, and I was immediately reminded of the fact that Rafael had told his uncle he had no secrets from me.

It aggravated me more than it should have just how effectively he made that happen only when it suited me. I wanted him to be the man who treated me as his equal in truth, his partner in all things.

And yet when it came down to it, I was trapped in a bunker and drugged for my safety. Tied down to a seat on his plane for a fast escape.

I'd never be his equal, and the worst part was I couldn't even blame him for that. Not when bullets carved through the air and flesh. Not when Rafe and his men had a lifetime of training that I would never be able to compete with.

I didn't even want to.

Hugo's steps retreated from the rear cabin, making their way toward the front where the rest of Rafe's men had undoubtedly begun to gather to give us privacy. Several more SUVs pulled onto the tarmac, a notably smaller number of men than had been living with us in the house in Chicago.

My heart sank, wondering which of the familiar faces I wouldn't see again.

Rafael distracted me by lowering himself into the seat across from me with a casual elegance that was so at odds with his appearance. Up close, the stain of blood covering his clothing was far more noticeable than it had been through the window, and it was all I could do to stare at the sheer amount of it.

There was no way the person had survived.

He leaned forward to rest his elbows on his knees as the sound of male voices carried from the other cabin where Hugo had left the door open. Some of the ruthless, cold expression faded from his features as his eyes met mine finally. "How are you feeling?" he asked.

I stared at him incredulously, twitching my arm against the restraint pointedly. "Untie me," I said.

The plane doors closed at the front, the energy within the plane shifting as I watched Matteo and his men clear all the vehicles from the runway. "Not just yet," Rafael said, holding my gaze with his. The pity and sympathy I found there drove my anxiety higher, making me struggle against the bonds that held me as the plane moved forward to get into position. He lifted a bottle of water he must have grabbed from the main cabin, uncapping it and lifting it to my lips.

I licked the suddenly dry flesh, realizing just how parched I was in the aftermath of being drugged. I'd been much more concerned with realizing I was tied down and what that might imply.

I let him pour the water into my mouth slowly, giving me breaks to swallow until I'd drained the entire thing.

"What happened?" I asked, watching as he set down the empty bottle and leaned back in his seat. The pilot's voice came over the intercom system, instructing that we'd be taking off in just a moment. Unlike flying commercial, that meant in *just a moment*. The plane accelerated before Rafael could answer, but the tired expression on his face did little to reassure me. "Rafe?" I asked as soon as the worst of the takeoff was over.

The plane continued to climb, and Rafe leaned forward in his seat, having never secured his seatbelt. I imagined such things seemed foolish to men like Rafael Ibarra who stared down the barrel of a gun without fear of death.

When we reached altitude, Rafe touched his hand to my forearm. Unfastening the strap that kept it tied down, he pulled my right arm into his embrace and rubbed feeling back into the numbed limb. He was eerily quiet as he worked, focusing all his attention on his task.

I swallowed back the tears that threatened and the sinking feeling that something terrible had happened. I stared down at my arm as he placed it back on the seat and moved to my left. He repeated the process on that side while I watched.

Something inside me died when he unbuckled me and pulled me into his lap as the plane leveled off, not bothering to wait for the pilot's instruction that we were free to roam.

The blood on his clothing was dry, as if it had been there for hours, and the fact that it touched my bare skin made me immensely grateful for it.

I might have stabbed a man, but I didn't think I was cut out to be a ruthless killer. The thought of all that blood on my skin made me nauseous. "What have you done?" I whispered, letting him tuck my face into his neck. Wrapping my arms around his shoulders, he lifted me and unfolded to stand.

Making his way toward the bedroom cabin at the very rear of the plane, he carried me straight through the room and to the small bathroom off to the side. Setting me on my feet, he wordlessly started the shower before turning his attention back to me. Raising his firm, calloused hands to cup my cheeks, he leaned his forehead against mine. "Our problems will be there in the morning."

"It is the morning," I pointed out in a whisper.

He sighed. "Our problems will be there after we've both gotten some sleep. Can we just have a little while where I'm just Rafe and you're just Isa? Without all the other bullshit and the weight of the world on our shoulders?" Something in the genuineness of his voice made me want to give him that, but the pounding dread rising in my veins made my heart race.

Rafael had never hesitated to give me bad news. To tell me things that he knew would worry me or stress me out.

Whatever had happened, had to be bad. My anxiety for Odina spiked, picturing her lying dead on the grass back at the house. Discarded, and not important enough for Rafael to bother with in his urgency to get out of the city.

I nodded in spite of my need for answers, observing his sigh of relief for the shock that it was. Whatever was bothering him, I didn't think I wanted to know.

I lifted my hands to his shirt, tugging the fabric up and over his head. It was so covered with dried blood that it crinkled as he raised his arms and let me pull it off him. Tossing it to the side, I ran my fingertips over the red stain on his skin until I reached the button of his jeans. Undoing it and shoving the denim down over his hips, I watched as he maneuvered in the small space to kick off his shoes, boxer briefs, and the pants. They joined his shirt in the corner, his hands going to my dress and raising it up over my head. His eyes dropped to my body, inspecting me for injuries as he ran his hands over me and stripped off my bra and underwear.

"Are you hurt anywhere?" he asked, the palm of his hand pressing against my belly. The meaning of the words washed over me, echoing the concern I felt.

"I don't think so. I haven't bled or anything like that, and I feel fine aside from being groggy and some sore muscles," I explained. Both seemed like they went with the territory, given I'd been hit with the blast from a bomb and drugged.

Again.

I very much looked forward to being back home on *El Infierno* where the night didn't erupt into an explosion and threaten to set my skin on fire.

"There will be a doctor waiting for you in New York," he said, moving to the shower.

"Why are we going to New York?" I asked, wanting nothing more than to be home.

"I have something to do quickly. We'll be safe." He stood under the spray while I watched, letting the water run red as it went down the drain. He waited it out, hanging his head and studying the swirl until it ran clear. Then he held out a hand, motioning me inside the small shower with him.

I walked forward, pressing the side of my face to his

unbloodied chest. Part of me hadn't been convinced that so much blood couldn't be his, that to be that covered he would've had to hold the victim close. "Who?" I asked.

He shook his head, touching his lips to the top of my head firmly. "Tomorrow," he reminded me. Grabbing the bottle of shampoo off the rack hanging from the shower head, he worked it through my hair. The massage of his fingers on my scalp felt like heaven, soothing the edges of my anxiety until I practically moaned from the sensation.

It seemed like no matter what happened in our lives, Rafael would always be able to bring me to the peak of whatever emotion he hoped to wring from me. Calm, content, horny, murderous, or stabby.

He brought out the best and the worst in me.

As he rinsed the shampoo from my hair, I settled into the gentle petting of his hands on me as he helped work the suds out. He made no move to touch me sexually despite the press of my breasts against his chest, instead taking care of me in the way I hadn't known I needed. I'd missed the intimacy of it in our more intense relationship that followed the turn in Ibiza.

So while he worked the conditioner through my hair, I sank into the feeling of his hands on my scalp and brushing against my spine as he worked it through the ends. "Your hair has gotten so long," he commented, grabbing the very bottom where it brushed against the swell of my ass with my head tipped back.

"I should have it cut," I murmured, lost to the sensation of his hand on me as he grabbed a loofa and squirted body wash into it.

"Don't. I like it long," he said, twisting the length around one of his fists. Despite the efficient, caring way he ran the loofa over my body, the heat of the statement washed over me. He didn't pause on my pussy, cleaning me methodically and sighing in relief when the loofa came away without the stain of blood that might have signified something was wrong with the baby.

I took it from his grip when he finished, scrubbing away the remaining stubborn traces of blood from his skin. "How much am I going to hate you when tomorrow comes?" I whispered, watching as his face twisted with reality.

"I'm not sure," he admitted, watching me clean him. I wasn't nearly as efficient, taking comfort in what very well may be the last time I touched him so willingly. I couldn't imagine what he might have done, but I shoved it away to enjoy one last night with my husband.

Before he again became my enemy.

My body felt light, sinking into the familiar trail of his fingers through my hair as he finally rinsed out my conditioner, turning off the water and stepping out to grab a towel. He dried himself first, then pulled me free from the shower as I stumbled with the gradually increasing exhaustion that caught me in its trap.

I hadn't thought I'd be able to sleep again so soon after waking from being drugged, but the undeniable exhaustion taking over my limbs made my movements sluggish. "Let's get you to bed," he murmured, wrapping me in his embrace and guiding me back toward the bed. He pulled the blankets back for me to climb inside, sliding behind me and enfolding me into his arms.

Tears stung my eyes with the sudden realization of what might have made me so sleepy so quickly. "You drugged me again," I whispered, thinking back to the bottle of water. Only the knowledge that Rafe would never endanger the baby with a medication that wouldn't be safe gave me any comfort.

"Just let me hold you," he returned, pulling me tighter into his grip. "Tomorrow you might not."

I sucked back a sob, sinking into his warmth and trying to shove away the ominous words. There wasn't time for a second sob before my eyes drifted closed and everything faded away.

4

RAFAEL

*I*sa stirred slightly as I pulled her to a sitting position and slipped a new dress over her head. Tugging underwear up her thighs with gentle hands, I took a moment to stare down at her sleeping face. At the peace written into her expression as her head settled back onto the pillow.

When we were in a better situation, Isa and I would need to have a conversation about the things I wanted to do to her while she slept. About the urge that had stemmed from the day I'd licked her pussy until she came in her sleep. I wanted to fuck her while she was unconscious and ask her what she dreamed when she woke up. I wanted to make her uncomfortable as she told me about all her darkest fantasies. It wasn't the right time, not with the grief that would come soon enough and the risk to her and the baby, but one day, we would play.

Joaquin seemed convinced that Isa had protected her stomach, that the effects of the blast hadn't been nearly as severe as the one that knocked her back several feet in that empty parking lot weeks earlier.

The doctor had assured me that the sleeping pill wouldn't harm the baby, at least not taken in moderation for the special circumstances. The stress that would follow her learning the truth would be far more harmful to her pregnancy, and I would never regret taking one last night with my wife before the uncertainty of her new reality overwhelmed her.

Death didn't come easy to *mi reina,* and the loss she'd suffered with those charred remains in the car may be the most difficult of her life.

I lifted Isa into my arms, smiling slightly when she groaned at me and half-heartedly swatted at my hands as if I would let her go and leave her to sleep in peace. "Go back to sleep," I murmured, kissing the top of her head as I stood from the bed and navigated through the doorway and the plane aisle, taking special care not to bump her head or legs.

Joaquin stood at the bottom of the steps, waiting for Isa and me while the others loaded into the vehicles around the plane. Joaquin made for the last remaining armored car, hauling himself into the passenger seat as I nodded my head at Nino. The executioner for Mariano Rossi was a brutal man with unusually shaggy hair. His tattoos extended up to cover his neck and the side of his face, looking like someone I'd expect to encounter in the cartels or the bratva. The Italians tended to favor their suits and clean cut appearances, making Nino stand out as something else entirely.

He opened the back door for me, watching with intense fixation as I gently placed Isa on the seat and then lifted her head so that it would rest on my lap for the drive to the Rossi Estate in Scarsdale. Though Mariano's son Luca had taken to staying in a Penthouse in the city while he lived the life of a bachelor, his father preferred the privacy afforded to him by his private estate outside the city limits. I greatly agreed with him.

Glaring at Nino as he closed the door softly so as not to disturb the woman sleeping on my lap, I watched as he made his way to the front seat. "She's a deep sleeper," he observed, and only the realization that he thought perhaps Isa was a drugged victim managed to calm the rough edges of my rage at seeing him look at my wife while she was vulnerable.

"Sleeping pills. It's been a rough night," I said, and he nodded as he started the car.

Mariano's fortress was the most secure place I could leave Isa while I went to Brighton Beach, aside from Calix's property in Philadelphia. Under any other circumstances, I would have chosen to spend time with the friend I hadn't seen in months, but he was only just finding quiet after the war that rocked his city.

The last thing he needed was me bringing trouble to his doorstep so soon.

The drive to the estate was mercifully short, with Mariano's father having built the private airport close to his home in case of an emergency. As soon as Nino pulled up in front of the house, I shoved open the door and carefully pulled Isa into my arms and out of the car.

She stirred, her eyes fluttering open as they met mine and she gave a sleepy grumble. "Where are we?"

"With friends," I murmured, tucking her face into my neck and encouraging her to go back to sleep. Joaquin stood inside the front doors, talking to the aging man I knew to be Mariano Rossi and his wife Anna. As soon as she saw me, Anna gave a sympathetic smile and moved to the stairs. Motioning for me to follow, she kept silent as she led me up and to the wing of the house that would be our refuge for a few days while Isa recovered from the initial shock of what was to come.

I stepped into the bedroom, lowering Isa to the bed and tucking her hair behind her ear. She closed her eyes sleepily when I kissed her forehead, leaving me free to go downstairs and find the doctor. Closing the door behind me, I greeted Anna with a brief kiss on the cheek. "Where is he?"

"Waiting in the kitchen," she said, leading me back down the steps and to the room where Joaquin and Mariano had gravitated. The doctor sat at the kitchen island, tapping his pen on his paper while Joaquin explained what had happened.

"The explosion knocked her off the couch," he said.

"Did she land on anything? Something bump into her stomach by chance?" the doctor asked, jotting down a note as I stepped into the room and listened to Joaquin's repeated summary of what Isa had been through.

The fact that it had happened in my own home and I hadn't been there to protect her was like lava in my blood, boiling and unstoppable until I showed the people who were responsible for her suffering what the meaning of true pain was. "No," Joaquin answered. "She's a quick thinker. She rolled and did what she could to protect her stomach."

"Did the force hit her in the back or front?"

"Back."

The doctor's eyes came to mine. "Has she had any bleeding?" he asked.

"None," I said.

"That's a good sign. I'd like to draw some blood and collect a urine sample, feel her stomach a bit and see if anything feels out of the ordinary. Is she awake?" he asked, standing from his seat and moving toward the door.

"She's sleeping, but you can examine her anyway," I said,

leading the way. His face twisted as if he wanted to tell me that he'd greatly prefer to conduct the exam when she was awake, but after meeting my gaze he sighed as if he knew just how pointless arguing with me would be. We climbed the stairs quickly, and I pushed open the door to reveal Isa sleeping in the center of the bed.

With her dark hair fanning over the white sheets, she looked like some kind of princess in the fairytales mothers read to their daughters. I wondered if Isa would read those to our own daughter one day. The doctor perched on the edge of the bed, raising Isa's dress to reveal her stomach while I clenched my teeth in frustration. His hands touched her smooth skin, making me hate every moment of the necessity.

I quickly decided the doctor who tended to Isa's pregnancies would be a woman, even if I had to kidnap her too.

He massaged her skin, pressing firmly and making her face twist as awareness threatened at the edges of her vision. Her eyes fluttered open and then closed. "Nothing feels out of the ordinary. There are no outward signs of a placental abruption."

"That's good, right?" I asked, clenching my hands into fists to prevent myself from interfering in his examination. He smoothed her dress back down her legs, moving to the bag he'd placed at the foot of the bed and pulling out supplies for a blood sample. He moved to her arm, going through the motions as I sat on the other side of the bed and pulled her free hand into mine.

If the needle poking through her skin woke her up, I wanted to be right by her side to reassure her. "That's very good. Make sure she holds still," he said, positioning the needle as I covered Isa's body with one of my arms. She twitched as he slid it into her vein, then he took several vials of blood before he was satisfied and pulled it free. Taking the gauze from him, I held it to the spot where Isa's blood pooled in the little wound.

I'd seen her bleed—I'd even been the cause of her bleeding—but the tiny needle prick of blood affected me on a whole new level knowing she was pregnant. There was no other explanation for the growing concern tightening my chest, only that my entire world was contained within Isa's body.

I'd never survive it if something happened to either of them.

*M*y lungs filled with a sudden shock of air as I sat up in bed. Touching my hand to my chest, I sank into the relief of the feeling of clothing against my palm. I sat there, breathing deeply and trying to calm my racing heart.

The last time I'd woken up in a bed I didn't remember falling asleep in, I'd feared for my life. I'd been violated and deceived, with no ability to begin to comprehend everything that would come my way soon enough. My hand slid down to touch my stomach instinctively, relieved there was still no pain to signal something might be wrong with the baby.

As my breathing finally calmed, I glanced around the room to take in my surroundings. The opulent bedroom had light gray walls with colorful painted canvases lining them. They spoke to a cool, modern luxury that felt far more impersonal than the home Rafe and I shared in Ibiza, with the warm neutrals and natural light flooding through skylights and windows.

Finally turning to the space where I felt Rafael's presence like a sear on my soul, I met his tired eyes. The dark circles beneath them made me believe he still had yet to go to sleep, instead taking to watching over me in my drug-induced unconsciousness. "You drugged me," I said, the faintest feeling of *deja vu* overcoming me as soon as the words left my mouth.

"A sleeping pill in your water," he confirmed, leaning forward to rest his elbows on his knees. He made no move to close the distance between us, instead watching me carefully from his seat next to the bed. His suit was rumpled, his hair disheveled as if he'd run his hands through it while I slept.

"And you don't see anything wrong with that?" I asked, my voice dropping low as I fought back the urge to strangle him. The drugging, the maneuvering and manipulating me until I did exactly what he wanted: I was so *tired* of all of it.

"The drugs are safe in moderation at this stage in your pregnancy, and far less dangerous than the ways you might have put yourself at risk should I have chosen not to give you a few hours of peaceful sleep. I won't apologize for doing whatever I have to do to keep you safe, even when you hate me for it," he said, and something in the tone of his voice on those last words felt more genuine than I could have expected given the circumstances. I'd forgiven him for drugging me before; I could hardly say that I wouldn't do it again.

I tried to remember what he'd said to me before I fell asleep, but the memory of everything was nothing but a hazy series of impressions. "Joaquin and Gabriel are safe, right?" I asked, the memory of Hugo's face in front of mine coming more clearly than the others.

"Yes, they're all fine," he said, his voice flat and even. Despite his exhaustion or maybe because of it, there was no inflection to his tone. No relief or satisfaction that we'd managed to walk away from what was clearly meant to be the final battle of our lives.

"Then what's going on?" I asked, pushing the covers back off my legs and moving to the edge. He moved then, touching a hand to my shoulder and forcing me to lie back in the middle of the bed.

"The doctor needs to do a more thorough exam now that you're awake," he said, slipping his cell phone out of his pants pockets. He typed off a text quickly, undoubtedly summoning the mysterious doctor. He sat on the edge of the bed, touching a gentle hand to my stomach that I covered with my own.

The worry he felt for the baby was tangible in those moments, when he lowered his forehead to rest against mine sweetly. His eyes clenched closed, his face twisting with a grimace. "When was the last time you slept?" I asked, reaching up a hand to cup his cheek.

He opened his eyes, staring down at me intently as he ran his nose up the side of mine. "I'll be okay, *mi reina.*" Those captivating mismatched eyes held mine, warmth chasing away the exhaustion in them. There was a pause of silence as he stared back at me. "*Amo cuando te preocupas por mi,*" he murmured, heat filling his eyes. Even not knowing what he said, Rafael communicated the meaning none-theless. "Tell me you love me."

A knock sounded at the bedroom door, but Rafe refused to take his face away from mine to go and answer it. He didn't call out, waiting and staring at me with rapt attention while he waited for me to give him the answer he so desper-ately needed at that moment. "*Ketapanen,*" I murmured, watching as his eyes widened. "I love you," I echoed, confirming the meaning of the word he'd probably never heard.

I so rarely spoke in the language of my grandmother's people, the use of it outside my family and the Menominee Center being all but futile, but in a way it almost felt like giving Rafe that one last piece of myself. Like bridging the final gap between the Isa who had existed in the life that came before, and the queen he'd crafted from her ashes.

"Do you know what I think?" he asked, the breath of his words caressing my cheek softly.

"What?" I whispered, my eyes tracking to the still closed door where the person on the other side knocked once more.

"I think we were always meant to be right here. That you've been a part of me for longer than either of us could have known, and there was never any possibility where you belonged to anyone but me," he said, putting his mouth on mine slowly.

The first brush of his lips against mine came in a smooth caress, the faint taste of him rolling over my senses as he teased me. I moaned in response, welcoming his hands as they touched my sides and he leaned more of his weight into me. He kissed me roughly, consuming me with his unyielding embrace as he steadied my body.

His right hand came up to tangle in my hair, angling me the way he wanted so that he could swallow me whole as if it might be the last time he'd be able to kiss me that way. Feeling the uncompromising gloom hovering on the horizon, I sank into his touch and welcomed the darkness of his soul into mine.

He was a part of me. A piece that I would never be free from, and that I suspected I would never want to purge from my soul. He made me feel like I wasn't so alone—like the people around me who somehow felt *different* didn't matter, because the echo of my heart beat within his chest.

I was breathless by the time he pulled back, his voice deep and guttural as he called out to the person in the hallway. I flushed from head to toe, knowing that my lips must have been red and swollen in the aftermath of Rafael's kiss.

"It's good to see you awake, Mrs. Ibarra," the doctor said, placing his bag on the foot of the bed as he stared at me. "My name is Dr. Hall. How are you feeling?" Rafe stayed close, clutching my hand within his and watching me intently.

"Groggy. A little sore, but fine otherwise," I said, pinching my bottom lip between my teeth.

Hot. Aching. Needy. Hardly seemed like the appropriate response.

"I'll need a urine sample," he said, pulling a clear cup from his bag and holding it out for me. Rafe stretched out a hand, taking it from him without hesitation.

I nodded through my embarrassment as the request doused the flames Rafe had put in me with his lips on mine, snatching it out of Rafe's grip as I moved to swing my legs out of the bed. "Do you need help?" Rafe asked.

"I think I can manage to pee in a cup on my own, thanks," I snarked.

"Just leave it in the sink, Mrs. Ibarra," Dr. Hall called. Retreating from the awkward situation, I closed myself in the bathroom and went through the process to get him the sample he needed. I straightened my hair slightly before returning to the bedroom, refusing to meet Rafe's eyes as the doctor stepped into the bathroom and emerged a moment later as I settled back into the center of the bed. Crossing my legs beneath me and pulling the dress down to cover my knees, I waited for what might come next. "Everything was fine with your bloodwork. Did you notice any bleeding when you were in the bathroom?"

"No," I said, shaking my head slowly. I knew well enough to know that blood during pregnancy, particularly after an accident, would be the first sign of something concerning. "When did you draw blood?"

"When you were sleeping," Rafe said. I should have known better than to think my husband would allow me any control over my body, especially when there was a risk to my health. "Can we do an ultrasound?" Rafe asked, continuing on as if the violation was of little concern to him.

I supposed it was.

"I don't suggest it at this stage in her pregnancy. It's too early for a heartbeat, so the results would be inconclusive at best, and probably cause more stress than it would be worth. I'd like to do an internal examination of the cervix, but other than that everything so far has been reassuring that the baby will be just fine. Why don't you go ahead and remove your underwear and lie back at the edge of the bed, Mrs. Ibarra?" the doctor asked, going to his bag and grabbing an exam glove.

I stood to do as he said, discreetly lifting my dress in the back to grasp my panties and slide them down my thighs. Rafe grasped my hand, tugging it away from my underwear and glaring over at the doctor as he averted his attention and waited for me to be ready. "Is that really necessary?"

"Is what really necessary?" Dr. Hall asked, turning to level Rafael with a confused stare.

"The exam. What will that tell you that the samples can't?"

"Rafe," I mumbled, snatching my hand out of his grip. "Don't be ridiculous."

"I promise, exams are a standard part of the first visit, even under normal circumstances," the doctor returned, his discomfort with Rafael's line of questioning obvious.

"Rafe, it's fine. It's not like it's my first time going to the gynecologist," I scoffed.

He leveled me with a glare. "It was a man?"

Rolling my eyes, I turned my attention to the doctor. "Do you perhaps have a female associate?" I couldn't repress the groan that came from my throat having to ask such a stupid question, but I suspected the doctor may find it difficult to perform pap smears in the future if Rafe severed his hand from his body.

The fact that it was a distinct possibility said mountains about the state of my life.

"I don't," he said, crossing his arms over his chest.

"Right. He'll control himself," I said, pinning Rafe with a look as I tugged my underwear down my thighs and let them pool on the floor. Kicking them to the side to avoid the awkwardness of having to bend down, I went to the opposite side of the bed and positioned myself appropriately so that Rafe wouldn't have an unobstructed view of the doctor's hand on me.

"You're going to have a female doctor from now on," he barked, taking a seat next to my head. I grasped his hand in mine, holding his eyes with my gaze as I released a chuckle. There were the faint sounds of rustling as the doctor got into position.

I kept my face neutral, refusing to show the uncomfortable grimace that I wanted to make as soon as unfamiliar hands touched me. Rafe glanced down my body and growled, and I caught his hand in mine and squeezed to reassure the nightmare within him that everything was as it needed to be.

The doctor's spare hand pressed down on my stomach, feeling my uterus while he went through the motions of his exam. "All done," he said, standing and giving us privacy for me to sit up and let Rafe wrap me in his arms.

I had to be impressed that the doctor had survived the ordeal, so I'd give Rafe whatever he needed to calm the raging possessiveness in his nature.

"Well?" he asked, his impatience coming through as the doctor moved to the bathroom to wash his hands.

"Everything looks good. I see no indication that the pregnancy has been affected at this point. It's not surprising that your body served as adequate protection at this stage. The uterus is tucked behind the pelvic bone, and I'm optimistic that you'll be fine. I'd like you to have a follow up in a couple weeks to confirm. Until then, I advise no penetrative sex."

"What?" I asked, blanching as I stared at him. Were Rafe and I even capable of abstaining for that long?

The doctor chuckled, lifting his bag off the foot of the bed. "Somehow I think you'll manage for the sake of the baby. It was nice to meet you and best of luck." He retreated from the room, leaving me with the caged animal holding me tightly in his attempt to restrain himself.

"He's gone. You can release the precious," I said, trying to restrain my smile. The silence that met my statement made me pause, freezing as I glanced over my shoulder to look at Rafe where his head touched my shoulder. "Rafe?"

"I don't think waiting for two weeks will be a problem," he admitted, lifting his head to meet my gaze. "I don't want to endanger either of you."

His hand trailed down to my stomach, touching me through my dress. I needed to shower, to wipe off the traces of another man's touch that left me feeling icky even knowing it was just an examination. Knowing what I would feel if the roles had been reversed made me want to get rid of that feeling for Rafe's sake. "Why do I feel like there's more to that than what you're saying?"

He blew out a breath, touching his lips to the name carved into my skin gently. They moved over my skin when he spoke. "My mother was prone to miscarriages. She evidently had two before I was born, and there were more after me. Unsurprising, given the state of her life in the last few years. I'll be on you constantly and annoy the hell out of you with how protective I'm going to be, but I won't be sorry for it."

"Only a fool would expect you to be genuinely sorry for the things you do," I murmured, a bitter smile transforming my face. I knew Rafe far too well to expect anything less from him. Silence met my response again, and I sat there and let him hold me for a few precious moments.

The reality of what was coming sank in, lessening some of the contentment I should have felt in his embrace. When I couldn't put it off any longer, I finally dared to ask the question burning in my brain. "I've waited. I've slept. I've been seen by the doctor. Now tell me."

He turned me on the bed, until I faced him, and his hands captured mine. The firm squeeze brought tears to my eyes, even not knowing what would come. "Is Odina—"

"Your father is in the hospital," he said, cutting off my line of questioning. "I've arranged for the best burn specialists to see to his care, and he's expected to make a full recovery. But there will be scars," he said, his voice trailing off as buzzing rang in my ears.

"I don't understand," I said, shaking my head as I tried to follow the turn in the conversation. Realization struck me suddenly, a direct impact to my chest. "He came to pick up Odina?" I'd been so desperate for her to get out of the house, to get her away from me, that I'd unknowingly put my father in harm's way by asking for someone to come get my sister.

"Dima and his men planted bombs on both your parents' vehicles. Your father's car that Odina drove detonated first, directly outside the house. That's the explosion you felt." I nodded, knowing as much even if it hadn't had the opportunity to really penetrate in the aftermath. I'd been looking at the car and felt like something seemed wrong, felt the moment it exploded deep within my bones. "Your father was at the gate when your mother's car exploded. He'd stepped out to speak to the guards at the booth. It's the only reason he survived."

Tears streamed down my cheeks, the knowledge that I'd caused my father so much pain making me feel every moment of how terribly I'd behaved as a daughter. I'd disappeared and left him to deal with the agony of his injuries that I'd caused. "I have to call my mom," I said, pulling at Rafe's hands to get him to release me.

He didn't relent, holding me tight as his face twisted. "*Mi reina*," he murmured, bringing one of my hands up to his face. He touched it to his cheek, twisting his lips to my wrist softly. "She was in the car."

My body went still, my weight sagging as I fumbled for the words to say. "Then why isn't she in the hospital?"

"Isa," he murmured as I yanked my hand away from his face.

"No." Shaking my head, I fumbled for the edge of the bed. I needed my phone. I needed to call, to hear her voice and know that he was being dramatic.

She couldn't be....

"She's gone, *mi reina*," he murmured, wrapping arms around my waist and hauling me into his grip. His chest pressed tightly to my spine, his arms encasing me entirely as a strangled sob shook my entire frame.

"NO! You're lying!" I yelled, shoving at his arms and forcing him to release me. I turned to face him, slamming a fist down on his chest. He took the hit, letting me follow it with another one, and another one after that.

"Isa," he whispered, his voice drowned out by the sounds of my crying. By the strangled screams that didn't seem human.

"She can't be gone," I whispered much later, my throat aching with the scalding tears that consumed me.

"I'm sorry, *mi reina*," he said, drawing me into his arms as the fight finally receded. He held me until there was nothing left, until only the broken shell of my grief remained.

I walked into the kitchen, dropping onto one of the stools at the kitchen island. Anna hurried to the counter, brewing a cup of coffee and busying herself with taking care of me. While I didn't know her well, I suspected most women would want to care for the man who had only managed to grab a few hours of sleep after holding his grieving wife for hours.

"How is she?" Hugo asked, wringing his hands as he looked toward the stairs.

"Sleeping," I said, accepting the cup of coffee from Anna gratefully.

"Did *you* manage to get any sleep?" Mariano asked, watching me pointedly. He was barely ten years older than me, and had a son who was older than my wife. It wasn't often that I remembered just how young Isa truly was, given she *felt* older than her age. I recalled her grandmother's words in one of the many conversations I'd listened to in the time when I waited to make Isa mine.

Isa had an old soul trapped inside the body of an eighteen-year-old.

"Not much," I admitted. "It took a while for her to cry herself to sleep."

"She didn't revolt against you touching her after what we did?" Gabriel asked, leaning against the far wall with his arms crossed over his chest.

"I didn't get that far. She knows about her parents, but not Odina yet," I said, taking a sip of the hot coffee and letting it rejuvenate me. The late hour didn't matter, since I had business to tend to that night and wouldn't find my way back to bed with Isa for a long while yet.

A glance out the window confirmed the sun had already set, hours prior from the look of things, and I'd been so preoccupied with comforting Isa through her grief that I hadn't even noticed.

I couldn't remember a time when I'd felt sadness as intensely as what I'd watched her suffer through; the loss of my mother being the closest memory. I only had vague memories of loving her, brief flashes of affection in stolen moments when my father wasn't around to witness them. I'd done everything I could to avenge her death out of the echo of that love in my life and how empty everything felt in the absence of it, but it had happened so many years ago, and I'd only been a boy. Until Isa entered my life, the kind of love that made you truly grieve when someone was gone seemed...impossible for a man like me. I wasn't sure I would be capable of the kind of sadness I'd seen wrack Isa's body.

Unless I lost her.

She was the one weakness that could bring me to my knees and break me, because a life without her in it would be empty all over again. Hollow, in a way I didn't plan to ever experience. I'd die right along with her.

"You have to tell her," Joaquin reprimanded me, giving me a stern look. I glared right back to remind him of who I was. No matter what his relationship with Isa had grown to be, he'd mind his place and do as he was told.

"Have we heard anything?" I asked instead of replying, wondering what the timeline would look like for my business in Brighton Beach. I suspected that Viktor Kuznetsov would quickly vacate his home once Pavel realized he'd taken Odina instead of Isa. "Does Pavel know yet?"

Gabriel nodded. "Pavel sent word to Alejandro, advising you to return his son to him in exchange for Isa's sister. Alejandro was vague in his response since he didn't know Timofey was already dead at the time. Pavel indicated that if a deal couldn't be struck for his son's return, then he would trade Odina for you or Isa."

"He knows that's never going to happen. No smart man trades his Queen for a pawn," I said, crossing my arms over my chest. Odina's wellbeing mattered little to me aside from the pain it would cause my already broken wife.

The room went still as the sound of creaking floorboards behind me alerted me to the presence of my wife. I'd had every intention of telling Isa the truth of what I'd done, but she deserved to hear it in privacy—without an audience who knew the truth before she did.

I turned to look back at her, taking in the sight of her tired, grief-stricken face for just a moment before she spoke. "What are they talking about?" she asked, her arms crossed over her stomach. She looked so painfully small, her face pinched and exhausted despite all the sleep she'd gotten. Dark circles were under her red-rimmed eyes, her cheeks and nose blotted and pink from the crying she'd done before finally falling asleep in my arms. Her cheeks were wet, and I knew without a doubt that she'd cried when she woke up alone—that I hadn't been there to comfort her like I should have been. The others exchanged glances, and

Mariano, Anna, and Luca nodded and left the room through the other hallway. I was grateful for the reprieve and the fact that Isa would only need to be around people she knew during the final phase of her grief.

"Sit down, *mi reina*," I instructed, standing from the stool and motioning for her to take it. She hesitated in the doorway, watching my face until she placed one foot in front of the other. She hadn't moved so slowly since the day we were married, the day she walked down the aisle as though she approached her final resting place.

"What's going on?" she asked as she perched on the edge of the stool. Placing my hands on her waist, I hefted her up onto the seat more fully and stepped between her slightly parted knees. I left enough space for her to not feel so vulnerable when I admitted the truth of what we'd done, but kept her trapped so she couldn't run until she heard me out.

"Pavel's son Dima mistook Odina for you and took her from the house in the middle of the shoot out," I said, tucking a lock of her hair behind her ear.

She bit her bottom lip, tears pooling in her eyes as she nodded slowly. Her nostrils flared as she fought to suppress the emotion. "It's my fault. I shouldn't have let her go off on her own."

"No, Isa. It isn't your fault," I said, glancing at Gabriel over her shoulder. "It's mine."

"Odina isn't your responsibility. You don't owe her anything, but I do. She's my sister," she murmured softly, the guilt in her voice giving me almost a sense of relief. Even if she would hate me for the choice I'd made, at the very least I would be able to strip that guilt away from her.

Her hand grabbed mine, clenching it tightly as she tried to work her way through her plan of action. Even in her grief, Isa's brain was always working. Always connecting the dots and searching for solutions, even if the problems weren't hers to solve.

It was why she'd spent so much of her life making other people happy, why she'd sacrificed her childhood in favor of responsibility. Because she wanted to fix everyone else's problems for them.

"We set her up, *mi reina*," I said, giving her the truth she deserved and freeing her from the blame she'd placed on herself.

"I don't understand," she whispered, staring up at me with rage building in her eyes. She didn't yet understand the depths of what I'd done, but she knew me enough to understand I'd thrown her sister to the wolves.

"It was my idea," Gabriel said, stepping closer to us. He kept his distance, his face neutral and not giving away any of the emotion I knew he must have felt. All the brothers loved Isa like a sister, and hurting her in this way wasn't a choice they'd made lightly.

But Odina'd needed to be dealt with, and Isa needed to be safe in that bunker.

"What did you do?" she asked, sniffling back the impending tears in favor of understanding. Of getting the answers she so desperately needed.

"I drugged her and put her in your clothes," Gabriel answered, glancing at Joaquin who nodded even though his face pinched with the ire he knew Isa would give him. "Then Joaquin led her out, pretending to be trying to escape the fire. She couldn't speak to warn Dima that she was the wrong sister because of the drugs."

"And then what?" she asked, turning her tightly pinched face until she stared Joaquin in the eye. "You just handed her over and they believed that?"

"They shot me," Joaquin said, tugging down the collar of his shirt to show the bruise from where the vest had caught the bullet meant for his heart, "and took Odina while I lay 'bleeding' on the ground."

"They could have shot you," Isa murmured, her voice twisting with anger.

"They did—"

"No! They could have *really* shot you! What the fuck were you thinking?" she asked, glaring at him as if endangering himself was a personal offense to her.

"*Mi reina*—" he started.

"Do not *mi reina* me. I forbid you from ever doing something so stupid ever again. Do you understand me?" she asked, her voice trailing off into a whisper as her bottom lip trembled. "My mother is dead. Odina is gone, and even if she's a complete shit, she's still my twin. Doesn't it matter to you what it would do to me to lose you too? Please don't make me lose someone else I love."

"I'm not—"

"You're not what? My family? If you truly believe that then you haven't been paying attention," she whispered, her voice trailing off.

"It's my job to keep you safe," Joaquin explained, his expression and voice softening with emotion as he stared at her. I'd never heard Isa speak of her bond with the brothers, of the relationship that had somehow survived the betrayal they'd dealt her over the months and grown stronger during her time at my side.

They grounded her. Gave her someone to love and spend her time with, aside from me, and as much as I hated knowing that there were other people who demanded her attention, I acknowledged the fact that Isa thrived on having people to love.

Even when those relationships were odd.

"Then you should have been in the bunker with me, not playing games with my sister's life," she said flatly.

"Using Odina as a decoy was necessary to end the fight quicker. It made them think they'd won, and it gave us the ability to get you off the property and to the airplane without risking you being trapped in the bunker with Hugo indefinitely. You needed a doctor as soon as we could manage it," I explained, touching her cheek and drawing her attention back to me. I didn't like the jealousy I felt over seeing her so bothered by another man's theoretical death.

"It was unnecessary. You couldn't have waited for help? You expect me to believe Matteo wouldn't have lent a hand?"

"That takes time, *mi reina*," I said, my voice trailing into a warning growl. "In the meantime, my men were dying. I owe Odina *nothing*, but I owe them my loyalty. I will always do what I must to protect you and to protect my people. Sacrificing your *pandeja* of a sister to save countless lives was no sacrifice at all considering what she's done to you."

Isa went silent, sliding her eyes to the floor as she processed my words. She must've known there was truth to them, but it was difficult for people like Isa to grasp the reality of the greater good.

One life did not justify a dozen deaths.

Mariano poked his head into the room, sympathy in his gaze as he locked eyes with Isa momentarily and then looked at me. "My men are suited up and ready to go whenever you are."

"Where are we going?" Isa asked, giving me her eyes once more.

Cupping her cheek in my hand, I leaned down to kiss her forehead. I hated to leave her, even knowing she wouldn't be alone. The fact that she was so willing to allow me to touch her despite her anger over the choice I'd made spoke to just how affected she was by what had happened to her parents. "You aren't going anywhere. You're going to stay here with Joaquin and Hugo. I have to do something in Brighton Beach."

"You can't just leave me here," she protested, shaking her head from side to side. The wide depth of her gaze made me wish that I could send someone else to deal with Viktor. That I could spend the rest of the night curled up in bed with her and doing what I could to distract her from the reminder of her loss.

"I'll be back soon."

"What's so important that you have to rush off in the middle of the night?" she asked, cocking an eyebrow in that way that she did when she knew I was up to no good, and that she would never approve of my plans.

"Killing Viktor Kuznetsov," I said.

"His brother has my sister, Rafael," Isa returned, pulling away from me as much as she could. She erected a wall between us, separating herself from me as much as she could, given our proximity, and shutting me out of her emotions as her tear-stained face went blank.

"I won't negotiate to get her back," I answered, placing a finger under her chin and tilting her face up until I could lean forward and brush my lips against hers tenderly. "My plans move forward regardless."

"But it's your fault they have her in the first place!"

"*Te amo, mi reina.* But I think you've mistaken me for someone who gives a shit about what happens to her. She doesn't deserve your care or protection. Let her go," I said, placing one last kiss on her startled lips. "I'll be back soon."

Nodding to the brothers, I followed Mariano out into the hallway to go join his men. Gabriel trailed at my heels. His abilities with tech equipment and disarming alarm systems would come in useful when we broke into Viktor's home while he slept.

We were nearing the end of my list of Kuznetsov scum to wipe from the earth, and nothing would derail those plans or my mission to make sure Isa was safe.

ISA

A woman strolled into the kitchen as Rafe disappeared, moving to stand behind the kitchen island as she stared at me. "Would you like to go back to bed?" she asked, tugging the tie on her house robe tight. The sympathy in her brown eyes made it painful to meet her gaze, and I sniffled back my tears as I turned to face the island and fought my way through the immediate reaction to that.

"No, thank you. I feel like I've slept all day," I said, touching the cup of coffee Rafe had left on the island. I couldn't drink it, and wouldn't have even if I could because of my distaste for it, but something about knowing it was his gave me comfort in his absence.

"You pretty much have," Hugo said helpfully, giving me a tight smile as he waited for the reaction I would give him. He had to know that drugging me wasn't something I would forgive easily, that it wouldn't simply be brushed under the table as if it never happened, and under normal circumstances, I thought that might have been true.

But I was so fucking tired of fighting. So exhausted from

feeling like I was in constant conflict with everyone I loved. Hugo had done something terrible, but even I knew it was with the best intentions.

He wanted to protect me and the baby, and in the moments where I'd already lost so much, all I could feel was grateful that what he'd done might have saved the life growing inside me. I'd have never forgiven myself for a stupid choice if I wasn't the one to pay the consequences of it.

Not again.

"I'll make you something to eat then," she said, moving toward the refrigerator and looking inside. "Is there anything you feel like?"

"I'm not hungry," I said, smiling through the revulsion I felt at the thought of food.

"You haven't eaten in twenty-four hours," Joaquin said to me before turning his attention to the woman who turned to look at me sadly. "Something light."

"Are you deciding my meals for me now?" I asked, glaring at him even knowing he was right. I needed to eat, but I didn't think I'd be able to tolerate anything.

"I'm making sure that you take care of yourself and the baby while you grieve, *mi reina*. There is nothing wrong with leaning on the people who love you; you don't need to worry about irrelevant choices right now," he returned, stepping forward and touching his thumb to my cheek to wipe away the moisture there. "Sour things help settle her stomach so that she can eat. Lemons, anything pickled. That sort of thing," he added.

She nodded, grabbing a mason jar filled with Italian pickled vegetables. "Start with *giardiniera* then," she said, grabbing a spoon and scooping one of everything out onto a little charcuterie board that she placed in front of me. "I'm

Anna," she said, holding out a fork. I took it, swallowing back the surge of nausea I felt as I stared down at the food.

"Isa," I mumbled, stabbing a pickled carrot and lifting it to my mouth. She smiled, going back to her activity as if she couldn't quite stop moving. Her hands flew as she grabbed the rest of her supplies, taking to slicing meats and cheeses and putting things on my plate one at a time. "I want to see him," I said, swallowing down the food bit by bit. Gradually the nausea faded, the *antipasto* settling that empty feeling in my stomach that brought morning sickness no matter what time of the day it was.

"That's not possible," Hugo said, taking the seat beside me and touching a hand to my back between my shoulder blades. "You have to know it isn't safe for you to go back there right now."

"He's my father. He just lost *everything*," I said, whimpering through the rush of pain that filled me with the thought. He'd lost his wife and both his daughters in a matter of moments, all of us ripped away without answers. He deserved to hear the truth from me, even if knowing that I was yet again at fault for all of it would make him hate me.

"You're still alive," Anna said, placing some crostini on the board to fill the last empty space. "He hasn't lost everything until that is no longer the case. As painful as it must be to have his daughters missing from his life, I can promise you he would much rather not see you than have you die simply so that you could be there for him through surgeries and skin grafts."

"How could you know that? What happened was my fault. I owe it to him—"

"You owe it to him to live and to allow what remains of your family to find a way through this on their own. I *know* how much it hurts to walk away from them, but that is exactly what you must do if you want them to be safe. Even if Pavel and Dima hadn't already struck against them to get to you, you will always be a danger to them. Being the wife of *El Diablo* does not come without hazards, and your husband can only offer so much protection to them while he lives on the other side of the world. The best protection you can give them is staying away," she murmured, her voice soft as her face twisted with the pain of what I could only assume was a choice she'd had to make.

I didn't know her story, knew nothing more than her name, but the kinship that came from being with another woman who lived the kind of life that demanded we make these choices couldn't be denied. The expression on her face was too somber for her statement to come from anything except personal experience. She'd lost her family. I didn't know whether she'd walked away from them in time or lost them in some other way, but they were gone from her life regardless.

"Can I at least call and tell them we're alive?" I asked, reaching up a hand to wipe away the stragglers of tears that never seemed to stop. I would have thought I'd run out, that I'd reach a point where crying was no longer physically possible.

That didn't seem to be coming anytime soon, and I sucked back the water Anna placed in front of me. The fluid went down easier than it would have had I tried to drink it before eating something, and it brought a strange sense of comfort to know that the symptoms I had during pregnancy were normal.

It seemed impossible that I should have any at all, and sometimes the pregnancy itself felt like a figment of my imagination. Life had been such a whirlwind of emotion and violence and *everything*, I wondered if I'd ever stop drowning.

"That wouldn't be a good choice right now. Your grandmother is with him, but he hasn't woken up, so I highly suggest waiting until we receive word that he's pulled through the worst of it. You can't call frequently in case someone is watching," Joaquin said, looking toward Hugo as if they might do whatever it took to keep me from disobeying that advice.

I understood it, logically and beyond the fog of sadness. To show I cared enough to call regularly would only put them more at risk, and I knew the complete severing of me from my family hovered just beyond the horizon.

I never should have come home in the first place. I should have stayed on *El Infierno* and let them think I'd died. At least then my mother would still be alive, even if it meant I had to live the rest of my life without answers about Rafael's father. That was a price I would have gladly paid.

"Eat," Anna reminded me, snapping me out of the emotional trance I'd sunk into. I nodded, happy for the distraction and knowing that retreating into that dark place inside me would be anything but comforting in those moments when my grief and loss threatened to pull me under the surface.

I shoved another bite into my mouth, chewing slowly and trying to focus on the flavor to distract myself. But everything tasted like ash in my mouth, and nothing existing beyond the realization that my mother had died in a fire. That the same flames that had terrified me after the car bombing that nearly took my life had been what tore her out of my life.

"My mother is dead because of me," I mumbled, needing to voice it to someone who wasn't Rafael. Someone who understood guilt and grief in a way he would never be able to relate to.

She nodded, and somehow the confirmation that someone understood was a greater comfort than all the denials in the world. Rafe could make excuses. He could take the blame or put the blame on Dima and his men since they'd been the ones to plant the bomb that had killed her. But it didn't change the fact that it wouldn't have happened if it hadn't been for me and my choices.

"But your father and grandmother are alive. That could easily change if Rafael were to give Pavel any indication that he cares for either of them," she said, confirming the words Rafe had said about Odina.

He could only protect me, in the end.

"He really isn't going to do anything to get my sister back, is he?" I asked, and the silence of Joaquin and Hugo as they surrounded me served as confirmation enough.

Still, Anna answered with the brutal honesty I had already begun to realize was just a part of her. "Sweetheart, my impression of your sister through your husband's eyes? Pavel did him a favor. Rafael Ibarra is not the kind of man to look a gift horse in the mouth."

I nodded, swallowing past the tightness in my throat.

Another life, another stain on my soul. At some point, I would have to confront the fact that I wasn't the innocent girl who had bad things happen to her.

There was something inside of me that attracted those bad things, that drew men like Rafael into my life.

There was something evil inside me, something I'd worked to suppress my entire life, but good things didn't come to those who resisted temptation.

Instead, it came to those who took what they wanted in fire and blood.

abriel sat at the computer in the van, typing away at the screen as Mariano's men pulled up at the curb. The blueprints of the Brighton Beach house were illuminated on his screen, and windows and doors with sensors highlighted.

"Is there any activity inside?" I asked, and he toggled the screen over to the security cameras he'd hacked into remotely. Flipping through the various feeds, he continued until he found the one of Viktor sleeping soundly in his bed — completely unaware of what was coming his way and content in the safety of his beachside mansion.

"Just the standard guards, but they're sloppy at best if they're awake. I haven't seen a patrol do a sweep since we left New York."

"What's our best access point?" one of the men in the back of the van with us asked. He'd immediately taken control of his men, serving as the contact point for me while we worked together in unfamiliar territory. It was less than ideal to have men that weren't mine, and I couldn't fully trust them, but they were far more suitable than taking a team of men who were exhausted or injured after the attack in Chicago.

"Beachside," Gabriel said, and the screen zoomed into the back of the house. The property was open to the private beach, only a team of two guards standing near the back patio and chatting to stand in the way of our silent infiltration.

If everything went according to plan, Viktor wouldn't wake up until I loomed over him in his bed. "Right," Mariano's man said, turning away to speak into the communication system he wore on his black clothing. In a neighborhood like this, filled with a mix of wealthy civilians and Russian allies to Pavel, the best we could hope for would be a quiet and efficient sweep.

I wanted nothing more than to get home to my grieving wife as soon as possible.

Mariano's men filed out of the van, and the night air was silent as the rest of them did the same from the other vehicles. They moved like they were part of the night, the impeccable training they'd been through an echo of my own.

Our lives were anything but simple, and they were far from peaceful.

We were born in blood and forged through pain, until all that remained was a mindless killing machine that thought nothing of snuffing out life repeatedly.

"You've got the alarms?" I asked, watching as the men checked their gear. They waited for me to step out of the van, taking their signals from me when it all came down to the time to strike.

"I jammed the systems with white noise, but they had countermeasures in place. I'm hacking the system to override them now," Gabriel announced, typing onto the screen filled with gibberish I would never hope to understand.

"How long?" I asked.

"Five minutes, tops," he said. I moved out of the vehicle, stepping into the night with Mariano's men. They were nameless faces to me, nothing more than soldiers to help me achieve the means to my end, but the network of alliances I'd worked to build already proved itself useful.

No matter where we were in the world, my men and I had friends nearby who could help in the event we needed it. All that was left was to dispose of our enemies one by one.

"Let's go," I said, having full faith in Gabriel's ability to complete the override by the time we were in position. He'd never met a problem he couldn't solve. Never met a computer or system he couldn't own.

We moved through the night silently, leaving Gabriel to do his job as we went through a yard down the street where the security system was practically nonexistent. Sand covered my boots, and even though I'd spent the entirety of my life surrounded by it, I couldn't help but think of the days I'd watched Isa step through the sand as if it was the most fascinating thing she'd ever seen.

We crept up to the fence separating Viktor's house from his next door neighbor's, staying out of sight until the signal from Gabriel. It spoke to his punctuality that we only had to wait less than a minute before his disinterested voice came over the communication system. "All clear."

Mariano's man signaled his people into position, and we moved like a trained unit. They surrounded me as they'd been taught, protecting the man occupying the position Mariano would usually claim for himself, but he and Luca had remained home. They lent their support through their men, but this wasn't their fight.

It was mine alone.

We moved in through the sides, overtaking the two

guards outside with a knife to the throat before they could communicate with the others. Dragging their bodies into the bushes, I watched as Mariano's men did what they could to hide the evidence of our insurgence.

With a last check for me, that I nodded in confirmation to, the lead pulled the sliding glass doors open and stepped inside before signaling his men forward with two fingers.

They moved in groups, and the unit that followed me headed for the stairs to make our way to the master bedroom where Viktor slumbered. We met little resistance until we crested the top of the staircase, the sound of a single shot ringing through the silent night.

I both cursed the interruption to Viktor's sleep and welcomed it, knowing that I greatly preferred it when my victims were able to fight back. It would make for a much more entertaining evening, but a longer one that meant Isa was without me for longer than I wanted.

The men took him down quickly, and we moved beyond with single-minded focus on getting to Viktor before he could try to escape through whatever plan he had in place for emergencies.

The bedroom door was closed as we approached, waiting to listen for sound on the other side. There was nothing but silence, the mark of something that was too quiet to be true after the errant gunshot had taken away our element of surprise. I raised my foot, kicking the door open so hard that the latch cracked beneath the pressure. The man hiding behind it grunted as I moved into the space, raising his gun as he forced his body around the door that had likely broken his nose.

I grabbed the barrel with my left hand, pushing the gun away quickly and removing my head from the centerline so that when he pulled that trigger, I wouldn't be in danger of being shot *again*. As much as I loved having Isa fuss over me, that was the last thing she needed right then.

The shot cracked off, shattering the window on the other side of the room. My right hand crashed into the inside of his wrist, bending it until I wrenched the gun out of his grip and delivered a downward kick to the top of his knee. He crumpled to the floor as I leveled him in the sights of his own pistol, his face grimacing as he stared up at me.

Raising his hands as if he was an innocent bystander and not the man I'd come to slaughter, he smiled to pacify me. "Is she dead yet?" I asked, the uncaring tone of my voice sounding inhuman even to my own ears. Part of me wished I cared for Isa's sake—the same part of me that wished my wife didn't have a terrible sister who made it impossible to tolerate her existence.

"I can tell you where she is," he said instead of answering. I resisted the urge to hang him from the ceiling upside down and carve into his stomach. Only the desire to get home to Isa kept me from ripping out his entrails and watching him bleed out. I pulled my bowie knife from the sheath attached to my pants, shoving his gun into the back of my waistband.

Tilting my head to the side as I stared at him, I didn't stop the cruel smile from claiming my face. "For that information to be valuable, I would have to care," I said, grabbing a fistful of his hair and wrenching his head back to reveal his vulnerable throat. He raised his hands to scrabble at my arm, raking his nails down the fabric of my shirt in a desperate bid to free himself as his horror mounted and he started to realize that he had nothing of value to offer me. "I don't."

"She's in Colombia!" he yelled, clinging to the last possibility that he could sway my decision.

He didn't.

I slashed my blade across his throat, cutting through sinew and flesh deeper than necessary in a sudden bid of inspiration from his reveal of Odina's location.

Even though I didn't care to save her and had absolutely no intention of wasting my men's lives on the pathetic waste of space that she'd become, nothing sent a message better than the head of my enemy.

Especially when that head wore a Colombian necktie.

His eyes went glazed as I finished the cut, and he was sadly already gone by the time I plunged my hand into the wound and gripped his tongue harshly. Pulling it back through the hole, I released it to lay against the bottom of his throat and drape there perfectly.

One of Mariano's men chuckled, confirming that I'd chosen a team who was just as fucked up as I was. Wiping the blood on his shirt and sheathing my blade, I turned for the door.

My wife was waiting.

*T*he sound of footsteps came through the foyer, and I studied Anna with my heart in my throat. Something about this murder felt different than the others, something about this one felt cruel in a way the others hadn't.

I couldn't explain it, because Maxim hadn't tried to harm us directly either. The only difference was the fact that the Kuznetsovs had my sister. I should have been doing whatever it took for her to be returned safely. Instead Rafael was out murdering them all one by one.

He'd already killed Timofey after they'd taken Odina, and I had no doubt he would continue to kill the rest of the line when the opportunity presented itself. The only problem was that Dima and Pavel were all that remained.

Rafael stepped up behind me, touching his lips to the top of my head. I would have recognized his scent anywhere, even with the metallic tinge of death and blood clinging to his skin. He didn't touch me aside from that, stepping around to the sink and washing his hands. The water ran red as he scrubbed beneath his fingernails, cleaning off whatever his quick solution had been while he was out.

I didn't think I wanted to know what he'd done to get blood in every crevice of *one* hand that way. I ran my eyes over the rest of him, noting the distinct lack of injury. Without a scratch on him, it didn't seem like he'd encountered any kind of resistance in whatever he'd done to paint his hand with the red stain of blood.

"Did everything proceed as expected?" Anna asked, hanging up her dish towel as she yawned. I immediately felt terrible for making her feel like she needed to stay up with me. I'd had Hugo and Joaquin for comfort, but given their involvement in Odina being taken, I was feeling less than chatty with them.

"In and out," Rafe said with a nod. "Let's get you to bed, *mi reina.*"

I grimaced, staring at the still darkened night sky. Despite the late hour, the last thing I wanted to do was go to sleep in the arms of the man I was completely torn between hating and *needing.*

I'd thought my family made me feel alone, made me feel different in a way that could never be reconciled, but having the distinct, final absence of my mother in my life made me realize that, in truth, I'd never really known what it was to be alone.

We'd had our differences, but she'd always been there. They all had, and I'd betrayed them to become a murderer like my husband.

"I'm not tired," I said, sinking my weight deeper into the stool beneath me. I wasn't interested in doing what he demanded, especially not after sleeping in a drug- and grief-induced haze for most of the day.

He stepped around the counter, closing the distance

between us and dropping his clean hands to my waist. He lifted me from my seat, setting me on my feet directly in front of him and sliding a finger beneath my chin until I turned my gaze up to his.

"Goodnight you two," Anna said, yawning once more as she retreated from the kitchen to find her way to her own bed.

"You're my wife," Rafael said, as if that was answer enough that I needed to go to bed just because he summoned me. To his demented mind, it probably was. "In the middle of the night, you're in my bed."

"That isn't your bed," I argued, latching on to the semantics. I hated that we both knew I was in no position to really argue with him, too desperate for the contact he provided. Even standing in front of him and trying to refuse to go to bed with him, my body sank into his embrace.

It remembered the way he'd held me while I cried, giving me the time I needed to just break. I still felt shattered, raw, and like I would never be the same again.

I wasn't sure I even wanted to.

"I don't want to sleep," I murmured, pursing my lips into a pout. Nobody seemed to care what I wanted.

I wanted my family to know I was sorry.

"What you want and what you need are two very different things," Rafael murmured, tucking a lock of hair behind my ear and grabbing my hand. He guided me toward the staircase, leading me up slowly. I didn't have the energy to physically protest, even knowing I should have had an abundance after all the sleep I'd gotten.

"I slept all day."

"You were also in another explosion, drugged, and cried for hours. All of those things mean you need more rest," he argued, pushing open the door to the bedroom we shared.

He wasted no time stripping off his clothes while I stood there awkwardly.

I understood his earlier comment that abstaining wouldn't be a problem. Between my rampant emotions and the fact that I couldn't help but blame him for what happened, as much as I blamed myself anyway, sex would be the last thing on my mind.

At least I had the doctor's orders to keep him from taking what he wanted, because I didn't think I would survive having that added to my inner turmoil in that moment.

Once he was naked, he moved toward me and grasped the hem of my dress and lifted it. As my underwear was revealed, he held my eyes and didn't glance down at the body that he so smoothly stripped almost nude.

The faint sound of a generic text tone came from his pants, his head dropping in disappointment. Indecision warred on his face, and he hesitated before finally groaning and moving to grab his cell phone. He stared down at the screen for a moment, his eyes darting over whatever message he received before he gave me his eyes again.

There was a slight smile on his face, a hint of good news shining through as he delivered the words that gave me hope for the first time since the bomb had gone off.

"Your father is awake."

*T*he phone trembled in my hands, the phantom vibrations making me wonder, making me *hope* that the call from my mother had come. That Rafael had been wrong and my mother was alive, and she'd called as soon as she had news of my father's health. It took me far too long to realize that it wasn't the phone trembling.

It was my hands.

When Rafael had told me my father was awake the night before, I'd been desperate to call. To find out his prognosis and what to expect in his recovery. To hear his voice and just know he still lived. Even if he hated me with every breath in the lungs that had likely been scorched by flames.

Rafe had insisted we sleep, that I call at a decent hour and not the middle of the night, and allow my grandmother to see to him in his first moments awake. He'd only just woken up, only just learned that his wife was dead. He needed time to grieve the loss of her privately.

It would be the only time I could call him for a while. I had to make it count.

"*Mi reina?*" Rafael asked, touching his hand to the top of

mine when I didn't touch my finger to the screen to place the call. My grandmother's number was displayed, just waiting for me.

"What am I supposed to tell her?" I asked, turning tear-filled eyes his way. My thoughts always ran a mile a minute, never ending and all-consuming in a way that seemed like I could never find silence in truth. I'd never thought there would come a day when I would be lost for words, when my mind would simply...

Go blank.

But there were no words for what I'd caused, and nothing would ever bring my mother back from the grave.

If there had even been enough of her remaining to bury.

I swallowed back a sudden rush of nausea with the thought, tossing the phone onto the mattress and vaulting to my feet as I made my way to the bathroom. I kicked the door closed behind me and barely made it to the toilet before my stomach heaved, attempting to empty itself in utter uselessness until my throat burned.

Rafe's hands slid the hair away from my face gently, gathering it at the back of my head and rubbing soothing circles over my back once he had it secured. I coughed, swatting him away as mortification pulsed through me. He needed to get out and leave me to be sick in peace, but there was no swaying the steadfast figure who fell to his knees beside me as I reached up a hand to cover my mouth when the worst of the nausea settled.

Tugging away from his grip, I moved to the sink and washed my face with cold water silently. Rafe pulled the toothbrush I'd used the day before from the holder on the counter, spreading a stripe of toothpaste over it and handing it to me without a word.

I accepted it even though I wanted nothing more than to

kick him out of the room and let me recover in privacy. "Are you alright?" he asked finally, stepping up behind me as I spit into the sink and rinsed my mouth thoroughly.

"I'm fine," I said, exasperated when his lips touched my shoulder. The contact was so sweet, so *gentle*, that it tugged at the memory of the man I'd first fallen in love with. He seemed a world away in everything that had happened, and I'd thought I would never see him again. I knew that his reappearance was Rafe's way of helping me cope, of comforting me through what he knew would be an impossibly trying time for me. Even with the inappropriate timing —I had bigger things to worry about in the immediate future—I couldn't help the surge of curiosity and wondering if that man had been real after all.

If Rafe would be that way with me when we weren't in constant conflict over the status of our marriage.

"I'll call Mariano's doctor. See if he has anything that can help with the nausea," Rafael offered, touching his lips to my cheek and making for the bathroom door he'd left open when he barged in on me.

"No. I'll be alright. It's just morning sickness," I offered, shaking my head and giving him a slight smile.

"I don't like to see you sick," he said, furrowing his brow in confusion. It was adorable in a way; every single time Rafe reminded himself of how unusual his obsession with me was, watching that moment of shock cross his face.

I wondered when it would stop surprising him that he cared.

"Then you shouldn't have knocked me up," I said, giving a brittle smile. "Let's not forget that one of us did this intentionally, and it wasn't me."

His nose nuzzled my cheek, and my eyes landed on the twisted little smirk that played at his mouth. "You want the baby too," he said, and while I didn't think I'd outright said as much to him, Rafael was capable enough to read me.

He'd seen the concern in my face that came with the thought of losing the baby after the explosion at the house. I glared at him, hating that I couldn't deny it, but I wouldn't ever tempt fate by saying something like that. Especially when it wasn't true. "I do, but that doesn't change the fact that you did this to me. If you didn't want to see me suffer morning sickness, then you should have wrapped it up. You made that choice, and now there is no one to blame but yourself."

"I'll do what I can to mitigate the symptoms. We can have the best obstetrician tend to you—"

"Stop," I said firmly. "This is...it's part of being pregnant. Yes, it's miserable, but I'm not so sick that our health is at risk. Leave the best obstetrician for the people who need it. Not just for the husband who feels guilty. In the meantime, if you don't like to see it, then stay out of the bathroom. I'd appreciate it."

"You're the one who has to carry the baby and all that goes along with that. I know that, but..." he trailed off, considering the words that would come next. He touched his finger beneath my cheek, turning me to face him as he stared down at me. "Is there any reason I can't carry *you*?"

My chest sagged, more of my weight leaning into his body as I held his stare. Tears gathered in my eyes with the unexpectedly sweet words.

Oh God.

A sob cracked in my chest, feeling like a cavern spreading through me as I leaned into his embrace. His strong arms wrapped around me, one hand cupping the back of my head as my tears touched his bare chest. "I know you want to stand on your own, and I want that for you too," he murmured, fingers running through my hair gently, "but I will always be here to carry you when you need it, *mi reina*."

He punctuated the words by sliding his hands down to my thighs and lifting me into his arms. My legs wrapped around his waist instinctively, clinging to him as I tried to push back the crushing weight that came with the knowledge that my father may not even have a body to bury. He would never get to set eyes on his wife again. There'd been a time when I couldn't understand how monumental that kind of loss would be.

But when I tried to picture Rafe suddenly...gone, a yawning chasm of *nothing* stretched out in front of me.

I would rather fight a hundred arguments with him than have any other man smile at me, and I knew down to my bones that would never change. If that was how my father felt about my mother, then I didn't know how he would keep going.

Rafe sat on the edge of the bed, positioning me on his lap and holding me. My gaze fell to the phone on the bed, staring at it with mounting dread of the conversation that would follow. Everything my father had lost in a single moment overwhelmed me, especially because all of it had been meant for me.

"I don't want to carry myself anymore," I whispered, feeling his body tense beneath me. His grip tightened, pulling me closer until my face pressed into his neck and I breathed him deep. He surrounded me, holding me through the stark realization that I was only ever a single moment away from losing him.

He felt like an unstoppable force, an inhuman being who could never be killed, but I'd seen him bleed. I'd felt his blood on my skin when he'd been shot.

"You never have to again," he murmured against the top of my head. Even knowing he meant every word, every syllable that he spoke with everything he was, I tasted the lie in the air. He couldn't make such a promise without a thread of doubt, not with the life he lived.

There was every chance that the day would come when he wasn't there to carry me, and when that day came, I wasn't sure I would be strong enough to carry on. "I love you," I murmured, my lips grazing against his skin. The sudden urge to make sure he knew exactly how I felt couldn't be denied, roaring in my blood as if summoned from the depths of my soul.

This man was everything to me: my devil, my savior, my husband, my heart.

"*Te quiero con toda mi alma*," he said, his voice hoarse as if he was overcome with emotion right alongside me. Had I ever said it first? Had I ever told him I loved him without prompting from him?

I didn't know that I had, and I knew I hadn't done enough to show him how I felt. Even knowing I had good reasons for that, that the guard around my heart was justi-fied considering all he'd done and would likely continue to do, I let all of it wash away.

I no longer cared what had led us to where we sat with his arms wrapped around me; all that mattered was that he was my rock.

My everything.

Staying seated on his lap, I pulled my head out of his neck to look at him. My vision blurred as I watched him, raising a hand and stroking gentle fingers over the strong line of his jaw. "What does that mean?" I asked, resting my forehead against his. His eyes filled my sight, that unique stare all I could see as I waited for his answer.

"It means, 'I love you with all my soul,'" he said, reaching up a hand to cup my cheek. His thumb pushed through the wetness of my tears, wiping it from my skin and just watching me process his words.

We sat in silence, me sniffling back the tears in my throat and him holding me through it. Carrying me, when I didn't feel like I could do it alone. Once my breathing calmed and my heart steadied, he reached for the phone lying on the bed. Placing it in my hands, he touched the screen to make the call before I could hesitate.

I lifted it to my ear, listening to the ringing as Rafe leaned forward and touched his lips to the corner of my mouth. "*Nōhsehsaeh*?" my grandmother's tremulous, exhausted voice said as the call connected.

"It's me," I confirmed, swallowing back the tears that came from the sound of her voice.

"*Isa*," she said, her voice catching on the word. "Are you hurt?"

"Nothing severe. I'll be okay," I said and there was a pause as the sound of my grandmother blowing her nose came over the phone. "How is he?"

Silence again. "Rafael arranged for specialists to treat him, but your father refuses to cooperate until you're home safe. He wants to go looking for you.

"We're not coming home, *Nohkomach*," I said, touching a hand to my eyes and clenching them closed to fight off the sting of more tears. How was I supposed to tell my grand-mother that my sister would probably never come home again? That it would never be safe for me to see her after everything she'd meant to me all my life?

"What do you mean you aren't coming home?" she asked, her voice a harsh whisper. I heard her rustling around, shifting and undoubtedly standing to pace. "You have to."

"I *can't*," I pleaded, unsure how much I could really tell her. I decided on the truth, the simplest version of it and in the end, the only one that really mattered. "It isn't safe."

"Whatever your husband is involved in, we can—"

"*No*," I said sternly. "Even if I wanted that, it's too late. I'll only put you in danger by coming home, and there's been enough suffering because of me, don't you think?"

"Nobody blames you for what happened. You have to stop shouldering the blame for the actions of other people."

"I'm not," I sighed in exasperation. "I know that I didn't...that I didn't kill her. I didn't set that bomb in the car, but it's just a different kind of responsibility. My choices led us here—"

"Did they?" my grandmother asked. "Or were they your husband's choices? Chloe was not lying or being dramatic about the kind of man you married, was she?"

"No," I agreed, nodding my head as my eyes met Rafe's. He pursed his lips, leaning forward to touch his lips to my forehead gently as if he knew that I needed him to confirm he truly accepted what my family would think of him going forward. "She was telling the truth."

"How could you be involved with someone like that, Isa? That is not the girl I raised."

"But it is," I said. "I just hid the demon inside me better than Odina did. I kept it from you where she flaunted it, but it's there. That's why I never really lived the way you wanted. I think I always knew what would happen."

"Where is Odina?" she asked, changing the subject as if she couldn't bear to discuss the line of thought with me any longer. I couldn't fault her, knowing that she'd pinned all her hopes and dreams for her legacy on me.

Another thing ripped away by my husband, even if it was just a casualty and not his goal.

"The people who were responsible for the attack took her. I'll try to get her home safe," I said, pinning Rafe with a look. The quirk of his eyebrow communicated how little he planned to do, but I owed it to my family to return one of their daughters to them.

I'd do it for my mother if nothing else.

"She has to come home. Just be careful," my grandmother confirmed. I agreed, giving her the confirmation I knew she needed. I had no idea how I would make it happen, not when I couldn't put myself at risk when I was pregnant.

If it came down to the baby and Odina, I knew who I would choose. Even if it destroyed what remained of my humanity.

"Can I talk to him?" I asked when an awkward silence descended between us. I wasn't quite ready to hang up the phone, not knowing that it could very well be the last time I spoke to her. Hanging up felt like closing a door and walking away from the past that could have no part in my future.

My future was bathed in blood and tears, but it was *mine.*

"I love you, Isa," my grandmother said, her voice tight. I knew without a doubt that she sensed the inevitable just the same as I did. That the goodbye felt final in a way neither of us wanted or should've had to deal with in the wake of my mother's death.

I hadn't only lost her, but *all* of them in one way or another.

"I love you too, *Nohkomach*. I always will." A pained sound escaped her throat, and there was a sniffle before the soft sounds of her talking to my father.

"Isa?" he asked, his voice too rough and weak.

"Hey, Daddy," I said, forcing a smile to my face as I spoke to him. "How are you feeling?"

"Please, Isa. Just come home," he said, ignoring the question and focusing on whatever tension he'd picked up from my grandmother. His voice grew tighter, as if the emotion worsened whatever pain speaking was causing him.

"Rafael has promised that he's going to take care of you," I said, not even bothering to question it. I knew Rafe would give me anything so long as it wasn't to leave him; taking care of my father's medical bills would be a no-brainer. "Go with the specialists. Let them do what they can."

"*Isa*," he rasped.

"I love you, and I'm sorry. I'm so sorry," I murmured, fighting back my own tears.

"The doctor said the same foundation that paid for your grandmother's surgery is paying for my treatment now. Tell me how that's possible," he said, and the desperation in his voice broke my heart. He knew that the conversation was ending, that I wouldn't last much longer before I fell apart.

And when that happened, he would lose me.

We would lose each other.

"Goodbye, Dad," I said, pulling the phone from my ear. I stared down at it, frozen at my father's shout, at the hollow and broken sound of his grief as I went silent.

"Isa!" he yelled desperately.

Rafe took the phone from my hand, touching the screen until my father's pained voice disappeared entirely. He dropped the phone to the bed, staring at the side of my face. I couldn't take my eyes off the phone, off the revelation in my father's last words.

"You paid for her surgery," I murmured, the quiet tone of

my voice sounding so broken that my breath caught. I felt numb inside, as if my body had been encased in ice and nothing could move or function until I found warmth.

It came in the feeling of Rafe's hands rubbing over my bare skin, of his reassuring touch that stimulated all the nerve endings that threatened to shut down in the shock of grief that plunged me into a state of agonizing stillness.

"I did," he said, drawing me into his chest and adding his warmth to my body.

"You saved her life."

"I have enough money, *mi reina*, but you only have one *Nohkomach*." He butchered the pronunciation, much the same way I was sure I would when I eventually tried to learn to speak Spanish, but it warmed my heart to hear his attempt anyway.

I only had one grandmother, just like I'd only had one mother. One father and one sister.

But with all that had happened, I no longer *had* them, not really. The ones who still breathed were lost to me.

There was only us and the family we were creating.

*I*sa's eyes watered, tears flowing down her cheeks as she processed the fact that she was alone in the world in a way she'd never thought to be.

I'd spend my life proving to her that she was never really alone, regardless of what needed to be done with her family. The ragged sigh that left her lungs sounded like it was torn from her soul, like a chasm opened inside her until there was a hole where her family had once been.

I leaned forward, brushing my lips against hers in a moment of tenderness. Her breath hitched, caressing my mouth gently as she leaned into the contact.

Of all the kisses we'd shared, of all the times I'd devoured her mouth and taken her as mine, *this* was one of my favorites. Something in her shifted, something in me embraced her, and I poured every emotion I felt for my wife into the contact between our mouths.

She whimpered, sounding half broken as she raised a hand to my chest and rested her palm against her name carved into my skin.

The same way she'd carved herself into my heart.

Her lips trembled as her fingers slid over the jagged skin, her body shaking in my lap as I shifted us back into the center of the bed. I laid her down beside me, resting an arm over her waist as I finally detached my lips from hers and looked down at her.

She pressed forward, touching her mouth to mine again. Her lips still trembled, and the caution in her touch took my breath away. She knew as well as I did that our lives had changed. That her grief and her pregnancy had shifted something in our marriage.

She'd loved me before. I knew that without a kernel of doubt.

But in that moment, I became the center of her universe. The only thing in the world that she had to cling to, and for the first time Isa needed me as much as I needed her. The raw vulnerability of her touch clenched my heart in my chest, intensifying the overwhelming urge to protect her.

I'd spent so many weeks determined to claim her as mine, I never stopped to wonder what would happen once I'd accomplished that goal.

Now that I had, and I knew it with every tremulous touch of her fingers against my skin and every contented sigh as my fingers coasted over hers gently, all I wanted was to protect her. To take care of her in a way that she'd never known, in the way I should have from the beginning.

I hated that I'd needed to hurt her, but I wouldn't change a moment of it if it led us to where we were now.

"Let me take care of you," I murmured against her parted mouth. Her eyes opened, widening as they connected with mine. Whatever she saw in my gaze, I only hoped that it was an echo of what I saw in hers.

Acceptance. Love. Light.

Her multicolored eyes weren't clouded with the nightmares that haunted her, only the openness of her grief as she nodded her head slowly. For Isa to concede that she needed to be cared for, that she needed me to take control for just a little while, I couldn't imagine the enormity of emotion swirling inside her.

Standing from the bed, I pulled her into my arms and made my way to the bathroom. I set her on the edge of the massive tub, turning on the hot water and letting it fill as she watched me. I grabbed the bath oils off the shelf, pouring some into the water until the scent of roses filled the space.

Grasping Isa's hands in mine, I tugged her to stand. Sliding one of the straps off her shoulder, I leaned forward and touched my lips gently to the skin it revealed as it hung down her arm.

Taking her chin in my hand gently, I tilted her head up until I could lean forward and kiss her again. Her lips parted for me, letting me sweep my tongue inside with gentle strokes that felt far too much like a first kiss.

In a way, I supposed it wasn't far off. No matter how many times I'd been with Isa, no matter how many times I'd plunged myself inside her mouth and taken what I wanted, it was so rare that she offered herself.

Not just her body, but everything that made her the woman I loved with every breath in me.

When I pulled away, I lifted her in my arms and placed her into the hot water gently. She stared up at me in confusion, her perfect, white teeth showing with her rounded mouth as she realized I wasn't coming in with her just yet. "I'm going to get you something to eat," I explained, tucking her hair behind her ear. I hated to leave her, knowing that the rawness of her loss lurked just beneath the surface.

Turning on my heel and resolving to find something

quick, I paused when the water sloshed and Isa's hand grasped mine. "Please don't go," she begged.

"You need to eat," I pointed out, even if the thought of leaving her when she wanted me to stay threatened to break something in me.

"I need *you*," she whispered, her voice catching on the confession. One day, Isa would get used to being vulnerable with me. She'd accept that there didn't need to be fear in laying out her feelings and needs with me.

Because I would never leave her, and I'd never be like most men who might freak out if she became needy or clingy. The more Isa craved me and depended on me, the better that would be for my own obsession with her.

I tugged my hand from her grip, but only long enough to step into the bedroom and text Joaquin to bring something up for Isa to nibble on. Isa hung her upper body over the edge of the tub, watching me through the open door to the bedroom as if she couldn't bring herself to settle. I watched her, knowing that I wanted nothing more than to sink into the water with her.

To hold her in my arms and feed her and care for her in the way she needed. The sensation was so foreign, so new and unexpected.

Even the urges to be gentle that I'd felt before she knew who I was couldn't compare, and I didn't think it was solely the baby that brought out the softer side of my love for her. It hadn't happened before the attack.

It only happened when she started looking at me differently. The thinly veiled suspicion that always lurked behind her eyes was gone, leaving nothing behind but love. Clear, unhidden, love.

The knock on the bedroom door came quickly, and I swung it open. Joaquin was silent on the other side, his brow raised with the question he didn't want to ask. I nodded to confirm that she would be alright, taking the tray of fruit and croissants from his hands and kicking the door closed behind me without another word.

Isa finally leaned her weight into the tub as I stepped into the room and placed the tray of food on the edge where she'd rested her upper body. She watched me while I undressed. Her eyes filled with the faintest trace of heat, her desire and attraction for me strong enough to show even through the sadness that I suspected would linger within her for the rest of her life.

I scooted her forward in the tub, slipping my body between her and the side. My legs slid along hers, the smooth glide of her skin on mine as she leaned back and her ass settled into my cock tantalizing, despite the circumstances.

I picked up a strawberry as Isa shifted sideways between my legs so that I could look at her. Guiding it to her lips, I watched as she opened and let me feed her. She didn't motion to do it herself or take it from me, chewing slowly and thoughtfully in silence. Unable to resist the urge, I licked my fingers clean before I reached over and pulled a chunk off the croissant to feed her. We sat in silence for a while, her head probably spinning as she ate and me simply enjoying the fact that she'd let me take care of her.

I wanted to spend the rest of my life just like this. Peaceful, with her in my arms and the problems outside our doors a world away when it was just the two of us, but tension crept back into her features when her hunger was satisfied.

The real world couldn't be held off forever.

"Talk to me," I said, touching a hand to her stomach. She covered my hand with hers, seeming to take comfort in it as we both held the child that I'd deceived her to create.

"I know she wasn't perfect," she said, her jaw clenching as she said the words.

"She wasn't," I agreed, wondering if Isa realized that nobody was. She'd spent so much of her life trying to live up to the perfect image her mother created, that I wondered if she ever really realized it had been an impossible standard.

"She wasn't even really the mom I'd thought I had, in the end, and it wasn't pretty for a bit," she said, her thoughts coming in a stream of consciousness that she didn't seem to have any control over. "But she was mine." Her voice broke, cracking as she leaned her weight into my chest. I wrapped an arm around her, touching my mouth to the top of her head and letting her work her way through the shock of all that had happened.

I knew Isa well enough to know that she'd give herself one more day. One day to grieve and feel the loss she'd suffered after the conversation with her father.

Then she'd pick herself up, shove it down into the depths of her soul, and come back ready to fight.

"I promise you, they will all die for what they've done, *mi reina*," I said, the soft murmur of my voice sounding so at odds with the words of vengeance.

"*Slowly*," she confirmed.

"They'll feel every moment of pain they've caused you by the time we're done with them." She nodded, burying her face into my skin and sinking back into my embrace.

One more day.

⚐♙♟♙♗♟

*I*sa sat in the center of the bed the next morning when I came back from checking with the men, making arrangements to have the plane ready for us to return home as soon as she was ready. Her hair was disheveled from her sleep, something hard in her gaze as she met my eyes.

"What is it, *mi reina*?" I asked, tossing my phone down on the ottoman at the end of the bed. She pursed her lips in thought, sinking her teeth into the plump flesh as I stepped around the side of the bed.

"What do they want with me?" she asked, her gaze so open despite the fact that she could clearly feel she was missing information. "I still don't understand. I'm *nobody*."

I studied her, watching her face for any traces of lingering suspicion that I might be keeping secrets from her. There was none to be found in her expression, and I knew I could continue keeping the last secret until the day I died if I wished.

For the first time, Isa had started to trust me for whatever reason. It was all out in the open and written on her face. My chest ached with an unfamiliar twinge of pain, and it didn't take a genius to wrap my head around what it was.

Guilt.

I couldn't remember the last time I'd felt guilty for something I'd done or a secret I'd kept, but knowing Isa didn't expect this?

That made it impossible to bear.

I stretched to the ottoman, grabbing my phone and unlocking the screen to search through my emails until I found the attachment I was looking for. The photo of the contract that had sealed Isa's fate stared back at me. "They want you because Dima has wanted you from the moment he first saw you at the river that day," I said, running a hand through my hair as her face twisted in pain.

"What are you talking about?"

"He was there with my father. From what you said, he

wasn't involved in throwing you into the water, but they were together." I turned the phone, placing it in her hands as she tore her eyes away from me and looked down at the screen.

"What is this?" she asked, zooming in to read the words.

"It's the contract my father signed with Pavel and Dima Kuznetsov," I said, pointing to her first name at the top of the screen. There was no other information regarding her whereabouts, ensuring my father and Franco Bellandi could broker the sale.

Even if Dima had known her full name and location, going into Bellandi territory and stealing a girl out from under him would have been a mistake. Paranoid men like Franco would have seen it as an act of opposition, something that could lead to a full-scale war under the right circumstances.

"To be delivered on her thirteenth birthday," Isa said aloud, the harshness of that settling over her. They'd have taken her from her home and given her a life of abuse on her birthday of all days. It shouldn't have mattered in the grand scheme of things, but from the way her face went slack, I knew it did.

"I killed my father on my mother's birthday. A month before your thirteenth," I said, pausing so the revelation of just how close she'd come to being taken could sink in. "I'd like to claim it was intentional, that I knew I would save you from the life they'd planned for you, but I can't. Until I saw you on that street, I'd all but forgotten about the girl my father sold to Dima. The rivalry with the Kuznetsovs didn't come until after I saw you and decided I wanted to rid the world of all the men like my father who would hurt girls like you." I touched my lips to hers gently, deepening the kiss when she didn't try to fight me off.

She stared into my eyes as I pulled back to look down at her, her brain processing everything she'd learned. "Your father sold me to Dima, and you." She paused, swallowing. "You knew? All this time."

"I didn't think you were anything other than just another one of my father's potential victims until you told me he threw you in the river, and even then, I hoped you would never have to know the truth about this. I wanted to protect you—"

"You wanted to keep me obedient!" she said, snapping back. "Don't you dare insinuate that you did this for me. That you kept this secret for *my* sake."

"It was for both of us," I said, reaching for her and grinding my teeth when she shook her head. "I knew that you'd never want to look at me again if you knew that I'd fucking sat there and watched them sign your life away and done *nothing*."

"You were there," she whispered, understanding finally dawning on her face. She'd thought I just discovered the truth when it had been said and done.

"You weren't the first he sold. I didn't think anything of it at the time," I explained.

"That's why you were so surprised when I told you the photos were from before the earliest dates," she said, nodding as she opened and closed her mouth and tried to find the words for what I'd done.

"I did what I could when I could," I said, meeting her eyes and hoping against all reason that the openness she'd shown me wouldn't be lost to the revelation of my deception.

"How am I supposed to believe that you aren't keeping more secrets? They never end, Rafael," she said, her voice turning pleading.

"I swear to you on my mother's grave, there is nothing else I'm keeping from you," I said, and her body went still with the words. My mother was the only thing that had ever mattered in my life until Isa, the only thing I could swear on that would mean *anything*.

Her eyes were wide as she stared at me, and then finally she did the one thing she could that shocked me.

She nodded, sighing as if she believed me. I somehow doubted it, but I'd take the concession for what it was.

*R*afael's eyes met mine as he pushed open the unlocked bathroom door. I ran the comb through my damp hair from the shower I'd taken alone while he made sure the men were ready to leave. The thought of returning to *El Infierno* didn't fill me with the same comfort it had only hours before. Not now that I knew what deals had once been struck long before I called the island home.

I never could have imagined the depths of the connection between Rafael and I, never would have begun to anticipate how entwined our pasts were. As if phantom hands guided us together, making us dance like puppets on a string.

I knew that couldn't be the case, knew that all the driving forces in our lives had worked to keep us separate. Between the river that should have killed me and his father's attempt to sell me when that failed, the fact that I still lived could be nothing short of a miracle.

If any *one* of the actions that had brought us together hadn't come to pass, would we still be standing where we were? If Rafael hadn't been drawn into the Bellandi war, would he ever have known I existed as more than just the ghost of a girl he'd allowed to be sold?

The answer wasn't clear. Even though logic said that a happenstance meeting on the street had been the catalyst that brought us together, every coincidental connection in our pasts made it feel like something else drove us toward one another. Whether it was the spirit of his mother or just a twist of the mind, I suspected we would never know.

Was it possible that Rafe had recognized me as the girl from that photo the first time he saw me? That deep down, even if he hadn't realized it, he'd seen in me a chance to make amends for the children he'd failed to save and protect?

Was it just his subconscious that caught his eyes on me initially, telling him he'd seen me before and his obsession developed from there?

As my eyes met his in the mirror and he stepped behind me, I didn't know that it mattered. Whatever had brought us to this moment, whatever had happened to make *this* possible, it was in our past.

I didn't want it to decide our future.

He took the comb from my hand, resuming the task of gently working it through the knots in my hair after a restless night of sleep. "Do you believe me?" he asked, and despite the harsh set to his features in the reflection, I knew my answer mattered to him in a way I wouldn't have expected.

"I do," I said, huffing a disbelieving laugh. I shouldn't have believed a word that came from Rafe's mouth, not when he'd fed me countless, beautiful lies and omitted the truth more times than I could count.

But whereas the times before had been lies that benefited him and kept him from having to deal with the consequences of my reactions, this one felt different. Yes, he stood to lose me if I reacted poorly to the news of what he'd done when I was a child—or rather hadn't done. But more than that, he protected me from knowing the truth of what my life had almost become.

He protected me from the knowledge that the man who wanted to rape me as a thirteen-year-old girl now had the twin sister who looked exactly like me within his grasp.

Something that Rafael had arranged, *knowing* what she would suffer.

"Out of everything you've done, keeping this a secret is hardly your worst offense," I said, thinking of the sister I needed to free. I was at a loss for how to accomplish that when Rafe himself had clearly stated he wouldn't risk his men for her.

I'd known he hated her, and that he would kill her if the time came when it was necessary, but the fate he'd condemned her to was unforgivable.

It was far worse than death.

Rafe set the comb on the counter, watching my hard face in the reflection of the mirror above the vanity as he rested his hands on the edge of the counter and leaned his weight into mine. "So where do we go from here?" he asked, and the question caressed my skin.

It felt like a choice, the first one I'd had since he came into my life. Even if I knew he would still never let me go, I'd stopped wanting that and it didn't matter anymore. But I'd gotten so used to him dictating where we went and what we did, that there was a moment of shock within me as I tried to remember what it was to *choose*.

"We go home," I said, letting warmth fill my eyes even as my jaw remained tightly clenched. His right hand lifted from the counter, resting on my hip as he sighed in relief. "And you teach me how to not be helpless anymore."

He paused, his fingers going still at my hip. "*Mi reina*, you're pregnant."

"The last I knew, being pregnant did not make me an invalid. You can teach me to take care of myself without kicking me in the stomach, and that is exactly what you're going to do," I said, grasping the hand at my hip within mine and dragging it toward my belly that would swell soon enough. "I need to do this."

He watched my face, searching for any signs of hesitation in whether or not I would be ready for this. "It won't change what happened, and it definitely won't get her back."

"I know that. After what you did, I don't truly believe that I *could* save her. She was already broken from when we were kids, but to be drugged and offered up in my place will push her over the edge. Of all the things you've done, that is probably the worst," I said, watching as his eyes widened in shock.

I knew he expected the fertility shot to be the worst for me, but while that had been a terrible thing to do, I had also always known Rafael wanted me pregnant. He'd left out some details, violated my body, but in the end the result was the same.

If he hadn't offered Odina up as a sacrifice, more of his men might have been killed. That was true, and I didn't doubt the sincerity of that assertion.

But it didn't excuse what Odina would suffer, and I found it difficult to reconcile the man who held me while I cried and fed me strawberries in the bath with the man who could condemn my sister to that kind of fate and never even bat an eye.

"She drugged you to help her friend rape you," he reminded me, and I nodded.

"She did, but she still didn't deserve what you did. Two wrongs do not make a right, and nothing is ever as simple as you think it is. Even if I hate her, she's still my sister. She's still a woman who deserved to have control over her own body."

"I won't apologize for doing what I had to do to protect you and the men who put their faith in me. I do not separate women from men when I decide what casualties are acceptable. Just because she has a pussy doesn't make her any less of an enemy to me, and when it comes down to it, I will always choose the people who stand beside me over my enemies," he said, his voice dropping low in warning.

I heaved out a sigh, not because I would heed the warning, but because I knew I could expect nothing less from Rafael. Part of loving him was loving the devil, knowing that I would never be able to change him into a saint who never stepped a toe out of line.

Loving every part of him—even the parts that were hand-carved from nightmares and sin—that was the choice I made. That was my power.

Loving the unlovable.

*A*nna hugged me tightly, pulling back to place her hands on my shoulders and stare down at me with a sympathy-filled look. "You'll keep in touch?" she asked. I gave her a small smile, nodding silently as I bit my lip. The odd emotion that flooded me seemed so disproportionate to how briefly I'd known her, but I didn't even bother to try to make sense of it.

Not when she'd kept me company in the aftermath of the revelation of how much I'd torn my family apart.

I nodded to Mariano and Luca, letting Rafe guide me up the steps to the plane and taking comfort in the familiar surroundings. Even knowing that *El Infierno* may feel differently now that I knew the truth of all that had happened there, I was resolved to not let Miguel take that away from me.

The island was my home, my sanctuary from the rest of the world and the one place on Earth where I felt safe. The place that had once been my cage became my refuge.

The doors closed at the front as we settled in the smaller back cabin, and Rafe reached into my seat to buckle my seatbelt for me. He fidgeted with it, making sure it was adjusted perfectly as I quirked a brow at him in amusement.

So far removed from the man who had carved his name into my skin, and I couldn't help but wonder when the devil would show his face again. I suspected I would be safe until the doctor lifted the ban on sex, since he couldn't punish me physically, *or* sexually as it was.

Maybe it would take time for him to believe I wouldn't fall apart at the first sign of something dangerous. Given all that had happened and how often I'd cried over the course of the days since my mother's death, I couldn't even blame him.

But something about today felt different. I'd woken up feeling resolved, determined to push through the sadness that would cling to me for the rest of my life and ensure that her death wasn't for nothing. I'd live my life to the fullest, and I'd be damned if the Kuznetsovs ever laid a hand on me, especially with the fragile life growing within me.

Rafe straightened, taking his own seat as the plane moved forward to line up on the runway. He stared at me in silence as we took off, grasping my hand from across the table between us and seeming lost in thought. I both loved and hated the consideration he'd shown me in the wake of my grief.

But I also missed the husband who didn't hold back, as odd as it felt to say such a thing.

Once we'd reached altitude and the pilot's voice came over the intercom, Rafe leaned forward in his seat. The hint of something dark lingered in his gaze before he shoved it away, reaching into one of the compartments tucked to the side of the table. He pulled out a chess board, setting it on the table between us and placing the white pieces in front of me.

"Shall we play a game?" he asked, the corner of his mouth tipping up in a seductive smirk that might have brought me to my knees if I'd been standing. A dark smile teased my lips in response, and he bit his bottom one as his eyes dropped to it.

Nobody could say no to the devil himself.

The twisted little smile on Isa's face took my breath away, watching with rapt attention as she moved her pieces with clear focus and determination. Her eyes gleamed and she bit her lip every time she studied the board to choose her next move. I moved my knight, taking the pawn she'd unknowingly put into my path and waiting for the moment she realized I was three moves from taking her Queen. She moved one of her pawns, sitting back in the chair like the Queen she was and it was her throne.

"Checkmate," she said, holding my eyes as I furrowed my brow, then I glanced down at the board again. She cocked her head to the side, smirking at me so arrogantly that I could feel it as I realized what she'd done. With my King pinned behind in all directions but the diagonal where she'd trapped me with her Queen, I couldn't move to escape her play.

The game hadn't been short, a group of pieces set to either side of the board as we'd conquered one another. But she'd won.

I couldn't remember the last time I'd lost at chess, but I

hadn't even seen her spring the trap. Let alone maneuver me into it. I tipped over my King, giving her the acknowledgement she deserved.

The King had fallen to the Queen.

The look on her face communicated just how intent she had been as she unbuckled her seat belt and slowly stood. She stepped out from behind the table, approaching me in my seat until she touched firm hands to the back of the seat and swiveled it to face the aisle. It was so similar to what I'd done on our journey to Chicago, so intense a reversal of our roles that my heart beat faster inside my chest, my body thrumming with need.

I'd thought my unending obsession with Isa couldn't get any more severe. That there were no corners of my being that didn't belong to her, but as she stared down at me with fire burning behind her arresting eyes, I knew that hadn't been true.

I had owned Isa, but *mi reina* would possess me in truth.

She leaned forward, touching her lips to mine gently but keeping her eyes on me as she bit the plump flesh and touched her hand to the belt at my waist. I stilled her hand, only the concern for her and the baby's health preventing me from letting her take what she wanted.

I was certain that the face of the commanding woman looking down at me could ask me for anything, and I would give it to her without question so long as it wouldn't hurt her.

"We can't—"

"I'm not planning to fuck you, my devil," she murmured, nipping my lip again as her lips brushed softly over mine. She unfastened the belt and my pants, reaching her small hand inside and pulling me free. Squeezing me with a firm stroke from root to tip, Isa pulled a ragged groan from me at the feel of her flesh surrounding me.

The power of defeating the devil at his own game shone in her eyes as she watched me, filling her with the desire I knew so well. It came from the adrenaline of winning, from the sensation of knowing that she'd finally bested her opponent.

Even if I was no longer her enemy, there had been days when we'd spent more time deep in a battle of wills than wrapped in each other's arms.

Those days were gone.

She dropped to her knees between my legs, working me slowly with her hand as she stared up at me. She leaned in, brushing her lips over my shaft with a smooth caress. Breathing slowly so that the slight and warm air tickled me, she nipped the side gently. My hips bucked of their own volition, seeking more contact with the way she teased me.

It wasn't lost on me that it was the first time my wife had gone to her knees willingly, the first time she'd initiated sex between us at all, that I could recall. She may not have been happy about what I'd done with her sister, and I was sure that would haunt her in the coming days, but Isa knew one single truth.

We were inevitable, and fighting the connection between us was as pointless as trying to count the stars in the sky. I was hers, and she was mine.

Finally drawing me into her mouth, the wet heat of her tongue dragged over my skin as she worked me to the back of her throat. Her hand twisted as it rose and fell on the length that she didn't take inside her, moving slowly and at the pace that she wanted.

My desperation from the days of abstinence after being inside her several times a day on a regular basis was too much, making my hips snap up toward her mouth. Wanting her harder, wanting her faster.

But she dug her nails into my thigh, glaring up at me as she shook her head and withdrew until only the tip of my cock remained inside her. Her message was clear.

She was in charge.

Settling back into my seat with a ragged groan, I watched her face as she worked me slowly. Her knees had to ache, her mouth had to grow sore from being stretched around me for so long, but she made no move to let me finish.

She worked me with experienced touches that came from knowing me and my body and what I liked, mimicking the way I tormented her when I wanted something from her. Pulling back until my cock sprang free from her mouth, she worked her hand over my shaft and slid through the wetness her mouth had left behind. "No more secrets," she said, gripping me more firmly until I felt like I might finally explode around her. She pumped me again. "No more lies."

"*Mi reina,*" I groaned, wanting nothing more than to fuck her face. She was injured, and she'd come to me, and that was all that kept me from taking what I wanted and saying to hell with her ultimatums.

"Say it, *El Diablo,*" she said with a stern look. "The only way I'll let you come down my throat is if you promise me and *mean it.*"

The challenge brought the desire to prove her wrong. To remind her that no matter what games I allowed her to play when she was on her knees, there was only one person who was in charge of our fucking. I could grab her by the hair, shove my cock down her throat, and fuck her mouth until I filled her stomach with my cum.

But I didn't, choosing to give her what I knew she so

desperately needed. What I could finally offer her. *Truth.*
"No more secrets," I reaffirmed, even if everything inside me
rebelled against the concession. Whether I'd intended it to
be the case or not, part of me didn't want Isa to win.

I didn't want to give her even more power over me.

"No more lies."

"No more lies," I repeated, grunting when she wrapped
her lips around my head and *sucked.* Her hand squeezed me
as she moved her mouth up and down my shaft, taking me
deeper and harder and giving me more of everything I
needed. I buried a hand in her hair, holding her but letting
her keep control of her pace as I struggled to control my
hips.

My release crashed over me like a blinding wave, darkness pinching at the edges of my vision until only the stunning color of Isa's eyes stood out in the darkness. I poured
myself down her throat, groaning as she swallowed it all.

I was still recovering when she stood from between my
legs with a smirk, lifting her dress around her hips and slipping her panties down her legs until they puddled on the
floor. She perched on the edge of the table between our
seats, leaning back onto her hands and lifting her legs to
give me an unhindered view of the perfect, swollen flesh
between her thighs. "The doctor said—" I protested with a
groan.

"He said no penetrative sex," Isa reminded me, slipping
a hand down to touch herself while I watched. "But I'm not
asking for your cock. I want your mouth," she demanded,
circling her clit with two fingers and then lifting them to
touch my lips. The taste of her flooded my senses, filling me
with the desperate urge to do exactly as she asked.

I parted my lips, letting her fingers slide over my tongue
briefly before she pulled them away and put them back to

her clit. I leaned forward, shoving her fingers out of my way and dragging my tongue over her. Her hand buried in my hair, holding me firmly against her pussy as she ground herself against my face and used me to find the pleasure she needed.

My tongue explored every part of her without ever going inside, watching her chest heave and her eyes hold mine as she took what she wanted. Wrapping my lips around her clit finally, I watched her tumble over the edge and into an orgasm that arched her spine and left her breathless.

When her breathing slowed, she lowered herself into my lap. Her naked pussy pressed against my already hardening cock, and I buried my face in her hair and breathed deep.

We might be going back to *El Infierno*, but I already held my home in my arms.

*T*he sun had set by the time Rafael pulled his car up in front of the house. After a nearly ten-hour flight and then a boat ride from the mainland, exhaustion should have crept into my body, but I'd taken a nap in the bedroom cabin while Rafe made arrangements for everything he'd missed while we'd been gone.

He opened my door for me, and I swung my legs out and stood. Looking at the face of the house that had somehow shifted from my prison to my home, I wondered briefly if my mother had ever been to *El Infierno* in her time with Andrés. "Have you spoken to your uncle yet?" I asked, wondering if the man knew I was the child of a woman he'd once been intimate with or that she was gone.

Would he care?

"Not yet. I'll call him soon," Rafe said, seeming oddly hesitant for the conversation he had to know needed to happen.

We went into the house, the smell of food reaching my senses the second we were inside the front door. Regina poked her head around the corner from the kitchen, her gaze landing on Rafe first as a smile transformed her expression. When her eyes came to mine, the smile faded off in favor of pity that I wanted nothing to do with. "I'm going to find Alejandro. Don't wait up if you're tired, *mi reina*," Rafe said, leaning down to kiss me softly before he sauntered off for his office.

I tried not to care that he'd abandoned me so quickly upon returning home, fully understanding that I couldn't attach myself to his hip indefinitely just because I didn't feel strong enough to be alone quite yet. I'd distracted him from his business since the moment I set foot in Ibiza and the timeline was undoubtedly much longer than he'd anticipated when he decided he'd make me fall in love with him in ten days.

It just went to show how little Rafael Ibarra knew about love. I'd absolutely fallen for him, but choosing to walk away from my family would never have happened with such a timeline. Apparently it took a kidnapping to change my mind.

My hand raised to touch the brand on my arm instinctively with the thought of how far we'd come, but I pulled it away as Regina hurried over to me. "*Mi hija,*" she said, closing the distance between us and wrapping a tender arm around my shoulder. I tried to push back the surge of emotion it brought out, determined to be *done* crying. The day when people no longer offered me condolences would make pushing forward easier. Most did it with the best intentions, never realizing how that brought my grief to the forefront every single time.

Regina guided me to the stool at the island where I'd spent so much of my time, even with how briefly I'd been on *El Infierno*. Juice and pickles already sat in front of me, and I suppressed the urge to cry once again at the thought of someone who reminded me of a mother figure taking care of me.

Guilt plagued me through my life now, reminding me that I'd never again have the opportunity to fight with my own mother.

"Rafael requested I make sure we were stocked with your favorites. His mother always took a bite of pickle before eating and then she would put the entire pickle right back into the jar," she said, laughing as her eyes turned wistful. "It means you will have a boy."

"Wonderful," I scoffed. "A little devil to torture me." The warmth of her smile told me she understood that I didn't say it as a woman who didn't want her child, but as one who knew how difficult it would be but wanted it anyway.

"Yes, well, you have me to help when he torments you," she said, smiling as the front door opened and the Cortes brothers stepped into the house. "Joaquin said you know about the fertility shot."

"I do," I said, popping a slice of pickle into my mouth. The vinegar flavor made my tongue tingle in the way I'd grown to appreciate, and as soon as I swallowed it, my stomach settled. Sometimes I wondered if it would be best to just start drinking pickle juice.

"You forgave him?" she asked, leaning forward until her elbows rested on the island counter.

I nodded, trying to find the words to communicate what I felt about that deception. "The shot was a secret, but I always knew his intention. He didn't hide what really mattered in the end. I guess he just sped up the process." I laughed. It hadn't mattered in the moment when I learned the truth, not when I was overwhelmed by the crushing reality of a life I wasn't ready for. "I can't exactly be all that upset when I didn't do much to prevent the pregnancy. I stopped protesting altogether at some point." The words felt more and more true as I spoke them, reaffirming the belief that while what Rafe had done was horrifically wrong and a violation, all that mattered in the end was that we'd both participated in making our child.

"I am glad. You'll need him in the coming months, moving forward with the pregnancy," she said. "Especially without your mother to give you comfort."

"I don't know that she would have been particularly involved in our lives regardless, but—"

"But it is another thing entirely to bring life into this world knowing the baby will never know its grandparents," Regina said, finishing the thought for me as tears stung my eyes. She moved to the fridge, taking out a dessert dish and handing me a spoon. It looked similar to a cheesecake, and she didn't bother to cut off a slice as she dug her spoon into the edge on her side and took a bite. "The solution for morning sickness is pickles. The solution for heartache is *flaó*."

I chuckled softly, sniffling back the tears that threatened and digging my own spoon into the cake. The crust was thin and flaky, and the cheese within was creamy with finely chopped mint to offset the richness.

"It will be alright, *mi hija*. You know that, yes?" she asked, holding my eyes as I nodded.

"I know. It has to be," I said, spooning another bite as my hand dropped to my stomach. There had yet to be any pain or bleeding, and with every day that passed I grew more and more confident that I would *know* if something was wrong.

I would feel it, because the baby was a part of me now.

"What happened to your mother is terrible. You will miss her for the rest of your life, but you are strong, and you'll find your way," she said, pulling another bite of *flaó* into her mouth.

"I'm not strong," I whispered, thinking of all that I'd allowed to happen to me. All that I'd forgiven, because I was too weak to live without Rafael.

"*Mi hija,*" she said, her voice soft but scolding. "You are the strongest person I know, and you are the only one who has yet to realize that."

I stalled, staring at her in shock as I let her words dance over my skin. I so wanted them to be true, to be strong enough to be everything I would need to be to survive at Rafe's side. "Will you teach me to speak Spanish?" I asked.

If the odd segue into a new conversation threw her, she didn't show it. She grinned instead, nodding her head supportively. "Of course. That is your strength. Your determination to carry on, to adapt to what life has thrown at you. I will teach you whatever you wish to know," she confirmed, pausing as she set her spoon on the counter. She reached across, taking my hand in hers and leaning to study me intently. "There are two responses to a loss like yours. To wallow in it and be lost to the sadness like I have done, or to rise up and do what you must to get revenge and make those who hurt you suffer. I think I know which type of woman you are." She released me, putting her spoon in the dishwasher as she went for the doors to the pool area so she could make her way to her own home. She paused, looking back at me with her parting words. "Do you?"

*T*ime passed. The days faded in and out. I spent time with Regina, learning to cook her favorite dishes and doing the groundwork for the Spanish I desperately needed to learn.

But restlessness settled in my bones, waiting for the day when the doctor would clear me for more activity. When Rafe could begin training me, and when I could go out and explore the island I called home without Rafael pressuring me to remain in the safety of the house, where he was only a shout away if something happened.

If I'd thought he would smother me with his toxic obsession before the pregnancy, I never could have imagined what the sweet version of him would do when he was concerned.

Finally, after a week, I couldn't take it any longer. I needed to get out of the house and explore. Rafael's people were my people now. I *needed* to know them.

Joaquin and I walked through the streets once Rafe finally conceded, making me promise to rest at the first sign of fatigue. The stroll through the grassy field beyond the pool area made my heart leap into my throat. The basket tucked under my arm was filled with *buñuelos ibicencos* I'd made that morning under Regina's supervision, and my hand trembled as I reached in and gave one to Joaquin. He groaned as he took a bite of the fried potato doughnut coated in sugar.

"You and Regina are going to make the lot of us fat," he said as we approached the main road that extended through the center of the village. I'd only ever ventured there during my run from Rafael, never truly realizing how large the town itself was. I knew some people lived outside of the central village, preferring the privacy that the more remote spots on the island offered, and that even more of Rafe's people lived on Ibiza itself since they conducted business there too regularly to commute.

I heaved a sigh as the bottom of my flip flop touched the road. We made our way down the street, nodding at everyone who looked my way. No one seemed interested in approaching, keeping their distance in a way I didn't want, and it felt hopeless.

I didn't know the first thing about interacting with strangers on this level, not knowing what they must think of me. A girl who wasn't one of them taking *El Diablo* from the potential matches I had no doubt the people who worshiped him had dreamed of for their daughters.

A young boy raced up finally, pulling free from his mother's grasp to hurry to stand in front of me. I knelt down with a smile, reaching into the basket as my eyes met his mother's. She nodded, though she looked tense as she did it and bowed her head with an apology on her lips. "*Mi reina*?" the boy asked, his eyes wide as I handed him the pastry.

"Now you see that's just not fair," I murmured with a laugh. "You know my name, but I don't know yours."

"Luis," he said with a beaming smile, biting into his doughnut and smiling around a mouthful of sugar. He ate happily, groaning his satisfaction with each of the bites that seemed far too big for his face. His mother watched, her wariness transforming to a subtle smile as I stood up. Reaching out a hand to touch the top of his head, I paused and held her eyes as I wondered if I'd crossed a line.

I didn't know her, and part of me completely expected to be an unwelcome figure in their lives.

An older woman approached at our side, and I watched her in uncertainty as Joaquin's face tensed. She studied my face with weathered eyes, the skin around them wrinkled with age. The hair upon her head was a stark white next to the deep tan of her olive skin, and I couldn't help but be reminded of my grandmother as I watched her.

Of a woman who saw through all the bullshit and straight into a person's heart.

Finally, her lips curved into a soft smile, her feet taking her a step closer as the boy scurried off. Her frail and wrinkled hand stretched forward, closing the distance between us to touch my belly that was still mostly flat. The slightest of bumps had appeared in the mirror a few days prior, making me question my sanity.

It was so small, it could have been a trick of the mind, but with her knowing gaze on me and that hand touching my stomach, I knew it hadn't been my imagination. "*Mi reina está embarazada?*" she said, her voice filled with wonder. Soft murmurs came from the people who'd emerged from the buildings and houses to observe our interaction, the weight of their gazes heavy on me.

Even though the words were a jumble spoken too quickly for me to follow, the hand on my stomach conveyed her meaning. "Yes," I agreed, smiling as I nodded for those who wouldn't be able to hear the soft admission. I covered her hand with mine, willing it to still be true.

And knowing in my heart that it was.

She pulled her hand from my stomach, reaching up with both hands to grasp my face in her hands and touch her forehead to mine. "*Nosotras pensamos que este día nunca vendría,*" she murmured, pressing a shaky kiss to the top of my head before she walked back into the crowd and disappeared.

"What did she say?" I asked Joaquin, trying to listen to the excited chatter of all the people around me as I waited for his response. They spoke too fast in Spanish, and my vocabulary was *far* too basic to understand even bits of it.

"She said they thought this day would never come," Joaquin said, reaching out to tuck a strand of hair behind my ear. "You have given them a gift, *mi reina*. One that I hope you will come to understand in time."

"What gift is my baby to them? I don't understand." I shook my head.

"A future," he said. "For our way of life here. A little *principito* or *princesa* to love as they should have been able to do with Rafael. His father took that from all of them. You've given them a second chance."

I thought over his words, turning a smile to the woman who approached at my side. She held a bunch of wild flowers in her hands, tied together with a blade of grass. She handed them to me, taking the basket from my other arm with a smile. "*Gracias, mi reina.* These look delicious," she said, turning and calling out to the group of children that I hadn't even seen. They raced forward, each taking one of the doughnuts until the entire basket was emptied.

Once that was finished, she tucked the basket back under my arms and placed the flowers from my hand within it. Slowly, the same children came from the fields beyond the buildings. Flowers were clutched in their grip, and one by one they dropped those into the basket alongside the ones she'd given me.

"That's really very sweet, but you didn't have to give me flowers. I'm happy to feed the children treats," I said with a laugh, reaching out to ruffle a little girl's hair as she dropped the periwinkle flowers she'd gathered in the basket with a playful grin.

"*Para tu madre,*" she said, and my heart clenched, because even not knowing much Spanish, *that* I knew. I bit back the sting of tears, forcing a smile to my face as another older woman stepped up. She touched my stomach compulsively, holding out a hand for me that I had no choice but to take.

Even knowing that wherever she would lead me might break me, I let her guide me farther up the hill. Just before the summit, she followed a narrow path off to the side and we made our way along in silence. Joaquin kept his distance, trailing behind us as if he knew I was absolutely safe with the older woman.

Light streamed in through the trees overhead, giving way to an opening that overlooked the Mediterranean Sea. It sparkled in the sunlight in the distance, but what drew my attention were the fine and glimmering stones a few yards from the overlook.

The first one was older, well-kept and clean despite the way that the name etched upon it wasn't as clear.

Daniela Vasquez de Ibarra.

Rafael's mother's name on the stone took my breath away, and the beautiful place he'd chosen to remember the woman who loved him fiercely enough to die painfully in her efforts to save him.

I owed her everything.

I ran my hand over the stone and stopped in front of the newer one. The name stood out more starkly, freshly carved as I dropped to my knees in the grass in front of it.

My fingers shook as I traced the name and thought about how much she would have loved this to be her final resting place.

Leonora Adamik.

The woman who'd guided me to the memorials disappeared quietly as I stared at the stones, but I felt Joaquin's presence hovering behind me like a silent sentry. Giving me the time I needed, but keeping me safe while I took it.

Tears fell as I laid the flowers the villagers and children had placed in the basket in front of the stone, moving to Daniela's and carefully arranging half of them against her stone.

I felt Rafael the moment he emerged into the clearing. He knelt in the grass beside me, touching a strong hand to one of the flowers in front of his mother's stone that had fallen over and straightening it.

He took my hand in his, holding it tightly as we stared at the stones that somehow united us even in death, and we sat together.

Grieving for what we'd lost, for what we could never have back.

And resolving to destroy the people who had taken it from us.

*S*omething shifted within *mi reina* in the week since she'd seen her mother's memorial. She visited often, laying flowers on the ground for both the mothers who had been taken from us too soon.

But having a place to go where she could feel connected and grieve seemed to help her pull out of the all-consuming grief she'd been overwhelmed by following her mother's death. I knew without a doubt the fate her sister faced continued to plague her, the reality that Odina had spent more than two weeks in the hands of men like Pavel and Dima.

It would be in her best interest if she was simply no longer living, because I knew better than most the kind of suffering she endured if she still lived.

In the time since, I'd had one of the spare bedrooms converted to an exam room and delivery room. The doctor would be brought in for regular check-ups, and when Isa's due date approached, she'd come to live with us temporarily. I wouldn't leave anything to chance when it came to my wife and child.

Not when money could easily buy the safety precautions necessary.

"Everything looks good," Dr. Perez said, smiling at Isa as she lay back on the sonography chair. With a sheet draped over her bare thighs, Isa rested as the doctor poked and prodded at her stomach gently. "You're starting to show. When did your last period start?" she asked with a smile, gently pushing on the little swell on Isa's lower abdomen.

"June 8th, I think," Isa said, and I nodded my head. Isa glared at me, clearly disgruntled by my insider knowledge of when her last period had come. Hugo had been a very useful spy in all ways, conveying all the information I needed to help with my plans for her at the official start of our relationship.

"So you're..." the doctor trailed off, doing the math in her head. "Just over nine weeks pregnant if I had to guess. Plenty far along for an ultrasound if you're ready to see your baby."

"Yes," I answered, not even bothering to wait for Isa's response.

She didn't pretend to be upset by my enthusiasm as the doctor woke up the computer and monitor at the side of the room and grabbed the wand for the ultrasound. The thought of some *thing* inside my wife didn't fill me with pleasant thoughts, and I could only hope that I'd be able to chase away the memory of it by stuffing her full of my cock soon enough.

Having her mouth on me at every turn had been incredible in its own way, but after two weeks of it, I was desperate to feel her pussy contract as she came.

Isa winced as the doctor slid it inside her, her pretty face grimacing in a way that wasn't pained so much as uncomfortable. Her cheeks flushed as our eyes met, and I had the horrible realization that another woman touching *mi reina* was only marginally better than a man doing it. There was static noise as the wand shifted around and the doctor's other hand pressed on Isa's stomach softly. Eventually, she froze when she found the positioning she wanted. She clicked away on the screen, measuring the bean-shaped white spot on the screen. "This is the baby's head," she said, pointing out the larger part of the body as I watched in rapt attention. "And you can see the beginning of arms and legs."

"It's so small," I murmured, grasping Isa's hand within mine and feeling overcome with the sudden emotion at the sight of our baby on the screen.

Peeling my gaze away from the image reluctantly, I turned my attention to Isa and the intense way she watched the screen. Tears pooled in her eyes, lingering there and never falling free as she refused to take her attention away from the image of our baby. Even with me squeezing her hand in mine, she still couldn't seem to take her eyes away.

If her face hadn't been filled with the same absolute joy I felt, I might have wondered if she regretted the baby.

"And this is the heartbeat," the doctor said, and the steady drum of the baby's heart filled the room. The tears that Isa had restrained herself from crying flowed down her cheeks, and we sat and listened to the confirmation of what we'd been hesitant to hope for. The baby was alive and well, and the attack hadn't cost us that on top of everything else Isa had lost.

The doctor cleared her throat, finishing with her measurements and then removing the wand to clean. "Measurement is consistent with nine weeks. I see nothing that's any cause for concern at this point. The placenta is firmly attached to the uterine wall despite what happened, so I think it is safe to say that negative ramifications are unlikely at this stage. I'm taking you off limitations, and you're free to resume normal activity," she said as Isa shifted to sit up. She smiled as I reached forward and wiped her cheeks with the sleeve of my suit.

"All activities?" I asked, earning a sharp slap on the arm from Isa.

The doctor chuckled as if used to the desperation that came after a period of abstinence. "Yes. There are no real limitations in terms of sex at this phase. Do whatever is comfortable, but if there's any pain then ease off. Let your body tell you what limits it has," she said, turning to Isa.

"Is there anything I can't do outside of sex?" she asked. "Like simulating a fight?"

"You mean like sparring in a training exercise?" The doctor shrugged. "Under very controlled circumstances, I don't see anything wrong with that. Nothing that would risk a blow to the stomach, but outside of that, I think it would be fine as long as you're careful until you're showing more."

Isa nodded, bidding the doctor farewell. A single glance at my wife's face and I knew without a doubt we had *very* different ideas of what our first activity should be.

Fucking shit.

♟♟♟♟♟

"Remind me how I got roped into this?" Joaquin asked, stripping the shirt off his head. I tossed mine to the side, kicking off my shoes and standing in the clearing where he'd taken Isa what felt like ages ago to teach her the very thing I'd forbidden.

The same thing that I'd been forced to concede after the attacks in Chicago. I hated the knowledge that my wife may find herself in a situation where she needed to protect herself, and I wouldn't be able to do it.

But I liked the thought of her stabbing our enemies enough to outweigh that.

"Just lucky, I guess," I grunted. "Gabriel is busy. Hugo is too small."

"I don't see the point in this," Isa sighed, curling her legs up underneath her on the blanket I'd set out for exactly that purpose. She'd showered and changed after her sonogram, looking too appealing in her clothes that hugged her curves tightly. "Shouldn't it be me you're fighting?"

"If you think you stand a chance fighting men like us in an even match, then that's exactly why you need to see this," I said. Joaquin nodded his agreement, kicking off his sneakers until he too stood barefoot in the grass. For the purposes of a demonstration, bare feet hurt far less than shoes. "I can think of other things our time would be better spent doing right now."

"Gross," Joaquin grunted, kicking out a foot and aiming for the top of my knee. I jumped back, evading the strike and glaring at him before I turned an exasperated glance to Isa where she watched with rapt attention.

"I don't know what this fuckhead taught you when you two earned your brands." I paused, watching Isa narrow her eyes in protest. She crossed her arms over her chest and waited for me to get to the point. When the woman dug her heels in on what she wanted, not even goading her into an argument could distract her from the task at hand. "But your *only* advantage at this point is the element of surprise. Men like Pavel and Dima have been trained to fight and kill since they were children, just like us. Until you have that kind of training, you won't stand a chance at winning a fair match."

"Even when you *have* had that kind of training, the odds are stacked against you. You're a relatively small woman. Women naturally have less muscle mass than men, so men hit harder." Joaquin held up a hand when outrage crossed her face at his blanket statement. "I'm not discriminating. There are some fierce women out there who give highly trained men a run for their money, but they're the exception, not the standard. It will be a long time before you're ready for that level of training, if ever," he said.

"So what are we doing here?" she asked, raising an eyebrow. "If this is all pointless?"

"It's not pointless. Pointless would be to teach you to fight the way we do. Your best fighting strategy will be to not get trapped in a fight at all. You wait for your opening and you strike fast and hard," I said, turning my attention back to where Joaquin stood very still.

The shadow of Ibiza's greatest strength came in staying hidden, in calling the least amount of attention to himself as possible and using that to his advantage. Mine was in killing quickly and ruthlessly, which was so at odds with how I liked to torture my victims.

The dilemma was real once it became personal, but under normal circumstances I was more likely to snap a neck and be done with it.

"Play to your strengths," Joaquin reiterated, stepping toward me in the center of the clearing. "Rafael can't do that unless he kills me, and then he has to deal with your wrath." The fucker had the nerve to laugh, chuckling as if he thought me being caught in a fake fight was entertaining.

I struck.

A fist zipping past his face, Joaquin jerked his head back at the last second to avoid the hit. He grabbed my forearm, jabbing an elbow for my face that I narrowly dodged, and then the fight continued. Punch for punch. Kick for kick.

Joaquin and I exchanged a volley of hits and strikes at the rapid kind of speed that only came when we sank into the feeling of a fight. Letting the violence wash over us and the world narrow down to nothing outside of the buzz of adrenaline in the air and predicting one another's movements quickly enough to block and evade.

He grunted when my fist connected with his stomach and then his eye in rapid succession, and the sound of Isa's gasp in reaction nearly pulled me out of the moment. Joaquin recovered without pause, hooking his foot behind my legs and aiming for my face so I had no choice but to take the hit or give up my balance.

My lip split and the taste of blood filled my mouth, but I jabbed an elbow into the side of Joaquin's neck to repay him for the blood he'd drawn.

"Okay! Okay I get it!" Isa yelled, but laughter tinted her voice. Joaquin and I drew apart instinctively, having no desire to bleed one another unnecessarily.

We'd fought enough to know that we could go on for hours, with neither of us ever being willing to concede to the other. Gabriel was the same way, though he much preferred to win fights before they ever began, through manipulation and control. Joaquin was the brother who used the raw power at his disposal.

"I don't stand a chance against that," Isa laughed.

"You don't," I agreed. "That's why you either end the fight before they touch you or you wait until your moment and kill them quickly, but only if you're sure they'll die, because if they don't then you've lost your advantage and the consequences will be severe. Protecting yourself is *always* a 'for when all else fails' plan for you. Do you understand me?"

"I do," Isa agreed, appeasing the nightmare that wanted to lock her inside my bedroom and never let her leave for fear of the danger she might fight outside those walls. What I'd come to learn about my wife in the time since we'd met made that an impossibility if I wanted our relationship to be a partnership.

She'd lived her life in a pretty cage of expectations, and she would never let someone make her feel like a prisoner again.

Not even me.

Joaquin went to the bag at the edge of the clearing, pulling out a throwing knife. "We'll teach you to use both these and a gun," Joaquin said, not even glancing at me as he threw the knife toward me. I caught it between my palms, the smooth edges of the blade gliding along my skin and making the thinnest of cuts along them as it came to a stop inches from my chest.

"But odds are there will be no weapons if you're in danger. So you make one," I said.

"Make one?"

"The environment around you. A fork, a light fixture," I said pointedly. She pursed her lips as she fought back her chuckle.

"How did you catch the knife?" she asked, her gaze snagging on the blade and the thin trail of blood as I shifted my grip to the handle. I glanced at Joaquin out of the corner of my eye, nodding to tell him his part was done.

I fully intended for the next part of the lesson to be much more hands on, and he had no fucking business seeing my wife when she was getting fucked.

*J*oaquin left without a word, retreating quickly as if he didn't want to be around for what came next.

Rafe's gaze landed on my face, mesmerizing as he stepped closer to me. With the knife in his hand, he approached like a panther stalking his prey.

And I knew that my lesson had come to an end far quicker than I wanted.

He touched his palms to the back of my hand, stroking delicate fingers over the flesh and up to the skin of my forearm as he drew me to my feet. Goosebumps rose in response to his touch, the warm air kissing me in a gentle caress as he brought them to the surface. Taking my hand to the one that held the knife, he wrapped my fingers around the hilt until I held it firmly.

His hand touched my waist, dragging over the fabric of my dress and around me slowly until he stood behind me. Arousal glittered in his eyes as he stepped out of my line of sight, running his hands over the skin of my forearm as he positioned the blade in my grip the same way Joaquin had held it before he threw it.

"Everything has energy. The greatest fighters and soldiers are able to *feel* that and unlock the instinct that taps into it. If you can know ahead of time what your opponent will do, then you can predict how to block and defend yourself. The knife is just another part of that. Joaquin exerted energy when he threw it, and the air shifted to accommodate it." I shook my head with a laugh, because what he talked about felt like something straight out of a training montage in a fantasy book.

It seemed too farfetched to be true.

He moved so suddenly I never would have seen it coming if I hadn't *felt* it. His hand left my hip, gliding away and in so smoothly that I only felt the light breeze on my skin before his hand clasped around the front of my throat and squeezed lightly.

He leaned forward, murmuring against my ear with a taunting lilt to his voice that raised the hair on my arms. My body reacted to it, my stomach clenching with desire as his forearm brushed against the front of my breast. "Did you feel that?" he asked, his breath warm against my neck and jaw.

"Yes," I said, swallowing past the nerves in my throat. I would never be able to move so quickly or suddenly. Never be able to compete against a man like that. I'd always known Rafael was a nightmare carved into flesh.

But the reality of it and the way he moved never ceased to amaze me.

He raised my hand with the knife in it, shifting my grip from the hilt to the blade itself. The cool metal touched my skin, contrasting the gentle way he maneuvered me exactly where he wanted me to go. We twisted to face the biggest tree off to the side of the clearing, and he raised my arm slowly and positioned my elbow just so.

My elbow bent in his hold, pulling the knife back above my shoulder and beside my head, and then he guided me through the motions of throwing slowly as he pressed himself into my spine tightly. I was too distracted, too wrapped up in the sinful man tormenting me with just his body against mine, that I wouldn't stand a chance of remembering anything he taught me.

I knew that was the point; this was his form of torture and the response to the delay I'd put on our sexual activities by insisting this needed to come first.

I should have known that Rafe would never tolerate such a thing, that the first task on his list would be to sink inside me after the abstinence. "Are you listening, *mi reina*?" he asked with a smile in his voice.

"Mhm," I murmured, not trusting myself not to give away too much of how he affected me if I spoke more.

He hummed thoughtfully, guiding me through the motion of throwing again, but faster. "Release when your forearm is perpendicular to the ground. The forward momentum will guide the knife where you want it to go." He positioned me back to the start, moving my arm up into the spot where the knife sat just next to my face.

Then he sprung, shoving my arm forward, and I did as he'd said, obeying the command even with my brain melting into a puddle that didn't feel capable of functioning. The knife slid between my thumb and forefinger, letting loose and gliding into the tree line.

I didn't hit the tree itself, but came close enough that I thought I would take it as a victory considering my lack of focus. "I don't think you're paying attention," Rafael murmured, tsking playfully as the hand that had guided my arm dropped to my waist. He slid it up and over my ribs, cupping my breast in his hand and sliding his thumb over my nipple through my sports bra and tank top. "Just say the word and we can change activities, *mi reina*."

"You're an asshole," I said, turning in his arms until I faced him. He stared down at me with all the triumph I knew he must feel in having me concede the day's lesson.

I'd seen enough, learned enough, to last me until tomorrow. "No disagreement there," he said.

"Take me to bed," I said, rolling my eyes and wrapping my arms around his neck.

"I have a better idea, my wife," he returned, scooping me into his arms and guiding me to the blanket he had so thoughtfully laid out for me to sit on. He laid me on my back, laying his body over mine gently and taking extra care around my stomach. I was tempted to tell him that it wasn't necessary, that the weight of my husband on me wouldn't hurt the baby at this stage.

But the thoughtfulness of it was so at odds with the Rafael who had taken me off the streets of Ibiza, that I let myself bask in the gentle care instead of arguing.

He leaned back, staring down at me intently, then shifted his weight onto his elbow as a hand tucked a strand of hair behind my ear. I bit my lip, turning my head to lean into the touch and wanting nothing more than to feel more of his skin on mine.

To remove all his clothes, until what remained was just our sweat slicked bodies beneath the Spanish sun.

His eyes hardened to cold fire, the blue seeming to glow as he pressed his lips to mine and ran his fingers through my hair. "*Te amo, mi reina,*" he murmured, leaving my lips in favor of trailing kisses down and over the column of my throat.

He left the tank top on, skimming his mouth and nose over my body through the fabric as he made his way down to my stomach. Flipping the shirt up to reveal my lower belly, his mouth touched it sweetly, and he murmured something softly while I stared at him and ran anxious fingers through the inky strands of his hair.

Smirking up at me, he curved his fingertips beneath the waistband of my leggings and pulled them down. He took my underwear with them, and I'd never before truly taken time to appreciate how easy it was to give him access to my body in my dresses. The painfully slow drag of fabric over my thighs seemed to take forever, tormenting me when he'd barely touched me.

Stopping with the material bunched at my ankles, he took his time taking off my sneakers and then he placed them off to the side neatly, and folded my pants to rest on top in his bid to purposefully drive me mad with need.

I spread my legs, giving him an unhindered view of my pussy when he didn't show signs of stopping with his torment and his mouth touched the inside of my knee. I slid a hand over my belly, touching the apex of my thighs and gliding through the already swollen and needy flesh that I found in response to the way Rafe tortured me. My fingertip dipped inside my entrance, barely making headway before Rafe growled in his throat and shoved it to the side.

His mouth covered me immediately, giving me the heat of him against me that I needed. His finger slid inside me, twisting and curling quickly as he loosened me.

How could it be anything else?

"I want your cock," I murmured, grabbing a fistful of his hair in my grip and tugging when his mouth wasn't enough. I'd had his mouth for weeks. I wanted *him*.

He seemed to agree, tearing his mouth away from my flesh and prowling over me. I shifted my hands down to between our bodies, pushing his athletic shorts down to free his length and wrapping a hand around him. I stroked him only once before lining him up with my entrance and pulling my hand out of the way, groaning in relief when he pressed forward and made his way inside slowly.

Pump after pump, shallow thrusts of his hips brought him further inside me until I was so filled with him that I could hardly see straight. I wrapped my legs around his hips, pulling him closer and wanting him to possess me completely.

He leaned over me, his face lining up with mine and hovering just out of reach as he moved slowly. There was no doubt that as much as we'd been deprived, he wanted me to feel not just his body but *him*. That thing that had shifted within our bond and our marriage pulsed between us, the love tangible in the air and hovering between us as he leaned forward and touched his mouth to mine.

The strangled groan that rumbled against my lips was enough to send me crashing over the edge and into my orgasm, my legs tightening around him as everything narrowed down to the feeling of his cock dragging through my tender flesh. He chased his own release, finding it within me as I settled and my grip on him relaxed.

We lay there catching our breaths together for a few moments, and then I let him help me back into my pants. He picked me up and carried me back to the house as I settled into his embrace.

We spent the rest of the day in bed, my training forgotten for the time being.

Love was more important.

♙♙♙♙♙

J smiled as I plated up the *pisto* Regina and I had made for lunch to bring to Rafe's office the following day. With everything that had happened, everything I'd lost, I'd come to the realization that love wasn't *only* more important than all the background noise. It was everything, in a way that I knew I could survive whatever life threw at me.

As long as I had him.

I navigated the steps down the hallway to his office, the shallow bowl of *pisto* for us to share clutched in my hands. The office door was open as I stepped up to it, moving into the space with a bright smile for my husband.

"Oh, I'm sorry, Alejandro," I said as I stepped closer to the desk. Both men looked up from the computer screen suddenly when I spoke, having been too absorbed in whatever they were looking at to notice me. Rafael froze, his body going solid as his eyes connected with mine and he shook his head subtly.

Furrowing my brow as I stared back at him, I tilted my head in question and took another step forward to deposit the bowl on the desk. Rafael and I didn't have secrets when it came to his work, especially not after he'd told me the last of his deception.

There was an openness between us that defied logic, that meant I would be welcome in his office no matter what he was discussing.

The shrill scream that came over the speakers was

muted, as if the volume was turned low so Regina and I wouldn't hear it. Even quieted, there was no denying the sound of my sister's voice, of her pleading whimper that followed after the sound.

I dropped the bowl on the edge of the desk, hurrying around the corner to see what had happened to make Rafe look so concerned. To make him lunge for the mouse next to the keyboard. I knocked it away from his hand urgently, desperate to know what answers he seemed inclined to hide from me.

I needed to know what had come of Odina, even if it broke me. I owed her that at the very least, since whatever happened to her was my fault entirely, thanks to my husband and the brothers I claimed as family.

The brothers who had done more to prove their place in my family than Odina ever had, even if they'd lied to me while they'd done it. Rafael grabbed me by the waist, using his arm to keep me out of line of the camera with a ferocity that took my breath away. It quieted the comment that I had ready on my lips, my eyes pausing on what little I could see on the screen. It wasn't a recording after all, but a live feed.

I could barely make out her face with the angle of the camera being positioned off to the side. The sunken, dark circles under her eyes seemed too big for her face, hinting at an exhaustion that I couldn't begin to imagine.

Had she slept once since she'd been taken weeks ago? I didn't want to think of what she'd suffered while I'd lived in my own little world being worshiped. Getting her back was out of my control. It was something I couldn't force Rafael to do, to the point that I'd barely bothered to try.

Odina screamed again, and I watched the glint of a metal blade as it pressed into the bare skin of her thigh and carved through her flesh. The wound was deeper than what

Rafael had done to my neck, meant to maim and *hurt* in a way that Rafe would have never done to me.

He carved her carefully, and I realized with mounting horror that he was drawing a replica of the scar on my thigh. Of the mark the barbed wire had left on me in the river that day.

"I thought she was lying when she said she wasn't Isa," the man in the video said, his cold gray eyes gleaming as he stared into the camera. "What a clever little liar to pretend not to be the twin I wanted, but do you know what I realized when I stripped her pants off and tied her to my bed?"

There was silence when Rafe didn't answer the question that could only be rhetorical. Given what he'd done to Odina, there could be little doubt as to what he'd expected to find. I covered my mouth to keep quiet, to force myself to shut up as he lifted the knife and touched it to her cheekbone. He didn't break the skin, keeping it only an inch from her eye in threat.

The fact that Odina never bothered to flinch was as horrific a sign as any as to what she'd probably endured.

"She doesn't have the fucking scar! Where is my scarred kitten?" he shouted, and the fury in it reminded me of the roar of a lion—a wild animal who had lost his dinner to another predator.

"My *wife* is not your kitten, Dima," Rafael said carefully, and the fury in his tone was darker. Quieter, and somehow all the more menacing for it. Dima would attack foolishly. He thought himself the baddest in all the lands and saw no consequences for his actions, but Rafael would sweep that out from under him with methodic planning.

And slit his throat before he ever saw it coming.

"She is not your wife," Dima growled, sinking the tip of

the knife into Odina's cheek. She whimpered in pain, and it was the final straw for me.

"Stop! Please don't hurt her anymore," I said, wincing back from the furious glare Rafe leveled at me. On the screen, Dima stilled and drew the knife away from Odina's face. He closed his eyes slowly, a shudder working its way through his body as he placed the knife on the table beside him. He pushed Odina's chair to the side, ignoring her and leaning forward on his elbows on the desk as his face filled the screen.

He was attractive, and it seemed horrific that someone capable of such atrocities would look so...normal. A black buttoned-up shirt was collared at his throat, striking against his fair skin. Light brown hair was styled short on top of his head, and a strong jaw curved the bottom of his face. Even with all the normalcy of his features, there was something so *off* within his stare, something crazed in the way he stared directly into the camera. "Come out and play with me, мой котик. Let me look at *my kitten*, and I'll have no need for your replica."

Rafe shook his head subtly, warning me against giving the man what he wanted, but I couldn't bear the thought of him hurting Odina if I defied him. For something so simple, taking the two steps until I stood in front of the camera felt harmless.

Like the only choice I could make.

His stare tracked up over my torso, and despite the distance and the knowledge that only the image of him was in the room with us, I shuddered at the feeling of his eyes on me. The day before, I'd wished I'd worn a dress.

Now I wanted nothing more than to cover every inch of my skin.

His gaze landed on my face, caressing up over my lips

and to my eyes finally. "*Isa*," he murmured. I swallowed back the revulsion in my throat, and let Rafe guide me back to perch on his lap. The claiming of his hands on my body steadied me and pushed me past the panic that threatened to consume me.

I couldn't shake the knowledge that I'd seen those eyes before. That they'd been the first thing I saw when I opened my eyes and took my first breaths after drowning.

"Hello, Dima," I said, resting my hand on Rafe's thigh. I used the feel of his strength beneath me to ground me against the disgust, and to reassure myself that the time would come when I could tell Rafe what I now knew to be the truth.

"You've grown to be so beautiful," he said, his lips twisting into a smile.

"I thought I was too old for you now," I spat in return, and he raised an eyebrow as a slow laugh came over the speakers.

"I see Rafael has been talking about me," Dima said, his eyes shifting to the space over my shoulder. Rafe leaned in, touching his lips to my cheek and pointedly baiting the other man.

"I keep no secrets from my wife. Especially not when it comes to a worm like you," Rafe said, and I could feel the malice in the words even if his tone didn't seem bothered in the slightest. There was nothing but complete dismissal in the way he spoke of the other man.

"I wonder if that is true of мой котик as well," Dima said, touching a finger to his lips and tapping it there. "Do you have secrets from *El Diablo*, Isa?"

I swallowed, his words all but a confirmation of what I'd slowly begun to realize when I laid eyes on him. "Not intentionally," I said, feeling Rafe go solid beneath me. I took his hand in mine discreetly, trying to reassure him that I hadn't known until the moment I saw Dima on that screen.

That even after the years that had been passed, traces of the boy who had saved my life on the banks of the Chicago River still remained.

Rafael didn't rise to the bait, not bothering to ask the question, but it didn't seem like Dima needed the verbal words to offer the information he was so desperate to reveal. "Tell me, *El Diablo*," he said mockingly. "If it is my breath that fills her lungs, do you truly believe your marriage can ever really claim her? I gave her life."

Even knowing in my soul that he was that same boy, hearing the confirmation was another thing entirely. The breath he spoke of expelled from my lungs in a sudden burst, my stomach caving in on itself as I felt hollow.

My memories of that day had always been hazy. Chaotic and vague, the details lost to time as I grew older and got some distance from the day I'd nearly died. I'd all but forgotten the boy who had saved me, his face a blur as he gave me mouth to mouth when my mother didn't know how. And he'd done it all for what?

To purchase my life down the line? To own me and abuse me?

None of it made any sense. He'd been there with the man who'd thrown me in the river in the first place, and for some reason chose to do what he could to ensure I lived. "Why?" I asked, hating the way my voice trembled. "Why go to the trouble?"

"I have my reasons," he said evasively. "I should have just taken you that day and let you be raised with a nanny here. I thought perhaps you would appreciate having a few more years with your family before you found your true purpose with me."

"Last I knew, you had a wife of your own, Dima," Rafael said, reminding me of exactly what that purpose would be. "Perhaps you should spend more time with her by your side."

"She is an alliance between families and nothing more. You know how it goes." Dima shrugged. "Men marry the wife for money. They keep the mistress they love. You're the one who broke those rules."

"You do not love me," I said, huffing a laugh as he grabbed Odina's chair and dragged it back beside him. His jaw hardened, as if the small rebellion of my words threatened to push him over the edge and carve his anger into my sister's flesh once again.

"Why is what I have done worse than what he did? You believe he loves you, do you not?" he asked, and I couldn't bring myself to answer the second question. I believed against everything that Rafe loved me with everything he was.

But Dima couldn't know that for certain without putting both of us more at risk.

"You sell people. That is all I need, to know that you and Rafe are different. That is a line I will never tolerate crossing—"

"Has he shown you how he murdered my brothers? How he carved them up and sent home pieces of them for my father to unwrap?" Dima growled.

I leaned forward, staring into the camera intently and willing him to understand that I wasn't the innocent victim I knew he thought me to be. "Not exactly," I said confidentially. "But he showed me how it felt to sink a knife into Maxim's heart. He taught me what it meant to watch the life bleed from his eyes. What part of him did Rafael send back to you after I killed him?"

Dima froze on the screen, his lip twitching as if he might roar his outrage from the other side of the world. But then the corners of his mouth tipped up, and a dark laugh erupted from his throat.

"Oh, мой котик, you are everything I ever hoped you would be."

*J*tightened my grip around Isa's waist and tugged her back, putting distance between her and the predator who stared at her as if she hung the moon in the sky and could be everything he ever needed.

She could only be that for one person, and it wasn't the twisted little maggot who touched her sister as if her very existence wasn't an insult to Isa. She could only be that for *me*.

"I believe this conversation has run its course," I said, striving to keep all inflection out of my voice. To show my hand so clearly when Isa was safely tucked within my grasp would have been a foolish and pointless endeavor. Even if my need to maim and kill threatened to take away all my rational thought and left me cringing internally like one of Pavlov's dogs waiting for a treat.

My treat just happened to be born of pain and suffering, of the blood and anguish of those who thought to claim what was mine.

"It is over when I say it's over," Dima growled his warning, trailing a finger over Odina's cheek. She shuddered in his grasp, faintly trying to pull away from him even though her eyes remained snared in that blank stare of hers that felt so similar to the way Isa looked when she retreated inside herself. "You haven't asked me the most important question yet, Isa," he said, twisting his lips into a smile as he turned his body toward Odina. He tugged her dark, greasy hair away from her neck, placing his mouth only a breath away from her ear and whispering something to her that we couldn't hear.

Odina whimpered, pouting despite the blankness of her features and shaking her head from side to side.

"What question is that?" Isa asked, swallowing her fury. I felt the tremble of her limbs as she shook in my embrace, her need to do something to protect her sister making her body rebel against the inability to move.

Against her helplessness, and I was immediately reminded of her request to never be helpless again. I'd do everything in my power, give her *anything* to make sure she never had to feel it. That she would never be the person sitting in that chair, restrained and resigned to the end of her life that was coming.

"What part of her will I send back to you?" he asked, touching his finger to a spot on the right of Odina's neck. "She has a freckle here. Do you have a matching one, or is yours a mirror?" he asked. Isa squeezed her hand on my thigh, trying to communicate something to me silently.

Isa reached up to the left side of her own neck, touching the freckle there. It was the largest one on her body, the most noticeable in the sea of them that I'd counted in the time since I'd started watching her.

"A mirror, then," Dima said with a self-assured smile, and Alejandro and I exchanged a glance.

"Who do you know that is a twin?" Isa asked the question rattling in my brain. To my knowledge, none of the Kuznetsov children had been twins. I couldn't remember a single one thinking back to my knowledge of the family I did my best to avoid.

Dima leaned forward, turning his head to the left and touching the birthmark on the side of his jaw line. The faint stubble disguised the darker skin, but he tapped it pointedly before returning those same digits to his mouth again and tapping his bottom lip. "Oleg was always the weakest of my father's sons. He was too soft, preferring to cuddle *kittens* rather than teach them to be *tigers*."

"What did you do to him?" Isa asked, the sinking horror written into the side of her face matching the storm I felt inside me.

In all the times the Kuznetsovs had visited my father, *Oleg* had not been with them.

"I put his head beneath the water during our evening bath. I hardly remember it now, of course, but I have never regretted it for a moment. The weak have no place in this world. Much like your sister," he said, reaching over to the table and grabbing the knife off of it.

He touched it to Odina's throat, drawing a whimper from the young woman who looked like nothing more than a girl with the glint of a blade against her skin. All traces of her hatred for the world were gone in the face of her potential death.

"Don't," Isa said, her voice a command and steady despite the wavering in her body. She wanted nothing more than to do what she could to help Odina, but there was *nothing*. Even if I would have allowed her to give herself up for someone who didn't deserve it, the baby made that an impossibility.

"Then come to me," Dima said, raising an eyebrow. "I

am more than happy to trade the weak twin for *mi reina*."
The sound of my name for Isa on his lips was wrong on a
fundamental level, making a shudder go through my body.

"I can't do that," Isa said. "But if you return her to me, I'll
convince Rafael to let you live. Surely your life is worth the
return of one girl you don't even want?"

"Ah, мой котик, even your pussy is not good enough to
convince a man to give up his thirst for blood," Dima
laughed, digging the tip of his blade into Odina's throat.
Blood welled around the knife, trickling down her skin
slowly. "Say goodbye to your sister, Odina."

"No!" Isa yelled, lunging forward as Dima dragged his
knife down over Odina's throat. The video feed cut off,
leaving just enough time to see the deep wound left at the
side of her neck and the knife continuing the path.

Isa may not have had to watch the life leave her sister's
eyes, but the stillness in her body confirmed that she understood exactly what had happened.

That her sister was gone, her throat cut by a man
obsessed after a day that never should have happened.
There were no tears as Isa tried to wrap her mind around
the turn of events, blinking as I shifted her in my lap until I
could see her face.

Alejandro stood, pushing back his chair and leaving the
office. He closed the door behind him and shut us in the
silent room. If I couldn't feel the expansion of her chest
against mine, I would have wondered if she even *breathed.*

"This is your fault," she mumbled, burying her face
closer into my chest.

"I know," I confirmed. "She was dead the moment I
handed her over."

"You don't even care, do you?" she asked, pulling back to
stare up at me. The first tear broke free from the maelstrom

in her eyes and more followed in its wake as she watched me, waiting for my reaction.

"No," I admitted. "I don't care that she's dead. Dima saved me the trouble of having to do it myself, and he saved both of us the heartache of you having to find a way to live with what I did." She released a strangled sob, her chest shaking with the force of it as she pressed her hand to her mouth and her chest lurched like she might be ill. I ran a soothing hand over her back, willing her to feel the truth in the words that would follow. "But I am sorry that it hurts you."

She nodded, sniffling through the hand touching her face as the other joined the first. Leaning her head against my shoulder, she felt as lost as she'd been the day I found her.

Trapped in the shadow of the vindictive twin who seemed to haunt her even in the death that had been decided thirteen years prior.

Death came for us all.

The shadow of grief wrapped me in a dark embrace, clinging to me from the sidelines and making me move through my life in a fog for the next week. I'd thought I'd been strong enough to push through the sadness and grasp onto the raging pit of anger inside me to cope with my mother's death. But the guilt of what had been done to Odina shoved me straight into the abyss all over again.

Regina watched me with concerned eyes when she thought I wasn't looking, making sure I ate all the food she gave me despite my grief for my sister. I did it for the sake of the baby, ignoring the fact that it all tasted like ash on my tongue.

There would be no recovering from what I'd done to Odina, from what *they* had done to her through me and because of me. I was the catalyst that ruined her life, and they were the weapons who'd delivered the fatal blows that stripped away everything that had been vital within my sister.

I wasn't foolish enough to think she might have survived

the second murder as intact as the first, and it left me in a horrible cloud of the unknown.

What had come of her after the camera disconnected? While seeing her with her throat slit was far from being something I ever wanted, I suspected it would have at least given me a sense of clarity. Hope was a shining light at the end of the tunnel, but if the tunnel never ended then that light was unreachable. It felt like a plague that would consume my life and strip away everything that was good.

Objectively, I knew I had to go on. I knew that I had to focus on my marriage and find a way to forgive Rafael for the part he'd played in Odina's death. I couldn't even blame him really, because we all did what we had to in order to protect the people who mattered the most. Odina was inconsequential to him: a thorn in his side and a threat to the life we were working to build. She'd proven that in our short time in Chicago, so I didn't really blame him.

I blamed myself instead. I could have forced her into that bunker with me. I could have refused to allow her to wander off on her own in the middle of the attack, but I'd let her go and left her open and vulnerable.

In the face of it, Rafe had taken to practically demanding that I spend my time in his office while he worked, needing his eyes on me to prove that I was okay and I was coping. I couldn't look at his computer without seeing Dima's haunting eyes staring back at me, the deranged touch of his stare on me feeling like a physical thing despite the distance.

I couldn't look at it without seeing the knife carving into Odina's neck. Living like a Queen with the King of Hell came with a price.

I just hadn't been the one to pay it.

I lay on my stomach on the sofa in the sitting area on the

other side of his office, turning the page in the fantasy novel that didn't consume my attention in the way I'd hoped. Reaching over to the bowl of orange slices sitting on the coffee table, I popped one into my mouth and tried to ignore the feeling of Rafe's pointed stare on me. My eyes roamed over the words, reading them and retaining nothing with the distracting way he seemed to accomplish nothing with me in the room.

The door to the office opened, and Alejandro came in. His eyes dropped to me briefly before he approached Rafael at the desk. Dropping into the seat in front of it, he cast one last uncertain glance over his shoulder to see if I was paying attention to whatever he had to say. Rafe had told him several times that he didn't need to hesitate to speak of their business matters in front of me since there were no secrets between us, and the thought comforted me after months of secrets and lies that had threatened to tear us apart.

I genuinely hoped we were past that, and that with Rafe's final admission of what he'd known for longer than I'd known he existed we could live our life together honestly.

What he did and who he was no longer horrified me. Sinking a knife into a man's heart had hardened me to that.

"You look tired," Alejandro commented, and I glanced up from my book to find his eyes on me. "Have you been sleeping alright? We can see if the doctor thinks there are any herbal supplements that could help you."

"She's fine," Rafe barked, his anger coating my skin in a thin layer. Everyone wanted to help, to offer whatever advice they thought might be useful to my coping and the grief that I needed to work through at my own pace. But the precious devil himself saw every question as an insult to his ability to take care of me and anticipate my needs. "I put her through her paces this morning."

"He's right. I'm just sore," I agreed, thinking back to the morning we'd spent in the meadow I was coming to think of fondly. While I never *felt* good when I left it, my body consumed by the exhaustion of the way Rafe worked me over and pushed me to the limits of what I could handle, he usually took care of me in an entirely different way once we'd finished.

That typically involved him reminding me I was alive with the slow work of his cock inside me, driving me higher and higher and refusing to allow me to separate from him mentally or emotionally. He didn't know that I had no intent to do that anyway, my guilt entirely focused on tearing myself apart rather than driving a wedge between our relationship.

Rafael Ibarra was the devil incarnate, and only an idiot would have expected him to be anything else.

"Was there something you wanted?" Rafe asked, raising a brow at his second-in-command and demanding his attention once more when he felt like too much focus went to me. To the baby that was somehow not just everything to Rafe and I, but to an entire community who had waited for the moment that *El Diablo* finally had an heir.

The people who said it took a village to raise a child had probably intended the statement to apply to something slightly less literal, but I'd certainly found mine.

"You have the summit in Stockholm this weekend," Alejandro said, then he paused, pushing a folder held tightly within his grasp across the desk until it stopped in front of Rafe. "Those are all the people who are attending. I don't think there's anyone you don't know on some level, but just to be safe I'd suggest going over the information briefly."

"I can't go to Stockholm right now," Rafe said, leaning back in his seat and furrowing his brow. "You'll have to go in my place."

There was a break of silence, and I closed the book held in front of me to stop pretending I was even capable of reading. A summit for criminals sounded...like something from a movie. "I think that would be a mistake," Alejandro said finally. "You've been separate from the face of the business for too long. Understandably, given everything that's happened, but with the tensions with Pavel rising and the hostile takeovers beginning, it's time for you to show your face again."

Rafe studied his second-in-command, sighing deeply as he scrubbed his hands over his face. "Do you understand how much I loathe you at times?" he asked finally, and Alejandro's cheek indented with a single dimple as he grinned at his boss.

"Someone has to be the voice of reason."

"I hate these things under the best circumstances, let alone going to be around a bunch of people who seem to think I'm their allfather."

"You are responsible for all of them coming together. I think saying that they worship you is a stretch, but you cannot possibly hope to solidify the initial bonds of an alliance if the person who orchestrated it isn't even present," Alejandro said, standing to his feet and moving toward the door to make his exit.

"It's alright. I'll be fine here," I interjected, leveling Rafe with a look that told him I could handle staying home while he conducted his business in Sweden. We would need to get used to it at some point. "You have to do what's needed for your business, and I will need to become more familiar with staying home without you here."

"You've misunderstood, *mi reina*," Alejandro said, his lips quirking up into the hint of a smile. "It would be considered a great insult for Rafael to leave his wife at home for this kind of outing. It is very much an opportunity for the wives to get to know one another and form their own friendships."

"Then I definitely don't want to go," I said, chuckling as my attention shifted back to Rafael. He was silent, studying me intently as if he could silently command me into going.

"This is the kind of event where marriages are arranged between children. Everyone will be expecting to discuss a potential joining through marriage with the pregnancy," Alejandro added. I went still, staring at him with wide eyes as my head drew back sharply.

I maneuvered my body to a sitting position, slowly turning my head to look at Rafe sitting behind his desk. He said nothing, giving me the first reaction to Alejandro's words and what they might mean for our future. "I will kill you before I *ever* allow you to do such a thing. Do you understand me?" I asked, clenching my hands tightly as I tried to convey just how much I meant the words.

Using the marriage of our children as an excuse for a business alliance was unforgivable, almost on the same level as human trafficking.

Rafe tapped his fingers on the desk, standing and walking around as he approached me. Those harsh, unyielding fingers grasped my chin and tilted my face up to his as soon as he stood in front of me. He towered over me, reminding me of how small I was in comparison to him. Something dark glittered in his eyes, the gleam of arousal sparking after my threat. "I do not believe in arranging marriages between children," he said, waiting until my features relaxed and the anger drained out of me. "But I will approve of the people my children choose for themselves, and I will *guide* them to make the right decisions regarding who might be an appropriate match."

"Right. Can't have your daughter end up with someone like you if we have a girl," I said, tearing my face out of his grip.

He smirked, his fingers snapping closed. "Of course," he said, shrugging as if it was the most obvious thing in the world.

It was comforting in an odd way, that Rafael wouldn't approve of someone like himself for his own daughter. That gave me hope that her future might be slightly less traumatic than mine.

If the alternative was me stabbing her father then well, *that* probably was the definition of traumatic.

Rafe spun in place, leveling Alejandro with a look. "Have Regina arrange a dress for Isa. Something fitted," he instructed. Alejandro nodded, leaving the office to make sure it was done as soon as possible. There wasn't much time.

"Not something fitted," I protested, dropping my hand to the soft swell of the baby bump that grew a little with every day that passed. "I'm not pregnant enough that people will be able to tell the difference between a baby bump and bloating."

"They'll know," Rafe said evasively, shrugging off my concern as his eyes dropped to my stomach and where I clutched it as I sat.

Sighing, I asked the real question that mattered in the choice of whether or not I could go. "What about Dima?"

"The Tessins have been allies for quite some time. The summit is being held in their private estate that will be filled with security and we'll be surrounded by friends who agree with our purpose. It's as safe as you can be off the island," he answered, reaching down to pluck an orange slice from my bowl. He pressed it to my lips, letting the citrus flavor explode over my senses. "I wouldn't take the risk if I didn't believe you would be safe."

"I don't know the first thing about making alliances and interacting with people like this."

"Women fight their wars with their words. They manipulate and strategize and befriend when they think it will benefit them. You have never had any lack of ability to communicate or play the game with words. You always know just what information to give to leave the biggest impact. You'll be just fine, *mi reina*," Rafe murmured, leaning forward to touch his lips to mine softly. "They won't know what hit them."

The ferry pulled close to the rocky shoreline, taxiing us to the mansion that gleamed in the Swedish sun. Isa had been silent for much of the trip to Sweden, and with every moment that brought us closer to the sprawling estate on the edge of the archipelago she tensed at my side. Her floral maxi dress wrapped around her body and disguised the beginning of the baby bump on her stomach, and part of me hated to know that she'd hidden it so effectively in the first outing where it was overtly visible.

The other part of me couldn't help but think about the great sense of pride I would feel when it came time for the evening and she slipped into the gown Regina had chosen for her under my guidance.

When the boat pulled up alongside the dock, I stood first and placed my foot on the wooden walkway. Reaching a hand in for my wife, I lifted her out of the boat until she felt more sturdy on the steady surface.

Even after her time on the yacht, she was still far more comfortable on land than in the water. Part of that was my fault, since I'd severely neglected taking her into the water of the pool and down to the beach on *El Infierno*. I'd remedy that when we returned home after the weekend away, reminding her that she was safe anywhere we went.

So long as she was safely tucked within my arms.

"It's beautiful," Isa said, though her voice betrayed her nerves as we walked up the planks toward the grassy lawn at the back of the estate. A cobblestone path led up to the white house with brick red and burnt orange rooftops, reflecting the fall foliage that would come shortly enough with the changing seasons. This far North, the fall came far sooner than it did in Spain. The beginning of September marked the shift, the air dropping just a bit cooler and losing the summer humidity.

"Rafael," a male voice said, and I turned my attention away from Isa to focus on the man waiting at the top of the cobblestone path. "We were beginning to wonder if you would come," Henrik said, extending his hand for me to shake.

"Henrik," I greeted, smiling tentatively. We'd been rivals as children, understandably considering our fathers had been in opposition to one another. But as I'd shifted out from under my father's thumb when I grew older and approached the day when I set him aflame, Henrik and I had begun to realize we had more in common than we'd initially believed. "How are your parents?"

"They're wonderful, around here somewhere mingling. Who is this enchanting woman?" he asked, turning his attention to Isa. He held out a hand that she placed in his with an awkward smile.

"Isa," she said, watching with wide eyes when he lifted the hand held within his up to his mouth and pressed a kiss to the back in greeting. It was innocent enough, a symptom of the aristocracy and old traditions that he'd been raised in.

That didn't stop me from wanting to cut the lips from his body and feed them to the fish. I wrapped my fingers around Isa's wrist, pulling her away from his grip and watching as confusion stole his features and I lowered our hands. My fingers shifted along hers, twining until I held her hand snuggly within mine. "My *wife*," I said.

Henrik slid his gaze from Isa to me, a sharp bark of laughter escaping him at the news of my marriage. While I'd never kept my wedding a secret, I also hadn't broadcast it for the world to know. His breath caught when he realized I wasn't kidding, a beaming smile transforming his face as he chuckled under his breath. "Is that true, Isa?" he asked. "*El Diablo* has finally taken a wife?"

"Yes," Isa agreed with a smile that was closer to the beauty of her *real* smile. There was still that undercurrent of discomfort, but she leaned her body into the side of mine more fully and took comfort in my presence. There would come a time over the course of the weekend when she did not have me to lean on in the moments when she wasn't certain what to do or what to say, but *mi reina* never failed to rise above the uncertainty of her situation.

She was *always* enough.

"Yes. So you see, it may be wise to inform the others that I am not a fan of other men touching my wife," I warned, communicating my meaning with the pin of a glare on his face.

"I meant nothing by it," Henrik said, shaking his head with an appeasing smile. "I will do my best to spread the word that she is to be greeted from a safe distance."

"You're ridiculous," Isa muttered, glaring up at me from my side. Henrik seemed to enjoy the challenge in her voice, giving a disbelieving chuckle as he watched me wrap my arm around her.

"Hej, Rafael," Henrik's mother, Sigrid, said as she stepped up behind her son. "*Välkommen till vårt hem.*"

"*Tack så mycket,*" I said, feeling Isa still with shock at my side. She'd been too isolated in our time together and she'd never been confronted with the reality of what it was to be a man who had allies all over the world.

I spoke the basics of several languages.

"*Mamma,*" Henrik said, turning an amused smile to face his mother. "This is Isa. Rafael's *wife.*"

She widened her eyes briefly, a bright smile transforming her luminously fair face as her bright blue eyes gleamed. "Congratulations," she said, her accent strong but eloquent as she leaned forward and kissed each of Isa's cheeks. "What magnificent news!"

"Thank you, Mrs. Tessin," Isa said politely, having latched onto the one piece of information she knew about our hosts. It was foolish on my part that I hadn't taken the time to educate her on them, but I'd also known that she would grow overwhelmed very quickly with the sheer number of people attending the summit.

"Please, call me Sigrid," she said, taking Isa's arm in hers. Staff members strolled by with our bags collected off the boat, and Sigrid pulled my wife away from me to guide her toward the gleaming house on top of the hill. "Let me show you two to your room. I'm certain you're anxious to get ready for tonight."

I watched as Isa murmured something in response with a polite smile on her face. Then I followed, because I'd follow *mi reina* anywhere.

*R*afe hung the dress bag on the back of the door, unzipping it slowly until the gleaming white satin came visible bit by bit. I gaped at it, the asymmetrical strapless neckline angular and unique in a way I wouldn't have expected.

If I'd thought to have the comfort of a black dress to make me blend in, all hopes of that were dashed by Rafael's choice. The white would stand out sharply against the fawn of my skin and my dark hair. The bottom was asymmetrical as well, and I knew it was very intentional that the leg that would be bared by the dress was the one with the scar.

"I can't wear that," I said, shaking my head in protest.

"You will," Rafe said, turning to me with a smirk. The bag with his tux was laid out over the bed, and he ran a hand over it until he was certain that the fabric wouldn't crease.

"I wouldn't even know *how* to wear something like that. What do I do with my hair? Makeup?" I asked, and he smiled at me and touched his lips to my cheek before moving to the door to the room we'd claimed as ours. It was truly more of a suite, with a living area and bathroom to ourselves as well.

Sigrid stepped into the room with a bright smile, waving a hand to welcome in two other women. "This is Zuri and Faye," she said with a bright smile. One of the male staff members wheeled in a cart filled with makeup and hair products, making my eyes go round as I turned to Rafael with a wide-eyed stare. "Your husband expressed concerns that you might be in need of some assistance this evening. Of course, he neglected to mention the woman he spoke of was his wife," she chuckled. Zuri smiled at me kindly while Faye went through the process of setting up the vanity in the corner of the bedroom.

"I..." I trailed off, fumbling for the words. I felt out of place with the knowledge that most women probably didn't need the help getting ready, but behind the tinge to my cheeks, all I felt was relief. He'd taken care of me, knowing I would feel much more comfortable stepping into the event later if I was dressed in armor.

And what was elaborate makeup and a gown but a woman's version of it, in a way? A pretty armor, but a shield between me and the rest of the party attendees no less.

"Thank you," I said finally, forcing a smile to my face as I met Sigrid's eyes.

"Think nothing of it," she said, stepping forward to take my hands in hers. "Pay me back by taking their breath away when you step into the ballroom on the devil's arm." She kissed my cheek gently.

When she walked out, Joaquin filled the gap she'd left, taking up a seat in the living room where he would be able to see into the bedroom and keep an eye on everything that happened. I was suddenly comforted by his presence.

Particularly when Rafael gathered his tux up to drape

over his arm. "I'll be in the next room," he murmured, catching my chin with his free hand. He leaned down, touching his lips to mine softly and hovering there longer than was appropriate. The heat of his mouth against mine tasted like fresh mint, his breath all-consuming as it flared out his nostrils with his need to restrain himself. I lifted up to my toes, brushing my lips against his in an invitation that never should have crossed my mind with the audience in the same room. He groaned somewhere deep in his throat, shifting his grip from my chin to my jaw and cupping my face to angle me exactly where he wanted me.

The swooning sounds of a woman in the background made me pull away slowly, my cheeks warming with the blush of embarrassment. Pressing my lips together, I looked toward the floor and waited for the moment to pass.

A moment that extended far too long when Rafael's deep chuckle of amusement filled the room. He leaned forward until his lips hovered next to my ear, and I felt the way that sinful mouth of his tipped up into a smile when it brushed against the curve of flesh. "After all the wicked things I've done to you, somehow you still manage to blush over a mere kiss, *wife*," he murmured, drawing back and touching his mouth to my forehead one last time. "I'll be back in two hours," he said to Joaquin as he departed the room.

Zuri nodded, her face still twisted as if she thought we were the sweetest couple she'd ever seen. I wondered if she would still think that if she knew the truth. People tended to think much less of a romance that was built on lies and kidnapping, but who was I to judge?

I'd fallen in love with my captor, and was in so deep that I couldn't even make myself regret it.

"Into the shower with you," Zuri said, grinning in a

friendly way as she swatted me toward the bathroom. After exchanging a quick glance with Joaquin to make sure it was safe, I did as she asked.

I wasn't sure I wanted to know what waited for me when the shower was done.

*T*he sight of my dramatic eyes in the reflection nearly took my breath away. I'd always thought them a bit of a muddled green, and the brown chunk in the bottom corner certainly didn't do much to dispel such thoughts. But the subtle smoky way Faye had done my makeup accentuated them, bringing out the slight angle to them. I looked like me, but somehow not.

"Hold still," she said, smiling slightly. Where Zuri had been incredibly outgoing and chatty while she dried and styled my hair into loose, fluffy waves, Faye had largely worked in silence while she applied product after product to my face.

"Faye is quite gifted with makeup," Zuri said, sitting on the edge of the bed and munching on one of the strawberries that had been brought for a snack while they worked. "She could make you look like a different person entirely. A whole new identity."

"I guess I'm just happy I still mostly look like me," I said with a laugh.

"You're beautiful as you are," Faye said, pursing her lips as she touched a brush to my lips and painted them a deep red. They were the only pop of color on my face, the eye makeup she'd chosen in neutrals with just the *slightest* hint of purple around my eyes to make the green stand out more. "To hide that would be a crime. Makeup should enhance you, not cover you up. Besides, I suspect your husband might strangle me if I gave him someone else for the night," she added, smirking as she finished painting my lips.

"Thank you, and I certainly hope you're right. If my husband wants another woman for the night, my lips might not be the only thing that's red by the end of the evening," I laughed awkwardly, ignoring the looks of shock on their faces. To work for people who had a business relationship with Rafael, I presumed they understood the nature of that business wasn't always squeaky clean.

Though most women didn't get their hands dirty, from what Rafael and Joaquin had said.

I stood, wincing when Zuri dropped to her knees with my shoes grasped tightly in her grip. I held out a foot, watching as she slid the delicate gold heels onto my feet. My toes matched my lips, painted that deep, velvety red as she clasped the strap around my ankle.

Once that was done, I moved to a corner of the room where Joaquin wouldn't be able to see me. I dropped the robe I'd dressed in after getting out of the shower. The strapless push-up bra was already uncomfortable around my chest, fitted snugly to hold its place even though it seemed to defy logic. The underwear were seamless, flowing over my body in a way that wouldn't show beneath the white fabric of the dress.

Faye held out the fabric for me to step into as Zuri held out a hand and helped me step over the pile of white. Faye dragged it up over my body, lining it up with my chest as Zuri grasped the zipper at the back and tugged.

The breath instantly left me as she sealed me in, the snug fit around my chest threatening to keep me from breathing all night. "It's too small," I rasped. "It probably would have been smart to try it on before we made it this far."

"It's not too tight," Faye said with a grin, taking my hand and dragging me over to the full length mirror. My eyes caught on the dramatic lines of my body in the dress, on the way the snug top of it clung to me like a second skin and pinched in tight at my waist before veering out slightly and draping over my lower stomach and down to the asymmetrical hem.

The small bump at my stomach was accentuated by the draping, looking just slightly bigger than it did when I ran my hands over the bare skin. My hands touched the fabric gently, hesitating as if I might stain the pristine fabric. "You look exactly like what the world will expect of *mi reina*," Joaquin said, leaning his shoulder into the doorway and meeting my eyes in the reflection.

"I'll go let him know you're ready," Zuri said, ducking out of the room as Faye worked to pack up their supplies. I moved into the living area, passing Joaquin in my need to pace while I waited. It was stupid to feel so much anxiety over seeing a man who had intimate knowledge of my entire body in depth, but the concern that he might not approve was there no less.

I fiddled with the clutch Faye handed me, smiling with something that felt tinged with sadness as she tucked the lipstick she'd applied to my mouth inside the open flap. Something moved behind her warm brown eyes, and it wasn't until I really looked at her that I realized something was off about the color of them. She looked away as quickly as our eyes had connected, swallowing and lifting a hand through her hair. She patted it briefly, fluffing the ends and then moving to gather up the rest of her things.

"Faye?" I asked, taking a step closer to her and touching

her arm as she worked to put brushes away diligently. She jerked back as if I'd struck her, cradling the arm to her chest. Her lungs heaved, far too sharply to be normal and not the consequence of a negative reaction. I pulled my hand back, giving her the distance she so clearly needed. "My husband is a very powerful man," I murmured, glancing toward the living room where Joaquin lingered. He watched her intently, having seen everything I did in her apparent fear of being touched. "And I do not tolerate women being harmed in the games that men play. If you need help, all you need to do is tell me, and I'll take care of it."

She shook her head, her small downturned mouth tipping up into a smile as she brushed off the statement. "You mean to tell me he's never harmed you?" she asked, tipping her gaze to stare pointedly at the carving of his name into my flesh. With my hair swept over to the opposite side, the not-quite scars stood out in the way I knew Rafael would want.

"I didn't say that," I said, grimacing as I turned my eyes away. "But that doesn't mean that I can't help other women who find themselves in similar situations."

The door to the suite opened in the living room, and Faye gave me a sad smile before she rolled her cart toward the door between rooms. "Maybe in the future, you might consider saving yourself before you offer to help others. They might take you more seriously." The sadness faded from her eyes, replaced by a steely determination. Her lips tensed with irritation, and then she was gone from the room.

Rafael swept inside, the warmth of his gaze landing on me and trailing up from my feet to caress every inch of my body slowly. The heady feeling of those remarkable eyes on me was enough to distract me from the concern I felt over

Faye's jumpiness, and I forced myself to shrug off the last of it that lingered.

I couldn't help someone who wouldn't let me.

"*Estás divina, mi reina*," he said, stepping closer until his chest brushed against mine. He reached his hand up, cupping my face and running a thumb over my cheek. "If I didn't know you any better, I would think you'd been sent to me from heaven itself."

My heart pitched in my chest, the oddly sweet compliment filling me with warmth in the wake of my insecurity. "If you didn't know any better?" I asked, furrowing my brow as I tipped my head back to meet his eyes.

He looked the same as he always did, and yet the tux that was perfectly fitted to his muscular form and broad shoulders somehow made him seem more normal than he did in his suits. Like the edge of danger that surrounded him all the time was replaced by an air of gentlemanly behavior. I knew better, but still Rafael Ibarra never ceased to surprise me.

"We both know you clawed your way out of the pits of hell, demon," he teased, leaning forward to brush his lips against mine gently. The contact barely existed at all, his caution not to mess up my lipstick making me pout as his eyes glimmered down at me.

He stepped to my side, touching a hand to the small of my back and guiding me to the living area and into the hallway so we could make our way down to the ballroom where the first event of the weekend was being held.

Nerves made my stomach swim, anxiety like a rock in the center of the sloshing liquid. I wasn't prepared to do this, to play the part of a society wife on Rafe's arm. I didn't know the first thing about holding a conversation with people who were more cultured and elegant than I could ever hope to be.

I'd consider myself fortunate if I didn't trip over my own feet.

But his fingers brushed against my stomach when he grabbed hold of me on the landing halfway down the stairs, backing my body into the wall on the landing until my spine touched one of the massive paintings hanging behind me.

"Rafe," I protested with a chuckle, turning my head when he moved to kiss me. The ferocity gleaming in his eyes was all the evidence I needed that this kiss wouldn't be so gentle. That he would tarnish my lipstick and never care that I was the one who had to go into a room full of people and pretend he hadn't mauled me on the stairs. "You'll mess up my makeup, and I promise you I am not talented enough to fix it."

He chuckled, pressing a hand to the artwork behind my head so harshly that the frame seemed to vibrate against my back. I had enough concern left in me to worry about the oils of his skin on the canvas, wondering if he would ruin something that might be worth more money than most people ever saw in their lives. He leaned in, those sinful lips tipped into a smile until his face disappeared from view. Warm breath kissed my ear, making goosebumps pebble the surface of my skin as he sank his teeth into the soft globe at the base of my ear. "And what if it's not your mouth that I intend to kiss?" he asked.

"Someone could see," I protested, turning my head to the side when his lips touched my neck, running over the mark of his name on my skin. Deft hands bunched up the fabric of my dress on the tops of my thighs, lifting it slowly while I squirmed against the wall.

"They won't," he said, nipping at my skin until I trembled in his arms. It killed me that I couldn't feel his mouth on mine, adding another element of something forbidden to the entire moment. "You wear my marks so beautifully. My name on your skin, my brand on your arm, my child in your belly, but your marks on me are all hidden."

"It's fine," I said, laughing uneasily as he pulled away. He dropped to a knee in front of me, running his hands up my legs beneath my dress. The cool metal of his wedding ring brushed against me, a reminder of at least one mark on him that others could see.

"I'm not going downstairs until my face is covered in my pussy," he growled, flipping the fabric of my dress up and holding it pinned to my stomach with one hand. The entire lower part of my body was revealed to the open air, sending a chill through me even as something twisted in my belly.

Something that felt a lot like arousal.

His bright eyes gleamed as he smirked up at me knowingly. "Do you trust me?" he asked, and despite everything that he'd done and all that had happened, I nodded without hesitation.

In this, I knew Rafe wouldn't risk me. In this, I knew with absolute certainty that I could trust him. The fingers of his free hand grasped my underwear and tugged them to the side, and then the heat of his mouth touched me. His tongue dragged through me, setting my soul on fire from that first brush where he licked me from my entrance to my clit. He worked me quickly, and my body was beyond my control. I spread my legs wider, grasping the back of his head as my fingers curled into his hair.

My other hand smacked against the wall when he worked his tongue over my clit in circles, driving me higher and higher and shoving his face into my core as thoroughly as he could manage. He'd be covered in me by the time he was done, and everyone would know what he'd done. Even as my cheeks pinked with the thought, I found an unbelievable thrill in the knowledge that I held that power.

That I alone brought the devil to his knees.

He worked me higher, devouring me until I was a gasping mess and my orgasm was only a breath away. I whimpered, ready for that moment where nothing existed but the pleasure he gave me, only for him to pull away.

He straightened my underwear as I gaped down at him, tugging on his hair with furious fingers. He dropped my dress, smoothing the fabric back down as if his greatest concern was making sure it didn't wrinkle. "What the fuck?" I asked, my lungs heaving with desire as I pressed my legs together and stood taller. "Rafe!" I gasped when he wrapped an arm around my waist and led me further down the stairs.

Hugo and Gabriel appeared at the base as we rounded the corner, their backs turned but preventing anyone from ascending the steps. I looked up at the top, finding Joaquin hovering there as a guard at the top. "Are you still nervous?" Rafe asked, smiling as he looked down at me from the corner of his eye.

"Not unless you count thoughts of castration as nerves," I growled.

He grinned in response, turning a wide smile my way. His lips gleamed with the essence of me covering them, and my pussy clenched in response. "Definitely not from heaven," he muttered.

I couldn't answer, because he guided me around the corner and into the open ballroom doors, leaving me to wonder who the hell had a ballroom in their home. Talk about ridiculous.

The space was filled with people milling all about, mostly groups that seemed to segregate based on their sex.

Women chatted together, their eyes falling on me with subtle smiles curving their lips. The whispers came almost immediately when eyes settled on my stomach, and I fought back my uneasiness.

As pissed as I was at Rafe for leaving me hovering at the edge of an orgasm, the anger I felt toward him melted a little with the realization that he'd given me a few moments of peace. I just hoped he didn't expect me to fend for myself with the women so soon.

I wasn't ready for that. Once we were in the center of the room, Rafe stopped walking and I stared up at his harsh features. Gone was the man who teased me about being a demon and who went to his knees in front of me.

This was the devil who ruled the world, who terrified people into submission with only a glance. The first of the men stepped up, and I settled into Rafe when he wrapped himself around my back. Despite the lack of tenderness in his face, his hands settled on my stomach as he introduced me to a man that I had no business knowing.

I was the only woman who remained with her husband as the first men introduced themselves, wishing us well and offering congratulations. Steadily the pattern changed, until more and more women came up with their husbands.

But it was clear that it was unusual for these events, that women were often discarded while the men discussed business. Any time something remotely violent or illegal came up, the women would duck out of the conversation.

But I stayed, wrapped in Rafe's arms and an active part of his business.

His equal.

And for the first time, I felt like *mi reina* in more than just the name he called me.

*I*sa sat at my side, smiling politely with an easy grace that spoke of the confidence she'd grown. If she could go toe to toe with the devil himself and not back down in fear, the roomful of people were nothing to her. At some point between having my mouth on her pussy, coaxing her to the precipice of an orgasm, and the time we'd settled down at our table along the edge of the room, she'd realized just how little she cared what they thought about her.

I leaned over, slipping my hand beneath the higher part of her dress beneath the table until I found the damp fabric of her panties clinging to her pretty pussy. My thumb stroked over it, nudging her clit gently. She jolted, turning an incredulous stare my way but keeping the smile on her face as she glared daggers at me.

Touching my lips to her neck briefly, I murmured against her skin. "You're stunning like this."

"Like what?" she asked, dropping her voice to a soft whisper to prevent the eavesdroppers watching our interaction with interest. Always watching, studying for weaknesses they wouldn't find.

We were each other's only weakness, us and the baby still growing within Isa.

I pressed harder at her clit, circling it more firmly and watching as her pupils dilated. "*Mi reina.* Standing next to me, *mine*, and belonging the way I always knew you would," I said, touching my lips to her throat when she tipped her head back to smile at someone who passed. Her smile proved to be enough of a distraction that the man didn't have a clue what I did beneath the table, working her up to that orgasm I'd denied her before.

That I would continue to deny her until I was balls deep inside her.

"I want to fuck you," I growled, pulling my hand away as her mouth tightened into a pout. I stood, holding out a hand and waiting for her to take it so I could guide her out to the floor where a few others had already begun slow dancing to the soft melody playing over the speakers. I guided her, touching a hand to her hip and tucking her into my chest tightly.

The feeling of her stomach against me felt as if I would never grow tired of it, as if I would be consumed by the need to keep her barefoot and pregnant for eternity.

Isa and I hadn't danced since that first night she met me in Ibiza, but she let me take the lead and guide her through the more refined movements that were entirely unfamiliar to her. "I'm glad I met you in the moonlight," she murmured, clearly having the same line of thoughts I had.

My hands clenched around her waist, my chin resting against her head. For the moment, I couldn't even be bothered to care that people in my world knew how much she meant to me. Let them know.

Because they had to know how slowly I would kill them if they so much as looked at her wrong, as well. My love for her was a double-sided coin, threatening to tear me open if I ever lost her, but giving me the strength to be a strong man —a better man—in whatever ways were possible for me.

The devil would never be good, but for *mi reina* I could be the best version of myself, and that would have to be enough.

"It wouldn't have stopped me if you hadn't," I said, giving her the words that she had to know were true. *Nothing* would have ever stopped me from making her mine.

Her eyes gleamed as she lifted her head from my chest to look up at me, leaning onto her toes to touch her lips to mine softly. No longer did the knowledge of my obsession scare her.

Isa had long since stepped into the darkness with me, making her home in the night I claimed as my own.

"Will they ever stop whispering?" she asked, chuckling under her breath when she pulled away.

"Probably not," I admitted.

"How wonderful," she muttered, making me laugh in response. With the evening coming to a close, all I wanted to do was take her upstairs and finally sink inside her.

So I decided to say fuck the event and do just that.

⚜

I shoved open the door to our suite, kicking it closed behind me as Isa wound her body around me. Her mouth danced over mine, an erotic tangle of limbs and mouths and *everything*. Those deft fingers of hers worked open the button of my tux jacket, tearing the bowtie from my neck so sharply that I thought she might take my throat with it.

The red painted nails on her fingers scraped against my

flesh as she worked open the buttons of my shirt. Reaching for her panties, I shoved the fabric of her dress out of my way until my fingers touched the waistband.

She wrenched her mouth from mine, swatting my hands away with a firm shake of her head. "No," she mumbled, working the buttons of my shirt open until my chest was bared to the dim lighting shining in through the floor to ceiling window at the back of the suite.

"The longer it takes me to get inside you—" I paused, leaning forward to sink my teeth into her bottom lip as she ran her fingers over the name carved into my chest. Her nails dug into the surrounding flesh, dragging over my chest and going for my belt buckle at my pants while I shrugged off my shirt and jacket. "The harder I'll fuck you."

"I'm counting on it," she said, giving me a saucy grin as she tore open my pants and wrapped her hand around my length. She dropped to her knees in front of me, covering my head with her mouth and enveloping me in the wet heat. With her lipstick already smudged from my assault when we'd reached the suite door, she looked like the desperate, needy woman I drove to the edge of her sanity.

The memory of her back against the Dali hanging in the stairwell, the precious art serving as the background for her ecstasy, threatened to be my undoing. Her hand and mouth worked me in tandem, pulling me closer and closer to the edge with each harsh suck of her stained red lips wrapped around me.

Yanking her to her feet, I spun her harshly and unzipped the dress that hid her from my view. My own pants fell down, tangling around my ankles as we moved toward the bed. Her dress fell into a puddle on the floor as I kicked off my shoes and pants, cracking my palm against the globe of her ass and watching as she reached up and unclasped her bra and freed her breasts.

She leaned over the edge of the bed while I watched, pulling her white panties down over her ass and slipping them off to toss to the side.

So far removed from the innocent virgin I'd taken that night in Ibiza, the queen before me crawled up onto the bed and lay on her stomach, raising her ass in the air in invitation. Another night, and I'd fuck that instead since she seemed determined to tempt me.

But I owed her an orgasm, and I'd be damned if she did it anywhere but on my cock.

I crawled over her, wrapping a hand around the front of her throat and driving inside her with a firm press of my hips. Her pussy clenched down on me immediately, finally having exactly what she had desired since the moment when I licked her pussy on the stairs with the apparent risk of someone seeing us.

But I'd never risk that.

I ran my tongue up the back of her neck, tasting everything that made her who she was. Tilting her ass up further for me, she took the hard drives of my cock inside her with sharp moans.

She was impossibly tight like this, with her thighs pressed together, and she fit me like a mold. She tumbled over the edge of her orgasm with a harsh gasp, her fingers grasping the sheets and clawing for purchase.

With her pussy clenching tight around me, I roared out my own release and filled her with my cum. I kept fucking her through it, moving slowly inside her and enjoying the wet glide of her pussy coated in me. It might have seemed redundant since she was already pregnant, but I'd long since decided that I would never tire of seeing her marked with my brand, with my release, with my *everything*.

I'd never tire of fucking her. Of seeing her face first thing in the morning or falling asleep with her in my arms.

This was the weakness of love bordering on obsession.

he white dress hung off my shoulders as I
stepped into the hallway. With my heart in my
throat, I glared back at the door as Rafael tugged it closed
and locked it using the key Sigrid had given him. Men like
my husband didn't sleep in an estate filled with ruthless
people without buying the extra time a locked door would
provide, even if that estate was filled with those he trusted.

I wouldn't have said he was capable of trusting anyone,
and yet, he trusted those present enough to bring me.
Considering what had happened in Chicago, it wasn't a
small concession.

"You'll be fine," he murmured, chuckling under his
breath and taking my hand in his. The feeling of his warmth
surrounding my palm and entwining between my fingers
was a comfort—even if I felt like I was flailing and the
reality of what I was about to do threatened to crush me.

Brunch with the other wives and daughters, while Rafe
went off with the rest of the men. After the way he'd
involved me in his conversations the night before, I'd foolishly begun to hope maybe I wouldn't need to be separated

from him. "You don't know that. You're relegating me to the typical wife role. That isn't where I want to be."

"And you'd rather talk about cocaine distribution between territories? Or is it the arms deals that interest you? The men talking about what stable girls they'd like to visit in Stockholm while they're visiting? Maybe you *should* be privy to that conversation. We could find a girl to join us if that's what you're inclined to," he said, the mocking glaze to his eyes the only thing that prevented me from ripping off his cock as soon as he said the words.

"Don't make me stab you," I threatened, blowing out a breath. "You know I would share you about as well as you'd share me. Is that your way of hinting you want to bring another man to our bed?"

Rafael scoffed, amusement lighting his eyes even as a dark edge tightened his jaw. "I would cut him up for even looking at you, and then I *still* wouldn't let you touch the pieces of him when I was done. Does that answer your question?"

"This conversation took a ridiculous turn," I said, rolling my eyes with a huff of laughter. It probably said something about me that his threat to dismember someone for looking at me no longer bothered me. Somehow, I found it endearing.

There was most *definitely* something wrong with me.

"I'm not asking you to go to brunch because it's where the men tuck their wives when they aren't needed. That may be the case for some of the assholes in that room, but anyone with half a brain knows that women are powerful in their own way. Those women make their own friendships. They go home to their husbands at night and whisper in their ears about all the things they want for the world. The changes may not happen overnight, but to think a man is not swayed by the sweet murmurs of his wife over time is naive. Most of the men in that room value their wives, even if they are not a love match," Rafe explained.

"I don't need to whisper in your ear at night. You've never made me feel like I can't express my opinion openly. So what good will that do me?"

"Because it will be your words that they whisper in their husbands' ears, *mi reina*. Not the other way around," Rafe said. "You are a queen in truth, and after last night they will know that for certain. You have what most of them have never dared to hope for, and they'll look to you to find a way to achieve that. You have power. Once again, all you need to do is step into your role and take it."

We came to the top of the staircase, and I let Rafe guide me down the steps slowly with an outstretched arm for me to take. Joaquin lurked behind us, a solid presence that fortified me against the terror I felt being away from my devil.

Being this far out of my element made me stand out enough as it was; I wasn't certain that Rafe setting me further apart from the rest of the wives would be as beneficial as he thought.

Women could be incredible. They could raise each other up and offer the kind of support that men would never be capable of, understanding that we weren't in competition with one another but a unit moving as one.

But there were those who ruined it, who saw a competitor where they could have seen an ally and a friend. Those who were ruled by their jealousy and pettiness. Those weren't my women.

I wanted to befriend the women who understood that a rising tide lifts all boats. I just had to hope this community I wasn't a part of would accept me enough to let me find them.

We hit the bottom of the stairs, and I turned toward the main dining room where I knew the women were holding brunch. Rafe stopped at the foot of the stairs, letting my hand slip along his suit-clad arm until his hand grasped mine firmly. "What?" I asked, letting him tug me back into him. His body pressed against the front of mine as he wrapped an arm around me and released my hand. That free hand came up to cup my face, and I leaned into the touch despite my best intentions to remain stubbornly irritated with the situation he'd thrust me into.

Sometimes, it felt like Rafe forgot that only a few months prior I'd been a barely eighteen-year-old girl whose greatest hope was to start college in the fall. Rafe didn't do anything halfway, and the transition of me from that innocent and wide-eyed girl who'd first smelled the almond flowers in Ibiza to the queen he wanted at his side had been nothing short of drastic.

"You amaze me," he said, leaning forward to touch his forehead to mine as if he could sense the thoughts trailing through my head. We were so in sync, so wrapped up in one another that sometimes it felt as if we shared a wavelength all our own. I wasn't even sure when it had happened or what had prompted the shift. There'd been a time when the man in front of me terrified me.

In spite of the marks on my body and the things he'd done, I knew I would never find a safer place than tucked inside his arm. His outbursts came from a place of possession, not of sadism, and I'd survived them even as I transformed.

"I amaze you?" I asked, raising a brow at him in an attempt to dispel the suddenly heavy conversation. I didn't *want* to be this deep in a conversation with him.

Rafael, when he was sincere and oddly sweet was...disarming. Like he saw straight into me and knew all the doubts that swirled in my head, when that should have been the one place I was safe from him.

"You're everything I thought didn't exist. So yes, *mi reina*, you amaze me. You gave me hope for the first time," he murmured, touching his lips to my forehead as I tipped my head further to look at him.

"Hope for what?"

"Even the devil himself can love," he said, giving me that rare and stunning smile that made the breath catch in my lungs every single time I saw it. He reached into his pocket, taking out a fine gold chain and dangling it in front of me. I reached out to grasp the queen charm, running my fingers over the smooth, solid gold. "I was saving it for a more private moment, but I think it would do you some good to wear it today. To remember *who* you are when I'm away from you, since you seem to forget in the moments when I'm not watching."

He reached out, clasping it around my neck and removing the diamond necklace Regina had packed for me, that dangled next to the hollow in my throat. My shaking fingers touched it, drawing strength from the symbol of all I'd become. "Thank you," I whispered, my voice cracking as I leaned forward and touched my lips to Rafe's. He'd given me exactly what I needed to feel strong enough to face the day, somehow understanding the self-doubt that crippled me.

He reminded me that I wasn't the girl from Chicago any longer.

I was the woman who'd bested *El Diablo* at his own game, and I'd be damned if I let a group of wives frighten me.

Sigrid stepped up to me the moment I walked into the dining room, locking eyes with Rafael as he turned back to me from the hallway. He smiled, giving me one last boost of confidence before he disappeared around the corner and went to conduct his own business.

And left me to mine. I didn't want to negotiate drug contracts and weapon sales, but building a foundation of my own within the wives of the men who did that was something I could do.

How difficult could it be to make friends?

I swallowed down my protest that I'd never been very good at it, even back in Chicago.

"Isa!" Sigrid said, leaning forward to kiss each of my cheeks. "I'm so pleased you decided to join us! Come. The others are simply dying to get to know the new Mrs. Ibarra." The way she said *new* grated on my nerves, because while Rafael's mother had been Mrs. Ibarra over a decade prior, to call her that when her husband was no longer Mr. Ibarra struck me as odd.

Women sat at small tables around the room, the main table filled with platters of bite-size food. Most didn't look as though they had any interest in eating, preferring to sip their mimosas. "Would you like a mimosa, Mrs. Ibarra?" one of the staff members asked as she made her rounds through the room with a pleasant smile that felt indicative of a familiarity with this lifestyle that I suspected I would never possess.

"Just water, please," I said, shaking my head as my hand dropped to my stomach.

"So it's true? Rafael is finally to have an heir?" one of the women asked from her perch on the edge of her chair. She was one of the older women in the room, her light grey hair pulled back into a severe bun in a complete contrast to my loose, dark waves that hung around my shoulders.

"Mother," one of the younger women scolded her, shaking her head as she turned her gaze to me. "Ignore her. Most of us do. She's evidently forgotten what it is to have manners. I'm Fleur, and my rude mother is Vera."

"Isa," I said, introducing myself as the other women went about giving me their names. There were too many of them for me to focus on any one face, and I immediately became lost in the sea of names I would never be able to remember.

"It's alright," Sigrid said smoothly, taking my arm and guiding me to one of the chairs at the edge of the room. "There are so many of us. I'm sure you're overwhelmed."

"I wasn't expecting Rafe to have so many...friends," I said, uncertain what to call them. Allies seemed like a man's word, something that they would use to describe one another but the women might find too harsh if they tried to stay away from the more brutal aspects of the business.

"Power attracts power," Fleur said. "And our husbands and fathers are wise enough to see when a man is amassing more of it. They've drawn their line in the sand between Rafael and his enemies. Human trafficking was more popular in the past generations, like my father's, but many of our generation have eradicated such things from our territories. We simply did not dare to dream of what we might be able to do on a global level."

"Rafael has always been a man of action in ways that most cannot comprehend," another woman said. "He has been a very sought-after prize for years for that reason alone, let alone the fact that he is a handsome and wealthy man."

I bristled at the mention of my husband being handsome, even if it was *ridiculous* to be jealous over that. He was a stunningly beautiful man, with darkness lurking beneath the surface and giving him a feral edge that I knew women found attractive.

I was one of those women, heaven help me.

"Now that the introductions are complete and we've gushed over the prize you've caught in your honey trap," Vera said, shooting a glare her daughter's way. "Has he knocked you up? It would explain such a rushed wedding."

I stilled, leveling the woman with a glare. I truly hated the assumption that the only thing I could have of enough value to warrant marriage was the child growing in my womb. "I'm certain you'll be happy to note we were married before we discovered I was pregnant," I said, not bothering to suppress the bite in my tone. "The pregnancy was very intentional on my husband's part, and I hardly used it to trap him. If you'd like to take up your concerns with Rafael himself, feel free, though I certainly wouldn't advise it. He's been known to react violently to insults against me."

The woman stared at me, watching as I shrugged as if her opinion didn't matter to me. In the end, it wouldn't. As much as it may aggravate me at the moment, I would shrug it off and move on with my life as soon as she was out of sight. I knew the truth.

Rafael had used the pregnancy to tie me to him, so he'd been the one to trap me altogether.

"I like her," Vera said, sitting back in her chair and smiling at me. "Most of you cower far easier."

"I'm pleased to know I meet your approval," I said, smiling sardonically as the woman barked a laugh. She turned to her daughter, continuing on with whatever conversation they must've been in the middle of when I entered the brunch. The server brought me my water, handing it to me before she scurried off.

I drank it quickly, hoping to quell the nausea churning in my stomach. Evidently I didn't do a good enough job of hiding it, because Sigrid stood and grabbed one of everything off the table and plated it for me. "Never hesitate to eat when you're pregnant. It is the one time you should be able to eat whatever you want, whenever you want, without fear of judgement."

I picked up a crostini and lifted it to my mouth, grateful for the bread even if something sour would be hard to come by. The women talked around us, and Sigrid involved herself like this was her court. It was enviable really, but not something I felt comfortable ever saying I would be able to do.

The conversations the men had with Rafael the night before had often gone over my head with talk of deals and such that I had no knowledge of, but the women's discussion of the latest fashion and gossip from their home territories was too superficial for my taste.

And something I knew nothing of, given my upbringing. I hardly recognized brand names being thrown about. I knew, without a doubt, that their conversation was more small talk than it might have been had I not been there, and I could appreciate their caution around a new person.

I just had to hope that I would make it through the small talk to one day be privy to the more serious conversations I knew they had. Most of them had intelligent eyes, their gazes bright and observing everyone around them.

But this conversation, I couldn't contribute to and my silence felt uncomfortable.

After I finished eating everything on the plate Sigrid had given me, I stood and resisted the urge to stretch like a sleepy kitten. "Excuse me," I said, stepping out of the room and going for the bathroom near the ballroom from the night before. It wasn't far from the dining room, just a stroll through the more open living spaces and to a long hallway that ran behind the ballroom.

Joaquin followed the moment I stepped into the hallway from the place where he'd stood keeping an eye on me. "Give it time," he said, seeming to sense my anxiety over what may or may not happen in the future. I wanted to be everything Rafael needed, but sometimes it felt like the expectations he placed on me were impossible.

I left Joaquin in the hallway just outside the bathroom, moving into the elegant space and staring at the luxury around me. Rafael's home was stunning and the details spoke to the wealth he had, but it was beautiful in an easy way that felt like it belonged on the island. The bathroom around me was opulent, with the walls lined with gold-painted stones and a bright light over the top of the off-white sink vanity. I shrugged off the overwhelming need to go back home where I was comfortable, moving to the mirror and staring at my reflection.

Several of the women in the dining room had to be my age, some maybe even younger—the daughters that came along with their parents. Yet somehow as I stared back at my face, I couldn't help but be confronted with just how young I truly was.

They'd had years upon years to become accustomed to the lifestyle they lived. It was new to me, and even with my harsh introduction to the world there was a quality to my face that they didn't have. It wasn't quite hope. It wasn't quite innocence—not given the things I'd seen and done.

It was just a part of me that I couldn't explain, and maybe it came from being firm in the knowledge that my husband loved me. I thought that was probably more than many others had.

I did my business, washing my hands and dreading returning to the dining room and putting on a fake smile with the turbulent thoughts swirling in my head. The sight of the chess piece hanging at my neck bolstered me, reassuring me that Rafael had faith in my ability to be this.

But did I even want to be? I didn't judge the others for the life they lived and the choices they'd made, but I wasn't sure it was the right one for me. Maybe I really was better off staying on *El Infierno*.

I'd taken my first step back toward the door when the wall to the side of the sink shifted. I froze in place, shock stealing over me as the entire thing seemed to just slide to the side and open up to a new hallway. Sigrid stepped into the bathroom, a kind smile on her face. I glanced toward the door, apprehension filling me despite the fact that she'd been nothing but kind.

"There's no need for that. I don't have any intention of harming you," she said, that kind smile remaining on her features to reassure me. I nodded and shifted myself closer to the door so that I could call out if something changed, hoping Joaquin would hear our voices and know that somehow I wasn't alone. "My husband thinks I don't know about the tricks in his house of mirrors or how he uses them to sneak around with other women in our home," she said, scoffing bitterly.

"I'm sorry," I said with a wince, glancing at the hallway behind her. It wasn't even bare bones or ramshackle in the way I might have expected of a hallway behind the walls, but looked like just another part of the house. I couldn't imagine the kind of pain that had to come from being trapped in a marriage with a man who would have an affair like that, let alone be disrespectful enough to do it in the place I called home.

She waved a hand as if it mattered little to her, and I imagined that at her age it had become just another part of her life. "I have my own fun. Not that the oblivious bastard knows it."

"I'm not sure what this has to do with me at the moment," I said, brushing a hand over the bare skin of my arm. My fingers felt along the brand on top of my tattoo, drawing comfort in *El Diablo's* name there. The things I'd once fought or thought I wouldn't want had quickly become a source of strength. If I'd survived that, I could survive anything.

Faye rounded the corner, her eyes wide and her breathing heavy. A bruise marred her cheek, staining the skin with a deep purple tint that didn't belong. I sucked in a breath, stepping away from the door to move closer to her. She swallowed visibly as she stepped to the side.

My heart stopped.

For just a moment, I couldn't breathe past the cloying mix of relief and confusion that took control of my chest.

It was like staring at my reflection in the mirror, seeing a ghost I'd thought lost forever. I had enough time to glance down at her neck, seeing Rafael's name carved into her skin as my breath returned in a sharp rasp.

I opened my mouth, a scream ready in my lungs at the triumphant look on my sister's face as she moved into the bathroom from the hidden hallway. I realized what was happening just a moment too late, the sound never making its way up my throat.

Pain erupted through the back of my skull, and I crumpled to the floor as everything faded.

Until there was nothing left.

J strolled through the halls from the library where the men had gathered to discuss the details of our trade. Some territories who'd been excluded from the meeting and the alliance had previously been key suppliers, like cocaine from Samuel in Colombia.

It was only a matter of time before we stole his territory from him, but in the meantime arrangements had needed to be made to ensure none of us needed to function without it. Cristiano in Peru would take care of that for us, stepping up his production as much as possible to make up for the difference.

I was just glad that the negotiations had gone relatively smoothly, prices set and determined without any guns being drawn or lapses within the tentative bonds of the new world alliance. I nodded to Joaquin as I passed, his brow furrowed but a smirk on his face when I practically glided into the room.

The smell of cigars clung to my skin, and I realized it would be the first time Isa was confronted with that scent on me. I wondered if she'd like it or need to grow to appreciate it with time.

She sat in the center of the room with Sigrid at her side, a beaming smile on her face as she threw her head back and laughed at something the older woman said. I tilted my head to the side and leaned against the door frame, watching the interaction with interest in the moments when Isa didn't know I was there.

Isa raised her hand from her lap, bringing it down to rest firmly on Sigrid's arm and squeeze, as if the two women had known each other forever. It warmed me to see her fitting in so well, something I'd doubted would come easily to Isa.

She wasn't one to thrive in crowds or embrace having attention on her, instead choosing to stay at the edges of the group and observe everyone. There was power in that, just as there was power in the way Sigrid worked a room and owned her outgoing personality.

Isa didn't need to be someone she was not to be *mi reina*, she just needed to own her place and demand respect, but I appreciated the effort on her part regardless. She'd figure it out for herself in time.

Joaquin stepped into the room alongside me, nodding his head toward where Isa sat. "Somethings wrong," he said, and I followed his line of sight to where Isa had yet to turn her head and find me.

Something was very wrong. Isa was as linked to me as I was to her. She *always* knew when I entered the room. I turned my head to meet Joaquin's fixated stare, sensing the worry that filled him. "Did anything unusual happen?"

"Nothing. She was awkward, normal Isa. There was a little tiff with Vera but nothing Isa couldn't handle on her own," he explained.

"What changed?"

"She went to the bathroom and seemed to collect herself. She had more energy when she came out," he said. I turned my eyes back to Isa's, watching as she finally shifted her attention over to me. Where I might have expected her to flush at being caught in her over the top performance or for her eyes to flare with heat like they usually did when she saw me after a brief separation, her eyes were oddly blank. The answer for that was very simple.

That was not my wife.

J unlocked the door to our private rooms, letting Joaquin enter with us as we stepped inside. Odina trailed behind us, smiling and looking around the suite subtly as if she needed to hide the fact that she hadn't been inside before.

Joaquin closed the door behind him, flipping the lock as he watched me. I didn't know if he'd come to the same realization I had yet, but he would understand soon enough.

It seemed impossible given I'd watched Dima slit her throat, but had I? He'd conveniently ended the call before we saw the blade drag across her skin, and the name carved into her flesh was fresher than Isa's. Healed beyond the point where it was an open wound, but definitely newer than the name that I'd cut into Isa.

Seeing it on Odina was an abomination.

I didn't know how she'd managed to pull off the switch, or how Joaquin had missed it happening, but I'd deal with him later.

After I had my wife back.

"Where the fuck is my wife?" I growled, staring Odina down as she moved into the center of the living space. She spun, staring at me with a furrowed brow and trying to mask the shock in her features as confusion. But predators could smell fear, and Odina's was potent. It was obvious she'd truly thought she would get away with it, that I wouldn't know she wasn't the woman I'd been obsessed with for nearly two years.

Only an idiot would have agreed to this if she thought otherwise.

"What are you talking about, Rafe? I'm right here," she said, stepping closer to me. Her hand touched my chest, fingers brushing against the fabric of my suit in the same area she'd kissed back in Chicago. I grabbed her wrist, tugging her hand away from my suit. She wore the dress I'd picked out for Isa earlier in the day, and the chess piece necklace lay clasped around her neck.

But her freckle was on the wrong side of her neck, leaving absolutely no doubt about who she was.

"Did they really think I wouldn't know you aren't Isa?" I asked, tearing the wedding rings I'd given Isa off her fingers. The tattoo and brand on her arm were a decent mockery of everything I'd done, but they weren't enough to fool me.

"You're scaring me," Odina said with a swallow, staring up at me with wide eyes. The hollowness in them faded a bit with her fear, and a better man might have seen the terrified girl lurking beneath the surface of her hatred.

I just didn't care.

"Lesson number one. Isa would call me an asshole and tell me to give her fucking rings back, not admit she was afraid," I said, shoving the rings into my pocket. "The longer you take to tell me where the fuck she is, the more pissed I'm going to get." I turned to Joaquin. "Get your brothers. Lock down this fucking city. *No one* gets out until I find her."

Odina pulled at her arm, defiance filling her eyes as she

seemed to realize that the deception was over and done with. She didn't speak or move to establish the truth of what I already knew, only glaring at me and waiting for whatever came next until Joaquin hurried out of the bedroom suite to do as I'd ordered.

I stared Odina down, inhaling deeply before I surged forward with a harsh, unforgiving grip. My hand pressed into the front of her throat, the flesh I'd thought Dima had parted with his blade tensing beneath my grip as I used it to back her toward the bathroom. "Rafael," she rasped, her eyes pleading as if she could deceive me into believing her lies.

My thumb touched the freckle on her neck, digging into the mark that was so different from the ones I'd memorized on Isa's face and body in the years I'd been watching her. "Why is there a fork on my wife's phone screen?" I asked, taking another step forward as her eyes widened. Her throat vibrated against my grip as we stepped into the massive bathroom. I kept my grip on her as I waited, watching for the reaction I already knew I would get.

"I don't know," she gasped, clawing at the skin of my hands in her desperation to breathe.

"Because you are not my wife," I said, lifting her until only her toes touched the tiled floor. I guided her backwards until her knees bent back over the edge of the bathtub, positioning her head above the drain and face up. She flailed as she fell in, kicking and thrashing while I held her with a steady grip. The hand towels were within reach, enabling me to stretch over and grab one without releasing my pinning grip on her.

I tossed the rag over her face, covering the part of her that was somehow so like Isa but not in any way that mattered. She spluttered as I turned the tap on, letting the flowing water soak the cloth and fill her lungs.

Waterboarding was a more *humane* torture than I usually preferred, but something told me it was Odina's personal brand of Hell considering that all of this had started with her drowning in the Chicago River.

I switched the tap off, pulling the towel off her face as she gasped for breath. "Where is Isa?" I asked, my mouth tense and uncaring. Her mascara ran down her face, soaking her cheeks with black streaks that would have been pathetic if she hadn't been a useless waste of life.

Of all the people in the world, I didn't know that I'd ever hated someone as much as I hated my father.

Odina just might have filled that void in my life.

"Fuck you!" she shrieked. Tossing the towel back onto her face, I ran the water even heavier. Leaving it to soak in her lungs and make her feel as if her entire body would fill with water, I pushed the limits as far as I dared. For the moment, I needed her alive.

She could die once I was done with her.

Every time she tried to tear the towel from her face, I knocked her hands away and pinned her down. There would be no escaping the fate that awaited her. The death Dima would have given her would be a mercy compared to what I'd do.

"You're too late," Odina rasped when I tore off the towel again. A menacing and evil glare filled her face as it twisted with brutality. "Pavel already has her by now."

"Are they going to the compound in Russia?" I asked, daring her to defy me by remaining silent.

"I wasn't exactly privy to his plans," she said, twisting her mouth into a snarl.

As much as I wanted to make my way to the airports and

insure that the Cortes brothers had been successful in preventing his plane from leaving, I had to have faith that they'd moved swiftly. There was one last aspect of Odina's treachery that I needed to know before I dealt with her. "Who helped you?" I asked. She balked at the question, as if whoever it had been could ever be more of a threat than I was.

Odina seemed determined not to accept the fact that she was as good as dead.

I smothered her with the rag, turning the faucet on once again and enjoying the way the water rattled the breath as it fought to escape her lungs. I sank into that hollow place where the only thing that mattered was answers, trying to ignore the growing dread pooling in my stomach and the rage that threatened to ruin everything.

"Who?!" I demanded when I let her up for air.

"Sigrid! That bitch couldn't have been happier to get rid of Isa. *Isa* always forgets her place, steps on everyone's toes to get to where she thinks she deserves to be. That was never going to go over well with these women who've strived their entire lives to have even a hint of what you seem determined to give her."

"She's still here. Who else?" I asked, watching as she considered her words.

"Faye is the one who took her off the property."

"The makeup girl?" I asked, narrowing my eyes at the depth of Tessin's betrayal.

"Yes," Odina said, glaring up at me. I watched her face for any sign that anyone else had been involved, but found nothing as she slumped into the tub. The bedroom door opened, and Gabriel stepped inside with his tablet in his hand and his face written in fury.

"Where the fuck is she?" I asked him. The city should

have been closed down by now, and we'd scour the streets until we found a sign of Isa.

"The plane left the private airstrip an hour ago," Gabriel said. "Cleared by Jakob Tessin."

The blood roared in my veins, filling my head with a red rage I thought I would never see past. "Do we know she was on it?"

"Yes. I hacked the security footage. She was definitely on the plane," Gabriel answered, turning a harsh, withering glare down to Odina. The man hated her almost as much as I did.

I couldn't think of a better jailor for her until I decided what to do with her.

"Watch her for now and then send her back to *El Infierno* with Hugo and two men you trust implicitly. I want her bound and gagged and locked in the basement until Isa decides her fate."

"Where are you going?" Gabriel asked as I stormed to the bedroom door.

I didn't glance back as I gave my answer on my way out the door. They'd have the opportunity to prove their loyalty to the alliance sooner than we intended. "To kill them all."

y mind spun through endless darkness, pain lurking at the edges of my brain as if a phantom memory. Cold grey eyes filled my vision as my stomach churned with nausea.

I jolted awake, my joints protesting the movement as I tried to propel myself forward. Metal rubbed at my wrists, stinging the already raw flesh as I peeled my eyes open. The pain at the base of my head made me groan, and I twisted my fingers to try to feel what had bound my wrists together.

It felt too familiar. Like the phantom of a memory I couldn't quite grasp.

"Don't move," a quiet, feminine voice said. I glanced up from the floor, my eyes trailing up pant-clad legs and eventually to Faye's sweet face. She'd abandoned the brunette wig she'd worn when she did my makeup in favor of white blond hair, icy blue eyes shining out of wide-set and angular eyes. "He tied you with barbed wire. It's...better if you hold still."

Her face twisted with regret as she met my eyes, and I resisted the urge to launch myself to my feet and force her to tell me why. I would never understand what I had done to warrant this kind of fate from a stranger. From someone I'd wanted to help.

"I know what you must think of me," she said, huffing a laugh even as her eyes filled with tears. "What would you do to save someone you love?"

"Not this," I said, wincing as I shifted my legs and met the same resistance that bound my wrists. Metal scraped against my ankles, tearing the skin apart and leaving me raw.

But the worst of the pain wasn't my abused flesh. It wasn't the memory of phantom shadows coming from me as barbed wire bit into my skin and held me beneath the water.

It was the hurt in my soul, the hollowness that settled inside me knowing someone had willingly put me in this situation. Someone had taken me away from Rafael, and she stared down at me with eyes full of regret. I wanted to hate her, to despise what she'd done, but even despite my words I had to wonder if there was anything I wouldn't do to protect the baby when the time came.

And I knew without a doubt, the baby would be in danger just as much as I was, if not more.

"I just want my brother back," Faye whispered, and I met her icy stare. Her eyes were filled with tears and she pressed the back of her hand to her mouth. "I don't...I don't do *this.*"

"Then what do you do that requires the skills to disguise yourself so effectively? I take it you aren't just a run of the mill make-up artist," I said, trying to shove down the empathy I felt for her. I shouldn't feel bad for her, but the remorse on her face was genuine.

"I'm a thief: art, jewels, anything that will fetch a high price with my contacts. *Never* people, Isa. I swear to you; I will do what I can to help you once I have Sacha back."

Footsteps sounded from the other side of the door and Faye darted a nervous glance that way before bending down quickly. "Pretend to be asleep. The longer you're unconscious, the more we can delay whatever he has planned."

She sat up straight in her seat, fiddling with her fingers hurriedly in an effort to look bored as I forced my eyes to close. The breath wheezed in my lungs as I heard the door open. The steps that made their way down the plane walkway were unhurried and steadily paced. I felt him standing beside me, forcing myself to relax and hold as still as possible.

"I hoped she would be awake by now," the male voice said.

"Sorry to disappoint," Faye snapped, surprising me with the amount of vitriol in her voice. She was either very brave or very stupid to be so openly disdainful to a man who had her brother as leverage.

"That mouth of yours will be your undoing one of these days, Faye Rousseau."

"Perhaps, but we both know I am worth far more to you alive than I am dead. Without me, who will find your precious diamond?" she asked, and I stored the information away for later. I wasn't certain if Faye believed I would never live long enough to be an issue for her jobs down the line, or if she hoped to give me something to use against Pavel in the event I got free.

But at any rate, her full name and something Pavel very clearly wanted was worth remembering.

I would remember everything that happened, everything that was said, and hope that I could use it against whoever I decided needed to die for what they'd done.

"Hm," Pavel grunted. "Eventually you will outlive your

usefulness. This pretty face won't last forever, and how will you find your way into art galleries and galas without it?"

"You underestimate what I can do with makeup, Kuznetsov. I could make *you* look fuckable, and that's saying something," she snapped back.

Faye grunted as the sound of a hand cracking against skin erupted through the space. She fell silent, and it took everything I had to remain still. No matter what he'd done to her, I was in no position to help her.

I shouldn't even want to.

The man shifted his weight, moving away from Faye as if he might walk back to the front of the plane. He stopped behind my back, pausing, and I felt his eyes on me.

Studying every breath as I fought for it.

The bottom of his shoe came down on the barbed wire wrapped around me, pressing my bound wrists into the floor and pushing the barbs deeper into my skin. I couldn't stop the pained scream that tore free from my lips as my eyes snapped open, and the gleeful chuckle that came in response to my pain should have surprised me.

It didn't.

The man from the beach at the hotel in Ibiza stepped around to my front, staring down at me as I glared at him. A fresh well of blood slickened my hands, trailing over skin to puddle on the ground beneath me.

"My son is very anxious to see you again, Isabel," he said, crouching down in front of my face. He reached out a hand to grasp my chin, turning my face from side to side as he studied me. "I hardly think you were worth all this effort." He grunted, releasing my face so suddenly that my temple smacked into the floor and spots danced in my vision.

He turned, striding for the front of the plane. "Then why bother?" I asked.

He glanced at me over his shoulder, a cruel smirk transforming his face. "What kind of father would I be if I didn't give my son the toy he's wanted for thirteen years?" he asked, chuckling under his breath. "And when he's finished with you, I'll send you back to Rafael piece by piece to repay his precious gifts he's sent me these last few months."

"He'll come for me. You're a fool if you think otherwise," I said, resolved to the fact that everyone knew it. Even if Rafael didn't love me, allowing his pregnant wife to be taken would show a weakness his reputation couldn't tolerate.

But he did love me, and he would burn the world to the ground to see me safe.

"Then perhaps he'll get to watch. How kind of him to save me some postage." He turned, slamming the door behind him and leaving Faye and I alone.

We didn't speak. There was nothing else to say.

*T*earing off my suit jacket, I tossed it over the stair railing and hurried down the steps. I rounded the corner at the bottom as I worked my tie loose and dropped it to the floor.

Joaquin and Hugo stepped into my path, and I watched as both men furrowed their brows in concern momentarily. Joaquin was the first to step out of my way, more familiar with the side of me that had come out to play than his younger brother, who hadn't yet seen the horrors men like us committed. "Your brother is waiting for you," I said, not bothering to glance Hugo's way as he moved to the side. His nervous swallow was the only response he gave, then he moved up the stairs quickly.

The shadow of Ibiza followed behind me, trailing at my heels like he knew his life depended on it. Given what he'd allowed to happen to my wife, the *only* reason he still breathed was the fact that some things would be unforgivable to Isa.

She'd moved past the tattoo. Past the branding and carving my name into her skin because in some deep, perverse way, she loved seeing the same marks on my body as I did hers. She understood my need to mark her.

Because the same pulse of darkness thrummed through her veins.

But murdering a man she'd come to think of as a brother, as much as it enraged me, would be the final straw that cost me my wife.

We emerged into the dining room where the women still celebrated and talked as if nothing had changed. I wasted no time closing the distance between us while Joaquin blocked the door. Lost to the red haze of fury, my fingers wrapped around Sigrid's throat and hauled her off her delicate perch on her chair before I even had time to form a conscious thought.

All around me, the hushed gasps and whimpers of the other wives filled the air with tension. But I ignored them as I walked Sigrid backward, waiting until her back touched the wall at the edge of the room. The women in my way clambered to escape my path, leaving their so-called friend to my mercy in their rush to save themselves.

"Rafael," Sigrid wheezed.

"Where. Is. My. Wife?" I asked, leaning my furious face into her space as my fingers tightened when a protest threatened to escape her lips. Her hands raised to my forearms, her manicured nails digging into the fabric of my shirt as she fought for freedom.

"She was with you," she rasped, glancing out the side of her eye to see if anyone would help her.

No one fucking dared.

"Where did Faye and Pavel take Isa, Sigrid?" I asked, tilting my head to the side and studying the way her lungs expanded with her desperate attempt to inhale more air.

When her breath settled down, something hollow

settled in her eyes. Recognition that her games had ended as soon as they began and a cool resolve that told me she knew *exactly* what would happen now.

She'd taken a gamble, a very fucking stupid gamble, with her life and lost.

"I'm as good as dead anyway," she said, shaking her head from side to side as much as my grip would allow.

"You can die very quickly with a bullet in your brain, or I can make sure you suffer for every second of pain Isa will feel until I get to her," I growled, intending every word. If I had more time, I'd make sure she suffered for it regardless. The red haze of irrational fury already threatened to consume me, to pull me into that blind rage where nothing existed except for my need for justice.

Only the knowledge that I had to act quickly kept it at bay.

"What is going on here?" Jakob yelled, his fury evident at finding me with my hand wrapped around his wife's throat and only moments away from strangling her until he was a widower. I looked over my shoulder at him, leveling him with a glare and gauging his reaction.

I released Sigrid, taking a few steps toward him. His confusion at seeing my hand on his wife was genuine, concern for her filling his eyes as he glared at me. "Were you aware of her plans?" I asked, my voice dropping low as I reached into the holster strapped across my chest and pulled my gun free.

"What plans?" he asked as Joaquin stepped to the side and let him stride into the room. He moved toward his wife, offering her comfort that she slapped away in spite. "Sigrid, what have you done?"

I spun, raising my gun to point at her and gesturing it down. She dropped to her knees wisely, obeying the silent command like she knew it would come. She'd wanted to live on her feet, with no one to command her.

Instead she would die on her knees.

"Rafael, surely whatever—"

"She gave my wife to Pavel Kuznetsov. She allowed people to infiltrate your home, and somehow took my wife out from under all our noses. Would you care to explain how your security saw *none* of that?" I asked Jakob.

He swallowed, clenching his eyes closed and then casting a nervous glance to his wife. "The hallways...."

"Yes, *husband*. I know all about your halls behind the walls that you use to disrespect me in my own home," she said with a menacing sneer. "Did you truly think I would not be aware after decades together?"

"Halls behind the walls?" Joaquin asked, his chest slumping as he finally understood how Isa had been swept out from under him. "When she was in the bathroom," he continued, scoffing. As much as I ached to punish him for the slip up, and I would when the time was right, even I had to concede that a secret entry to the bathroom insinuated something far more deceptive than we'd been expecting.

Something more skeevy than I'd thought Jakob capable.

"They're always willing," he said, casting me a nervous glance when he realized what I'd started to consider.

"I don't fucking care about your spying kink right now," I growled. "I want to know who else was involved."

"No one," Sigrid hissed, snarling with her rage. "The pleasure of getting rid of your wife who forgot her place is mine alone."

Something about her statement felt like the truth, but still... "How did you get her out of the building?"

"Faye's cosmetic cart has wheels. All we had to do was get her stuffed into the bottom and off she went.

Odina swore she could play the part of her sister and that she'd done it more times than she could count. How did you know? They looked identical to me," Sigrid said, fishing for information. I had no doubt that she suspected Odina had turned on her, given the information required for me to know about the switch. She never could have understood that I'd have recognized Isa anywhere.

Because she was the other half of my soul. It would have been impossible not to miss that in the eyes staring back at me.

I nodded, turning back to glance at Henrik as he stepped into the room. His eyes swept over the scene in front of him: his mother on her knees in front of me with his father staring down at her nervously. Jakob had to know what would come next, and still he didn't speak to defend the choice his wife had made.

"What the fuck?" Henrik asked, stepping into the room. He hurried to his mother's side, laying a supportive hand on top of her shoulder. She didn't meet his eye as he stared down at her, as if the condemnation she would find in her only son's eyes would be too much for her to bear.

"Make sure the plane is ready, and have Gabriel track her location," I barked back at Joaquin. He disappeared from the room, hurrying to ensure we would be able to follow Isa to Moscow as soon as possible.

"How much of a head start do they have?" I asked, watching as confusion laced Henrik's face when he met my glare.

"Three hours or so," Sigrid answered, fiddling with her hands in her lap.

"Who?" Henrik asked.

"Your mother conspired with Pavel Kuznetsov to abduct

my wife," I said, leveling the younger Tessin with a look and studying his reaction.

His confusion gave way to shock, his chest sinking as he furrowed his brow and studied his mother in horror. "She's pregnant," he said, shaking his head from side to side and taking a step away from her. "How could you do something like that?"

She didn't answer, keeping her head bowed and refusing to meet her son's probing stare. I touched my gun to her forehead, lifting her head until her final moments were filled with everything she didn't want to see.

Filled with her son's hatred.

The trigger felt firm against my pointer finger when I placed it there, finding an odd sort of calm in the midst of the cold fury that wracked every bone in my body. I wanted her to suffer, but I couldn't leave enough men behind to guard both her and Odina.

I'd need them to get my wife back.

I met Henrik's gaze as he looked up from watching my finger tighten, the pressure of the trigger meeting my digit as the final resistance before the woman who had raised him would no longer exist. He winced, clenching his eyes closed before backing away from her and retreating to the back of the room where he wouldn't be touched by the bloodshed.

In our world, there would be no forgiveness. In our world, all that separated us from the people we stood against was the fact that we did *not* traffic women. We didn't sell them or give them away when they became an inconvenience.

We didn't have many lines, but she'd broken every last one that we did have.

I pulled the trigger, watching as her blood stained her

husband's chest and the rest of the women winced at the show of violence. Their husbands may not be pleased that they'd been exposed to my brutality.

They'd see worse by the end of the day if I discovered any more rats in the house. "Go kiss your husbands good-bye. They're coming with me to Russia."

"If they don't?" Aaron asked as the armed guards I'd brought with us filled the hallway outside the room.

"Then they aren't loyal. I'll expect them ready or dead within the hour," I said, shoving my gun back into my holster. "Will you be joining me?" I asked Henrik. He nodded, proving his loyalty.

His mother lay on the floor, her body still warm. Still, he would push through the grief and guilt on his face to make amends for her crime against me.

He'd save my wife and unborn child.

*M*y body jostled as the plane landed hours later. My shoulders ached and throbbed with being restrained behind my back for the entire flight. I'd lost track of how long we'd been in the air since I awoke, and with no idea how long I'd been unconscious at the start of the journey, it was impossible to predict where Pavel might have taken me, but it didn't seem too far.

Only the knowledge that he resided in Russia gave me any kind of affirmation that we had arrived there, but it was also the place Rafe would expect Pavel to take me. My knowledge of the world might have been limited, but I suspected Stockholm and Russia weren't all that far from one another, depending on *where* in Russia they would take me.

I resisted the urge to groan as my body shifted along the carpeted floor with the force of our landing, sliding forward so harshly that the rough fabric rubbed the skin on my arms and legs until it felt raw and the wire at my wrists and ankles tore through my flesh.

Faye unbuckled her seatbelt, but made no motion to get

up from her seat when the plane came to a stop finally. She waited in silence, looking far too cowed and obedient for what I knew of the woman who seemed to want to defy the men that thought to control her.

I suspected it had far more to do with the proximity to the brother she was willing to sacrifice her humanity to save. Her very soul rested in the balance, but I understood better than ever the desperation to protect those we loved.

I shuddered to think of what I would do to save my unborn child's life should it come to it. My only real hope was that Odina had kept that one fact to herself.

That even though she hated me, she hadn't been able to bring harm to her own niece or nephew. Considering my predicament, that didn't seem likely.

The door at the front of the cabin opened, and the footsteps that glided along the fuselage were smooth and even. Somehow less heavy than Pavel's; the physical vibrations didn't jar my body in the same way his had.

The shoes that came into my vision weren't the same brown loafers Pavel had worn, and I swallowed back the saliva that filled my mouth. Staring at the black dress shoes in front of me, I hesitated to glance up at the man who wore them.

Even knowing who I would find, even feeling his eyes on me like a stain on my soul that I would never be rid of, I couldn't bear to see those grey eyes in person. Not when I'd thought him a hero for so many years, a mysterious specter who'd saved my life and disappeared in the chaos following the accident.

To know he'd be the one to rip it all away, and to stare that kind of evil in the face, I sank my teeth into my bottom lip in an effort to restrain the burning at the backs of my eyes.

I'd had thirteen years of freedom wasted in a cage of my own choosing. A few months of captivity where I enjoyed the freedom to discover the woman I was meant to be.

I was not a frightened little girl any longer. I was not the *princesa* who did as others expected for fear of upsetting them.

I was *mi reina*, and I would not bow.

Dragging my eyes up the fitted suit slacks, my gaze faltered on the sight of the gun held firmly within his grasp. He squatted down next to me, making it easier for my glare to land on his face. His square jaw was clenched as if he couldn't contain his fury, those icy grey eyes firm on mine when I finally met them. "мой котик," he murmured, reaching out a hand to grasp my chin between his fingers. He glanced around the rest of the cabin quickly, nodding his head to dismiss Faye. She gave me one last rueful glance, but then ultimately left me to the fate she'd decided for me.

To the pain she'd sacrificed me to in order to save her brother.

Dima's thumb touched my bottom lip, rubbing against the flesh that felt dry and cracked after the plane ride. His focus narrowed in on the place where he touched me, his eyes drifting closed as he pressed that thumb in tighter. The minute he pushed through the barrier of my lips, I sank my teeth into the tip and bit it as sharply as I could.

He didn't retract the appendage, in fact he made no movement to even show that I'd hurt him. "Don't be like that," he said, smirking and pushing his thumb further into my mouth. I resisted the urge to gag as the taste of his skin coated my tongue. It was so wrong to have *any* part of a man who was not my husband inside of me, I knew I would do almost anything to protect my body from his assaults.

I had chosen my King. Had given him everything despite

all he made me endure. Everything he put me through, he'd suffered alongside me, until we were equals. Molded in the flames and united through the marks on our skin.

Dima would never be worthy of me. He would never be able to compete with the man who possessed me body and soul. No matter how long I spent trapped with him.

I would not bow.

I bit down all over again until the sharp, coppery taste of blood filled my mouth. He finally grimaced, withdrawing his thumb and staring down at the bloody mess I'd left when I sawed through the base of his appendage with my teeth.

Even as thirsty as I felt, as desperate for fluids of any kind, I spit his blood from my mouth so that it stained the pristine carpet beneath my body. He watched me in silence, staring down at my glare and considering something as he drew his thumb to his own mouth and licked the blood from the wound.

Dima shuddered when his tongue touched the wet skin that had been in my mouth, sliding his gun into the holster strapped across his chest. His eyes drifted closed, savoring the taste of me on his skin and mixed with his own blood.

I ground my teeth together, resisting the overwhelming urge to wrap him in the barbed wire that pierced my skin, undoubtedly leaving me with more scars.

The thought of it damaging the ends of my tattoo made a pang of sadness pulse through me, and I spent a moment reflecting on how furious I'd been when Rafe marked me. When he branded me, I'd sworn I wouldn't forgive him.

I didn't know that I had, or that I ever would claim forgiveness was the right word for what I'd done.

In the end, there was nothing to forgive. In the end, I loved seeing my name carved into his chest and *mi reina* burned into his skin. I liked to know that I owned him so fully that he felt no shame in wearing the signs of that for the world to see.

If I felt the same, how could I fault him for what he'd done? I couldn't, because we were two halves of the same whole.

I missed him, and with the horrific realization that I may not ever see him again, *none* of what I'd suffered felt like it mattered. The only thing that I cared about when it all came down to it, was getting back to the man I loved with every part of my soul.

"I don't blame you for being angry," Dima said, and I jolted as my eyes refocused on his face. "*This* was not the reunion I'd planned." He shuffled toward my ankles, unwinding the barbed wire slowly.

Each prong slid from my skin, sliding through the swollen tissue and bringing a fresh well of blood and pain until my ankles were entirely free and I sagged with relief. They throbbed with pain, but at least I could move them if I chose to brave the agony.

"You mean you didn't want me hurt? I thought you liked your bitches scarred?" I asked. He touched his hand to the raw skin at my ankle, making my face contort with the burning pain that shot through my flesh. Those fingers trailed up over my calf, caressing the skin until I shivered against the goosebumps that raised in response to his touch. He didn't stop until he touched the scar that wrapped around my thigh.

"I like my women scarred, because *you're* scarred, мой котик. That doesn't mean I want you to be marked against my wishes." He removed his hand, dragging my dress down to cover me more fully before he moved around to my back. His hands brushed against my skin as he unwound the wire from my wrists, and it wasn't until he had fully extracted the barbs that he brushed his hand over Rafael's brand on my skin. "This I do not like."

"He's my husband," I said, shaking my head. The rings that were missing from my finger had been a nuisance— easily removed by the sister who'd betrayed me—but the names carved and branded into my skin would serve as a reminder to Dima about where I really belonged.

"You cannot be married to someone who no longer breathes. I'll take care of him soon enough," Dima growled, moving in front of me. He stood, bending down and putting an arm beneath my knees and back. He lifted me into his arms, ignoring my weak protests that I could walk on my own.

We left the plane, walking into an uncertain future where my dread rose higher and higher with every passing second. As much as I hated his touch around me and the feeling of my face pressed against his shoulder, I knew I would need my strength to fight when it mattered.

I forced my body to go still, observing my surroundings as he made his way down the steps from the plane. The landing strip was surrounded by fields of marigolds, the yellow flowers seeming so bright and sunny compared to my pulsing horror over what would come next. In the distance up ahead, a building that reminded me of St. Basil's Cathedral sat in the center of a garden of lush, colorful flowers that reflected off the colorful architecture.

It was the exact opposite of everything I'd expected to find in the home of a human trafficker in Russia, even knowing it was summer. I'd expected the property to feel cold, even if it lacked the snow that came in the harsh winters.

Dima carried me toward the structure, never pausing to

catch his breath as he closed the distance. When he finally reached the palatial estate, he moved to the steps around the side that led down rather than the ones that went up to the grand front entrance. "Am I to be hidden away like your dirty little secret?" I asked, perhaps foolishly trying to poke at him and irritate him in my anger. To be kidnapped and treated like dirt, hidden within the confines of the earth, *that* meant I could have been anyone.

I wasn't special to Dima, no matter what he had convinced himself.

"Just until you prove to me that you can behave on the upper floors. My wife is not pleased with your arrival, and I will not risk her wrath until I know you'll do as you're told, мой котик," he explained. At the bottom of the stairs was a pair of heavy doors, and there was a brief moment where I wondered how Dima would pull them open with me in his arms.

They opened for him, two bulky guards parting ways and enabling him to slip inside without issue. He walked down the sterile white hallways, going past countless locked and guarded doors until he came to the very end.

Another guard input a code into the security panel next to the door, and it slid open to allow us through. The room was filled with all sorts of things I didn't recognize. There were odd black benches, a free standing x-cross, and all forms of terrifying implements hung on the walls.

A bed waited in the corner of the room, looking plush and opulent with dark grey bedding. The thought of everything that had happened in that room, of all that I might live through, threatened to overwhelm me.

But it wasn't the most prevalent furniture in the room. That title belonged solely to the person-sized water tank against the rear wall. The lid was open now, but it gave no sense of security. Even knowing how to swim, all Dima would need to do is pull the lid closed and I would drown with no escape.

Dima set me on the edge of the bed, and I forced myself to sit up. I couldn't lie down with him in the room with me, but I also couldn't take my eyes off the tank. "Ah, yes," he said, following my gaze to where it lurked, tormenting me. "Your sister in particular hated my tank. I cannot say that I blame her considering what she survived in the river. I have to wonder, would you be the same? Are you afraid of water, мой котик?" he asked.

"I know how to swim," I said, admitting the truth. "Not that it would matter in that."

"Don't worry, my love. I have no intention of drowning you. That has always been intended for the girls who came before you. To see if they were strong enough to survive as you did. Only then were they worthy of having me as their master," he said. He moved to the nightstand next to the bed, pulling out a first aid kit. He poured hydrogen peroxide over the wounds on my ankles, seeming uncaring about the stains and moisture on the bedding.

It gave me hope that he didn't plan to sleep in the bed with me.

He cleaned and bandaged the wounds on my ankles and wrists quietly, seeming to fixate on the care and making sure they were treated to the best of his ability. I swallowed back nausea as he finished, looking around at all the foreign objects surrounding me. Uncertainty about what he would do first was almost as bad as the knowledge that I would be powerless to stop whatever came.

I could fight, but with nowhere to run, I would never win.

After he'd finished with the bandages on my wrists, his

hands slid over my forearms and his thumb and fingers kneaded the skin as if he was looking for something. He hummed thoughtfully as he worked, and it wasn't until his fingers brushed over the small bump on the back of my elbow that he froze in place.

I stared up at him, watching his eyes narrow on mine as he pressed down on that bump more firmly. "Did you know?" he asked, pulling my arm harshly. He forced me to lay on my stomach, the feeling of the sheets beneath me sending a throbbing shock of panic through me that only worsened when he reached into the stand next to the bed and pulled out a knife.

"Stop!" I screamed, thrashing in his grip and trying to escape. He straddled my lower back, holding me still and wrenching my other arm beneath my body.

"Did you know?" he repeated, his voice seething against what he must have thought was my first betrayal against him.

There would be many others.

"Yes, I fucking knew!" I spat, snarling when he pinned my arm to the mattress and the tip of the blade pressed into my skin. White hot pain spread through the back of my arm just above my elbow, shifting and writhing as he cut through me. I clenched my teeth, resisting the urge to yell against the pain.

He didn't deserve my screams.

It all stopped as quickly as it had begun, the tracker making a dull clunk as he dropped it to the top of the stand by the bed. I held perfectly still, willing him to make the assumption that it would be the only tracker implanted inside my body.

Because who bothered with more than one?

The hilt of the knife came down on top of the tracker

while I watched Dima destroy the device that would bring Rafael to his home. I breathed slowly, wincing when he wrapped a bandage around my elbow delicately, as if he hadn't been the one to cut me in the first place.

When he was finished he crawled off of me and stood from the bed, holding out a hand for me to take. Even with the relief that he hadn't bothered to look for a second tracker, I couldn't do it. Not knowing how similar it felt to the way Rafael had asked me to go up to his room that first night in Ibiza. I hadn't known what I was doing then, but I did now.

"Come, Isa," he said when I didn't take his hand.

I shook my head slowly, sitting up and curling my legs up to hug against my chest and refusing to meet his eyes. I didn't want to go wherever he wanted me. I knew, somehow, that whatever would come was far worse.

He pinched his brows together, casting a cursory glance around the room. "I do not like you here. I thought it wouldn't bother me to know it was a temporary arrangement, but you were right. Locking you away like a dirty secret is wrong. I only want to bring you to your rooms upstairs for now."

"At least this cage makes it clear what it is. I don't want the pretty, gilded cage that makes you feel better about what you plan to do to me. I'd much rather stay here, where we *both* know exactly what I am and what my place is," I snarled in defiance.

He went still and then nodded his head slowly. He faced away from me, breathing heavily, and continued nodding.

He turned so suddenly I never saw the open palm coming, the sharp slap of his hand cracking against the side of my face so harshly that my entire body twisted with the force of it. I crumpled to the mattress, my lungs heaving against my shock.

I shouldn't have been surprised, but somehow I was, even after everything.

"Have I not shown you kindness? Have I not been gentle?" he yelled, grabbing at my ankles. I screamed as pain flooded my body when his hands wrapped around the bandages, dragging my feet off the bed and twisting me until I was bent over the edge in front of him.

I shoved my body up until I stood, turning in front of him and trying to keep myself out of the kinds of positions that were vulnerable.

Even if they all were.

"Will you be gentle when you rape me inside my pretty cage?" I demanded, my face grimacing at the heat blooming on my cheek. It throbbed, and his eyes narrowed in on what I knew must be a red mark at the very least. "Because no matter how *gentle* you think you are, it will *never* be anything but rape. I will never want you, and I will *always* choose him."

The back of his hand cracked against the other side of my face, sending me tumbling to the floor in front of him. I panted as I forced myself up to my hands and knees, running my tongue over my bloody lip.

I would not bow.

The mantra played in my head even as my wrists throbbed with pain. I turned my head to glare up at Dima where he stared down at me.

The movement of his leg caught my attention, a shrill scream tearing free from my throat as he pulled back to prepare for the kick to my stomach that would bring my entire world to an end. "I'm pregnant!"

I twisted my body, shoving myself forward to take the

kick somewhere else. *Anywhere* else. Dima pulled back in shock, the kick driving into the back of my thighs with less force than he intended as I twisted, making my body protest.

He went still above me, glaring down at my stomach, and then lunged. Grabbing me by the hair, he yanked me to my feet and laid me out on the bed in front of him while I thrashed. My dress was shoved up my legs, leaving my underwear revealed as he bunched the fabric around my breasts. He stared down at the swell of my stomach in shock, and I knew Odina hadn't told him.

She'd kept one secret to herself, and I wondered if there was at least that small trace of humanity left inside her. It would hardly matter once Rafe realized what she'd done.

With Dima's eyes on my bare body, I couldn't stop to think about my husband with my twin, even as tears stung my eyes to think of how irreparable our marriage might be if he'd fallen for her tricks.

But I had to have faith. I had to believe he would know the difference between us.

I pushed my dress back down when Dima took a step back, running a hand over his short, styled hair and turning it into a frantic mess. He stretched out his hand suddenly once more, grabbing me around the throat and lifting me to my feet. He shifted that grip to the back of my neck, collaring me and forcing me to walk toward the door. "Where are you taking me?" I asked, limping through the pain in my ankles.

"To decide what to do with the spawn the devil planted inside of you."

*G*uards hauled open the heavy wooden doors, and Dima wasted no time shoving me inside with his grip on the back of my neck. I stumbled in, my ankles burning with the jarring motion and leaving me to fall forward. I caught myself with palms smacking against the inlaid wood floors, hurrying to get my feet back underneath me. Pavel sat behind his desk, eyeing me with disdain briefly before going back to the paperwork in front of him.

"Tired of your new toy so soon?" he asked his son, his throaty and accented voice forming the words I knew had to be for my benefit. If he hadn't wanted me to hear just how disposable I was, he would have asked in Russian.

His cold stare came back to me as I stood, holding my chin high and glaring at him. "She's pregnant," Dima growled, tossing an arm my way. Pavel studied me, that cold gaze dropping to my belly and studying it intently as he leaned back in his chair and steepled his hands over his chest. Dima accused, "You wasted too much time. If you'd only brought her to me sooner—"

"This is good," Pavel argued, leaning forward with a

cruel smirk. "Do you know what our buyers would pay for an Ibarra brat to play with?"

"She's mine. I have waited this long, and I will not sell her," Dima said, approaching me. He grasped my dress in his hands, tugging the fabric until it laid snugly against my stomach to show the small bump to his father. "I want to get rid of it."

"You will do no such thing," Pavel said, standing and moving around the desk. He grasped my chin, turning my face side to side and studying the marks his son's hand had left. "You can keep your precious pet, so long as you do not endanger the child. I want it alive, and I will decide what we do with it in the end. Just think of how we can torment Rafael. We not only have his American whore of a wife, but we have the only heir to the Ibarra legacy. We can control *El Diablo*, Dima."

"He will never give you what you want if you allow your son to touch me. You must know that," I spat, wincing at the way the twist of my face hurt the swelling of my cheekbone.

"Surely you must know that he assumes you've already been raped and used. That is the Kuznetsov way, and your husband is very aware of what we do with the women under our control," Pavel said, stepping back. He eyed the bandages on my wrists and ankles and leveled his son with an unimpressed stare.

I had a feeling if it had not been for the baby, he'd have tied me in barbed wire all over again to undo the small kindness his son had shown.

"Take her to her room. I'll send Karine and the kids to the summer house until you have your new toy under control," Pavel instructed Dima.

Dima nodded, reaching out to take my hand in his.

I slapped it away, the crack of my skin against his

echoing through the still office. He wrapped that hand around my wrist, pressing into my wounds. I refused to cower, to show the pain he caused on my face. Holding his glare with one of my own, I knew he would break my wrist before I gave in.

Rafael had earned my submission. He'd shown me what it was to be loved by him, and how things could be on the other side of our battle of wills.

I would not allow Dima to break me, not when I'd survived so much just to be reborn.

"Gentle, Dima. Isa is now our guest, and if you were wise you would remember that she is vulnerable. No matter how she may bluster and put on a brave face right now, she's already given you her weakness," Pavel said, grinning as he moved to sit behind his desk once more. "After all, what mother wouldn't do anything to protect her child?"

I turned back to Dima, watching his face twist with satisfaction. He took my hand once again, grinning happily when I didn't slap his touch away. "I have something I want to show you, мой котик."

He dragged me out of the office, his frenzied pace up to the second story of the palatial property straining my ankles. Blood soaked the bandages as the movements continued to aggravate my wounds.

The room he brought me to practically dripped with amber and gold, from the patterned wallpaper to the cream bedding with gold threads. It couldn't have looked more like a gilded cage if he'd tried, the rich luxury of European royalty had to be a play on the notorious Amber Room that was lost to history.

"I had it designed for you," Dima said, leading me into the intricate room. "A queen should have nothing but the best."

"I may be *a* queen," I snarled. "But I will never be yours."

"And yet here you are, in the rooms I designed for you. In the bed I will share. I have already won, Isabel. The time has come for you to accept it," he said, forcing me to sit on the edge of the bed. "I'm sure you must be tired. I'll allow you to take a nap before dinner, but first..." He stood, grabbing a remote off the nightstand. A screen popped down from the ceiling, and after the press of a few buttons, my face filled the blank screen.

No. Not mine. Odina's.

"I'll leave you to it," Dima said, clasping my chin in his grip. His lips touched mine softly, raising bile I wouldn't even attempt to push back. Perhaps if I was sick all over him, he wouldn't risk touching me again.

He pulled away, staring at my lips and then making his way to the door. It closed behind him, the mechanical sound of the passcode-controlled locks clicking into place.

With trembling hands, I lifted the remote and found the play button. I hesitated, wondering if I really needed to hear whatever my sister had to say. Rafael's name had already been carved into her neck, and she wore the same dress I now wore.

The one they'd changed me into after knocking me unconscious. I hadn't even had a moment to realize the dress wasn't my own, but I longed for the one I'd chosen earlier that morning.

It seemed like a lifetime ago.

Pressing the button, I watched Odina's face contort with hatred. Listened to her tell me how she hated me. She detailed her suffering at Dima's hands, the feeling of water filling her lungs in his tank and his knife carving through her to mark her with Rafael's name.

She hadn't known what he'd planned to do that day, truly believing it would be her final breaths.

He'd beaten her.

He'd told her over and over again that the only reason he hadn't raped her was because I would never forgive him for it. That the knowledge that a man had been inside my sister would be enough to keep me from allowing myself to love him.

Always precious Isa.

He told her if she hadn't made herself useful, he would have allowed his men to take turns with her. But she told me it wasn't only her desperation for freedom that drove her to make the switch, but the outright desire to see me suffer the way Hugo had promised all those months ago.

"And while you're suffering, while Dima is shoving his cock so far up your ass that you feel like you can't breathe, I hope you remember that I'll be with your precious *Rafe.* It will be me in his bed. Me taking him inside me at night and me that he can't get enough of. I want you to know that you were never special to him, and I want you to *die* with that knowledge haunting you. I hope you never find peace, dear sister," she said, leaning toward the camera. "Just like me."

The screen went black.

My guilt couldn't outweigh the pure hatred that flooded my veins with her parting words. With her determination to blame me for a ruined life that she'd caused with her own toxicity and bullshit.

If, *when*, I saw Odina again, I would cut her throat myself.

I couldn't sleep, and after watching the video of my sister and the realization that I wore *her* dress, I couldn't bear to wear it any longer. I went to the antique armoire at the side of the room, pulling open the doors and rifling through the clothes hanging inside.

Pants would have been ideal, a barrier between me and Dima where it mattered most. If only the sexist dick had provided me with any. I snatched a floral dress off one of the hangers, hastily ripping Odina's over my head with my eyes on the door.

The fabric settled over my curves too snugly, the chiffon dipping lower than I wanted between my breasts, but it was the only even remotely covering option.

I hoped the white base would be stained in blood by the end of the night, and I promised to do everything I could to make sure it happened. I might not have been the strongest fighter, but I'd be damned if I didn't use everything at my disposal to rid the world of the Kuznetsov scum that insisted on plaguing it.

As soon as I was changed, I paced back and forth in the

room, exploring the confines of my pretty cage with only my eyes in case someone watched. It would have been naive to think there wouldn't be cameras hidden somewhere, eyes on every move I made.

The best weapon at my disposal was being underestimated. I would let Dima and Pavel underestimate me until they found themselves buried six feet underground.

I lost track of how long I paced, certain that I would wear a hole in the area rug if I'd worn shoes. Eventually, the beeps of the control panel on the other side of the door made my feet freeze in place. Dima came into the room, his eyes full of condemnation for my defiance.

"You're meant to be sleeping," he sighed.

"How thoughtful of you to creep into my bedroom while I'm asleep," I said, tilting my head to the side and refusing to look at him. I felt his eyes bore into the side of my face as he closed the door behind him.

"If I didn't suspect it might be traumatic to your pregnancy, you probably would have woken up with me inside you," he said, closing the distance between us. He touched the swelling on my cheek, running the backs of his fingers over it gently as if he felt regret. "How long do you think it would have taken for you to realize that I'm not *him*?"

"The moment I felt you touch me, I'd have known just how vile it felt," I said with clarity. My skin crawled when he touched me, my soul protested the contact.

"We'll find out soon enough," he said, raising an eyebrow. "My father neglected to mention you'd been this defiant with Rafael in Ibiza."

"I wasn't," I said simply. The urge to tell him that Rafe was ten times the dominating man he could ever dream to be sat on my tongue, but I withheld it. As much as I wanted to insult him, forcing him to prove his manhood didn't seem wise given the proximity to the bed. "Does your wife have a gilded cage too?" I asked, glancing at the amber and gold walls.

"You seem to think that just because I gave her a ring and my name, that makes her my queen. She's a bargaining chip. An alliance with another family in Russia that keeps the Kuznetsov empire in power. She birthed my legitimate children, and she has done her part as expected of our marriage contract. She's served her purpose," he said, shrugging and stepping over to the vanity against the wall. He lifted an expensive glass bottle of perfume, bringing it to his nose and sniffing briefly before turning back to me.

"So why stay married?" I asked. It wasn't as if I *wanted* him to divorce his wife, but my heart hurt for someone who was trapped in a marriage where she mattered so little. Surely in that case, divorce would be better.

The bandages at my wrist prevented him from spraying it there, so he spritzed it on the crook of my unhurt elbow. The floral scent was mixed with notes of vanilla and some kind of blackberry to temper the intensity. "There is no divorce in my world, мой котик," he explained, tilting his head to the side as he studied me. "If it would please you, she could meet an untimely death. Accidents happen all the time sadly."

"That's...no," I said, taking a step back and staring at him with every bit of the hate I felt for him. "She's the mother of your children."

"All boys." He shrugged. "Boys their age should be peeling away from their mother and learning to be men anyway. As men, they'll understand the usefulness of women and their place in this world."

"And how long until you do the same to me? How old

will I need to be before you decide I'm no longer interesting enough to be useful?"

Dima pursed his lips at my question, truly seeming to consider the answer. "I do not know," he said, not bothering to lie and tell me that the attraction would last forever. From what I knew of him from Rafe, I was already older than he preferred. "My interest in you has never been the way I typically feel about a woman. I cannot say that you would follow the same pattern."

"You're disgusting."

"Perhaps," he agreed, taking my elbow in his grip and guiding me toward the door. "Or perhaps you merely need to understand the bond we share to appreciate that I may never grow tired of you. Only then can you see just how we're meant to be."

I swallowed back my revulsion, letting him guide me down the hallway. At the other end of the second floor, another locked door stood out against the opulence. The panel for an access code stood out starkly against the opulent wallpaper and decor of the hall itself.

"Why do you think the stranger pulled Odina out of the river that day?" he asked, making my body go solid when he stopped in front of the door. "Did you think he had a sudden desire to be heroic?"

"Why does anyone need a reason to pull a drowning girl from a river?" I asked, glaring at the door in front of me.

"Olezka worked for my family. He did what he was told to do while I made sure that you breathed. I gave you life from my lungs. I *breathed* for you. What can *El Diablo* ever do to compare to that? He can mark your body however he wants, but the very air in your lungs belongs to me."

"I don't understand," I said, wincing with each beep of his finger on the control panel. The door clicked open, and his hand touched the knob. Turning it and pushing it in, he motioned for me to step into the dimly lit room first.

A wheelchair faced the windows overlooking the court-yard outside, and a man's head lolled to the side as if he were sleeping. "What is this?" I asked, backing away a step.

Dima came up behind me, settling his hands on my shoulders and pressing me forward with his chest at my spine. He guided my steps further into the room, until a few more paces would put me next to the wheelchair.

Dread filled my body, claiming it for itself. "Would you like to know what I hoped would become of Odina that day?"

"No," I said, shaking my head and turning to the side as if I could escape what was coming. The answers I'd wanted since Rafe told me the truth felt like they were finally within my grasp, but I realized I didn't need to understand the motivations of a cruel man. All I needed to know was that he enjoyed the suffering of others.

"I hoped she would become like Oleg," he said, grasping the back of my neck and pushing me forward slowly. The side of the man's face came into view as we made our way to the window and then turned to face him. He was an exact replica of Dima, an identical twin down to the most minute of facial features, except there was no life behind his eyes. No menace or darkness.

They were just...blank.

"This is what Odina was meant to be, because you and I are one and the same. I shoved Oleg beneath the water. I held him below the surface and watched his body thrash. I drowned him, just like you did Odina."

"We are not the same," I argued, spinning to glare at him. "I did not drown Odina."

"Didn't you? It was your choice that put her in that river.

Just because you didn't hold her down doesn't make you any less culpable for what happened," he said, raising an eyebrow and reaching up to stroke my jaw. "You have always been bloodthirsty, мой котик."

"It was an accident. I didn't mean for any of it to happen. You deliberately drowned your own brother! Why?" I asked, shaking my head from side to side. He stepped forward, backing me into the window at my spine until the cool glass pressed against every inch of revealed skin.

He leaned into me, folding his body over mine until his lips hovered just beside my ear. "He touched my favorite toy."

"Your favorite...toy? How old were you?" I asked, turning my neck to meet his icy gaze.

"We were five," he murmured, his full lips tipping into a smile as the breath stalled in my lungs. "So you see, my love, we were meant for one another. Even you must see it now. *You* are the feminine version of me."

"I'm not," I gasped, shrinking back into the glass as his hand came to rest on my belly.

"You are, and when you're ready to accept it, I'll protect you from my father's wrath. I'll dispose of Karine, and if you behave for me, I'll even let you keep that spawn for yourself," he said, guiding his hand higher until his open palm cupped my breast in his grip. I grabbed his wrist, moving to tug it away, but he was too strong and the hand didn't budge. "I may have been raised by Pavel, but I spent a great deal of time watching Miguel get everything he ever wanted from the women he took by using their children against them. We both know you will give me *everything* I ask for if I'm only patient enough. Once you realize that Rafael cannot save you, then you'll give yourself to me."

"Don't touch me," I snarled, earning a pinch to my

nipple in response. He spun me to face the glass, my battered cheekbone colliding with the unforgiving surface and drawing a pained wince from me. He lifted the hem of my dress up while I struggled to slap his hands away, baring my underwear to Oleg's gaze.

"Do you think he knows what sex is? Do you think he sits trapped inside his body and wishes he could feel your tight little cunt wrapped around his cock?"

"Stop it!" I yelled, wincing when he cracked his hand against my ass in warning. When Dima pressed his body tighter into mine, I did the only thing I could do to buy myself some time.

Time for a plan. Time for Rafael to come.

I whipped my head backward, cracking the back of my skull against his nose and finding pleasure in the sound of his pained grunt. He released me, stepping back as liquid splashed against the wood floors in small puddles. When I spun, he held his broken nose in his blood-covered hand. "Do. Not. Touch. Me," I warned. "I swear to God I will cut every appendage from your body before I gut you."

He took a step toward me, his face twisted in fury as he released his nose. His mouth was a bloody mess, his teeth stained with red.

Only the sound of the beeping control panel froze him in place, and then the sight of his father stepping into the room with a disgruntled sigh. "Your husband is demanding to see you," he said, looking as if he was genuinely amused that I'd managed to harm his only remaining son.

I didn't suppose I posed much of a threat.

"How?" I asked, panic flooding me. If they'd somehow captured him, I would never survive that loss.

"Come, girl."

*J*akob Tessin's office surrounded me as my allies gathered up the men they'd brought along with them to prepare for the attack we would launch to get Isa back. I stared at his computer screen, the image of Pavel's antique bookcase all I could see in the moments since he'd left to find my wife.

The fact that he'd left her alone with Dima Kuznetsov didn't speak highly of what she might have already suffered, and my hands clenched the arms of my chair tightly. My skin vibrated with the need to have her safe in my arms, my body pulsing with the thirst for the blood of my enemies.

Everything she'd suffered, I would ensure they felt it more. If she'd been raped, I would watch as men took turns shoving their cocks so far up Pavel and Dima's ass that they tickled their brains. If she'd been hurt, I would beat them bloody and cut them apart piece by piece while they watched.

"I don't understand," a feminine voice said so softly I could hardly hear it. I leaned toward the laptop, straining my ears to listen more intently. Pavel filled the screen, taking the seat behind his desk and settling in as if he didn't have a care in the world. He didn't bother to look at me, continuing to ignore me in favor of whoever stood behind the camera.

There was the sound of shuffling, and then a woman who was not my wife brought in an antique chair to sit beside Pavel's. Dima took the seat, smirking at me arrogantly despite the blood staining his mouth as he met my eyes in the camera.

"Did you just get a sense of *deja vu*?" he asked, the humor lighting his eyes as he considered just how the tables had turned. "Come here, мой котик."

Isa stepped up to the edge of the desk, her eyes landing on my face. A shudder rippled through her body, her chest sagging forward as she raised a hand to her mouth. "Oh my God," she murmured, a bitter smile on her lips when she drew her hand away. "You're okay."

My jaw clenched with the realization that they seemed to have led her to believe I'd been hurt, and my palms twitched with the need to reach out and touch her. To brush her hair back from where it fell into her face and reassure her that it would be over soon.

The swelling bruises on each of her cheekbones did nothing to soothe my ire and convince me that they might not have harmed her. Despite the rage simmering in my veins, I did everything I could to keep my face impassive.

Disinterested in a way that it pained me to do. I had to hope Isa would see through the act and know it was for her benefit. The edges of my short nails dug into my palms with how hard I squeezed them together to keep the emotion off my face.

Dima reached out, grasping Isa around the waist and pulling her toward him. She slapped at his hands, twisting her body to try to avoid the contact as he manhandled her between his spread legs. His hands drifted lower, until his fingertips brushed the fronts of her thighs. "Return my wife," I ordered, the low bite of my words the only thing that even remotely conveyed the storm churning inside me.

I wanted to destroy everyone who stood between us. Needed to watch them burn on the pyres of Hell for taking her from me and for daring to touch what was mine. Dima tugged her back until the backs of her legs touched the edge of the chair, the force of his hands on her maneuvering her until her legs were swept out from under her and she fell into his lap.

She squirmed in his grasp, touching her hands to the arms of the chair to try to lift herself out, but Dima held her steady. Pavel's gaze was amused as he watched her struggles, somehow at odds with how I'd always envisioned the way the man would perceive defiance from *anyone,* let alone the wife of his enemy.

He pulled out a drawer, the squeals of the slides sounding impossibly loud. Isa went solid, her body freezing in place as Pavel drew a knife from that drawer. He touched the tip of it to the floral fabric that covered my name carved into her skin, cutting it delicately and letting the knife slip just enough that a bead of blood welled where he'd nicked her.

My teeth ground against each other with the need to withhold my reaction, to leave any hint of doubt that I would come for her. It was in Isa's best interest if they thought they had time with her.

When Pavel dragged the knife down over her breasts and pressed it to her stomach, I realized that they already knew about the pregnancy. I'd hoped to have more time before they discovered the truth of that realization, because with it came power and control over me.

Children may not be valued in the same way by men like Pavel, but even he understood the importance of a man's sole heir. Mine was so vulnerable, trapped inside the body of the woman I loved.

I'd killed all but one of his, and now he had mine at his disposal.

"But she's such a good kitten for Dima," Pavel said, catching the fabric of Isa's dress with the tip of his knife. Dima grinned over her shoulder, leaning forward to run his tongue over the bead of blood at the scar of my name on her neck. Isa shuddered in revulsion. "She even brought him a gift."

As Pavel guided the knife away to set it on the desk, Dima's hands glided up to her belly. Cupping the swell of her stomach, he put his hands on everything that was mine.

"You've made your point," I grunted.

"After everything your father loved to do, it seems only fitting that we have your child to control your wife. Life has a funny way of coming full circle, no?" Pavel asked. On the other side of the room from the place where he observed the call and paid witness to his failure, Joaquin went solid. He stared blankly ahead of him, undoubtedly lost to the memories of his mother's screams and everything she'd endured to protect him and his brothers.

"You will not touch her," I warned, leaning closer toward the camera until my face undoubtedly filled his screen. I wanted nothing more than to drink in the sight of my wife, of her mostly unharmed body and take comfort in the fact that as we spoke, I gathered an army to take her back.

She was less than three hours away by plane. She only needed to hold out for a few more hours, and then in the cover of darkness I would take back what was mine.

In fire and blood.

"It would be incredibly foolish of you to waste your bargaining chip by harming her or the child," I said, feigning casualness. My eyes drifted over to Isa, taking in the shock on her face at the indifference she must have seen when she watched me and listened to the heartless words.

Just hold on a little longer. I wished I could tell her.

Instead, I studied the bandages on her wrists and noted every injury she'd suffered, cataloguing them for the suffering I would force on those who had harmed her.

"She's mostly unharmed," Pavel said, turning over to study the lines of Isa's profile as a tear broke free from the welling moisture in her eyes. It trailed down her cheek, breaking a part of my soul as I watched it and was powerless to do nothing to convince her that it was all a ploy.

I loved her with every part of me, with all the pieces I'd thought dead and gone years before I saw her. If I hadn't yet convinced her of that, at the very least, then I'd failed as her husband long before I'd trusted the wrong people and allowed her to be hurt.

"But as you can see, my son is already quite partial to her. I don't think he's in any rush to return his new toy," Pavel went on to say. "Especially not when he's only just begun to play with her."

"Has he touched you?" I asked, the words sounding sharper than I intended. I needed to know, even though I understood it would matter very little in the coming events. All that mattered was Isa's healing, with the trauma she might have endured. The irony of that coming from me after everything I'd put her through wasn't lost on me, and a moment of regret threatened to consume me.

When I had her back, things would be different. When I had her back, she would *know* that she was the center of my universe.

When I had her back, she would understand her place in my life and that everything I'd done hadn't been to tear her down. But to show her how strong she was on the other side of everything she'd believed she needed to become.

"He tried," Isa answered, grasping his hand in her grip and tugging until he removed it from her stomach. "I broke his fucking face."

Pride welled in me, and the satisfied nod didn't seem like enough. Even in the face of what had to be terrifying for her, my wife was unbroken.

She hadn't even bent.

A queen knelt only for the man she chose, for the one who deserved her submission. That would never be Dima Kuznetsov, no matter how he tried to force her hand.

There was beauty in submission that came from a woman who gave it of her own free will in the end. Isa may have been my captive physically, but she'd become *mi reina* because of her own choices.

"You must know this will not end well," I said, leaning back in my chair. "What do you want for her safe return?"

Pavel grinned, his mouth twisting in pleasure as he leaned to the side and cut off my view of Isa. "You. That will do just fine."

The screen went black as he ended the call, and even though it hadn't been anything less than I expected, I swept the laptop off the desk in my rage. Jakob moved from his place, jumping back when I shoved the heavy antique desk with my foot and sent it tipping over.

"Tell them we're moving within the hour. I will person-ally hunt down anyone who isn't ready when I'm finished with the Kuznetsovs." He nodded in response to the order, moving to see the message conveyed.

Picking up his desk chair and hurling it into the window

on the opposite side of the room, something in me soothed as the glass shattered. Still, I kept going. Destroying every last inch of his office without feeling the slightest bit of guilt.

Considering what his ignorance had caused, I hoped the man died in Russia.

*P*avel barked orders at his son in Russian, and Dima shifted me off his lap so he could stand. The motion of his hands on my waist guided my body through the movements, imitating them as if I was still alive.

As if my heart hadn't stalled in my chest the moment I realized that Pavel wanted to trade me for Rafael. He had to know they would never follow through on that deal. He had to know that it would only end in both of us being held captive and in danger.

He had to know that would be the final straw that broke me. I could survive most anything.

Just not that.

In the corner of my eye, I watched Dima step around the desk. His gaze felt heavy on the side of my face, but I couldn't tear my attention off the black screen in front of me. Off the lack of Rafe's face.

Even as cold as he'd seemed, I'd taken a few moments of comfort in the sight of his face staring back at me. The cold surface was a ploy, a deception to make Pavel and Dima believe I didn't matter to him as much as I did.

"Behave, мой котик," Dima said, finally nodding his head at his father where he stood behind me. There was nothing but silence when he left the room, and Pavel studied me relentlessly as I dealt with my grief.

"It is a shame," Pavel said finally, standing beside me and taking my elbow in his grip. "I hoped for Dima's sake that you didn't truly love *El Diablo*. It will pain him to realize you will never truly love him in the way he hopes." He lifted me to my feet, ignoring the way I stumbled and clenched the edge of the desk in my desperation to remain next to the one connection I had with Rafe. It didn't matter that it had been severed, that his face no longer filled the screen.

I couldn't bear the thought that it might have been the last time I felt his eyes on mine, the last time I looked into that dark and dangerous stare.

No matter what he led the Kuznetsovs to believe, Rafael Ibarra loved me, and he would come for me. I knew that with every fiber of my being, and I knew that no matter what happened, we wouldn't go down without a fight.

We'd protect one another. We'd struggle and be together again. We would find a way, until the moment that death parted us forever.

Pavel guided me to a shelf against the wall opposite of his desk, lifting a file from the organizer on the top. He opened it, extracting a photo and handing it to me while he studied my face. I took it in a trembling grasp, my thumb running over the photo of a girl. It was like looking at a ghost, a girl who was barely alive and suffocated in the weight of her own mistakes.

How long had I lived that way, suffering and unable to cope with the choices I'd made to the point that I never truly experienced anything?

"I didn't recognize you at first," Pavel said, reaching over a veined finger to touch the photo where the scar showed on my thigh. It was summer in the photo, one of the rare instances my mother had managed to maneuver me into shorts before I was older and my protests made it not worth the effort. "But that scar of yours is unique. I've sold hundreds of young girls, scouted out thousands as potential products. Never have I come across that scar," he said, shifting his eyes down my body. From his vantage point and being taller than me, I knew there was no way he could see the white lines that wrapped around my thigh, but I still felt the weight of his stare as if his eyes caressed my skin.

"You're a fool," I said, handing him back the photo. I wanted nothing more than to deny that the girl in the photo was me, but he and Dima knew enough. I'd all but confirmed it that day when I video chatted with Dima unintentionally, and anything I might not have provided would have been confirmed by Odina anyway. "All of this for one girl? I'm not worth a war."

"Your husband would seem to disagree," he observed. He replaced the photo in the file on the shelf, using his grip at my elbow to steer me from the room. "He's spent the last several hours preparing for exactly that, gathering the forces he has at his disposal and local enough to be of use to him."

"How do you know that?" I couldn't imagine a world where Rafe hadn't yet discovered that Sigrid had betrayed him, that he hadn't been as relentless as a bloodhound in the pursuit of finding everyone who'd been involved in her betrayal.

I wasn't sure if my sister still breathed, and something empty inside me pulsed with concern. Not for her life, but for my lack of capacity to care. Was it possible to be human and not care if my twin was dead?

Could I be any better than the monsters I claimed to hate?

"Sigrid is most likely dead, but that doesn't mean I do not have spies within Stockholm who can see preparations being made."

Pavel led me down the hall, not pausing to give me time to fully take in my surroundings. The flash of columns on one side supported a nook with a sitting area, the other side covered in heavy blue and gold curtains that I suspected covered windows. Why anyone would want to hide the view of the flowers and grounds outside was beyond me, but I wasn't about to ask my captor why he shunned all things beautiful.

We crossed through what had to be the front entryway, the grand foyer of marble gleaming as he tugged me with a relentless grip. A woman and two children hurried down one of the curving staircases, her feet freezing in place as her eyes locked on me.

There was disbelief there, accompanied by a flash of hurt. She turned her eyes down to her children, touching the tops of their heads softly. One was a little boy who couldn't have been more than six, and the other boy was even younger than that. "This is why you're sending us away?" she yelled after Pavel. "So one of his whores can come out of the basement?"

Pavel froze, wrenching my body around when he spun so suddenly I almost couldn't catch my balance. I stumbled, only that hold on my elbow keeping me upright. "I am sending you away to keep you alive. What do you think Dima will do with the woman he's grown tired of when she becomes too much of a nuisance for him to truly enjoy his favored pet?" he asked, the growing harshness of his tone making me blink back my shock.

The woman was the mother of his grandsons. To be so calloused when discussing her murder at her husband's hands... I'd thought I knew what monsters were. I'd thought Rafael was a nightmare given flesh.

I'd been wrong. He was a dark knight, too tarnished to be white, but sweeping in to protect me from the evil who sought to break me in his own twisted way. To use me until there was nothing left and then burn the shell of who I'd been to ashes in the wind.

I couldn't meet the woman's eyes as she nodded, putting hands on her children's backs and ushering them out the front door. The kids disappeared, accompanied by a woman dressed in a black uniform that they seemed comfortable with. She turned at the last moment, clearing her throat until I met her gaze. "He'll tire of you too."

"I hope so," I said back, my gaze torn from hers as Pavel took me toward an elaborate path of rooms. She steeled her shoulders, stepping into the light outside and disappearing from sight. I had the uncomfortable realization that if Dima had his way, she might never return to her own home.

She might not continue to breathe at all.

We finally stopped in a formal dining room, the space occupied by Faye and two men I didn't recognize. Dima wasn't present, but I was sure he would come looking for me soon enough. I didn't get the impression that he wanted to leave me with his father for long, not after he'd tied me in barbed wire on the plane. It would seem that, in Dima's eyes, the only abuse I was allowed to suffer would come from his hands.

Pavel led me to the chair to his left, dropping me uncere-moniously into the seat and taking his own at the head of the table. Long and rectangular, there were places set for the three people who sat across the table, as well as one unoccupied on my other side where I presumed Dima would join us. The rest of the long piece of furniture was empty, and I imagined the vacancies reminded Pavel of all the sons he'd lost to Rafe.

"You have no daughters?" I asked, perhaps stupidly as I glanced over at Pavel. I didn't remind him of his sons directly, leaving the words unspoken.

"I do not tolerate imperfections. When my wife began to bear me daughters instead of sons, I disposed of her," he said, leveling me with a cold stare that made my blood turn to ice. "As to my daughter, she was married off as is to be expected in families of our stature. She ceased to be my family the moment she served her purpose."

For a fleeting moment, I wondered if she would be better off dead as part of Rafael's kill list and mission to eradicate the world of the Kuznetsovs. I had no response to the dark words or the implications they held. Dima's daughter would be married off in the same fashion.

"I believe you've already met Faye," one of the men on the other side of the table said. His dark brown hair was artfully arranged, the thick slash of eyebrows across his brow ruthless and unyielding despite the formal and polite words. "This is her brother, Sacha." The man on Faye's other side was older than I'd expected. Her brother had to be in his late twenties, but I'd mistakenly assumed he was a child given his vulnerability to Pavel and his men. He nodded, his face looking too thin in contrast to Faye's rounded heart shape. His clothes fit him well, so I didn't suspect they'd starved him while they'd held him captive, and there were no signs of brutality. The bruises on my cheeks and wounds on my wrists and ankles were far more prominent than any damage he'd suffered.

"And you are?" I asked, studying the man who'd made

the introductions with a quirked eyebrow. He seemed unconcerned that he might step on Pavel's toes by taking charge of the conversation, completely at ease when he leaned back in his seat with a relaxed, but not slumpy, posture. His face was clean shaven, deep brown eyes studying me with something that felt too knowing.

As if he could see right through the shell of me, and understood what he would find when he looked inside.

"Dimitry Turgenev," he said, leaning forward and steepling his hands on the edge of the table. "It is nice to finally meet you, Mrs. Ibarra."

"Don't let Dima hear you call her that," Pavel inserted with a laugh. "He seems to be quite territorial over his latest plaything."

"I mean your son no disrespect, *Pakhan*, but for the time being, that is her name. I will call her as is proper, and should he like to change her name then I will address her otherwise," he said, smiling at the elder man. Pavel gave him an indulgent grin, the likes of which I had yet to see him give his own son.

"Dimitry is my most trusted advisor," Pavel explained.

"Bully for you," I said, placing my hand on the table as a staff member brought in trays of food and set them in the center of the table. The sheer number of covered trays was astounding, and totally unnecessary to feed a grand total of six people.

I was so busy watching the staff member remove the lids from the trays that I never noticed Pavel picking up his steak knife. The movement caught my attention from the corner of my eye, the swift downward swipe driving toward my hand at the exact moment his hand caught my wrist. Burning pain erupted through the wounds his barbed wire ties had given me, and he pinned me still for the stab that came just between my ring and pinky finger.

The knife wedged itself into the wood of the table beneath my hand, my breath coming in sharp pants as I tried to wrap my head around how close I'd come to losing a finger. The staff member gasped, a squeak escaping her as she finished her duties and hurried the cart she'd wheeled food in on out of the room. "What is wrong with you?" I asked, tugging at my hand and trying desperately to get free of the edge of the blade that was so close to my hand. Pavel lifted the tip out of the wood ever so slightly, angling it so that it came closer to my hand and pressed against the skin without cutting.

"You will not disrespect me at my own table, girl," he ordered.

"Technically, she disrespected Dimitry," Sacha said, his lips curving up into an arrogant smirk as he drew the attention away from me.

"Quiet," Dimitry said, the order cold and monotone and lacking all traces of humanity. "Pavel, I appreciate the efforts to correct her behavior. Given it is her first night in Russia, I believe we can allow her some time to adjust to our ways. Clearly, her husband has indulged her far too much and allowed her leniency where it was not deserved. That is no fault of hers, but of her weak husband. I'll forgive it this time as she truly does not know any better."

As tempted as I might have been to tell him I didn't need his kindness, the reality of having a knife pressed to my hand and threatening to carve my finger from my body stifled my snarky response. My need to have a voice was not greater than my need to have a finger.

"Her punishments will remain my domain," Dima said, stepping into the room with a thunderous expression on his face. He glared at his father in challenge, and I tried to wrench my hand away while the two men had their stare down. Dima had cleaned up, washed the blood from his mouth and clothes. While his nose was mostly straight once more, there was a slight crook in it that hadn't been there before.

It filled me with a sense of pride to know that I'd done that. He'd always bear a sign of my defiance, and I would do everything I could to make sure that he had more of them by the time I was done with him.

"Keep her in line, Dima," Pavel said, withdrawing the knife and setting it beside his plate. Dima took the seat next to me, dropping an invading hand to the bare skin of my thigh. His fingers dug into the flesh, kneading it in warning and silently telling me to keep my mouth shut as he reached forward and filled my plate with the food from the platters in front of him.

"Of course. She'll be suitably punished when we retire to bed later tonight," Dima said, lifting his fork and knife. He cut through a green bean, stabbing it with his fork and guiding it to my lips. "Eat, мой котик. You'll need your strength."

Despite my misgivings about potential poisons, I watched as everyone else loaded their plates with the food from the platters and parted my lips.

Dinner continued in the same fashion, Dima alternating between feeding himself and me and refusing to allow me to feed myself. He treated me like the kitten he called me, a pet to be cared for and disciplined.

It would only be a matter of time before he discovered that even the most innocuous kitten had claws.

*D*ima took me to the library after dinner. With his father and Dimitry leading the way and Sacha and Faye trailing behind us, it felt more like a funeral procession than anything resembling a group of dinner companions moving to another room for drinks.

The library seemed to be the only room in the house I'd seen where the curtains were thrown open. The sun had only just started to set despite the late hour, thanks to the summer season this far North, and the brilliant colors flooded the mahogany and gold room with warmth despite the overly extravagant decor.

Dima moved to the bar in the corner of the room, pouring vodka into two tumbler glasses. He carried them over to me, holding out one for me to take. "I'm pregnant," I said, raising an eyebrow at his disregard for drinking during pregnancy.

"Right," he said with a slight laugh that hinted that maybe, at one point in time, something other than a monster had existed within him. It was so unsure, so hesitant as he downed the vodka himself and placed the empty glass on the corner of the desk that Pavel sat behind. Dimitry sat in a chair opposite the older man as they discussed something in Russian, Sacha and Faye lingering on a sofa nearby and speaking hurriedly in a language I only recognized a word of here or there with the quick way they blended the words fluently. I suspected it was French, but I hadn't detected an accent from either of them.

"What are we doing here?" I asked, wincing back my own distaste for the choice of words. I should be grateful to be in the semi-public library instead of locked in Dima's bedroom with him. My own dread over what would come when night fell made me ask stupid questions, made me stumble over my words when I should have stood strong.

I would not bow.

"I've heard Rafael likes to teach you to play," Dima said, touching my waist and guiding me to the chess set waiting on a table positioned in a nook by the windows. The pang of longing that spread through me for my breakfast nook, with my chess board and my scratched pieces from the streets of Ibiza, nearly took my breath away. "A waste of time if you ask me. Any smart man would spend that time inside you."

I refused to flinch, to show a reaction to the crude words as he guided me to a chair behind the white pieces. He'd given me the advantage of the first move, automatically discounting me as a true opponent.

It would be the mistake that cost him his life.

I stroked my fingers over the edge of the board, using the familiar feeling and the sight of the checkered pattern to ground myself. To draw myself back to the place where all that mattered were the moves on the board. "Would you like to play?" I asked, forcing my mouth to curve into a soft smile.

Dima took the seat across from me, unbuttoning his suit

jacket as he lowered himself gracefully. Bruises had started to form under his eyes, taking away from what I distantly noted was probably a face so handsome it disarmed his victims, but I knew the truth.

I knew the monster that hid behind the pretty facade, because the devil was a gentleman after all.

"Sure, мой котик. I would love to play with you," he said, his lips twisting into a beaming grin. The innuendo sat heavy between us, and I swallowed thickly.

"Should we make it interesting?" I asked, pushing past my nervousness. I'd beaten Rafael, learning and absorbing everything he taught me until the student surpassed the master. Winning against a man who greatly underestimated me would be easy enough.

There were always ways to distract him if it came to it, because nobody said I needed to play fair.

"What did you have in mind?" Dima asked, those grey eyes blazing with molten steel as he leaned into the table. He stretched a hand across, pressing his thumb to my bottom lip and dragging it down. The memory of my first wager with Rafe, the one that had ended in a way that felt so horrific at the time, brought a flush of heat to my face.

If Dima confused it as something he caused, it could only work to my advantage. At least, for that moment in time. All of that would change when it came time for bed.

I needed to buy time.

"If you win, I'll go to your bed peacefully. I will not struggle or fight," I said, knowing it would be the best offer he could believe. So soon after my kidnapping, to offer to participate in my own rape would only raise suspicions. But not fighting was in my best interest in the end, and would be better for the baby. I felt certain as his eyes blazed with fire that he could imagine that being true.

That he would know even if I didn't fight physically, it would still be rape in my mind.

"And if you win?" he asked, licking his lips and nipping at the flesh of the bottom one. "I presume I will not touch you tonight?"

"You do not touch me, and I am allowed to sleep in a room alone," I agreed. Even if I wanted to tell him he would not win, I refrained from the boast. Better to let him underestimate me. The moment of shock when he lost would be worth suffering through the arrogant grin that claimed his features.

"You have a deal, Isabel," he said, shifting his hand away from my face and holding it out for me to shake. I did so, pretending that it would mean anything when the very person I negotiated with would renege on his part of the deal. I knew it without a doubt, and I suspected he must know I would too.

But he hoped I would be gullible enough not to, so I pressed forward, stalling for time as I looked down at the board and considered my openings. I went with the Spanish game, knowing it was one of the more common ones and he might assume that meant my education into chess had been basic.

"The Ruy Lopez," Dima said, clicking his tongue and continuing through his move. "How disappointingly common." We continued on in silence for several moves, Dima's eyes feeling too intent on me and studying me far more closely than I would have liked.

There was a moment of curiosity, wondering if he'd not underestimated me as much as I thought he would, but the thought quickly drowned out when Faye stood from the sofa where she and Sacha waited and made her way to Pavel's desk.

"I did what you wanted," she said, touching her palms to the surface and leaning into him. "Now we have diamonds to find. Let us leave."

Pavel leaned back in his seat while I watched, waiting for Dima to make his next move, but his jaw clenched in frustration as he stared down at the board and realized the trap I'd sprung. In one more move, he would be in Check.

In two, Checkmate.

I met his eye, trying to ignore Faye's muffled argument with Pavel. That was her battle, and it was one she needed to fight on her own. I could not, and should not, help her after what she'd done. Even though it pained me.

Dima huffed a laugh, leaning over the board and studying it intently to search for options.

There were none.

"I'm impressed," Dima said finally, moving his pawn with a casualness that spoke of just how little it mattered. He knew he'd already lost.

"Check," I said, ignoring the way he never took his eyes off me. He moved another piece. Another distraction from the main game that would only buy him a single move of reprieve, and then I delivered the crushing blow, and what I had thought would wound his pride. "Checkmate."

Instead of growing angry, he smiled at me and shook his head from side to side. "You are quite the little mystery, aren't you, Kitten?"

"Not really." I shrugged, leaning toward the table. His eyes slid down to the line of cleavage the position revealed, his jaw clenching as he realized he would either need to break his word and set the precedent for our future encounters where I would never make a bargain with him again, or sacrifice his first night with me within his grasp. "I'm actually very simple to understand."

"And what is the key to this understanding," Dima asked, leaning forward to hover with his face only inches from mine.

"I will not break," I said, smiling at him sweetly. "Once you come to understand that? Then you'll understand me."

"Every woman has a breaking point," he said.

"I believe that. Unfortunately for you, a greater man than you has tried and failed." Dima began to respond, anger finally clouding his gaze.

"Alright, I'll permit you to leave. I need you to find my diamonds, after all," Pavel said. Silence filled the room, the shock of his concession striking me in the chest. Something was wrong, and the worry building in Faye's face told me that she saw it too.

I pushed out my chair, moving to stand before I even realized what I'd done. Dima followed quickly, catching me in his arms when I took my first few steps to where they stood at the opposite end of the library. "Don't get in the way," he murmured, restraining me with arms wrapped around my torso and his low voice echoing in my ear.

Faye hurried back to Sacha. She rushed him to his feet and they made their way to the library doors. I hoped they'd be able to find their way to the closest city, but Pavel stood behind his desk as they approached the doors.

"Faye?" Pavel asked. Faye and Sacha froze, and Faye turned slowly to look back at him. "I never did understand why you needed a partner."

"He handles the technology," Faye said, her voice a quiet whisper as her dread rose to match mine. Her eyes turned pleading, and I watched with increasing horror as Pavel opened a drawer in his desk.

"Dimitry will handle that element of your operations

from now on," Pavel said, gesturing to the man on the other side of the desk who blinked in surprise.

"I don't work for you. I need someone who I can trust to be impartial," Faye said, turning to usher her brother forward in a hurry.

"You do now," Pavel said. The gun went off, the sound so similar to the backfiring of my mother's Toyota that I felt my heart stall in my chest with a pang from the memory. My ears rang, the room going still as time seemed to stop.

Blood splattered across the side of Faye's face, the thump of the bullet embedding itself within Sacha's neck seeming simultaneous to the streaks of red in the air.

He fell, dropping to his knees as his hand raised to cup his throat. Blood coated it, his hand disappearing in the endless torrent of red that poured from his wound.

"No!" Faye screamed, dropping to her knees on the bloodstained carpet at his side. She covered his hand with hers, frantically trying to stop the steady stream of blood. The back of her body obscured most of Sacha from my view, the sounds of her whimpered pleading as she tried to hold the blood in his body.

His hand fell away from his throat, hers pressing more tightly to the wound as his raised to touch her cheek so gently that my heart throbbed with pain watching it. He swayed to the side, and Faye fought to hold him upright, to keep him on his knees as he toppled to the side. She leaned over him, tears covering her entire face as her lips kept moving.

It took me a few more seconds to realize she wasn't whispering to him, but singing softly as his eyes drifted closed and her lips trembled. Mine trembled in tune with hers, her hands shaking as she stood and stumbled.

She turned her tear-streaked face to Pavel, the glare in

her light eyes haunting. They watched one another silently for a moment, her jaw clenching as she steeled her resolve.

She lunged, darting across the room with speed I hadn't expected. Dimitry pushed to his feet quickly, grasping her around the waist and fighting to restrain her through the screaming rage. She kicked, elbowed, and punched him in rapid succession that compared only to what I'd seen from Rafael and Joaquin when they sparred. Dimitry met her for every strike, blocking and only trying to restrain her.

When she finally exhausted herself, he smoothed the hair back from her face and murmured to her gently despite his position as Pavel's right-hand man. Something about the way he soothed her seemed odd, like most men who associated with a human trafficker wouldn't have bothered. I watched the interaction in fascination, trying to keep my eyes off the still bleeding body of her dead brother next to their feet.

Maybe it was the knowledge that he would be responsible for managing Faye in the future that made him show her kindness where most men would not.

Maybe that made him even more twisted than the rest.

"Put her in her room," Pavel ordered, and Dimitry moved to do exactly that. The moment they'd shared where he offered her solace in the raging storm of her grief was over, the bubble burst as reality intruded. Dimitry lifted her up in his arms, not even looking down at her tear-stained and blotted face as he carried her from the room like a disobedient child. They left her brother's body on the floor as he stepped over him, and Pavel called someone to dispose of it with only a grimace for the mess he'd made.

Dispose.

As if Sacha hadn't been a person at all, just the garbage to take out at the end of the day.

"I did everything you asked!" Faye screamed from outside the door as Dimitry carried her off. Pavel didn't show even a hint of remorse or care for what he'd done, sitting back behind his desk and returning to work while I watched in horror when two men came in with a tarp and nudged Sacha's body with their boots until it rolled onto it. They carted it out, and housekeepers came to clean the blood from the hardwood floors.

It was all so methodical, so careless. It was something well-rehearsed, that they'd likely done countless times with countless men and women. I didn't want to think about what would happen to his body and how Pavel would rob Faye of her final goodbye.

"Why?" I asked, glaring at the elder Kuznetsov. Dima's grip tightened around my waist in warning, but I ignored it in favor of shrugging off his grip. "You had what you wanted." My lips trembled as the housekeepers deposited the red, soaked rags into their buckets of soapy water and fled the room.

"Hush, Isa," Dima urged me, tugging me tighter into his chest. Even surrounded by the coppery scent of blood and death, none of that seemed as repulsive as the feeling of his body fitted snuggly against mine.

"No one tells me what to do. Now she has a new handler, and he'll teach her how to stay in line. Her skills are valuable for now. She won't be hurt so long as she learns to do what she's told," he explained.

I went to reply, but the words stuck in my throat. Helplessness like I'd never known overwhelmed me, knowing there was absolutely nothing I could say that would make a damn bit of difference. Even at his worst, with Rafael my words had power. Here, I was nothing.

Dima released me finally when he seemed to realize I

had no intention of attacking his father. I wouldn't do anything so foolish. Faye had nothing left to lose, but I still had everything I'd never known I wanted but couldn't imagine my life without: my husband, my baby, and the new family I'd created unwittingly with Regina and the Cortes brothers.

Dima stepped around me and moved closer to his father, saying something in Russian as he went. I ran my fingers over the chess board behind me, trying to draw strength from a symbol that had once given me the most terrifying moments of my life. I forced the memory of Faye's pain away, needing to focus on what was coming.

The sun had fully set outside while we played our game of chess, and the time would soon come to know if Dima intended to keep his word. Sleeping alone on my first night in Russia was the best possible outcome I dared to hope for.

Pavel's phone rang with an alarm, the noise shrill as it vibrated on his desk and the buzzing sound seemed to echo through the room. "What is it?" Dima asked, stepping away from the desk and moving toward me once more, like he already knew that whatever it was, he wanted to have me close.

"Radar spotted a plane approaching. They'll be here soon," Pavel explained, meeting his son's eyes intently and holding the stare past the point of comfort. It left me with the distinct impression that Pavel was testing Dima, determining what he would do in the situation if he had been the head of the family. I supposed he was used to having a number of sons to choose from in terms of taking over after he was gone. Suddenly, he was down to only one, and I didn't get the feeling Dima would have been his first choice.

But my breath stalled in my chest as I pondered the meaning of his words. *A plane?* I didn't dare to hope as I reached behind me, grasping one of the chess pieces in my hand and turning it until my thumb touched the flat bottom and I held it firmly. Drawing strength from the familiar feeling of smooth marble in my grasp, I fought back the urge to panic. If Rafe's lesson where he'd worn a mask had taught me anything at all, it was that my own fear was my greatest enemy in these moments.

"Shoot it down," Dima said with a shrug. Pavel nodded in approval as Dima turned his attention to me. I leaned back against the table, hating the way the movement jutted out my chest and his attention dropped to it. I resisted the desire to yell out for Pavel to stop, knowing that he wouldn't listen to me anyway. I needed to wrap my head around my options, around the limited choices I could make in the next moments, but with life and death hanging in the balance, those moments flew by far too quickly.

I felt the moment I had to make the choice like a crack of lightning resounding through my body, threatening to tear my heart in two if Pavel successfully downed the plane and Rafe was on it.

Even my devil couldn't survive a plane crash.

Dima closed the distance between us, his hand falling to my waist and snapping me out of the moment of dread that had flashed through me. His body was close enough to mine that when Pavel picked up his phone and moved to follow through, everything inside me went still.

Time slowed to a crawl.

Nothing existed but the satisfaction on Dima's face when he lowered his head toward mine, his eyes on my lips as if he could steal them for himself.

But they didn't belong to him. They belonged to *El Diablo*.

I moved as quickly as I could, striking fast and hard like

Rafe and Joaquin had taught me. I drew my hand away from my back, the chess piece clutched in my grip becoming a weapon as I drove it toward his face.

The grey, glinting eyes that were so vivid in a sea of hazy memories widened in shock. His body flinched back just enough to give me the extra space I needed. I put all my weight into it, propelling my body forward toward him and fighting back the urge to gag when the crown on the queen piece pierced through the flesh of his eyeball. It sank into the socket, a sickening pop rippling through the air and shuddering up my arm as I pushed forward. Still, I drove it deeper, raising my leg and kicking it down on top of his kneecap until he collapsed in front of me.

Pavel shouted from beyond his son, his voice a blur as I yanked the queen piece back. My vision filled with red, the haze of blood and gore consuming me as I looked down at the crown of the queen piece and the empty hole where Dima's eye had once been. His hands raised to touch what he no longer possessed.

Suddenly, he looked like the monster I already knew him to be.

"You fucking bitch!" Pavel yelled, and I threw the bloody chess piece at him with all the strength I could manage. There was a moment of satisfaction when it struck him in the forehead and the marble left a trail of red on his skin, and I wished it had been a knife like Rafe had taught me.

It bounced off as I sprinted forward and out of Dima's reach. Pavel and I fought for the phone in his hand, his elbow glancing off the side of my cheekbone as I grabbed the cell and threw it to the floor. I stomped my heel down on it twice in quick succession, reveling in the feeling of the screen cracking beneath the pressure even as he shoved me to the side and I toppled over.

Pain exploded across my nose and mouth, taking my breath away, when Pavel kicked me in the face. Everything ached as the taste of blood welled on my tongue. I spit it out, leaning onto my hands and taking a moment of satisfaction in the red stain on the area rug beneath my body. Pavel glared at me, but didn't move to touch me again.

Not when the baby in my belly was too valuable for him to risk.

"The first rule of chess," I spat as Dima approached me. One of his hands covered his eye socket where his gleaming grey eye had once been, taken from the phantom memory of a child and turned into a nightmare. "The Queen always protects her fucking King."

"You'll suffer for that," Dima said, but he swayed on his feet. His hand was covered in blood, the thick fluid leaking out of his empty eye socket and trailing down in thin lines onto his wrist.

"Go see Ivonova. See if he can do something to fix that," Pavel barked to Dima. The disgust in his voice was evident, and I didn't think it had to do with the blood. Considering his propensity to violence, I suspected it had more to do with the fact that I'd damaged his son.

Dima only glanced my way briefly, his lips twisting with a moment of concern that his father might hurt me. Despite his insinuation that he would protect me, that he would be the only one to punish me, he left me with Pavel so he could deal with his eye. I'd earned whatever consequence his father deemed appropriate.

The elder Russian turned his attention to me as soon as Dima was out of sight. "I will very much enjoy watching him break you slowly. Piece by piece, bit by bit until there's nothing left of the bitch that Rafael Ibarra allowed to run rampant," he said, closing the small distance between us. He wrapped a hand in my hair, hauling me to my feet and dragging me into the hallway. My feet scrabbled along the floor beneath me, struggling to find purchase and unable to support me given the fast pace he set. "You'll do whatever he tells you by the time he's done with you, and when he finally gets bored, I'll enjoy renting *El Diablo's* wife out for use. If you thought his precious little island was Hell, you've seen nothing of the world."

His voice strained with effort as he dragged me up the stairs. My limbs thumped against each step, my knees aching with the blows as my scalp screamed in pain. I dug my nails into the back of his hands, bleeding him as he pulled the hair from my head with his ironclad grip. He didn't so much as flinch.

I screamed finally when he shoved open a door with his foot, dragging me into a bedroom. Flashes of my face stared back at me as he moved through the elaborate room, stepping up to the platform where the bed lay.

I was only a girl in the photos, the scar on my thigh gleaming in the sun as I tried to hide it on the rare occasions that it showed. Revulsion slithered through me as Pavel grunted with exertion and lifted me onto the surface of the bed.

I wanted to weep with relief when he let go of my hair, the pain lingering but not as sharp. It was short-lived, replaced by agonizing terror when he reached for the landline phone on the bedside table and dialed. Surging forward, I was pushed back with a strong hand at my throat. The breath left my lungs, stolen by the harsh grip as I gasped to try to suck in more air.

I kicked my legs, struggled and clawed at every part of him I could reach. But the edges of my vision went black, his voice lost to the overwhelming lightheadedness that consumed me. I'd have sworn I could hear the blood coursing through my veins, the sounds of everything around me deadened.

But even through that darkness, the twisted smile that consumed his face seemed to gleam like a Cheshire grin, while my heart fell into my stomach.

I'd tried to buy enough time, and if Pavel didn't allow me to breathe soon enough, I would die with the knowledge that I'd failed. When he dropped the phone to the bed beside my head, he leaned closer. The smell of vodka and cigar wafted over my face as he ran the knuckles of his free hand over my cheek.

"Such a pretty little widow," he said, squeezing his hand tighter around my windpipe. The confirmation of the strike against the plane stripped me of any lingering hope. There would be *nothing* left to live for without Rafael. The baby and I would be doomed to a life of misery, and I wondered if I was better off dead.

There had been a time when I would've said it would be a mercy for Odina. That a life of abuse was worse than a quick death.

Pavel released my throat suddenly, leaning back to stare down at me. His head cocked to the side as he waited, as if he was listening for something. I fought the urge to struggle, sucking back greedy breaths and raising a trembling hand to my aching throat. With his stare fixated on me and that eerie tilt to his head, he looked more animal than man.

The windows rattled, a boom resounding in the distance as a grim smile transformed his face. I knew, without a doubt, that he believed the explosion to be the plane. The house was too quiet in the moments following the blast, as if even the staff who moved about the manor constantly waited with bated breath.

The phone rang on the bed, and Pavel grinned at me as he lifted it and pressed the button for the speaker phone. A male voice said something in Russian on the other end of the line, and I stared at it. Swallowing my fear, swallowing the grief threatening to consume me, I touched a hand to my stomach and resolved to get free.

Somehow, some way, I would protect the baby. Even when I wanted to crawl into a hole and die alongside Rafael, for my baby I would not bow.

"In English for my guest," Pavel said to the phone, interrupting the man's slew of Russian.

"Direct hit," the man said, his accented voice making something inside me clench. I couldn't believe it, and I wouldn't. Not until I saw a body. I'd been burned once before, thinking my sister dead while she lived on to take part in my abduction.

Pavel opened his mouth to speak, gloating on the tip of his tongue with a vindictive, evil smile taking over his face. He leaned forward, coming into my space once again as if he was compelled to taste my grief for himself.

He paused as sharp bursts of rapid gunfire came over the phone, the sound of a man's shouts and pained grunts accompanying the noise. "Igor?" Pavel asked, the glee falling from his face. As if the gunfire had been the cue, the building shook with the force of an explosion.

I'd had the misfortune of being around enough bombs to know what it felt like when the noise reached us. When the pressure from the explosion itself sent a shock of pain through my head, the windows rattled in their frames and the walls shook in place.

Pavel's face twisted with his panic, the smile that had been his finding its way to my mouth. My lips parted, revealing a broad, toothy grin. It wasn't the relieved smile of

a girl who knew she'd be rescued, but the deranged muta-
tion of all things good, that came from a woman who was
ready to shed blood. "I hope that wasn't anything important," I said, pushing myself up to a sitting position to face
him more fully.

Bolstered by the reality that Pavel was under attack, that
my husband and my family had come for me, I glared into
his face as it twisted with fury. "Miguel was right about you
all along wasn't he, little witch? I guess it's time I fulfill the
promise I made him." He reached into the nightstand while
I vaulted off the other side of the bed. I was halfway to the
door by the time he turned his attention back to me.

A rough rope around the front of my neck stopped me,
and he used it to haul me back to the bed as I wheezed and
gasped. I fought for air, clutching at the rope with frantic
fingers and thrashing my body to try to dislodge him. He
pushed me onto my back, pulling the rope free from my
throat and using it to tie my hands quickly. I kicked, aiming
for his face, and screamed, but he was relentless in the way
he wrapped my wrists.

The rope burned the wounds beneath the bandages,
making me hiss in pain as he lifted me up to my feet. He
draped the rope over a hook hanging from the ceiling,
moving to the cord draped by the bedpost and pulling until
the hook retracted into the ceiling once more.

It raised higher and higher as I screamed, until only the
tips of my toes touched the top of the mattress. My wrists
blazed with pain, my shoulders throbbing as all my weight
hung from them. "Dima likes his women scarred," he said,
reaching up to pat my cheek sharply before he stepped
down from the bed. "This would have been where he strung
you up to whip you until you bled and then had his way

with you. How fitting that it should be where you die slowly to distract your husband long enough for me to get away."

"He's going to cut you into pieces," I seethed.

"Perhaps," Pavel agreed, moving to the dresser at the other end of the room. He came back toward me, striking a match against the box he picked up and lighting the curtain closest to the bed. The stark reds and oranges of flames burned a path up the fabric, slowly consuming everything as they grew larger.

"Pavel!" I screamed as he made his way to the bedroom door.

He turned back to me, murmuring his final words so softly that I almost didn't hear them as the fire on the curtains blazed higher toward the ceiling. "But you'll already be dead."

Then he was gone, leaving me to the fate that had been written from the moment I'd survived the river.

Death by fire.

*G*abriel furrowed his brow after a cursory check on the security system he'd hacked. "No sign of Pavel outside the house yet." He locked his phone screen and tucked it safely into the pocket of his black cargo pants. We continued forward, prowling through the woods on Pavel's estate.

One call to my man inside and he'd cut a hole cut in the fence line at the back of the property and made a guard disappear to give us a window to sneak in. The closer we could get before the diversion went off, the better.

Pavel and Dima would be dead by the end of the night, my contact inside taking over their operation as we'd always intended from the moment he first came on my radar, but the transition had to be seamless. There couldn't be any remaining men loyal to Pavel and his sons, no heirs left to claim his position as their birthright.

His young, American wife had been trafficked by Pavel and his men, sold to one of the local brothels for her virginity to be auctioned off to the highest bidder. That would have been her fate if he hadn't seen her and claimed her for himself.

Love didn't always start out as a pretty fairytale. Sometimes it was brutal and ugly and reflected the realities of the world around us. But when it grew, it outshone anything that was rooted in the beautiful lies society tried to tell us were the truth. In the end, though, they would always be false—deceptions to keep people complacent.

Men like me ruled the world, whether we worked for a government or a criminal organization. We were power hungry. We were selfish, and we'd destroy anyone who got in our way.

We were the only real law that mattered.

We moved through the yard next to the house, stepping out from the tree line in the moments when the guards patrolling were on the other side of the building. Aaron was already at work, his explosives secured to the side of the house as he stepped back to join our group and retrieved the detonation device from his pocket.

The explosion rocked the south corner of the house as the first bomb detonated. Rubble and chunks of the building sprayed through the air, and I waited for the dust to settle.

The commotion would bring any guard worth his weight to the scene, and I needed to be well on my way to retrieving my wife before that happened. When everything stilled finally, Aaron motioned us on. I followed Gabriel as he raised his assault rifle to rest against his shoulder and moved into the new opening where there had once been a door. We moved quickly, sweeping through the hallway that we stepped into. The two brothers flanked me, acting as guards even though the person they should have been protecting was already inside and hurt. Aaron and some of the others veered off toward the basement, going for the women imprisoned there, while the rest remained behind to fight the response to our attack.

Blood boiled in my veins at the memory of the marks on Isa's skin. I was the only person in this world who was allowed to touch her, to leave her with the imprint of possession that would never go away.

Dima had dared to touch what was mine, and I would make him bleed slowly for it.

We turned the corner, heading toward the library where Dimitry had said Pavel liked to take his after-dinner drinks and force his guests of the evening to sit and indulge him or talk business. After reviewing the blueprints of the house, we made quick work of the labyrinth of hallways and stairs in the old manor. We met little resistance along the way, which only served to raise my suspicions higher.

Pavel had to have known we'd come, the explosion to break down the doors couldn't be mistaken. Gabriel kicked open the double doors to the library when we found them, stepping into the space first despite all of Joaquin's insistence that he should take point.

I followed, cursing when we found the room empty. Only a wet stain of blood on the carpet remained and offered even a hint of a struggle.

My blood ran cold at the sight of it.

"It's not hers," Joaquin said, reassuring me even though he couldn't possibly know if that was true. There was no way to know, and I suspected the words were just as much to reassure himself as they were me.

He stepped over to Pavel's desk, picking something up off the surface and grinning at whatever he saw. That beaming smile turned my way. "That's my girl," he said, pride blooming on his face when he held up the bloody queen piece from the chess set.

"Is that an eyelash?" Gabriel asked, tipping his head to the side and turning for the door back into the hallway.

Joaquin pocketed the piece as we moved. "The basement is cleared of hostiles. No sign of Isa," Aaron said, his voice coming through the radio confirming his team had swept through the basement and the torture chambers we knew were located down there.

It was where, the last time we spoke, Dimitry had claimed Isa would sleep for the time being. Her absence there did not reassure me, but if I knew I was being invaded I would keep my best bargaining piece at my side, too. Isa would be with Pavel, if she hadn't already killed him with a chess piece.

We moved to the staircases, hurrying up them as quickly as we could while keeping quiet. My assault rifle was heavy in my grip, but my arm showed no hint of tiring. It never would, not when it was all that stood between me and the people who wanted me dead.

A dead man couldn't protect his wife.

I would not die unless she was safe.

The first of Pavel's men stepped out from the top of the stairs, firing rapidly as the three of us moved to make ourselves the smallest targets possible. Gabriel fired first, catching the man between the eyes. He fell to the floor, his gun blasting holes in the ceiling until his finger finally let off the trigger when Gabriel kicked it out of his hands.

Another jumped forward while he was distracted, earning three rapid shots from me that took him down before he ever fired off a single bullet. We continued through the halls, searching the abandoned bedrooms for any hint of my wife.

Eventually we came to a junction in the hallway, looking both ways before I signaled Joaquin and Gabriel to each take a hall.

"We stay with you," Joaquin insisted.

"All that matters is finding *mi reina*," I ordered, taking the hallway to the right. He looked as if he might protest more but nodded and did as he was told. The secondary team would catch up once they cleared the ground floor and offer assistance, but Joaquin had something to prove.

He'd failed us when he allowed Isa to be taken in the first place. He'd be the luckiest man alive if he survived my wrath when we were home.

Never in my life had I cursed the size of a home so much as I did in those moments when I kicked open door after door hoping to find my wife. I continued through the halls, searching until the smell of smoke finally drew me toward the room at the end of the hall.

My feet couldn't move fast enough, instinct driving me toward the place where I knew without a doubt, my wife waited for me.

With her life hanging in the balance.

S moke filled my lungs, drawing a ragged cough as I fought for air. Looking above my head to stare at the hook, I fought to pull myself up enough to get the rope off where it hung. It was too far, the curve of the metal too deep to allow me to lift my body with the way I dangled. My feet ached with how harshly I arched them to touch my toes to the surface of the bed, and the way the soft material compressed beneath me gave me no leverage to push up.

I coughed again, wincing as the flames progressed from the curtain to the area rug surrounding the bed. It went up in flames all around me, surrounding the bed in fire while I waited for the moment that the bedskirt would come next.

"Help!" I screamed, hacking up deep, wrenching coughs and thrashing my body from side to side. Hoping that something would jar loose in the ceiling or the ropes might loosen. "Rafe!" I yelled again, a strangled sob cutting off my desperate cry.

I wouldn't die like this, alone in the bedroom of my would-be rapist.

I stretched a leg behind me, kicking at the pillows and

slowly maneuvering one beneath my feet. It wasn't enough, the plushness of it sinking too much beneath me, and a growl of frustration came free from my throat. I swung until I grabbed another one, pulling it forward and trying to stack it on top of the other.

But the fire came too close, catching around the bottom of the bed skirt finally. I knew I would have only moments before those flames engulfed the bedding itself, licking at my ankles before they could consume me entirely. I wouldn't be given the mercy of dying of smoke inhalation before they reached me.

I sobbed, curling my legs beneath me and glancing around. There wasn't enough time. I'd never be able to stack the pillows high enough to get myself free.

"Rafe!" I screamed again, my lungs heaving with the force of resisting the cough that tried to claw its way up my throat. Everything hurt, and I let my eyes drift closed as the flames crept up over the foot of the bed to touch the surface.

With a whimper of fear, I pulled my legs back and tried to make myself as small as possible. I tried to picture the view of the ocean on *El Infierno*, the memory of the first moment Rafe stalked toward me from the pool at *Moon* in Ibiza.

Anything but the flames dancing toward me.

A deep bang reverberated through the room, making my eyes fly open. Rafe's thunderous face filled my vision, relief warring with his fury as his eyes landed on me dangling from the ceiling and huddled in the center of the bed.

"Isa," he rasped, the sound of his voice barely audible over the roar of the flames. He threw his gun to the side, stepping forward as I stared at him and wondered if he was real, or if my mind had created his image to offer some relief from the pain that was to come.

I could conquer anything, so long as I had him to hold me up.

The specter of my husband didn't pause at the edge of the rug, striding through the flames as if they couldn't touch him. Like the shadow of a former life, the memory of everything I had to fight for, he didn't flinch back from the fire that licked at the hem of his cargo pants.

The heat had to be scalding. The pain had to be blinding.

But the phantom of my husband didn't care.

He grabbed one of the bed posts at the foot of the bed and hauled himself up onto the surface with me. Fire touched his legs through his pants, his hand where he'd touched the post coming away seared bright red from the heat when he drew away and came to me.

He moved quickly, his body seeming to move faster than humanly possible. But I watched intently, memorizing the lines of his face and his body for what felt like would be the last time. Even if he wasn't real, even if I'd made him up to not feel so alone, all that mattered was he was there with me in my final moments.

"I'm sorry," I whispered brokenly, my voice trailing off. The thought of him going on without me, of him finding my burned body and mourning the style of death that seemed to haunt him throughout his life, that hurt me almost as much as the sweltering heat of the room that made my skin slick with sweat.

His hands dropped to my waist, touching me as I gasped through the shock that he was real. That he wasn't a figment of my imagination designed to protect myself from the agony to come. I whimpered as he lifted me without a word until the rope knots at my wrists came free from the hook. He draped me over his shoulder, my world inverting as he jumped down from the bed and jostled me around in his hurry to get away from the fire.

He stepped through it again as if he couldn't feel the flames. As if he was truly the devil incarnate, and even the fires of Hell couldn't harm him.

Once we were free of the fire, he set me to my feet. His hands encompassed my face, his mouth slamming down on mine as he pulled me against him. There was no finesse, only the brutal possession of his lips against mine. The furious pressure that came from the desperation of thinking he might not ever see me again. I returned the passion he gave me, wishing that my hands were free so I could wrap my hands around his neck instead of them being trapped between us like a reminder of the remaining danger. I buried my fingers in his hair and reassured myself that he was real–that dreams or illusions couldn't touch.

He pulled away, bending down to pull a knife from his boot and sawing through the ropes binding my wrists. "You came for me," I murmured.

His eyes went shocked for a moment and he growled low in his throat, as if he couldn't quite believe that I'd doubted he would for even a moment, but the insecurity that I could ever be worth this kind of risk was something that couldn't be denied.

In my relief that I no longer felt it, I realized just how uncertain I'd been.

"I will always come for you, *mi reina*. Even when you do not want me to," he said, tangling his fingers in my hair. He tugged lightly, forcing me to meet his eyes. My scalp burned with pain, sensitive from Pavel's assault, and I watched Rafael's eyes darken once again.

When we were safe, I had no doubt he would count

every mark, every bruise on my skin and wish he could kill the Kuznetsovs all over again.

"Are you alright?" he asked, his stare pointed and conveying everything I needed to know. Some hurts couldn't be healed; some violations would never go away. His fingers trembled as they touched what I imagined had to be the beginning of bruising on my throat.

"I'm alright," I agreed, nodding slightly. He touched his forehead to mine, sighing a breath of relief as his hand came to rest on my stomach. We gave ourselves that one moment, the opportunity to breathe together and then he pulled away. His face turned stony, the devil who sought revenge taking over his features as Rafe faded away and *El Diablo* came to life.

I buried my face against his chest, breathing in the scent of him one last time even as it was disguised by the smell of burning fabric. When I released him with a shuddering breath, he bent to pick up his discarded gun and led me into the hallway.

"Pavel's getting away," I said, desperate for the man to be caught. For him to suffer for all he'd done and would continue to do if he managed to escape.

"I'll find him, *mi reina*," Rafe said, turning back to look at me. His eyes filled with warmth, with love and affection, even as that dark nightmare lurked beneath the surface. Rafael wanted blood and retribution, but my husband wanted me safe even more.

I wanted to hide away and stay wrapped up in his arms, but the need for Pavel and Dima to suffer meant I stayed with him, trailing behind in my bare feet. My shoes were nowhere in sight, and I realized that they must have fallen off when I fought with Pavel as he dragged me up to Dima's bedroom. I hadn't even realized it at the time, too focused on surviving.

We moved through the hallway, with Rafael clearing each room we passed and keeping me tucked behind him to the best of his ability. The hall curved to the left; a little alcove tucked away where heavy curtains covered the windows.

Somewhere in these halls, there was an amber room made to be my gilded cage, where the last remaining bond with my sister had snapped in two. We rounded the bend, coming face to face with Dima standing in the center of the hall. Rafael stilled in front of me, shoving me firmly behind him as he observed the other man.

He wasn't armed, lumbering along as quickly as he could. He stumbled occasionally, as if the loss of his eye made him incapable of balancing the same as before. A blood-soaked bandage crossed his face, covering the void of the eye that I'd taken from him, and it appeared as if it was doing very little to control the bleeding.

"What's wrong, Rafael? Don't recognize me?" he asked, spreading his arms wide as if he welcomed death.

"Where's your father?" Rafael asked, handing me the gun. I didn't know what I was doing with a weapon so large, but I took it and kept my fingers as far away from all the important parts as I could.

"Long gone by now," Dima said, dropping his arms to his sides. He trailed his eyes up from my bare feet and over my legs, taking in the marks on my body. "I never should have left you with him. I'm sorry, мой котик. I won't let that happen again."

I stilled as I stared at him, watching him raise his hand toward me. He was truly delusional enough to believe that I would go anywhere with him, that I would ever choose him.

Rafael stepped forward, approaching him with fury written into every line of his face. His fist shot forward like a whip, the crunching sound of Dima's nose breaking echoing through the hall as the Russian man groaned. He raised his fists to block his face, jabbing toward Rafael far too slowly to do any good.

I'd watched Rafael and Joaquin fight, a battle of speed and masterful violence. Dima was no more frightening than I would have been in a fistfight, and the sight of his pathetic attempt was almost enough to make me pity him.

But I thought of all the women he'd hurt; of all the children he'd violated and sold. They'd been weaker than him. They'd been vulnerable, and he hadn't hesitated to exploit that.

It was his turn to bleed.

It was his turn to hurt, and I wanted to be the one to deliver that final blow on behalf of the victims who hadn't been as lucky as I was.

Rafael's fists landed against the flesh of Dima's stomach in rapid fire, the breath knocked out of the other man as he leaned into the assault. "By the time I'm done with you, there won't be anything recognizable for your wife to bury," he growled, striking the underside of Dima's jaw with an uppercut.

Dima fell back, his head bouncing off the wood floor when he landed. Rafael kicked him in the ribs, nudging him as if he wanted his plaything to stand back up so he could keep toying with him. "Pavel, Rafe," I reminded my husband, stepping forward and looming over Dima.

He was curled in on himself, cradling his legs to his stomach as if that would do much of anything to protect them from Rafael's booted assault.

I aimed lower as Rafe watched me, his lungs heaving

and nostrils flared with the need for violence. Drawing back my right leg, I kicked Dima in the balls hard enough that his shrill scream clattered off the gaudy papered walls and sounded like music to my demented ears. Rafael laughed darkly, pressing the toe of his boot down on top of Dima's throat while he thrashed from side to side. "Did you take his eye?" he asked, nodding down at the bandage covering it.

"Yes," I said, and he tore off the bandage to look at the damage. To take that moment to memorize the injury I'd inflicted. I thought it would be a fond memory for him, a reminder of how blood thirsty I could be thanks to the nightmare he'd turned me into.

"And now you crushed his balls. Seems fitting," Rafael said as he pressed down more firmly on Dima's throat. Dima clawed at his boots, the sound of his short nails on leather like nails on a chalk board as he gasped and fought for breath. His face turned red, his remaining grey eye bulging from its socket.

I watched in captivation, wondering for a moment if that was what I'd looked like when Pavel had strangled me. "Alive, Rafael," I said, taking his forearm in my grip. His eyes met mine, understanding and something twisted dawning in his expression even as I took away his newest toy to torment. "I want him alive."

His lips twisted into a sinister smile as he lifted his boot off Dima's throat. "Anything for you, *mi reina.*" He accepted the gun from my grip, slamming the butt of the weapon down against the side of Dima's head. He stilled on the floor; his eye drifting closed as his consciousness dropped away.

"Stay close," he said pointedly, as he stepped over Dima's limp form. He notched the gun against his shoulder and continued down the hallway.

"We can't just leave him. What if he wakes up?" I asked. I hurried after him, anxious to keep up but not wanting to take my eyes off Rafe's back long enough to really glance back at Dima lying in the middle of the hallway.

There'd been a time when he was my savior; then he'd been my enemy. In the end, I would be the woman who murdered him slowly.

"I'll send someone back to watch him," Rafe said, continuing through the hall in his mission to find somewhere safe for me so that he could go after Pavel. The thought of him leaving me left me conflicted, torn between wanting him to stay at my side for the rest of my life and not wanting Pavel to escape.

We came to the place at the center of the building where the four hallways intersected, the sound of footsteps hurrying down the halls toward us. Rafe pushed me between him and the wall, giving me his back and flattening us against the surface as best he could while we waited for the people to appear.

My fear kicked up a notch, my breathing coming in rapid huffs that I tried to calm by counting backwards from ten in my head.

Joaquin rounded the corner, his eyes going wide when he came face to face with Rafael's gun. The men both sighed in relief, lowering their weapons. "Isa," Joaquin said, his voice strained under the guilt I knew he must have felt.

"It's not your fault," I said, shaking it off and giving him a look that conveyed this was not the time to get sentimental on me. I wanted out of this house of horrors, and then we could deal with the damage that had been inflicted by Sigrid and Faye's betrayal.

Even though it had been my body at risk, my soul that had nearly died in the arms of a man I didn't want, I wasn't the only one who would bear the scars of my abduction. Joaquin would wear the mark of his failure for the rest of his life.

That was the way of life on *El Infierno*.

"Take her and get her to the rendezvous. If anything happens to her, I will personally gut you, Joaquin. I no longer care who you are to her if you fail her again," Rafael ordered.

"I don't want you to leave me," I protested, shaking my head as Rafe leaned forward and kissed me. His lips moved against mine slowly, gentle finesse in the way he touched me as if I was his everything. I reached up with a trembling hand to cup his cheek in my hand, feeling the stubble of his jawline against my skin as I rose up onto my toes and pressed my mouth more firmly into his. The added pressure made him deepen the kiss, hunger in the contact between our bodies that we wouldn't be able to sate until our nightmare was over.

Until only we remained.

"He will *not* get away with this," Rafe said when he wrenched his mouth away from mine. The devil played at the surface of his gaze as it darkened. His need for revenge was too great for him to let Pavel walk away, but the thought of being separated from him again was too much to bear.

"Please don't make me go," I argued, shaking my head. The men both snapped to attention when Gabriel strolled down the hallway, his hand wrapped tightly around Faye's bicep. She struggled in his grip, her face streaked with the line of tears from when she'd cried before.

"I'll deal with you later," Rafael said, glowering at her. "I want your eyes on her." Faye had the brains to swallow, tearing her arm out of Gabriel's grip. He stared at his hand where he'd touched her for a minute before he raised his gun higher.

"We've got her," Gabriel agreed, and I wasn't sure if they meant me or Faye. I hoped for Faye's sake that they were talking about me, because it would be in her best interest to slip away at her first opportunity.

The shifty look in her eyes told me she knew it.

Rafe nodded, darting down the front hall that led to the staircases to go down to the main floor. He spoke into the radio strapped to his chest, a rapid burst of Spanish orders where only Dima's name was recognizable with how quickly he spoke.

"Move," Gabriel said, raising his chin for Faye to walk in front of him. She huffed, holding her head high and crossing her arms over her chest.

"Make me," she snarled, her pretty, ethereal face twisting into a challenge. Gabriel tilted his head to the side, his lips twisting as his brown eyes darkened. There was something in the expression that frightened me for her, something almost demonic about the way he watched her and waited for her to back down from her challenge.

Faye swallowed, only the slight tremble of her bottom lip giving any hint of weakness in her resolve.

Gabriel's mouth split into the hint of a smile. "If I have to make you, we're gonna end the night with you on your knees and begging for my cock, *mi sirenita.*" Faye's cheeks turned pink with his dirty words, and even Joaquin shot him a look of shock before she turned on her heel and strode forward in the direction he'd pointed.

"I thought so," Gabriel chuckled as he walked behind her.

"Did you get the women from the basement?" I asked in

an effort to distract the two of them from the tension cracking between them.

"There's a team down there now," Joaquin answered, clearing his throat as we made our way down the hallway to the rear of the house.

"We have to help," I said, turning to look at Faye. She nodded her head in agreement once, and we leveled the men with a glare when they looked as if they might protest.

"I'm not leaving them. A group of men charging into the basement with a bunch of traumatized women will scare the shit out of them. Let us help," Faye said, meeting Joaquin's questioning stare and pointedly ignoring Gabriel's fixation on her face.

"Fuck," Joaquin groaned, nodding finally. Gabriel seemed even less enthusiastic to be disobeying Rafael's orders and going to the basement, or maybe it had more to do with the extended time he would have to keep an eye on Faye. Whether it was the tension strumming between them that made him watch her so obsessively or the need for penance that I knew *El Infierno* would demand for her involvement in my abduction, I couldn't say.

All I knew was that he watched her like a tiger pacing in a cage, a wildcat ready to lunge at the first sign of weakness.

The way her eyes shifted to the side to watch him as we descended the second set of stairs quickly was all too familiar, reminding me of the way I'd felt in those first moments when Rafael stalked me through the streets of Ibiza. She'd been a prisoner of Pavel for who knew how long, but there was something different about men who obsessed the way Gabriel and Rafael did.

Despite myself and my better judgement, I reached over as we walked and drew her hand into mine. I couldn't say that I wouldn't have done the same thing if it had been a brother I loved more than anything who was taken, and that scared me more than I wanted to admit.

I didn't know if I'd be able to live with myself afterward, but I didn't think her choice was as black and white as I had originally thought. Anyway, between her own guilt and the loss of her brother, I thought she'd suffered enough.

She stumbled awkwardly, something that seemed so out of character for the woman who seemed to glide just above the ground, her feet never really touching the surface. When her glacial blue eyes met mine, something in her softened. Her face relaxed, and she let out a breath as she winced.

"It's okay," I told her. At the back of my mind, all that mattered in that moment was being better than Odina. Being better than the twin who'd taken an accident and wielded my guilt as a weapon for years.

I wanted to forgive. I wanted a life without hate, without pain and suffering over the choices we made to protect the ones we loved. Whether she and Gabriel became a thing or she was punished and went on her way after it was over, I wanted to live knowing that her fate wasn't hanging over my head.

That my hatred didn't consume me from the inside out and turn me into *her*.

"I forgive you," I said, using my hand to guide her forward when her body seemed to get heavy all of a sudden, as if she couldn't bear the weight of supporting her impossibly rigid posture. Like the show she was so used to putting on for everyone who watched her was suddenly stripped away.

"I don't deserve it," she whispered, shaking her head from side to side slowly. Tears welled in her eyes, but she sniffled them back as we rounded the corner at the bottom of the stairs and made our way into the basement.

"Maybe not, but I do anyway," I said with a smile as we stepped into the chaos of Rafael's men trying to evacuate the women.

Many of them cried out, clinging to the doorways as men tried to coax them out. I moved, stepping out from the safety of Joaquin and Gabriel to help a man who was trying to pry a woman's hands from the door frame closest to me.

I grabbed his hand, guiding it away slowly and nodding him away as I smiled at her. I didn't move to touch her, letting her decide for what I imagined was the first time. The bruises covering her skin were like a map of the abuse she'd suffered.

"It's time to go," I said softly, not bothering to give her false promises about how everything would be okay. We both knew that after everything she'd suffered, everything these women had seen and experienced, nothing would ever really be *okay* again.

But they'd be free.

"Master wouldn't want me to go," she said, meeting my gaze with her own brown-eyed stare.

"Who's your master?" I asked, wincing as I said the words. I wished I could erase them and the fear in her eyes as she met mine and shook her head. Refusing to speak the name. "Dima?" I asked.

She bit her bottom lip, nodding ever so slightly as Joaquin watched me from the next doorway. He worked to coax a somewhat less traumatized woman out of her room, never venturing too far. Gabriel and Faye worked a few doorways up, moving in tandem as if they'd been born to do it.

"Can I tell you a secret?" I asked, leaning closer as if it

was truly a secret and not something that I would proudly announce if given the chance. "I'm going to kill him. You don't need to worry about what he thinks anymore."

She blinked up at me, biting her bottom lip and glancing to where her hand clutched the doorway. Finally, her fingers relaxed and she stepped free of the room that had been her prison. One of Rafe's men swept in, gesturing her forward to the exit from the basement where Dima had carried me in from the plane.

I heaved a sigh, continuing on my way to the next woman who struggled. We all worked together, until most of the basement was empty and only a couple of the more resistant ones remained.

"He loves you," a small voice said as I walked past an open doorway. I froze, peering inside the darkened room to try to find the girl who'd spoken. There was nothing, only white walls and a distinct lack of furniture inside.

No place for her to hide.

My foot crossed the threshold as I stepped into the room, called by the sound of a child. Maybe it was the mother in me that couldn't leave anyone behind, but something else inside me forced me to stop. Like the whisper of a woman's voice inside my head or the tickle of the wind on my skin making me pause.

Stop. It seemed to say, and I froze in place. Heeding the warning inside my blood, I stepped back into the light of the hallway just in time for a body to collide with my side and push me out of the doorway.

Gabriel surged into the room before Faye and I had even stopped moving, Joaquin appearing at my side.

It had been one step into the darkness, one heartbeat, and then it was over. Something wet dripped onto my arm where Faye clutched me, her eyes dancing over my face intently. "Are you okay?" she asked, pulling back to run open palms over me and my stomach.

I furrowed my brow at the question, tilting my head to the side as my gaze dropped to the slash in her bicep. Gabriel pulled a girl from the room. She was kicking and screaming as he handed her off to one of the guards, something wild in her eyes as she looked back at me.

"He loves you! Ungrateful whore!" she yelled, and the word in her childlike, singsong voice made my heart clench.

"I don't understand," I said, shaking my head. Whatever had happened, the action had been too fast for me to follow.

Faye had moved before I could even register that a girl had stepped into the light from the doorway, a knife clutched in her hand. I glanced at the wall opposite the door, finding the blade embedded there.

"I think you've earned my forgiveness now," I said, swallowing as I wrapped my arms around my stomach.

Faye laughed lightly as Gabriel and Joaquin came over and pried us apart. Joaquin rested his hands on my shoulders, his face heavy as he glanced at Faye. "It's time to go." The seriousness in his stare left no room for argument, so I nodded my head with a last glance toward the stairs back up to the level where I'd seen Rafael disappear.

This house was full of horrors, and I just had to hope he was strong enough to survive them.

The knowledge that Isa was finally secured with not one, but two of the brothers working to get her to the rendezvous, where more of my men waited, bolstered me. I walked forward, making my way toward the front of the house where I suspected Pavel must have gone to escape the reckoning that was coming for him.

With my wife and unborn baby safe, I was free to ensure he died a very slow, painful death that would somehow still never be enough. I owed him one last thing before I fulfilled the promise I'd made.

He would watch all of his sons die before him, and only after he knew his line had been all but eradicated would I allow his personal suffering to begin. His grandchildren would be raised by carefully chosen guardians around the world, my allies who were beyond reproach and I trusted completely to snuff out the toxicity of their lineage.

If I'd been able to bring myself to slaughter children, I'd have removed them from the equation entirely, but even I had to draw the line somewhere if I wanted to stand apart from the very monsters I hoped to rid the world of.

I stepped out into the night, spinning slowly and scanning the grounds at the front of the house for where Pavel might have disappeared to. My allies stood guard around the plane, some of the remaining of them scattered through the front of the property.

There was no chance that Pavel had gotten through undetected. Not with the sheer number of men peppering the property and his security bleeding on the ground.

I pulled the radio from the strap against my bulletproof vest, clicking the button. "Gabriel, did you see any tunnels on the blueprints? I have a hard time believing Pavel wouldn't have some kind of escape plan."

"No, there's nothing on the blueprints," Gabriel confirmed, undoubtedly having double-checked the schematics on his phone before he answered me. Dimitry's voice came on the radio. "There are rumors about the old dog kennels. Ground floor of the Eastern wing. Pavel had to move them out to a barn when Dima was a boy because he's terrified of them, but it's unlike him not to convert the space to something new."

I turned, making my way toward the East wing as my irritation stirred. Even if it was solely based on a rumor, that kind of knowledge would have been useful *before* Pavel made his escape attempt.

"On my way," I grunted, charging through the groups of people coming my way. Allies who had cleared the main floor and were on their way to help the crew in the basement. They didn't follow me, as if they could sense that taking Pavel down was something I needed to do on my own.

The kennels were tucked underneath a deck on the second floor, with enough height for me to stand up and have room above my head. I rounded the corner into them, moving past the abandoned and eerily clean cages that had held dogs at one point in time.

At the back corner of the space, I came to a storage room. Pushing the door open, I moved inside and searched the room quickly for threats. When I found none, I felt along the walls that connected to the house itself.

Nothing.

I moved around the corner, pressing on every inch of space and hoping for that moment when something would snap into place with a resounding click. From what I knew of Pavel, Dimitry was right. He would never allow this space to be an eyesore if it wasn't serving a purpose.

Finally when I reached the opposite corner, the wall gave way beneath my hands ever so slightly. I pushed, applying more pressure until the mechanism and aging gears ground into place.

The wall shifted, retracting back as if it had been sucked away by sudden pressure. Then it slid to the side on a smooth path, leaving just enough space for a single person to slip through undetected.

I pulled one of my longer knives free from the sheath at my belt, dropping it into the track on the floor where the wall would undoubtedly reclose in time. Hoping it would be enough to keep that from happening until the others could follow me, I stepped over the threshold the track created.

Darkness surrounded me, welcoming me home like an abyss as I descended the slight decline into the earth. My steps were fast and sure, moving along the darkened path and toward the dim lights in the distance. They illuminated a walkway that seemed to lead to tunnels that ran beneath the house, with stairs at the end that went further underground.

To get there, I needed to walk through the complete absence of light that surrounded me in the open space.

But the devil didn't fear the dark, he came to reap what his enemies had sowed there. Where other men might have hesitated, I moved through the inky darkness like one of the phantoms Isa had seen in the waters of the Chicago river.

I didn't slow, striding through the open space to follow after the soul that was mine to claim. Pavel thought he knew Hell.

He knew nothing.

As soon as I was within the dimly-lit tunnel, I picked up a slow jog. Hurrying to catch up with the head start Pavel had, I wished I knew where the tunnels let out. To be standing on the other side, waiting for him to emerge, would have given me the greatest satisfaction.

Taking his moment of triumph and twisting it back to show him he'd never had a chance at all. There was no escaping death when it came at the hands of *El Diablo.*

I hurried along, moving as quietly and swiftly as I could in an attempt to channel Joaquin. The man moved with more stealth than should be possible, blending into the shadows seamlessly until there was no hint of anything else remaining.

The exit loomed ahead, the dim light of the moonlit sky shining through as I rounded the corner quickly.

The swing of a pipe came across the tunnel, and I ducked to avoid it as I spun to come face to face with the eldest Kuznetsov. With one of the only people alive in the world I hated almost as much as I'd despised my father.

"Rafael," he said, tilting his head to the side and hefting the pipe in his grip. He swung again, moving quickly for his age with the understanding that if he didn't move fast and hard, he would stand no chance of winning. "I always thought you were far too sophisticated to murder me with something as simplistic as a gun."

"I am," I agreed, lowering my aim as I stepped back out of his reach. I fired a single shot through his right kneecap, watching him crumple to the concrete beneath our feet. "I have no intention of killing you right now. *That* would be a far quicker death than you deserve."

"If you need a gun to win this fight, then you're hardly a man at all," he spat, swinging uselessly with his pipe. The absence of a gun of his own was odd, given his personal preference toward them. I hadn't imagined I would find him mostly unarmed.

What man runs for his life without a gun?

"I am merely a man who is impatient to tend to his wife after you tried to burn her alive. She just refuses to die, doesn't she?" I smiled as he realized I'd already found and saved Isa. "You should have known you cannot burn the wife of the devil."

"No. I suppose you can't," Pavel said, a slow smile taking over his face as he dropped the pipe to the floor. The blood from his knee stained the concrete, but a cruel smile claimed his face as I hefted the pipe into my hand.

His own hand tightened around something he clung to, squeezing gently. It wasn't until I looked down at it that I saw the blinking light held within.

Too late to stop the explosions that detonated around me, I dove toward my prey and the exit just on the other side of his body as the tunnel collapsed.

Rubble rained down; chunks of concrete and building foundation and rock surrounded me and pinned my limbs. The exit disappeared, only a few feet away as all the moonlight was blocked by debris.

My world went dark.

I helped one of the women from the basement to her feet when she stumbled over a tree root. The woods surrounding us were thick and pressed against my sanity, blocking out the light from the starry sky above our heads. The trek to the boundary where SUVs waited to take us to the plane that had landed just outside of Pavel's radar seemed never ending.

"Not much farther," Joaquin promised.

Even able to see the lights of the house in the distance, the colorful spires of the towers and unique architecture, it seemed like we walked forever. That was probably more due to the weak women who made the journey with us, than the actual distance. The fact was that many of them couldn't handle contact with the men who would have helped them, if they weren't too traumatized to accept it. Faye had taken up a place at my side to help get the women away from the danger of a burning building, but we were only two women, and there were so many survivors who needed us.

Gabriel watched her as intently as he watched me, seeming to understand that she would fade into the woods the moment he took his eyes off her. I wasn't sure what his interest in her was about, but I didn't get the impression she would be walking free anytime soon.

Even after Rafael was done with her.

Joaquin watched her with growing curiosity every time I interacted with her. Her face was stained with the ghost of her tears, of the splitting of her soul when she'd sung to her brother while he bled out in her arms. Whatever the price should have been for what she'd done, she'd more than paid for it in my mind, especially with her action that led to the blood trickling down the deep gash in her arm.

Gabriel closed the distance between them, ripping fabric from the hem of his shirt and tying it around the wound as they walked. She pointedly ignored him, not so much as sparing a glance for the man who seemed to want to tend to her, even though she should be his enemy.

Obsession blurred all lines of right and wrong.

"Just a little farther," I murmured softly to one of the young girls. I hoped my words were true. Her face was too pale, drawn too thin for the youth that she was. She couldn't have been any older than I had been when Rafe first spotted me, but her eyes held the wisdom that came from seeing the world as it truly was.

Full of horrors that no child should ever endure.

The ground shook beneath our feet as we walked, a deep rumble that seemed to come from inside the earth itself.

Whatever remained of the birds on the property fled from their trees, taking to the sky as I stumbled and went down alongside the girl in my place between Joaquin and Gabriel. The woods around us were eerily silent despite the mass of men surrounding the group of women at a careful distance.

I spun on my hands and knees, looking back to the house where I'd last seen my husband. The lights in one of the spires seemed to crumple inward, until they rested on the ground itself. The breath left my lungs as I lunged to my feet, watching as the corner of the manor collapsed.

I bolted forward, slipping through the press of women on their knees where they'd fallen from the force of the shaking ground.

My feet couldn't carry me fast enough. They couldn't keep up with the panic pressing on my lungs. Arms wrapped around my chest, hauling me back and pinning me against a broad chest. "Let me go!" I shrieked.

"There's nothing you can do, *mi reina*," Joaquin urged, lifting me off my feet. I thrashed my legs, clawing at his arms in a desperate bid to get free.

"Rafe!" I screamed, trying to twist my head to look back at the house where I'd left him.

I left him.

The thought of a life without him in it was unbearable, and I knew I could never go back to who I'd been before. I'd never be the Isa who did what her father told her, and I didn't even *have* a mother to boss me around any longer.

Death was everywhere. Waiting to take everyone I loved until there was nothing left.

"Shhh, Isa," Gabriel murmured, his face filling mine as he cupped my cheeks in his hands. He leaned his forehead against mine as I struggled in his brother's grip, kind eyes holding mine. "I'll find him. Not even death could keep him from you."

Joaquin barked orders at some of the men lurking at the edge of the group, and I watched from the corner of my eye as they nodded and turned back. They led the way, jogging back toward the crumpling house we'd only just escaped.

To find the man they all followed by choice, the man who held their utmost loyalty.

I sobbed, stilling my body as his words penetrated, feeling the truth in them and shocked by his proximity to me. Gabriel guided my hand away from Joaquin's forearm and to my stomach. Pressing into the bump there, he reminded me that even if Rafe was gone, there was still something to live for.

I nodded, tears streaming down my cheeks as he pulled away and turned to follow the group of men who'd gone back to search. He spared one last lingering glance for Faye, pointing a finger at her intensely.

"Do not make me hunt you down, Little Thief," he ordered, and then he sprinted back to find my husband.

"I want to wait," I said, turning to look at Joaquin as he released me finally.

"We keep going. For them," he said, looking at the women all around me. They needed to feel safe, and standing in the woods, still trapped on Pavel's property wouldn't offer them that. I nodded, swallowing past the grief looming and threatening to render me incapable of functioning.

Rafe would find me. I had to believe that, or I wouldn't be able to keep going.

Joaquin returned me to the girl I'd been helping walk, and I forced through my fear to wrap an arm around her waist and support the weight she couldn't on her own.

We walked, and we walked some more. My arm and leg ached on the right side of my body where I supported the girl who wouldn't allow Joaquin to touch her.

And then finally we made our way out of the other side of the woods, the trees opening into a clearing where the chain link fence had been peeled back to give us room to walk through. I recognized people from the Tessin's house in Sweden waiting to help, standing around the vehicles parked there to take us to safety.

Women stood among the vehicles, wives and daughters who had come to do what they could to help but couldn't leave the safety of the cars. Just the fact that they'd come, that they'd stepped outside of their comfortable lives to help women who were less fortunate, gave me hope.

Hope for a better future. Hope for a world where families like the Kuznetsovs were dead and buried where they belonged.

Zuri swept in beside me, helping me with the girl until she was tucked safely within the backseat of one of the vehicles. The group of women eyed Faye curiously, and it didn't take an expert to realize that they knew she'd been involved.

My attention went to the others, helping load them into vehicles with reassuring words that they'd be safe. When I turned back to check on Faye, the space she'd occupied before was empty. I spun, peering into the windows of all the cars but knowing I wouldn't find her there.

She was gone, like a ghost in the wind.

I wrapped my arms around my waist as the vehicles left one by one, hoping that wherever they were taken they'd be safe. That there'd be someone gentle to receive them.

What would happen to them from here, I couldn't even begin to comprehend. Would they go back to the lives they'd lived before? Would they choose to become someone new, never trying to reconcile the person they'd once been with the one they'd been forced to become?

I hoped they found comfort in loved ones' arms, no matter where they ended up.

I turned my back on the evacuation, staring at the woods and the burning building in the distance. I watched. I waited. For what felt like hours, I stood there and kept my eyes peeled for any movement in the woods. For stragglers, and for my captor who had become the love of my life.

My reason for living.

My fingers dug into my stomach, staring at the stars above and begging for him to come back to me. "You have to go back for him," I said, not bothering to turn my head back to where Joaquin watched over me.

"The last time I took my eyes off of you, they took you from us. We have to go, *mi reina*," Joaquin said gently, touching a hand to my shoulder. "I'll send back more of the men to find the others, but we need to get you to a doctor."

"I'm fine," I said, brushing off his touch. "I'm not leaving."

"You're leaving even if I have to put your ass in the vehicle by force," Joaquin argued, the deep notes of his voice leaving no room for argument. I knew he would do it, especially with his guilt over my being taken at all plaguing him. "I care about Rafael too, and do not forget that my brother went back for him. We all have people we care about in that house right now. The right thing to do is make sure you and the baby are safe."

Joaquin would never be able to live with himself if something happened to the baby that he could have prevented with medical attention, but there'd been no injury that caused me concern.

"Just a little longer," I begged, watching the dark woods. He tightened his grip on my shoulder before releasing me, and then his presence at my back disappeared. I knew my time was limited, that I'd only delayed the inevitable.

I lowered myself to the ground anyway, sitting on the cold grass and letting the sharp blades dig into the bare skin of my legs. The scratching feeling rooted me in the moment, keeping my thoughts from wandering as I watched the tree line.

But then there was movement in the woods, and the soot-stained face of Rafael emerged as he limped his way over tree roots and stepped into the light from the starry sky. The other men who'd gone with Gabriel followed behind him, all except for Gabriel himself.

Rafael looked up and froze when he saw me, stilling and heaving out a sigh of relief that I felt within my soul. Those eyes shifted from relief to that same intensity I recognized from the first moment I'd seen him in Ibiza.

I moved without realizing it, bolting to my feet, racing forward, and closing the distance between us. I crashed into him, his pained groan reaching my ears when he staggered back a step onto the leg that seemed to be the source of his pain.

He chuckled deep in his throat, raising his arms to surround me as his mouth came down to touch the top of my head. "*Mi reina*," he murmured.

"I thought you were dead," I sobbed, staining his vest with my tears.

"I was made to love you," he said, sinking to the ground beneath us and pulling me into his lap. "Not even death could stop me."

Despite the foreign landscape surrounding us, I was home.

*I*sa's warmth in my arms felt like perfection, like contentment and something I hadn't known I was missing until I found her. She was my home, the one who mattered to me most.

"The baby?" I asked.

"We're fine," she mumbled against my chest.

"Have you seen a doctor?" I asked, staring at the almost empty rendezvous point. Most of those we'd brought along with us who had medical training had already evacuated, tending to those with physical injuries.

"They went back to Dimitry's home," Joaquin said, opening the door to the last remaining SUV. I stood, ignoring the pain that I suspected was a broken ankle in favor of standing with Isa in my arms. She put her feet to the ground, determined to walk alongside me as we made our way to the vehicle. "Where's Gabriel?"

"Guarding Pavel. His legs were crushed in the explosion, so he's probably not going anywhere. Aaron has Dima," I explained. Joaquin raised a brow, asking if I had Isa without voicing the words. Nodding, I gestured him on and he retreated back into the woods to go for his brother.

They knew better than anyone that I wanted the Kuznetsovs alive, so that I could kill them slowly, but only one of their deaths would rest on my shoulders in the end.

Dima belonged to my vicious little nightmare.

Isa fussed over me as we climbed into the backseat of the vehicle, making our way to Dimitry's estate that wasn't far from Pavel's. It served as the perfect jumping off point to find where the women from the basement belonged.

"What happened?" she asked, grabbing me around the calf and shifting me until my legs were draped over her lap. Peeling up the pants carefully, she stared down at the burned flesh in horror. Her fingers hovered over it, trembling along with her bottom lip.

"Pavel blew his escape tunnel. My leg was caught in the rubble," I said, explaining the limp.

"The burns," she said, the well of tears making her beautiful eyes shine an even brighter hue of green. "Did this happen when you came for me?"

"I'll be fine, *mi reina*," I promised, looking down at the bright red, patchy skin where the flames had burned my legs briefly when I walked through them to get to her. "Better me than you."

I touched my fingers to the brand on her arm, not regretting the mark for a single moment. Hers echoed the contact, seeking out her name on my skin and I knew in that moment that she understood what I'd sought to do.

I'd made her mine, but not just as property. I'd marked myself alongside her to make her my equal in every way, the queen to my king.

La reina y su diablo.

Any woman could wear a brand on her skin, that was

put there by force, but only Isa could see the beauty in my mark. Only she could understand what it meant to be mine.

Only she could possess the devil himself.

The vehicle pulled into Dimitry's driveway, the Russian himself standing on the steps in front of his home that was straight out of a gothic fairytale. His wife, Montana, stood among the women at the foot of the steps, guiding them where they needed to go.

"Rafael," he said as Isa threw open the door and I slid out of the seat. She fussed, trying to help me stand. I didn't need it, but the care she showed in helping me to my feet warmed something inside me that I'd feared might die forever.

If I lost her, there would be nothing worth living for. Nothing worth saving left within me.

I would burn the world down to get my vengeance for what it had taken from me.

Two of the medics in his employ moved to take me from Isa, muttering as they glanced at the burns on my legs where she'd left my pants rolled up. She trailed behind, talking in a rush with the female doctor who peppered her with questions. "Have you had any bleeding or cramping?" she asked, jotting notes down on the clipboard she held in her hands.

"Nothing like that," Isa said after only a moment's consideration.

"Where were you hurt?"

Isa detailed all the injuries she'd suffered since being taken from Stockholm, and, knowing that I would consider them minor had they happened to anyone else, I needed the exam and medical attention to be over and done with.

I had a Russian to kill, as did my wife.

"What's he doing here?" Isa asked suddenly, coming to a

stop in front of Dimitry. She glared at him, glancing toward me in concern when I wasn't bothered by his presence.

"You didn't really think he had no one to keep an eye on you from the inside, did you?" Dimitry asked, smirking at her with more warmth than he usually afforded. The only hints of anything resembling affection from him had been aimed his wife's way, but I knew without question that whatever had happened in Pavel's estate, Dimitry liked my wife.

"So why not just get me out?" she asked, crossing her arms over her chest and giving him a challenging glare. "You weren't very helpful, were you?"

"How far do you think one man and a woman would get before Pavel's dogs found us? Escaping without taking out the source of the problem was never going to be a solution. I was supposed to get you somewhere safe to wait out the invasion, but you and Faye just had to go and do something stupid," he grunted.

"Oh, so I was supposed to just let him shoot down the plane I thought my husband was on?"

"Yes," Dimitry said. "It was a drone and there was no one on board. Nothing but a distraction."

Isa pursed her lips, considering something. "I still don't regret stabbing him in the eye," she said.

"And you shouldn't. You wouldn't be *mi reina* if you did," I said, stepping into the house and letting the medic tend to my ankle and bandage the burns while the other continued to ask Isa questions. She deemed her pregnancy as safe as it could be given the circumstances, the stress of the events more dangerous than any injuries she'd suffered.

"You said something about Pavel's dogs?" Isa asked, looking back to Dimitry with a funny expression on her face. For a moment, I thought she was concerned about them in the fire and collapse of the building.

Dimitry nodded. "He has to keep them in one of the smaller buildings. Dima's terrified of the things," he said, shaking his head with a laugh. "Can't exactly blame him, given what Pavel uses them for."

"What are you thinking, *mi reina*?" I asked, tilting my head to the side through the sting of ointment being applied to my other burned ankle and shin.

"Dima likes to use a person's worst fear against them," she said, turning her cold gaze my way. The green of her stare glittered with something cruel, darkness lingering in the depths. "He's mine to kill."

Despite the pain of my burns being wrapped, a demented smile claimed my face as I followed her line of thought. "You're my vicious little nightmare," I purred, shifting my leg as the medic finished with the worst of the burns. Isa smiled at me, the first hints of a mood more normal for my wife filling her face. "I love it."

"And I love you, my devil," she said, leaning in to press a sweet kiss to my lips. I needed to get her somewhere completely safe, to bury myself inside the brutal, twisted woman that matched me so perfectly. But in spite of the doctor's confidence that there were no signs for concern, I knew she needed to rest.

She needed to heal from the injuries that had taken root on the inside and recover from the fear that must have been all-consuming from the moment she woke up without me.

Besides, there were a few last matters of business to tend to before I could feel her writhing beneath me, and I wanted to do it as far away from the Kuznetsov's horror house as I could. "Why don't you go get washed up first?" I asked, nodding my head toward Montana.

Isa nodded, looking more than pleased to wash the blood and dirt from her skin. Something about knowing what she had planned for her would-be rapist and knowing she would carry out those plans looking pristine made the monster inside me rage with the need to fuck her afterward.

To be the one to dirty her up all over again.

She kissed me once more, making her way up the stairs with Montana to shower and change. Something in me clenched the moment she was out of my sight, fearing the worst. Aaron nodded, following the girls up the stairs as if he could sense my torment in her absence.

"Well, that solves what to do with Dima," Dimitry laughed, shaking his head from side to side as if he couldn't quite decide if he was impressed or horrified. "What about Pavel?"

"I have something in mind," I said, grinning as I started to lay out my plan for the elder Kuznetsov.

If I had it my way, he would live for a very long time.

He'd just wish he was dead.

*J*oaquin dragged Dima's limp body into the center of the kennel. The dogs on the other side of the gates where they were locked away snarled and bared their teeth viciously enough that even with the barred gates separating us, my heart stalled in my chest when I followed him.

Joaquin flipped him to his back, and I watched the moment his remaining eye widened and his mouth went slack. The bruising on my cheek and bandages at my wrists and ankles were the only sign that he'd ever laid his filthy hands on me, while he couldn't so much as twitch from the neck down. I stood beside his body, kicking him with the pointed toe of my heel and prodding to see if he could feel the pain.

The lack of response on his face muted just a little bit of my fun as I squatted down beside him, reaching out a hand to cup his cheek tenderly. "мой котик," he rasped, looking as if those two words drained him of energy.

"I'm not your kitten. I never was," I murmured softly,

enjoying the moment of pain that flashed over his features. Rafe was a silent sentry at my back, staying out of the cage and letting me have my moment even though I knew it must have pained him to give up control over a death he'd wanted for so long. "I'm *El Diablo's* wife."

I reached back, accepting the knife from Joaquin when he handed it to me. I touched the tip of the blade to Dima's skin, carving through his flesh and watching as it parted to reveal the muscled sinew beneath. Blood pooled on the floor, staining the shoes Montana had given me with full understanding that they would be ruined.

She could buy more.

She watched on, her face a blank mask that I related to all too much. There had been a time when I'd realized that not all violence was horrific, when I'd lived through the moment when I realized that there was something beautiful in watching the blood of those who would hurt me spill to the ground like paint on a canvas.

I reached over, carving through his other arm in the same way and exposing the raw meat beneath his skin. His legs came next, and then I cut through the cloth of his shirt and made shallow cuts in his chest and stomach so I wouldn't hit anything vital and deliver him a death that was too swift for what he deserved.

Then when his bottom lip trembled, I brought the knife to his face and cut from his jaw to his good eye. The moment the tip of the knife came too close to his eye, he clenched it shut like it might protect him from losing it. I laughed, a deep, twisted sound that I'd never made as I drew the knife away finally. "Don't worry," I whispered. "I want you to see your death coming for you."

I stood, handing the bloodied knife back to Joaquin and

grabbing the gallon of blood the men had secured by stringing up the bodies of Pavel's dead men and letting the thick, viscous liquid collect in a horse trough.

I smiled as I poured it over his body like gasoline, watching as the blood of his men filled his mouth and his nose and he sputtered and coughed. It covered his chest and torso, filling the gaps in his skin where I'd cut him and mixing with his own blood as it poured from his wounds. When the jug was empty, I stepped back and looked down at my handy work.

"I've heard you're afraid of the dogs," I said, squatting beside him again. His face was a massive red stain, covered in the blood I'd poured on him as that one eye fought to stare at me.

"Please," he begged.

"Do you think you'll feel it when they sink their teeth into your flesh? When they chew through your organs and devour the black hole where your heart should have been. Or will you only feel it when they eat that pretty face?" I asked, standing and looking down at him.

"Woman, you better watch yourself," Rafe called, a deep chuckle resounding in his chest when I turned back to him. I left Dima in my rearview, making my way toward my husband—the most beautiful man I'd ever seen. His stare was unnerving, a glare in it as I approached him with a smile on my face. "I know you did not just call him fucking pretty."

I stepped out of the kennel, feeling Joaquin do the same at my heel as we left Dima in the central room. He pulled the cage door closed behind us.

I reached up, cupping Rafe's cheeks in my hand and stretching onto my tippy toes to touch my lips to his. "He is pretty," I said, doubling down on my words and enjoying the moment of rage that I earned when his hands came around my waist finally and grabbed at the top of my ass. "To anyone who has never seen you."

"Oh, please gag me," Dimitry said, a smile in his voice as he flipped the switch. The gates that restrained the dogs lifted, and the frenzied racing of massive paws over the concrete came. Claws scratched the surface as I turned to watch over my shoulder, hearing Dima's terrified scream echo over the walls as they came closer.

The growls of them erupted through the room. Goose-bumps raised on my arms when they tore through Dima's flesh, the wet, snarling sounds something that would haunt my nightmares for a long time.

Even still, it was worth every moment of knowing that I'd turned his worst fear back on him like he'd done to so many others. Even still, there would be no regret for the stain to my soul.

He deserved every ounce of terror he'd suffered and then some for the women and children he'd sold, for those he'd raped. I only wished he hadn't been paralyzed and unable to feel pain, because then he might have suffered the same fate as his father.

That would have been a sight to see.

"Good puppies," I murmured, drawing a laugh from Dimitry where he stood beside Montana. "What will happen to them?"

"The dogs?" he asked, huffing a second chuckle. "I'll take them home with me. They're good dogs, particularly when they're well fed. Pavel just has a tendency to keep them hungry because they're more vicious that way. They'll have a good life now."

If there'd been any doubt that Pavel deserved what was

coming to him, it disappeared with the reality that he'd starved his dogs to use them as weapons.

Dima's screams faded out as he died, his blood mixing with what was already on the concrete floor, and when they finished?

The dogs were no longer hungry.

$\mathscr{I}$sa slept upstairs, her body exhausted and her mind settled. She knew the truth of what would happen to Pavel, and after what she'd chosen as the way Dima had to meet his end, there was nothing left inside her that would object to the torture he would suffer through.

He would experience everything he'd done to his victims, until his mind was a broken shell and only his body remained. Only then would I return to Russia and give him the mercy of death. Dimitry guided me to the bunker below ground in the woods that surrounded his house. The concrete walls of the underground room were cracked, water dripping through them and I quickly understood that it was not a bomb shelter or panic room designed to keep people out. *This* was where the butcher of Russia kept his personal victims stowed away, out of sight from his gentle wife who likely wanted nothing to do with the violence of his life and his mission to slowly rid his home country of men like the Kuznetsovs.

He wouldn't have any need to do it in secret now with Pavel gone.

"This is Ivan," Dimitry said, introducing me to the man who stood guard at the door to the very back cell within the prison bunker. "He's my warden for the prisoners with special circumstances who survive longer than a day or two. He's willing to do what you require."

"Ivan," I said, shaking the man's hand. He input the passcode to Pavel's cell, and the door slid to the side to allow us to enter. Pavel was strapped down, his wrists bound in barbed wire above his head and looped around the metal corner posts to the cot he would sleep on. Entirely nude, there wasn't a stitch of clothing or a blanket in sight. No luxuries would be afforded for him as my prisoner through Dimitry.

Terror blazed in his eyes as I stepped around the cot to stand in front of him. At my request, he'd not yet been raped. I wanted to watch the pain on his face, to witness him feeling, for the first time, the suffering he'd inflicted on so many others.

To watch him experience what he'd intended for my pregnant wife.

He struggled against the barbed wire binding him, flinching when it tore his skin open. He would bear the same scars he'd left on Isa, every day for the rest of his short life. "Beg me," I ordered, crouching in front of his face and removing the ball gag from his mouth momentarily. He rolled his jaw to relax the ache, staring up at me with pleading eyes.

"Please, just kill me," he begged, his voice pathetic and weak even though his suffering had barely begun.

"Like you killed them? Why should I give you mercy when you couldn't spare it for your victims?" I asked. He glared up at me, finally wrapping his head around the fact that I only wanted to hear him debase himself but would never actually give him what he wanted.

I reached into my jacket pocket, removing the ball of napkin from within and holding it in front of his face. "Do you know what this is?" I asked, unwrapping it bit by bit. The grey of Dima's remaining eye that the dogs had somehow left untouched came into view as the napkin parted. "Isa fed him to your dogs. This is just about all that's left of him," I said, grasping him around the jaw and forcing his mouth to open as he thrashed from side to side. I ignored his breath of relief when I set the eyeball on the chair next to the bed. The only furniture in the room, it would give him a perfect view of all that remained of his last son while he suffered day in and day out. "I made a promise that you would see all your sons dead before I came to finish you off. I always keep my promises."

I stretched up, grabbing a knife off the wall where Ivan's toys hung. The blade was heavy as I flipped it in my hands, walking around the cot to decide where to begin my fun.

He needed to be alive for Ivan to torture in the most poetic way, but that didn't mean he couldn't be in pain first. I grabbed him by the hair, ripping his head back harshly until his eyes met mine. The tip of the knife pressed into the skin just below his eye, dragging down his cheek and away from it as he clenched it closed in relief. "I should take your eye and put it next to your son's. In a way, you could watch yourself get fucked. I've heard you like that."

Instead, I moved the knife down to the star tattoo just below his collarbone. Applying pressure until the tip dug into his skin and blood welled, I carved in a circle around the tattoo and then slid the blade through his flesh until it pulled free.

The strip of skin dropped to the cot beneath him,

leaving me to pick the grisly piece for him to see. "I don't have any sons for you to send it to," he said, his voice pained.

"I think I'll keep this one for myself," I said with a smile, patting his cheek with my bloody hand as I shoved the flesh into my pocket. I shoved the ball gag back into his mouth. "He's all yours," I said, turning a sadistic grin to Ivan. I didn't watch him fumble with his pants or anything that happened on the other side of Pavel.

I watched his face, watched his eyes clench closed in agony the moment Ivan shoved inside him.

And my vengeance began.

⚐⚐⚐

"*P*romise me you'll come visit," Isa said, drawing Montana in for a hug. "I'd really love to get to know you better under less bloody circumstances."

"Of course we'll come visit. I wouldn't miss this little one for anything," she said, touching Isa's stomach affectionately. The two women were the same age despite the fact that their respective husbands were much older, their entrance into our world entirely different, and yet somehow the outcome was the same for the both of them.

Married to monsters who corrupted them with the sins of flesh and blood.

"I don't recall inviting the butcher to my home, *mi reina*," I scolded.

"Fine, then I'll come visit them," she said, sticking out her tongue at me and turning her attention back to her new friend.

"That, we will most definitely do," I said, hinting at the man I planned to pay visits to regularly to ensure he was being taken care of properly. There weren't many men I trusted, but Dimitry Turgenev was high on the list thanks to the woman at his side. They had a love like Isa's and mine, one that most wouldn't understand.

But we did.

I guided Isa away, getting her to the plane that was already overcrowded with people we needed to return to Stockholm. As much as I wanted to fuck her on the plane, we had a too-long journey home.

Then her ass was mine.

*T*he face staring back at me shouldn't have reminded me of myself. There was nothing of me that still lived in her, despite the identical features. Her face was contorted with malice when I stepped into the basement where Rafe evidently kept his torture victims, her hands bound behind her back and secured to the chair in the center of the stark room.

"You don't have to do this, *mi reina*," Rafe said, lingering at my spine. As soon as I'd learned my sister was still alive, determination drove me to see her. To look her in the eye and make sure she saw with her own eyes that I lived.

That I'd escaped the clutches of the fate she'd sacrificed me to.

"I do," I said, nodding at him. He kissed my forehead gently, sighing as he retreated up the stairs and left me with the twin who didn't deserve my kindness.

She didn't deserve my mercy. But even looking at her and remembering how much I'd recently wanted to feel my knife cut through her skin and into the heart that beat within her chest, my hands shook as I stared at her.

"Well?" she asked, cocking her head to the side. "Has the wife of a criminal come to kill me?"

"Does this make us even?" I asked instead. "Can we *finally* move on from this ridiculous feud over an accident that happened thirteen years ago? I nearly caused your death with my choice. You have now returned the favor."

I crossed my arms over my chest, leaning onto the table at the opposite end of the room and staring at her across the empty space. Her brow furrowed in confusion, as if she couldn't quite wrap her head around the question.

"We will never be even," she said, leaning forward in the metal chair as much as the binds at her wrists and on her arms allowed. "I will never forgive you for not listening to me, and for pretending to be so fucking perfect for so long. Precious fucking Isa could do no wrong, and Mom did nothing but remind me of that every day of our lives."

"Mom loved you," I said, clenching my eyes shut. "But you won't have to worry about feeling like she's judging you anymore, will you?"

"What are you talking about?" Odina whispered, shock crossing her features. I hadn't stopped to think about the fact that she'd been taken before she could learn the truth. That she had no clue our mother had died on the same day Rafe sacrificed her to save me.

"She's gone, Odina. Dima planted a bomb on the car. You know, the man you were so keen to work with? He murdered our mother in cold blood, just to break down the gates at the house in Chicago," I explained.

"What was she even doing there? It was the middle of the night," Odina protested.

"She was coming to get *you*. I couldn't let you drive your-self home when you were trashed."

"You're trying to blame this on me?" she asked, sniffling

back tears as a tiny sliver of humanity and love for our mother showed through. In all the years she'd wasted yelling and screaming at our parents, the unusual emotion caught me off guard.

"No," I said. "That's not what I'm saying at all."

"Because you know it's *yours*," Odina hissed, her face twisting with cruelty all over again. "You brought them into our lives—"

"Actually, Mom did," I corrected. "The man who threw us into the river was there because he was keeping an eye on Mom. She knew too much information about his business and his family to just walk away. He was deranged and twisted, but all of this began before we were even born, Odina. That *still* doesn't make it her fault. It's no one's fault except for the sick bastards who tried to hurt us or kill us."

She sighed, hanging her head forward as if she could block out the logic in my words. Nothing mattered to her, not when she was so blinded by her own rage that she couldn't see straight. "What do you want?"

"I want my sister back. The one I had when we were little," I murmured, uncrossing my arms and shifting them down to clutch the edge of the table. "Is she anywhere in there?"

"No," Odina snarled. "You killed her."

I nodded, exhaustion creeping in through the last clinging emotion I'd tried to share with her. To salvage whatever still remained after the years of being torn apart. "Okay."

I stood, straightening my body and making my way to the stairs. I grasped the railing at the bottom, taking that first step and leaving her behind.

"Where are you going?" she asked, something akin to panic leaking into her voice. I knew she worried what would happen to her if I left her death to Rafe, but she didn't know it wouldn't come to that. I'd never be able to forget the knowledge that he'd killed my only sibling.

Even if she deserved it.

"Just fucking kill me, you stupid bitch!" she screamed as I came closer to the top of the stairs.

I paused, turning to look back down at her, with all the pity I felt over the uncertainty in her future. "I'm not the monster you want me to be, Odina. I'm not like you," I said, turning the knob on the door. I stepped out as she screamed after me, plunging her into darkness as the overhead lights switched off.

"Isa! You don't deserve a single fucking thing that you have! I hope your husband slits your throat and fucks his next wife on your corpse!"

I closed the door, and I walked away from the ghosts of my past, leaving them with the sister determined to live in her own misery.

*I*sa stepped out of the basement, closing the door behind her and leaning her forehead against it as the breath left her body. I gave her the moment, stepping up and rubbing soothing circles on her back. Her hands and clothes were free of blood, and the distinct sound of Odina's shrill screams coming from the basement when the door had been open left little doubt to the fact that my wife hadn't been able to follow through.

That was okay, because I would always be strong enough to do what it took to keep her safe. Even if she wasn't.

"I'll take care of it," I grunted, wincing when she grabbed my hand in hers. Her glassy eyes stared up at me, and she guided me away from the kitchen and toward the hallway that led to our bedroom. It felt like it had been so long since we'd lain in our own bed together, since we'd made love in our own space.

"You can't," she murmured when we stepped into the open living room. "I wouldn't want to hold it against you, but I don't know that I could ever let go of it. Not really." The admission hurt, knowing that something would hang over our heads even if it was done for her protection.

"What am I supposed to do, Isa? We can't let her go free. Not after what she's done and what I'm sure she'll do again, given the first opportunity. She has to die," I told her, touching my forehead to hers lightly.

She stared up at me, and I watched those green eyes process and look for other options where there were none. "She doesn't necessarily have to be dead. Just not free," Isa said, swallowing as if she couldn't believe her words.

"You can't honestly expect us to keep her here with us. After everything she's done, I don't want her anywhere near you or the baby," I argued, feeling harshness snap onto my face. I wouldn't risk her for anything. Especially not for her delicate sensibilities regarding the sister who didn't deserve her protection.

"No," Isa agreed. "I don't want her anywhere near *you* either. Isn't there somewhere we could send her? Someone who could...look after her?"

"You mean someone who could lock her up and keep her cared for without hurting her?" I considered my options, running through them silently, before I nodded. "I have a friend in Peru. I trust him. I don't like it. I want her to suffer, but if it will make you happy, I'll call him in the morning."

"Please, Rafe. This is the only way that her death won't hang over us like a black cloud. I just want to move on and put it all behind us."

"Anything for you, *mi reina*," I said, letting her walk backward. My ankle twinged with pain, but it wasn't broken after all and supported my weight as she led me to our bedroom.

The satisfied smile that transformed her face made it all worth it when she sat on the edge of the bed and pulled her dress over her head slowly. The fabric fell to the floor when she tossed it to the side, reaching behind her back to unclasp her bra and toss it to join the dress. Her shoes were next: a pair of flat flip flops Montana had given her so she could be comfortable on the plane.

The panties she pushed down her legs came last, revealing every inch of her body to my gaze as she watched me wrestle for control.

After everything she'd been through and everything that could have happened, she deserved someone who could be gentle with her and not maul her like an animal. But I was overcome with the need to drive inside her, to feel her pussy wrapped around my cock and *rut.*

She seemed to sense the battle within me, no trace of insecurity on her face as she closed the distance between us once more and touched the button at the top of my shirt. "I want you," she murmured, staring up into my eyes with the mesmerizing stare that had always taken my breath away—even before I was smart enough to see it for what it was. "You won't hurt me."

I pounced, shoving her hands away and tearing my buttons open as my lips crashed down on hers. I invaded her mouth, conquering her in the way that I hadn't been able to for so long. Her hands worked my pants open, pushing them down my legs furiously as if she was as desperate to feel my skin on hers as I was.

I kicked them off my feet, fumbling momentarily with my hurt ankle. By the time I stripped them off entirely and my cock bobbed up toward my stomach, Isa had perched on the bed and backed into the center. Legs spread, pussy already gleaming for me, she crooked that single wicked finger and summoned me toward her.

Where she went, I would always follow. Where I went, I

would drag her kicking and screaming. Such was the volatile, toxic nature of the love we shared that few could understand.

It wasn't built on hearts and flowers, but forged in blood and fire. Consuming everyone who dared to get in the path we set, we'd burn the world to the ground before we allowed anything to separate us.

I crawled between her legs, the heat of her enveloping me as she wrapped them around my hips. We fused our mouths together, sharing breath as my hands roamed over her sides and cupped her breast.

She gasped when my thumb stroked over her nipple, her back arching and pussy grinding against me in her need. There might have been a time when Dima's breath filled her lungs, but it was me who owned her body and soul. It was me who lurked inside her brain and claimed her heart.

She tilted her hips ever so slightly, running her wetness over my cock until the head notched at her entrance. Later, I would wish that I had her taste on my tongue.

Later, I would devour her entire body until she was a throbbing mess of need.

For this moment, I drove inside, taking her more roughly than I should have. Her body clenched around my invasion, pulsing as the force of her desire crashed over me. A better man would have stopped, would have given her time to recover from the harsh possession before battering at her pussy and taking it as his.

But I was not a better man.

I covered her body with my weight more fully, lifting her hands above her head and pinning them to the mattress beneath her. Carefully avoiding the bandages at her wrist so I didn't hurt her in ways I had no interest in, I plunged in and out of her depths.

Her cries of pain mixed with ecstasy only fueled me on, driving me to fuck her harder. To remind her that she belonged to me and me alone. Just as I was hers alone. I shifted her hands to one of mine, using the free one to grasp her around her jaw and squeeze until she opened her mouth to mine. I devoured her mouth with mine, kissing her like there may not be a tomorrow or a future for us.

Because there nearly hadn't been.

She gasped into my mouth, her orgasm washing over her with the relentless drives of my cock through her tender insides as my pelvis rubbed against her with every thrust. I fucked her through it, shoving away my own orgasm for just a few more minutes inside the heaven of her body.

When it finally claimed me, I roared out with the release that sucked the cum from my balls and finished inside my wife.

Many would look at our relationship and pity the woman for what I'd done to her, but anyone who knew us well enough understood the one simple truth.

Isa had owned me from that very first stare.

When my breathing returned to normal, I gathered *mi reina* in my arms and strode for the bathroom and the shower that waited for both of us. Desperate to wash Russia off our skin entirely, I set to doing just that.

*T*he door opened silently, and I slipped inside quickly before I could risk anyone noticing me.

With a hand on the railing, I made my way down the stairs with careful, cautious steps through the dark. I didn't want anyone to know that I'd wandered into the basement.

Not yet anyway.

Only a single, dim light was on by the table where Rafael kept his tools, illuminating the terrifying knives and instruments vividly for the victims. It was all they could see in the light on the rare occasion that someone made it back to *El Infierno* alive.

More often, Rafael dealt with his victims in Ibiza itself, preferring to keep the island clean of the violence that happened elsewhere. This was his sanctuary, a land of life born from the shadows of all the death his father caused.

Death like my mother's. Slow. Torturous. Painful.

I stepped in front of the chair, staring down at Odina's sleeping face with contempt. She'd been a pain in my ass from the first day we started watching over Isa, and I always knew it would come to this moment.

To the choice to do what was necessary to protect Isa. Even when she didn't want it.

Even when it was against her wishes.

I would do whatever it took to give her a life of true freedom, even knowing it might mean she hated me for the rest of my days. If she couldn't look me in the eye, at least I would know she was alive to ignore me.

There would be no regrets.

I drew the knife from its sheath, the blade dragging over the leather as I stared down at Odina's sleeping form and considered my options. The darkest part of me wanted to make her suffer, wanted her to feel every bit of pain she'd ever caused the girl I'd long since come to think of as a little sister.

But the knowledge that Isa would at least want it to be done quickly, to be more humane than Odina deserved, drove me to line the knife up to slip between her ribs.

She startled awake at the first press of the point against her skin, her eyes flying open as a shocked gasp escaped her lungs. The pain that lurked in them faded quickly when I shoved the blade forward, sinking it into her flesh as blood dripped free from the wound.

She groaned once, the sound cutting off as her eyes went glassy when I pulled the knife free from her heart and wiped the blood on the dress she'd stolen off of Isa's body when she switched places with her.

Her head lolled, dropping forward to hang over her corpse as what remained of her wasted life poured out of the hole in her chest.

I swallowed, sheathing my knife and making my way for the stairs to find my brothers and tell them what I'd done. There would be no pretty lies to hide the ugly truths of what happened to her sister.

All that mattered was that Isa would be safe.

I strolled from the bedroom the next morning, finding Regina waiting in the kitchen with a fresh batch of lemonade waiting for me. I took a sip of the sour concoction, stepping into her waiting arms and the embrace she offered.

In the aftermath of arriving home late the night before, of discovering my sister was still alive and I didn't need to deal with the conflicting thoughts about what Rafe might have done to her when he discovered her deception, I'd been too distracted to think about the woman I'd missed while we'd been gone.

"It's so good to have you home safe," she murmured, resting her hand atop my head and soothing the frayed edges of my own emotions. I wondered in a distant sort of way if there would ever come a day when I didn't feel a twinge of guilt over the mother figure in my life. If I could ever just love Regina without missing my own mom.

"It's good to be home again. I don't know if I ever want to leave again," I said, huffing a laugh at how much had

changed in such a short time. My prison had become my
sanctuary. The only place I ever felt truly safe.

Home was wherever Rafael was, but this place was
special. It was a part of me I didn't think I'd ever want to be
rid of.

"That will change in time," she said, stepping back with
an odd look on her face.

"What's wrong?" I asked, feeling it in my bones that
there was something I was missing. First Rafe was gone
from our bed before I woke up when I'd felt sure he would
stay with me so that I could wake up in his arms. On our
first morning home after everything that had happened, it
seemed unusual that my husband wouldn't cling to me for a
time.

"You should eat something," she said, grabbing a piece
of homemade bread and popping it into the toaster. The
lack of a gourmet breakfast waiting for me was the next sign
that something was seriously wrong.

"Where's Rafe?" I asked, turning to stride for his office.

"Isa!" she called, following after me as I barged toward
the office door. I pushed it open, not bothering to knock and
feeling shocked to find the three Cortes brothers in there
along with Rafe and Alejandro. Rafe's hand was on the back
of his neck and he stood suddenly the moment I burst
inside.

"What's going on?" I asked, crossing my arms over my
chest. After everything, the thought of being left in the dark
was too much for me to bear.

Rafael sighed, the breath heaving out of his lungs
suddenly as he stepped around to the front of his desk and
leaned his ass against it. His hair was disheveled, only a pair
of deep navy silk pajama pants hanging from his hips that

he must have slipped on when he got out of bed this morning.

It was so rare to see him in anything other than his suit — because when we were in the privacy of our bedroom we rarely wore clothing. "Come here, *mi reina*," he murmured, gripping the edge of the desk with white knuckles.

I closed the distance between us, choosing to trust him for a moment despite the dread consuming me. My father was at the front of my mind, wondering if he'd taken a turn for the worst.

If something had changed with his treatment.

When I stopped in front of him, he released his grip on the desk and touched a palm to each of my cheeks. Encompassing me in his gentle touch, he sighed one last time before delivering the harsh truth. Later, I would be grateful that he hadn't tried to hide it.

"Odina won't be going to Peru to stay with Cristiano," he admitted, his voice sounding too soft for the fact that he'd chosen to go against my wishes. "She died last night."

I jolted back from his grip, stepping away and glaring at him with all the hatred I felt. All the disbelief that he'd known what the betrayal would do to our relationship. It wasn't so much that Odina didn't deserve to be punished for what she'd done, but I hadn't needed to suffer alongside her.

I didn't need her death on my conscience and a stain on my marriage. "You promised me," I protested, shaking my head from side to side. "How could you do this?"

"He didn't," Gabriel said, shocking me when he stepped forward and came closer to me than he normally would have risked with Rafael watching.

"How do you know?" I asked, furrowing my brow as I watched him stand tall in front of me.

"Because I did it," Gabriel admitted, his face even and not a hint of regret or shame on it. I felt tears fill my eyes, the burn of my throat stinging as I swallowed around my nausea. "She didn't suffer, and it was more kindness than she deserved."

"Why?" I asked, shaking my head from side to side and turning to look at Hugo and Joaquin who seemed to stand behind their brother and the choice he'd made. "There was another solution! There was no reason to—"

"She was never going to stop," Gabriel said, stepping forward and touching a palm to my cheek. He willed me to stop, silently staring down at me and imploring me to listen. "She was never going to let you ride into the sunset of your happily ever after, because she was determined to make you as miserable as she was."

"She was going to be locked away! What could she have done from Peru?" I asked, gaping at him as if he'd lost all his sense of reason because of his hatred for Odina.

"Manipulated a guard. Escaped. Any number of things, *mi reina*," Gabriel sighed, his face twisting in sympathy. "Even with everything you've survived, you still see the best in people. You still want the best *for* people. But there was nothing good left in Odina, and I did the world a favor by getting rid of her. Now...you can be free."

"How am I supposed to look at you and not feel that? Not see what you did to her? This is why I didn't want her dead! This is why I wanted to lock her away where she couldn't take anything else from me. Now she took you," I protested, dropping my forehead forward until it rested on his chest. His arms raised, wrapping around me and squeezing me in a brotherly embrace.

Rafe's growl sounded through the room, but he refrained from interfering in the moment. In what felt like a goodbye.

"You'll have some time to come to terms with what happened. I'm leaving *El Infierno* for a while," Gabriel murmured, staring into the shock in my eyes when I turned my head up.

"I don't want that either," I whispered, looking over at the two other brothers I loved. Would they go with him? Would they stay?

I didn't think I could cope without them in my life either.

"Faye is still out there," he said, toying with the ends of my hair playfully. "She needs to answer for her part in what she did."

"No. She was just protecting her brother—"

"This is how our world works, *mi reina*. I have no intention of killing her, but she needs to face the consequences of her actions. She needs to pay her *penitencia.*"

"Her brother is dead. He bled out in her arms. I think she's suffered enough, and I'm the one she wronged. Leave her alone," I ordered.

"Sadly, *mi reina*. She owes her penance to *El Diablo.* Not to you," he said, smirking and turning his eyes to where Rafael glared at me. There was no forgiveness in that cold stare, no willingness to understand that her circumstances had been challenging.

The breath left my lungs, knowing that no matter what I said or did, Gabriel would hunt Faye to the ends of the earth.

He would find her, and he would bring her home to punish her.

44

---

ears flowed down Isa's cheeks as we stood on the docks, Gabriel's bag packed for his trip. The yacht would serve as his headquarters while he hunted for Faye. He tossed the backpack with the last of his clothes onto the loading deck, his laptop and tech equipment already safely loaded and stored on board.

"Where will you start?" *mi reina* asked, her voice nearly breaking.

"It's better that you don't know the details," Gabriel said, pulling her into his chest for a quick hug. The fact that my wife seemed so lost, so uncertain of how she was supposed to feel didn't sit well with me. There'd been a time when I would have been nothing but jealous over the relationship she had formed with the brothers, but there was something else in its place now.

A hollow feeling at the realization that they were her family—the family she'd chosen to embrace and who had shown her that they loved her as she was and not who they expected her to be.

As much as my possessiveness drove me to pull her from

his embrace and into mine, I restrained myself. I could give my wife the goodbye she needed with the man who had been able to do what I could not.

The one who'd been brave enough to risk Isa never being able to look him in the eye again, so long as it meant she would be alive to hate him.

"It's okay to be angry with me," Gabriel said, staring down at her as she took a step backward so that his brothers could have their goodbyes.

"I am," she whispered brokenly. A sob claimed her throat, and her hand came up to grasp it like she could refortify it with strength through the contact. "But I don't want to be."

"I'll see you soon, *mi reina,*" he said, nodding as she took a few steps back toward the end of the dock. She went to the beach, dropping off the wooden planks and burying her toes in the sand. I resolved to take her swimming in the water soon enough, because after everything she'd survived, there was no doubt my wife was ready to conquer that fear in truth.

We had all the time in the world.

I stepped forward, my own goodbyes hanging heavy on my chest. "Thank you," I said, raising an eyebrow at the man who'd become more serious since Isa became a part of their lives. He'd been rambunctious when he was younger, caught in an eternal loop of humor and technology that I wasn't sure would ever be of use outside of his hacking skills.

He'd proven himself and then some, taking matters into his own hands when he knew that my love for my wife had rendered me unable to make the only choice that could be made. He'd saved me from being culpable for Odina's death, giving us the greatest gift I could ever ask for.

A future.

"It needed to be done," he said, his eyes tracking over to where Isa stood and shifted her toes around in the sand beneath her feet.

"It did. But thank you for being the one to do it," I said. "Now I don't need to live with the guilt of her falling victim to an unfortunate accident in Peru." I smirked at the other man, knowing that he knew me as well as anyone.

Odina would never have been allowed to live, but sometimes the truth was too ugly to know.

Sometimes a beautiful lie was the greatest gift.

"Find her. Bring her to me, and I'll make sure Isa has come to terms with Odina's death by then. This will always be your home," I said pointedly, ignoring the swell of emotion in his throat as I turned and left him to say goodbye to Joaquin and Hugo.

I left them to their private moment, collecting *mi reina* and taking her into the car. We drove up the hill slowly, the winding roads curving until we reached the village just beyond the house. It was a detour for sure, but I wanted Isa to understand something before she wandered there on her own inadvertently.

"I've had Odina buried next to your mother's memorial," I said, watching as she snapped her head toward me. Tears stained her face, and I hoped it hadn't been a mistake to do it without consulting her. As much as it had pained me to see her name so close to my mother's, knowing that I would have sooner disposed of her in an unmarked grave where no one could mourn her, I'd done what I thought Isa would want. "I can have her moved somewhere else if you'd prefer—"

"No," Isa said, easing the nerves I felt over the choice. "I'm just—I'm not ready to see it yet."

"Whenever you're ready, *mi reina*. We have all the time in the world," I told her, and finally, she smiled.

I still had one last thing to show my wife, and then I intended to spend the rest of my day, the rest of our lives, inside her.

*R*afe led me to his office, his focus intent there despite that I'd expected to be directed toward the bedroom. Something inside me clenched, both apprehension and arousal warring within me, in spite of the conflicting emotions from saying goodbye to Gabriel and the death of the sister I shouldn't have cared about.

He was everything I wanted, but fuck if he didn't scare me when his eyes went hard with that glint. Rafael's schemes never ended well for me.

The moment we walked into his office, I saw the blood-covered queen chess piece on his desk, gleaming in the sunlight streaming in through the windows. He had to have taken it from the library at Pavel's house.

He picked it up, touching the cleaner part of the base and carefully avoiding the blood and gore at the top. "I was wrong," he said, smirking at the shock he must have seen on my face. He moved to the bookcase at the other end of the room, placing the piece high on the top shelf where he could see it from his desk every day like it was a point of pride. "I'm glad you knew to aim for the eyes, but I still don't regret branding you."

I laughed at his audacity, shaking my head to show how ridiculous he was. "Does that mean there are more lessons in my future?" I asked, approaching him and shoving him down to the sofa. He let himself fall, grabbing me around the hips and hauling me into his lap until I straddled his legs.

"I'll give you all the lessons you want, my queen," he murmured, grasping a fistful of my hair in his grip and tugging me forward until his face buried in my neck. He nipped at the skin sharply, his teeth sinking into my flesh like he needed to remind me just who was in charge.

I might have been on top, but there would be no doubt about who controlled our sex.

His free hand lifted my dress up my thighs, exposing my underwear to his wandering hand so that he could shove a hand inside and stroke his fingers through my folds. He found my clit with ease, bumping against it with his thumb and drawing a ragged moan from me.

Two fingers slid inside me, and I was powerless to stop the writhing of my hips above him as I fucked his hand.

He chuckled into my neck, the whisper of his breath over my skin making it pepper with goosebumps. "Did you want something else to ride, *mi reina*?" he asked, his deep voice setting something loose inside me when he finally released his grip on my hair and reached his other hand between us. His fingers left my pussy, so he could free himself from the pants he'd slipped on before going to the dock to say goodbye to Gabriel.

The moment he pulled himself free, I reached between my legs and tugged my panties to the side. When he guided himself to my entrance, I sank down on him and groaned at the mix of pleasure and pain that filled me.

He'd been voracious the night before, taking me over and over until I all but passed out in his arms from exhaustion. My flesh felt swollen and sore in the wake of that, but I wouldn't have changed anything.

He didn't give me time to adjust to the sudden fullness, his hands steady on my hips lifting me and guiding me until I shattered around him and he followed me over the edge into a fast, blinding orgasm.

I had the feeling it would be the first of many through the day. After all, he was right.

We had all the time in the world.

♟♟♟♟♟

We lay together in the bathtub later that night, the sun starting to set over the horizon as I thought through everything that had happened in such a short time.

"I don't want my family to know the truth," I murmured, watching the sky tint with purples and oranges. It was beautiful, a stark contrast to all the evil in the world. In the face of that, I wanted to offer them something that was just as beautiful as what I saw when I looked out my window every day.

"They'll always wonder what happened to her. I think that's worse," Rafe said, running gentle fingers over my arms. With his strength at my back, I felt like I could conquer anything.

Except giving my father more heartache.

"I want to send them postcards from Odina. Little notes about the places she's visited on a whirlwind adventure. It wouldn't be unusual for Odina to go and see the world, especially after everything that happened. She's always been impulsive," I murmured, turning my body to look up into Rafe's face.

He stared down at me, understanding exactly what I intended. "We can take pictures of you. They'll never know that it isn't her."

"We would have to leave the safety of the island for it to work. Is that...is that okay?" I asked, hesitating. I had been so sure that I never wanted to leave my sanctuary.

"Give it some time. Send the first few postcards without photos, and once we're sure it's safe, I'll take you to see the world," Rafe agreed.

"Do you think it's a bad idea? Will it only hurt them in the end?" I asked.

"You're letting them believe that Odina is out living her best life. You're giving them peace," he murmured, leaning down to touch his lips to mine.

That peace might not have been the ugly truth, but it was such a beautiful lie.

EPILOGUE
RAFAEL

*S*ix and a half months later

She ignored the warning signs. She pushed me to my limits and didn't seem to care what that might mean for Joaquin or Alejandro when I took out my fury on them.

My wife was far too pregnant to bear the consequences of the rage she instilled in me. Two weeks past her due date in fact, something she drilled into my head every time she disobeyed me to go for a walk through the village with Regina. *Walking is a good way to induce labor*, she'd informed me repeatedly.

Walking was a good way to cause me to have a coronary and murder my own men, that's what it was.

The women in the village who had taken Isa in as one of their own, especially as her knowledge of Spanish grew with the months of learning from Regina, seemed to take delight in my concern for my wife.

It was only a matter of time before she dropped a baby in the field beyond the house when I wasn't with her, no matter how much she liked to remind me that first babies didn't typically just pop out without a fight. The only reassurance I had was the doctor who had come to live with us for the last month of her pregnancy, but even she grew antsy with Isa's insistence on letting the baby decide when the time was right.

She wouldn't be induced, not if she could help it, but sadly the time quickly approached when it would no longer be in her control.

I watched her stroll through the very shallow waters of the cove with Hugo clinging to her arm to support her. The water was still, as calm as it was on most days, but still the fear that she might be swept away in the tide drove me to slam the McLaren door behind me and walk down the steps from the street to the beach.

She squealed when Hugo dove into the water at her side, his hands plunging below the surface. He came up with a fish held in his grip, the pale blue thing flopping from side to side as Isa laughed and fumbled her way toward the shore as quickly as her stomach would allow. She refused to let it hinder her movement, but it got the best of her.

She was the only one who didn't see just how adorable her pregnant waddle was.

She faltered when she saw me standing on the beach just at the edge of the water, my shoes just out of reach of the swaying tide. With her dress hiked up in her hands to avoid the water, the golden glow that had taken over her fawn skin couldn't be missed.

Her face was radiant, an unmistakable happiness settled there that couldn't be denied. I'd thought it would be enough to know she loved me, that even if I hadn't been able to make her *happy*, I'd accomplished that.

Instead, I realized how important her happiness was to

me. I could no longer live without seeing that smile every day.

She groaned, dropping her head forward even though the smile never left her lips. The way the sunshine played on the surprising copper notes it had brought out in her hair still took my breath away, the picture of everything I could have ever wanted as she made her way toward me.

She dropped her dress as she stepped up onto the dry sand, moving into my chest as if she could sense the nightmare playing beneath the surface. Hugo wisely left my wife to me, retreating back to the dock and starting the hike back up to the village.

"You walked all the way down here." My voice was every bit as scolding as the fury pulsing in my veins. The risks she took with her safety would never be something I could tolerate, like her personality had swung from being too well-behaved and mild-mannered to being impulsive and choosing to live every moment to the fullest.

Even if doing so might mean it was her last.

"Stop it." She laughed, stretching up on to her tippy toes and offering me her mouth. With her belly between us, she could no longer reach me to kiss me.

It had been a stretch for her before, now it was just impossible.

"What if you went into labor?"

"Then I would call you and you'd be here in two minutes. You have to stop worrying all the time," Isa complained. She took my hand in hers, leaving me to scoop up her sandals and guide her back to the McLaren. I opened the door for her, leaving her to lower herself into the seat before I knelt on the pavement and used the towel from the floor to dry her legs and shake what I could of the sand from her skin.

The marks on her ankles had faded over the months, but the scars remained as constant reminders of just how close I'd come to losing them both forever. *Nothing* would ever come between us again, not even Isa herself.

"Don't make me lock you in the bedroom," I warned her, eventually determining that she was as sand-free as possible and lifting her legs up so I could shift them into the car. She helped me by using her arms to lift her butt so she could pivot, narrowing her eyes on my face when I grabbed her seatbelt and buckled her in protectively.

Maybe I should've had the armored SUVs from Ibiza brought here to drive her around, after all. They'd have been safer if there was an accident.

"Sure, you could do that," she said, shrugging her shoulders. I closed the door on whatever protest she'd been about to voice, walking around the front of the car and making my way to the driver's side. "I don't suggest it if you want to have more than just one child though."

I smirked, glancing at her from the corner of my eye. "*Mi reina*, what makes you think you'll have any more say in the other pregnancies than you did this one?"

She gasped, reaching an arm across the seat to smack me in the chest. Even despite her lack of training in recent months, the pound of her fist against my chest resounded through the confined space of the car. I chuckled, leaning over to kiss the side of her jaw as she broke out in laughter.

She knew it was true, as much as I did. But it was just part of our history, part of the complicated future we'd carved out for ourselves. No one else would understand.

"How many kids do you think I'll be popping out, *El Diablo*?" she asked, staring at me and gaping in shock.

"Five more," I murmured. "The devil likes the number six, right?" I asked, shifting the car into drive. Her nose wrinkled as if it was too many, but I knew she'd come around to it in time. Neither Isa nor I had been gifted with healthy sibling relationships. We'd never known what it was to have that kind of bond.

Her because my father had derailed her life, and me because I'd been an only child, but we could do better by our own kids.

"How about two more instead?" she asked, narrowing her eyes on the side of my face.

"Odd number," I dismissed, pulling onto the main, winding road that took us up to the house.

"Okay *one* more then," she growled in warning, turning her head to stare out the window like she'd settled the issue. When the time came, we'd see who was triumphant.

My queen would give me just about anything I asked for, so long as I did it on my knees and ready to worship at her altar.

Because she owned me, body and soul, heart and mind. All of it was hers for the taking, just as she was mine.

I pulled the McLaren into the driveway, hurrying out to help my moody wife from her seat even though she wished more than anything that she could still do it herself. Her face twisted with pain as I pulled her to her feet, and all thoughts of future babies were swept away in the rush to make sure she was alright.

I'd never knock her up again if it meant I didn't have to see that look on her face.

"What's wrong?" I asked, watching as she leveled me with a stare.

"Contractions," she answered, shaking off my grip and slowly making her way toward the house. "They're about six minutes apart."

"You've been having them? And you stayed at the

beach?" I asked, my voice raising louder than it should have given my wife could have been in fucking *labor* and needed my peace.

"How many times have I had Braxton Hicks in the last few weeks?" she asked, spinning and putting a hand on her hip to remind me of all the false alarms we'd been through. I couldn't truly blame her for being doubtful that it was really time.

That was, until water splashed on the ground at her feet, her hand clutching her stomach in shock as her eyes flew wide open in disbelief.

"Regina!" I yelled, lunging forward and wrapping an arm around Isa's waist. I hurried her through the house, her face twisting with pain much more regularly than her six minutes of timed contractions would have been before.

"Fuck!" Isa yelled, curling over in pain when we were halfway to the guest bedroom we'd set up to be her birthing space. Regina was quick to take up her other side, trying to wrap Isa's arm around her shoulders but *mi reina* shrugged us both off and made her way to the bedroom. "Walking helps," she explained, pacing once she'd gotten into the privacy of our bedroom.

"Get Dr. Perez," I ordered, sending Regina scurrying from the room to find the doctor who was quickly losing patience and wanted to return to her other patients.

It seemed like her wish would come true soon enough.

The baby was coming.

Isa

*O*ne look.

That was all it took for life to just...make sense. For love like I'd never known to flood my veins and fill my body.

The first glimpse of those dark blue and brown eyes staring up at me from the sweet face of my son took everything I'd thought I knew about myself and changed it to something different entirely. His little hand wrapped around my finger when I cradled him to my chest, my body exhausted but somehow lighter than it had ever been.

I would spend the rest of my days loving this boy.

"There's mommy's little lion," I whispered, rubbing my thumb over the back of his hand where it clasped mine. Rafe sat on the edge of the bed, staring down at the bundle in my arms and leaning over me.

"Leo," he murmured gently, reaching forward to rest his palm against his son's tiny head. Leo had nursed while Rafe watched with rapt attention, unable to take his eyes off the little boy in my arms, but this was the first time he'd come close enough to touch.

As if he didn't trust himself around something so precious, something so tiny and fragile.

"You should hold him," I said, looking over at the uncertain stare of the man I loved with everything I was. A few months before, if someone had asked me if I trusted him with a baby, I might have laughed.

But I knew, without a doubt, that I trusted my devil with anything and everything that mattered to me. He moved to the armchair beside the bed where he'd held my hand through the screams, through the agonizing contractions that rocked my body and the labor and delivery that brought the worst pain I'd ever felt.

I shifted my weight, swiveling my body carefully until my feet touched the floor and I bounced as I walked the few short steps between us. He gaped up at me nervously as I smiled, twisting to place Leo in his arms.

Rafe shook his head quickly, swallowing as emotion washed over his features. I lifted one of his elbows so that it supported Leo's head, the baby curled up in a single one of Rafe's long, muscular arms, looking so much smaller in his grasp than mine.

Rafe's panicked gaze dropped from my eyes, going down to the little boy who raised the hand he'd broken out of his swaddle blanket and caught his pinky finger in his grip. Dragging it down to his body, he held his daddy's hand close to his chest and opened his eyes.

I watched my husband's world disappear, narrowing down to the sight of that tiny hand on his. To those all-consuming eyes as they held his. I fell back onto the bed, my shoulders heaving as I sighed and relaxed.

"Sleep, *mi reina*. We'll be right here," he said, standing and leaning over me to press a kiss to my forehead. He walked toward the end of the bed, bouncing carefully in his attempt to mimic the movement I'd made when I brought him the baby he'd seemed so terrified of.

I lay back on the bed, my eyes drifting half-closed as I watched him softly murmur to his son. It wasn't until the moment that my eyes drifted closed that I realized he wasn't speaking.

But singing softly in Spanish, some kind of sweet lullaby that I'd never heard pouring from his lips while he walked back and forth.

For the son named after the stars he'd stared up at with his mother. For the son named after mine.

For our new beginning, I'd give him anything.

Leonardo Ibarra Adamik.

My little lion looked up at his father's beaming face and the eyes that were more wet than he would ever admit.

And he smiled.

The end.

Remember Calix from the prologue Until Memory Fades? His story begins in **Dreams of the Vengeful** as part of the Tangled Sheets anthology, releasing July 13th. Continue reading for the first chapter.

>>Pre-Order now.

Download the exclusive Beauty in Lies Extended Epilogue for a look at life three years later when the Ibarra family goes to Capri.

>>Download the Extended Epilogue.

Fall in love with a Bellandi? You can find Matteo, Ryker, and Enzo's stories in Adelaide's Bellandi Crime Syndicate series.

>>Start with Bloodied Hands.

DREAMS OF THE VENGEFUL
CHAPTER ONE
CALIX

Twenty years prior.

The air inside the Karras home turned suffocating as soon as I scrawled my signature on the page, on the contract that bound me to a future no boy would choose for himself. Just like my father, Origen Karras built his empire on lies and suffering, on business arrangements and on the arrogance of the figurehead who sat behind a desk, striving to unite the six families for his own selfish greed.

Anyone could see it if they merely looked hard enough, seeing past the proper veneer of the image he tried to present. Glimpsing the monster residing beneath his skin.

I stumbled out the back door of the house, my lungs heaving with the ridiculousness of it all. The arranged marriage that loomed on the distant horizon, to a tiny slip of a girl I'd only seen in passing, sent me spiraling out of the stuffy estate and seeking fresh air.

The girl was five years old, far too young to already contemplate which monster would share her bed when she was old enough to breed, and yet that was precisely what a group of grown men had chosen to do on a sunny Spring afternoon.

At thirteen, I'd already lost my virginity and appreciated what girls my own age could do with their changing bodies. The thought of that with a girl less than half my age made my skin crawl.

I leaned against the railing at the edge of the elaborate wood deck, my eyes catching on the bright green blades of grass that had only sprouted from the frozen ground weeks prior. As my gaze dragged up to the expanse of yard at the back of the estate, my focus narrowed on the form of a young girl twirling between the gardens of narcissus that her mother must have been fond of to have so much growing on the property.

She looked at me, a smile on her heart-shaped face as she spun and completely oblivious to the contract that had been signed only moments before. The ink of my name probably hadn't even dried on the page as of yet, as our fathers and her brother toasted to the agreement.

To cementing the alliance between our families despite her mother's obvious desire to stall it. But there was no stopping tradition and there would be nothing to save little Thalia from becoming mine after she became a woman.

As a kindness to her mother, they'd agreed Thalia didn't need to know until she was old enough to understand. She could have her childhood and enjoy the promise of freedom when she would come of age.

Even if it was a lie.

My legs guided me toward her, closing the distance between us even though I knew I should stay away. To get close to her and never tell her the truth of what was to come felt like a cruelty she didn't deserve, and nothing about the five-year-old girl would last until our marriage. She'd be a new person by the time she became mine.

Our lives dictated that.

She continued spinning until dizziness consumed her, falling to her back in the grass and staining her yellow sundress. My mother would have disapproved greatly, because young ladies should always present themselves properly. Not be stained with grass after rolling in the dirt.

She stared up at the sky, the sun sparkling off the unique amber of her eyes—completely oblivious to my approach. "Shouldn't you be inside?" I asked, stuffing my hands into the pockets of the suit pants my father made me wear.

Already a man ready to take the city by storm in his mind, I was no longer a boy.

She startled, pressing a hand to her chest as she flung up to sit and that distinctive stare landed on mine. She squinted at me, fixating on something on my face as she tilted her head to the side. "Why?" She rolled her eyes and shrugged, dropping back to the grass as if she couldn't be bothered to concern herself with what the adults might be doing inside.

Despite my better instincts, I moved closer and risked my mother's wrath to sit on the ground next to her. Kicking my legs out in front of me and feeling strangely awkward, I picked at the blades of grass beneath my hands. "That's a good question," I admitted and huffed a laugh.

"Being inside is so boring. Out here, I don't have to be so quiet." Her face pinched together, not quite pretty enough to be adorable. Her eyes were too big for her face, her lips puffy, and her ears had an odd sort of point at the top like she was something straight from a fantasy book. Her face was intriguing, her features bright as she turned a smile my way, but between her odd face and the tiny frame that looked far too young for a five-year-old, no one would ever call Thalia Karras pretty.

Perhaps that would change by the time we married.

I swallowed back the despair that tried to settle over me, knowing that the future waiting for us wasn't one either of us would have chosen for ourselves, yet still trapped by the forces working to drive us together.

"What do you like to do?" I asked, thinking maybe I could send her gifts. Get to know her a little, bit by bit, without ever truly being a part of her life. Just enough so it wouldn't seem so agonizingly painful when the contract came due and her life became mine.

"Draw, but Daddy doesn't like it. I like to draw flowers, but the colors are always wrong, and—" She cut off suddenly as if she'd realized she'd said something she shouldn't.

With a swallow, she sat up, curling her arms around herself protectively. "You're five. Flowers can be any color you want," I said in an attempt to comfort whatever nervousness had settled over her.

"Can they be black and white?" she asked, her eyes turning hopeful as she leveled me with that wide-eyed stare.

"Wouldn't you rather they be pink?" I asked, furrowing my brow. What little girl painted black flowers?

The hope faded from her eyes as she pushed herself to standing once more, leaving me staring after her from the ground. "I have to go."

I moved to follow, taking up a slow walk at her side as her little legs worked to make her way back to the house. She was so painfully thin that it seemed as if each step required too much energy. Still, there was a stern determination on her face that didn't belong on anyone her age.

As if she had to do it for herself, or the consequences

would be dire. "What color flowers do you like best?" I asked, resolving to send her some that she could draw.

She paused, her steps halting as she hit me with a concerned stare. "I'm not supposed to talk about it," she said, biting that too-large bottom lip and staring nervously toward the house. Her eyes darted from window to window, swallowing when she found no one watching us.

"About your favorite color flower?" I asked, grinning down at her in my confusion. She was such an odd child, and if her parents truly forbid her from talking about the flowers, then I couldn't imagine what kind of life she had with them.

"I don't know," she answered. "I can't see them." She picked up her steps, quickening her pace as her lungs heaved with exertion. I was half tempted to lift her into my arms, knowing her tiny frame couldn't weigh much.

"Flowers?" I asked, laughing at the ridiculousness of the notion. I'd only just seen her twirling in the fields surrounded by narcissus and never harming a single flower.

"Colors," she whispered as she reached the back door, taking the handle in her grip. She turned back to me, her eyes silently pleading to keep her secret. Whatever she saw on my face must have reassured her, because she nodded once and pursed her lips thoughtfully.

Looking far too old for her body and for her age, she turned the handle and swept into the house. She was gone by the time I followed, disappearing like a ghost in the wind.

Like she'd never been meant to exist at all.

Pre-Order Tangled Sheets to read the rest of Dreams of the Vengeful.

ALSO BY ADELAIDE FORREST

Manufactured by Amazon.ca
Bolton, ON

26006203R00195